AND ALWAYS

The Porn Star Brothers Series

L.J. DIVA

★ Royal Star Publishing ★

Chances is an imprint of Royal Star Publishing
www.royalstarpublishing.com.au

First edition paperback published in 2021
All Rights Reserved, Copyright ©L.J. Diva 2021
Song lyrics reprinted with permission

Trade Paperback ISBN: 978-1-922307-47-7
Dust Jacket Hardcover ISBN: 978-1-922307-48-4
E-book ISBN: 978-1-922307-46-0
A catalogue record for this book is available from the National Library of Australia.

Cover design: Royal Star Publishing and Odyssey Books
Cover photos: sondem/shutterstock.com
Typesetting in Minion Pro by Royal Star Publishing

 Dedications

In 2014 a vague idea to write a book about a porn star came to me. In 2015 the idea brewed and grew and when my idol, Jackie Collins, passed away, the idea flourished with a vengeance.

Jackie Collins is the only inspiration in my life when it comes to writing. She had the passion, the brains, the ballsy rollicking attitude, and the kind of life that made me want to *be* her.

Without her, these books would not exist, for I would not have had the inspiration to follow in the same 'write whatever you want' league. Without her, I will continue trying to write the kind of books she wrote. Real, ballsy, and bonkbustingly good.

Jackie,

the Porn Star Brothers book series is dedicated to you as so many of my other books are. I thank you for the inspiration you have given me and hope you continue giving me, to go on and write more. I hope that you are well and having a good laugh wherever you are. I miss you and will continue doing so. Sometimes I think I feel you egging me on with my writing. Maybe that's true, and maybe it's just my rampant imagination; the same imagination that has given me the books I have written so far in my life. And sometimes, I really wished I could be you. You will forever be my idol and inspiration and I thank you.

RIP, Miss Jackie C.

And to the three Stefanovic brothers, Carlos, Pedro, and Tomas, without whom I would not have had names for my porn stars.

Alena & Luca - 2010

"Ugh, I can't believe I'm thirty-two and *still* single. How did you get married and have a child before me?" Alena Stephanopoulos asked her cousin, Diana Stephanopoulos Kensington, who sat beside their grandparents on the sofa.

"Because I just did," Diana replied, casting a quick glance at Alena before turning back to her two-year-old son on his great-grandmother's lap. "Don't worry, you'll find someone just like I did, just like Cabot found Tony, and Mama and Daddy found each other, and Grandma and Grandpa…" She looked at her grandmother. "I'm just glad you get to see him and spend time with him. That's four generations in the family now."

"I'm only eighty-two, sweetie," Jenny Stephanopoulos, the family matriarch, said. "Not dead."

"I know. But none of us knew, or know, when we're going to have children, or get married, and I wasn't sure I'd be married with kids by thirty. So I can see Alena's point. *I* can't believe she's thirty-two and *still* single, either." She threw a sly glance at her cousin. "You *are* getting old, cuz."

"Old!" Alena shrieked and sat up straight in the easy chair opposite them.

"Tone it down," her father called from the kitchen where he was munching on grapes and waiting for his brother and brother-in-law to finish lunch for the family. "The whole of Mykonos can hear you when you shriek like that."

"Sorry, Daddy," Alena called. "But she called me old."

"I don't care." Pedro threw a grape at Tomas who caught it in his mouth. "Stop shrieking like a banshee." He shook his head at his wife, Angie, and brothers Tomas and Carlos.

"Banshee!" Alena exclaimed. "Daddy, how could you!"

"Oh, for goodness sake, *stop it,*" Jenny told her. "*You are not old,* Alena. By the time I was thirty-two I already had your father and uncles. Diana has Adam." Watching her granddaughter fall back in the chair, she shook her head. "Look at you. You're a beautiful, *stunning* woman who'll find the right man when he's ready to come along. Not a moment before and not a moment after. Stop worrying." As much as Jenny loved her grandchildren, Alena did still carry on at times.

"That's all well and good for *you* to say, Grandma," Alena scoffed. "You met Grandpa at twenty-two and married him at twenty-four. I'm *thirty-two* and over the hill!"

"You *will be* if you keep carrying on like that," Alexis said from the doorway. "Whew, it's hot out there." After shutting the door, she kissed her grandparents' cheeks and ruffled Adam's hair. "Hey, kid." Turning to her sister, she added, "You *need* to stop whining like a little kid. Hell, Adam doesn't even whine as much as you."

"Easy for *you* to say," Alena muttered, eyeing her sister up and down. "*You're* still *twenty*-two. *You've* got plenty of time." She changed tack. "How's the centre?"

"The centre's fine, which you'd know if you bothered to drop by. You haven't in months." Alexis walked over to accept the cool lemonade her uncle Tomas offered her. "Thanks, Uncle T."

"*You know* I'm rehearsing for my European tour. I don't have the time," Alena whined and twirled a dark tendril of hair around her finger. "It's not that I don't want to, but it's *your* thing. *Yours* and Cabot's. Mine is singing and making music."

The Mykonos Assault and HIV/AIDS Support Centre, that Alexis and Cabot had set up in 2007 after both of their assaults, was going extremely well. They had used their trust fund money, along with the money the family had put in, and a share of the Poulos fortune Angie's dad had left after his death in 1977, and Jenny had given them one of the many Stephanopoulos properties on the island. Alexis had been running it ever since with the family dropping by to donate time, food, and clothing to those in need.

"That doesn't mean you can't stop by and help out," Jenny told her, tickling Adam's chin and making him giggle. She bent him backwards so he was lying across her lap and onto Spiros's who was beside her. Spiros pulled faces at him, making him laugh harder. "We all help out from time to time," she added.

"Yeah." Alexis sat on the arm of her sister's chair. "You're not going back to the old selfish Alena we all had for twenty-nine years, are you?"

Alena stared up at her sister. "Of *course* not, I just…" She glanced away. "I don't particularly feel helpful, or useful there, and don't feel comfortable being there. I'm more at home in the studio, or on a stage. It's not my thing, that's all." Looking back at Alexis, she gave her a smile. "But I'm extremely proud of you and Cab for setting it up and helping people."

"Ah-ha," Alexis muttered dryly and took a sip of her drink.

"Look, sweetie." Angie came over to her daughters. "Everyone finds their person when the time is right. If and when you're meant to meet yours, you'll do so regardless of how old you are." She sat on the other arm of the chair and stroked Alena's long jet-black hair. "Just because *we* have been lucky enough to have found our person, doesn't mean it won't happen for you. Danté, Dom, and Antonio are still single, and Alexis is dating. But just because Diana is married with a child doesn't mean *you* should be. You're still young and gorgeous and could date any man you wanted. And speaking of, why *aren't you* dating? There are so many men out there."

"Because I haven't found anyone interesting enough to date since James Gardo." Alena sighed and flopped back in her seat.

The silence that followed was deafening.

At least, in the lounge room.

In the kitchen, the conversation had continued without pause.

"Why would you bring his name up?" Angie urgently whispered. "We haven't mentioned his name since…" Glancing at her parents-in-law, she saw Spiros's shocked expression and Jenny's passively neutral one.

"That's not to say we *can't*," Jenny said. "He *is* entwined with the family. Most of us choose *not* to discuss it. *Or* him." Inspecting her granddaughter's embarrassed face, she asked, "Has there *really* been no one you've been interested in since him? That was 2007."

"Three years that I've had no one," Alena grumbled and looked away. "I was *so* ready to fall in love with him. He was gorgeous. But the whole damn family…" She crossed her arms and scowled.

"I know it was hard," Jenny murmured. "It was on all of us and that was one mess we didn't need. But, we survived, and you both moved on. Are you telling me you haven't dated since?"

"Gone out on a date with? Sure." Alena blew her fringe out of her eyes. "Had an *actual* relationship with? *No!* And Alexis has my ex, so it's not like I could go back there."

"Alena!" Alexis bit back. "*You* dumped *him* and it was a hell of a long time before *I* started dating him." She was dating Lorenzo Gavalas, a local doctor who'd also dated Alena many years before she had.

Alena waved a dismissive hand. "I know, I know. And it's one rule I follow. Don't go back to a previous partner, so I wouldn't anyway. But I just feel so…" Trying to find the right word, she sighed. "Single… lonely…alone…"

"In this family?" Diana retorted. "You're hardly alone."

"I *mean* romantically." Alena tucked her hair behind her ears. "I want a man to hug and kiss and do stuff with. You know…" She waved her hands at the family. "The kind of stuff that produced all of us."

"Sex! Is that all you girls think about? No wonder I'm still single," Danté, her youngest brother, proclaimed from the doorway.

"You're single because you're seventeen and only think about music," his best friend, Nick Gatos, retorted as he shut the door behind him. "Ain't no other reason."

"And we don't *just* think about sex, you know," Alena told him. "We think about, and want, a lot of things." She watched him kiss their grandparents and ruffle Adam's hair. "Sex runs in this family. You'll have it one day."

Danté screwed up his face. "Ew! No, thanks, rather have my music."

He walked into the kitchen for something to drink with Nick hot on his heels.

"We're here." Cabot and his partner, Tony DeLuca, came through the door and saw that not everyone had arrived. "Where's Antonio?"

"Not here yet, sweetie," Vivian, his mother, called from the kitchen. She was setting the tables and talking with her husband and brothers-in-law while Jenny and Spiros spent time with their great-grandson.

Cabot wandered over to his mother and kissed her cheek. "Huh…I haven't seen him in a couple of days. Figured we'd be planning our birthday next week."

"That's already planned." Viv set the napkins by the cutlery. "I think he said he was going to spend the week relaxing. Getting some sun, meeting girls."

"See!" Alena threw her hands up in exasperation. "*He's* off meeting girls; *I* should be off meeting boys."

"I thought you wanted a man," Alexis reminded her.

"Yes, okay, I *meant* a man," Alena snipped. "I'm sick of being single and I want sex."

Cabot's eyes grew round. "Well, you can get plenty of that around here, cuz. You should have asked; I would've directed you to the best places."

"Not gay sex, Cab." Tony touched his lover's arm. "Straight sex."

Cabot glanced from Alena to Tony and back. "I know the best places for that, too."

"Gross, Cabot," Alena muttered. "Just gross. My gay cousin telling me where to go for sex."

Cabot shrugged nonchalantly. "I used to like women too, you know. Had sex with them before realising that wasn't for me. There *are* straight bars here where you can pick up, or just go to the club. Put yourself out there. Women are hanging out all over the place for Dom, and girls for Danté. Get yourself down there and tell the world you're single and see all the men come flocking."

"Flocking would be *really* nice right now," Alena told everyone. "Because I want to *flock* a lot. And I *mean* a lot. I want to flock a man's brains out and have my own flocked out."

"Ew, Alena," Alexis complained and walked into the kitchen. "Ugh, Alena's talking about sex and being single. I'm over it."

"Just because you're currently happy and in a relationship, Alexis, doesn't mean she's not entitled to feel left out." Pedro wrapped his arms around her and watched Alena in the lounge room. "She's been working hard these last few years. She took over *Haus of Stefan* when Diana had Adam. They set up *Styled by Stefan,* and you've all released books and music since then. She's been busy and a relationship just hasn't happened for her. Unlike you." He pulled back to look at her. "You're still with Lorenzo. How's that going? Is he coming to lunch?"

"It's going well, and no, he's got a shift at the hospital today, so I'll see him later." Alexis knew the subject of her dating Alena's ex was still a touchy one. Even after three years.

"I'm just glad that at least *one* of my children is happy in a relationship," he added.

"What's that supposed to mean?" Danté narrowed his eyes and took a sip of lemonade, watching his father over the rim of his glass. "I'm seventeen, I don't need no girlfriend. I have DJing and our IT business to run. I'm too busy for girls."

"Too busy for girls?" Nick muttered and stared at him. At a year older than Danté, he'd already dated a lot of girls. "*How* are you too busy for girls?" He scored a dirty look in return.

"No, you don't *need* a girlfriend at seventeen," Pedro agreed, watching his son in return. "But it *does* sound as though you need grammar lessons." He saw Danté frown and slink off into the lounge room with Nick following. Turning to his brothers and Roger, he added, "I don't need to worry about Danté and girls yet, do I?"

"Probably not." Carlos popped a grape into his mouth. "But considering he's a year off the age you were when you started having sex…"

Pedro's face fell. "Oi! Jesus."

"Ew, gross. Can we *stop* talking about sex," Alexis complained and flung her head back in exasperation "Ugh! Uncle T, when's lunch ready? It smells good."

"Doesn't it always?" Tomas smiled at his niece. His mother's roast chicken happened every Sunday come hell or high water, summer or winter. And if the family members were in town, they all came unless previously occupied. Which was rare these days. He glanced at the large windmill clock on the wall. "About fifteen minutes. In time for Dom and Antonio."

"Uncle Mike, Maggie, and the girls coming?" Alexis was best friends with Summer and Melody Gatos, just as Danté was best friends with their brother. And their parents had been best friends for decades.

"Running late, but they'll be here, as will Dan and Derek." Tomas gave the pot of gravy a mix. "And here they are now." He nodded at the door.

Dan Ardent and Derek Blaine, the doctors who'd been with the family for over three decades, walked through the door, followed by Dom and Antonio who were both sweating from the midday heat.

"Jesus it's warm out there." Dom wiped the sweat from his brow and headed to the kitchen for a beer, which he guzzled back. Once finished, he sighed and added, "When's lunch?"

"Ten minutes," Pedro told him and watched Antonio follow suit with the beer. "I know it's hot, but you two might want to take it easy on those things until you get some food into your stomachs."

Memories flashed through Antonio's mind. "I seem to recall a scene almost like this about three years ago now, but it wasn't me you were telling that to." He glanced over at his twin in the lounge room kneeling in front of their grandmother and playing with their nephew, and thought back to their birthday in 2007, when Cabot had thrown a beer bottle across the kitchen in a tantrum, and stormed off, only to be assaulted later that night.

"So, which one of us will smash the bottle on the floor this time?" Dom asked him. Standing side by side, they were quite similar in looks and height, with Dom being dark and blue-eyed and Antonio golden-brown and green-eyed.

Antonio grinned. "Probably you since *I'm* the good child and would *never* do such things. And I seem to recall—" He cut off Dom's protests. "That you had quite a few issues yourself that year."

"Mmm," Dom grumbled. "I came good."

"So did Cabot," Antonio reminded him. "And that's what *he* says."

"Yeah, but he got slapped by Grandma, and I didn't, because I *definitely* wasn't as bad as him." Dom grabbed his cousin's bottle and set them both in the crate in the recycling cupboard under the island bench.

"Very true," Antonio agreed. "Guess it should be me, then."

"Don't even think about it," Carlos warned his son. "One bad seed in this family's enough."

Antonio snorted and went to say hello to his grandparents with Dom.

"You still calling Cabot the bad seed?" Dan asked as he and Derek sat at the island bench next to Carlos. He accepted an icy glass of lemon-lime mineral water from Roger. "He has come good."

"He was. And for all I know, he still is," Carlos argued. "Time will have to tell, or have you all forgotten that *years'* worth of his garbage only came to a head three short years ago?" He looked at his brothers and Dan and Derek. "We'd been dealing with his rubbish since he was eighteen or twenty. And it only stopped when Mama took charge. How long till lunch, T?" He swigged back the last of his beer and set the glass down.

Tomas checked the roast and pots. "Five minutes everyone," he called out and saw Summer and Melody rush through the door.

"Sorry, we're late. Mom and Dad are coming in a few," Summer told everyone and went to stand under the air-conditioning duct. "God, it's hot out there."

Simon and Deidre came in next. "Sorry, we're late; the kids had birthday parties to go to." They headed for the kitchen to see Roger and grab glasses of ice-cold mineral water.

Within minutes, Tomas and Roger started plating up and handing out Jenny's delicious roast chicken as each member of the family took a plate and found a seat at one of the two tables. Lunch on Sundays had become a process line where everyone grabbed a plate from the kitchen bench and passed by.

Mike and Maggie arrived and came up the rear. "Sorry, we're late." Accepting plates, they made it to the adults' table and took their seats.

"Hey, D. Where's Charlie?" Alena asked as they converged at what was known as the kids' table even though none of them were kids anymore, and the next generation only had Adam so far.

"At home finishing up some things. He should've been here by now." Diana settled her son into his high chair and sat beside him. "And you know he *hates* being called Charlie."

"Sorry, I'm late," Charles Kensington called from the doorway and quickly rushed over. "Lost track of time." He kissed his wife and son, took his plate of food from Tomas, and quickly sat down.

"You must have been lost in your work to be running this late," Jenny said from her seat at the head of the table. She cast an eye over both tables and made sure everyone had everything they needed, and that the carafes of drink and pots of gravy were readily available. "I hope we're not working you too hard."

"Of course not." Charles shook his head. "It's just easy to lose a sense of time when processing photos in a dark room." As a photographer, Charles was still old school and used film.

"That's good. Dig in everyone." Jenny sliced into her chicken breast and let the aroma waft up to her nose. "Mmm… Smells good."

"Tastes good, too, as usual. But can we get back to my issue?" Alena asked.

"No!" came the resounding chorus from her siblings and cousins.

"What issue do *you* have now?" Dom asked his sister. "What hairstyle of the week is next, or what outfit will look hottest on Twitter and Facebook."

Antonio snorted. "Good one." He saw Alena's frown and grinned.

Danté snickered and said, "She's worrying about sex."

"Ew, Alena!" Dom screwed his face up. "Keep *that* conversation for your bedroom."

"*That's the problem!*" Alena dramatically exclaimed. "It's not happening *there* either."

"Ew!"

Diana rolled her eyes and updated the others. "Alena's feeling left out because I'm married and have a two-year-old already and *she's* still single and *alone.*" She eyeballed her cousin.

"Suck it up, princess, you can't always have it your own way," Dom told Alena.

"Princess Alena doesn't always get what she wants," Alexis added. "*Especially* in the last few years." Princess Alena was a long-standing nickname that had started way back when Alena was three and had first gone to Disneyland.

"Just because *you're* fucking *my* ex-boyfriend, Alexis, doesn't mean *you* get to torment *me* over *my* lack of sex," Alena sniped.

Charles had quickly covered Adam's ears, and a clatter of cutlery and silence followed.

"Ouch! Burn!" Cabot murmured and stared wide-eyed at his cousins and brother. They all looked at each other in shock.

"Did I just hear right?" Pedro demanded across the tables.

Alena looked up from her plate to see everyone staring at her and shrugged. "What?"

"Well, maybe if *you* fucked yourself as hard as you fuck your vibrator, *you* wouldn't be such a bitch now, *would you*?" Alexis glared at her sister on her left and then turned to the girls on her right. "Summer, let's swap seats."

"Double fucking burn!" Cabot whispered in shock and clasped his hands over his mouth as he watched Alexis trade seats with Summer, so she was now beside him.

"*Do not* fall back into your old habits, *either* of you," Jenny warned, watching Alexis change places, so she and Alena were separated. "I won't tolerate it from either of you."

"That's fine, Grandma. I'm sure we'll be back to normal when she apologises." Alexis went back to her food as if nothing had happened. It had been a long three years of her and Alena getting to know each other again. After Alena had ignored her for nineteen years, it took her assault back in 2007 for Alena to finally wake up to herself and get to know Alexis as not only her sister, but an adult.

"Actually, that *was* a good burn," Alena agreed. "I need to remember that for the next person I have to whip out a one-liner for. Well done, Alexis."

Alexis casually swiped her fringe away and glanced at Cabot on her right, who was seated at the end of the table with Tony, and scored raised brows and wide eyes in return. "I thought so. One of my best, I'd say."

Cabot nodded vigorously in agreement.

Slowly, the family went back to eating and Alena went back to complaining.

"Seriously, D," she said to Diana on her left. "Have you got any friends you could hook me up with? Dom? Antonio? Cabot offered to take me to places before, but as much as I want sex, I also want a relationship. Got any friends you could introduce me to?" Looking from siblings to cousins all she saw were grimaces.

"Seriously?" Dom asked. "You're *that* desperate? *So* desperate you'd ask *us* to set you up? If anything, Cabot's gonna know more men than us."

Antonio, who was beside him, snickered. "I think I still have that list somewhere." He was referring to the list he'd kept, of partners, one night stands, and quick fucks Cabot had done over his short lifetime. He'd made it to 4242, that Antonio actually knew of. With Tony supposedly being 4243. And the last.

"Ugh, Antonio, gross, you kept it?" Cabot complained and gave his brother a withering look before turning to his cousin. "Look, Alena, as the resident champion of how many partners one can have, I'm going to offer my advice."

A collective groan went around the table, but it just amped Cabot up.

"You're a gorgeous girl," he declared, "who could have *any* man you want. *Your* problem is you're not getting out and about to meet them. You're *here*, on *Mykonos*. And while summer is on speed with all of the tourists, many of them are gay, so out of the running." He settled into his spiel. "But they're *just* tourists. You need to get out to London, or L.A., or New York to meet other men."

"I met a man in New York once..." Alena distractedly muttered.

"We *all* met that man in New York once," Cabot replied. "And he was a hunk and a half of hot male flesh, but the point is," he noticed everyone staring, "*the point is, your* dream man may not even be here. He could be from somewhere else entirely. Like *my* dream man." He gazed fondly at his partner of three years, Tony DeLuca, son of Antonio and Cynthia DeLuca. They'd met when Tony had flown in from London to try and find his attacker. The rest was history.

"Just because *you* got lucky with a man from somewhere else, and Diana got lucky with a man from somewhere else—" Alena started but was interrupted.

"And *Grandma* got lucky with a man from somewhere else," Alexis said.

"And *Mama* got lucky with a man from somewhere else," Diana added.

"Then it doesn't mean that *you* won't get lucky with a man from somewhere else," Cabot finished. "*Seriously*, cuz, you gotta think big. Think outside the scope. You're going on tour again; maybe you'll find a man in one of the many places you're going to this time. And *not* in New York."

"Mmm, I think she's just pissy that James is getting married to his lovely *fiancée*, Sarah." Alexis wiped her mouth with her napkin and picked up her glass. "Did y'all see the engagement photos in the paper?"

"No, when?" Cabot asked.

"Back in Feb. He proposed on Valentine's Day. How *romantic*," Alexis told him.

"Imagine that." Cabot leaned toward her and rested his elbow on the table while his chin settled on his hand. "Alena's ex is dating you, and Alena's ex-potential is engaged to someone new. Is it just me, or does *no man* seem to want out little pop princess? And I do *have* to add that both men are *delectable* dishes." He saw Alena's scowl out of the corner of his eye.

Alexis giggled and swatted her cousin's arm. "Yes, they are, and both moved on rather rapidly."

"For *all* of your information," Alena piped up. "*I* dumped Lorenzo, and me and James never got started."

"And you know why," Tomas said over his shoulder, partially turning in his seat to look at her. "Can you stop talking about him, please?" James Gardo was still a touchy subject for him three years on.

"*I* didn't bring him up," Alena argued. "But *I* got to miss out on a relationship with him because of all that crap."

Every adult at the other table turned their gaze to her and the frown on Tomas's face burned into her heart.

Sighing, she relented. "Sorry, Prince Tomas. I'm just…" Her gaze darted down to her plate and she knew she was redder than a tomato. "Lonely, and single, and depressed about it."

Tomas relented and his frown slid away. "It's okay, Princess Alena. You know that period of our lives was rough. But times are better, and they will be for you, too. Someday your prince will come."

"Yeah…but when's *that* supposed to be?" she mumbled and stabbed at the breast of her chicken.

*****

"Why do I feel so lonely? Why do I feel so blue?
Is it because I miss you? Is it because of you?
I feel so lonely without you, feel so lonely,
I feel so lonely without you, feel so damn lonely…"

The words drifted off as Alena stopped singing, and stared across the vast expanse of the concert arena in Athens. It was the first stage of her tour that started that night. Sighing, her body deflated. "Why do I feel so fucking lonely?" she muttered and closed her eyes.

"You okay, Alena?" Rodney asked. As her sound engineer, he needed to know if anything was wrong, and right now he had no idea if it had been the microphone fading out, or Alena.

"No, Rodney, I'm not." Staring at the back of the venue she let out another sigh. "I'm depressed, not happy, not loving this, not loving being here. I just don't feel like doing it." She flopped down onto the stage and lay on her back, staring up at the metal ceiling.

Maria Baugh rushed on stage and over to her one and only charge. As a member of the Stephanopoulos staff, her only job was to worry about Alena's career, management, publicity and bookings. "What is it? Are you ill? Why are you depressed?" She stared down at Alena. "And what was that song? That's not on the setlist, is it? Are you having a heart attack?"

"Calm *down*, Maria," Alena told her. "It's just something I was singing."

Maria managed to get down on her knees next to her. "What is it?

What's going on? Why are you depressed?"

"Because I'm lonely and single and haven't had sex in God knows how long," Alena replied, trying to think back. "Hell! *I* don't even know when."

"Oh…well…" Maria's brow furrowed. "You're not the *only* one, you know. Although I am surprised, considering how gorgeous you are."

"So everyone keeps telling me." Alena looked at her. "Do you know how depressing it was being at my cousins' twenty-eighth birthday and my grandfather's eighty-eighth birthday as a single, lonely woman? Meanwhile, my sister's dating my ex, and another sort of ex is engaged. I haven't had an *actual* relationship in…" She counted on her fingers. "Since Lorenzo, and oh, my God," she wailed. "2002."

"What do you *mean* you haven't had a relationship since 2002?" Maria demanded. "You've had plenty of dates."

"Dates, yes. Relationships, as in, more than a week or month, long-term. *No.*" Alena rolled over onto her stomach and leaned up on her arms. "I want a *long-term* relationship where we walk and talk and hang out and go to parties together. And sex. I want lots and lots of hot steamy sex."

"Who doesn't?" Maria argued. "But right now you have a concert to prepare for tonight and a tour to produce over the next six weeks. Imagine all of the men you'll meet and can take back to your hotel room."

"Or tour bus." Alena screwed up her nose. "Yeah, coz *that's really* romantic. And taking guys back to my bus or hotel room makes me sound like a whore and I'm not."

"Nobody said you were." Maria sighed at the juvenile dramatics.

"That guy I had a fling with last year certainly did," Alena scoffed. "Couldn't wait to tell the whole tawdry story to the tabloids. We dated for barely a month before he ran to the press with lies and gossip. Thank *God* for the family lawyers. Shut that down pretty damn quick, because it made me sound like a nymphomaniacal whore."

"It's 2010, and you're a consenting adult," Maria told her and slowly set herself back on her feet. "If you want to have sex with men, and they consent too, that's fine. It's up to you. Unfortunately, some people are just scumbags and want a quick buck or two." She brushed down her pants and straightened her blazer. "But for now, you have a show tonight, so you need to finish rehearsing. Come now; stand on your own two feet like an adult instead of rolling around on the floor like a child."

"Argh! I'm *not a child*, Maria." Alena stomped to her feet. "See, I'm an adult."

"And yet you just stomped your feet." Maria raised a brow in amusement.

"Argh!" Alena growled and stormed off stage.

"Are we…" Rodney muttered into the mic.

"Give her a few minutes to cool off and grow up," Maria called out. "Meanwhile, is everything else ready to go?"

"We've rehearsed for weeks, but need to get this sorted out today," Randy said. "The first show's tonight."

"And we all know the first show always has teething problems." Maria sighed and wondered if she should go after the pampered princess.

"True, but if she doesn't get this done today, there will be more than usual."

"Okay, okay, I'll go." Maria waved a dismissive hand and walked towards the dressing room, coming across Alena's support act for the tour.

"Ah, Maria, how are you today? And it is a beautiful day, no?" Luca Saint, thirty-five, Italian American, tall, dark, and devastatingly gorgeous was a singer-songwriter-musician and currently the hottest thing in Italy. His debut single had scored a top five position in the charts for ten weeks, five of those being in the number one position. He was hot property in Europe right now and had been chosen for the spot on Alena's tour.

"Hello, Luca, nice to see you again. Been keeping to yourself?" She extended her hand for him to shake, but he kissed it instead, in that charming European way. "We haven't seen much of you."

"Ah, yes…" he smoothly replied with all of his Italian charm. "Busy doing phone interviews and promotional work, photo shoots for magazines. Busy, busy, busy. But then, you would know all about such things working with Greece's hottest pop star…Alena."

"Yes, yes I do." Maria was quite charmed by the sexy Luca Saint, as were most of the women throughout Europe.

"And when do I get to meet Greece's pop royalty?" Luca kept a hold of her hand. "Our first show is tonight and we have not crossed paths, yet."

"Well, I'm sure you'll meet sometime." Maria smoothly extracted her hand. "She's been busy rehearsing, costume fittings, book promotion, running her design empire."

"Ah, yes, and she and her siblings and cousins have new books out with the family publisher." Luca's smile dazzled like a million halogen lightbulbs. "I found her music books to be…" His expression became somewhat patronising. "Entertaining. The same for her brothers' books."

"Oh…well. Nice to know. I'll pass that on, shall I?" Maria watched him intently, knowing full well what he was up to.

"You do that, and let the pop princess know I'm *very* eager to meet her and cannot wait." He bowed. "Good to see you again, Maria."

"You too, Luca," Maria murmured and continued on her way to Alena's dressing room. *Jesus Christ on a freakin' unicycle he's hot. No wonder he's got the world buzzing right now. The sexual heat coming off him alone would set fire to the place and burn the whole damn building down. Maybe I should set him up with Alena…*

*****

"Okay, where are we sitting?" Nick asked as the family filed through the door from the backstage area into the arena.

"Down front as usual," Danté replied, trailing after his brother and sister.

The whole family had hopped their private plane over to see the start of Alena's latest tour, including Dan and Derek, Mike, Maggie and the girls. All of them had dressed up for the show, and waved to the fans as they walked past. The whole of Greece knew the Stephanopoulos family and all were considered royals and celebrities.

Danté thought that an absolute riot since all his side of the family did was make music and sing, or DJ. The golden-haired side of the family was the best known. These ranged from movie director, writer, producer Carlos, to Vivian, Diana, Cabot and Antonio, four supermodels that were world-famous. All he did was DJ in the family club and make music, and run an IT business on the side.

"This is so cool," Nick crowed. "Look at all the girls here." He scanned the audience of more than fifteen thousand and saw it was a good half and half mix of men and women.

"Can you stop perving for God's sake?" Danté rolled his eyes and looked at the hangers-on that had come with the family. Namely, Lorenzo, who was acting all protective of Alexis by keeping an arm around her and almost shoving Summer and Melody aside. Frowning, he looked to his parents and grandparents who didn't seem to be amused by it, or by him being there. He watched as everyone seated themselves and Cabot waved and primped for fans, even running over to take selfies with the crowd. "Doesn't he ever stop?"

Antonio glanced over his shoulder at his twin. "Nope. You know he's always on like the Duracell bunny. But stop worrying about him. I see some fans screaming for you."

"Yeah, right," Danté scoffed, but then he noticed that some of them were and blushed before going over to take photos.

"Ugh, why don't they scream like that for me?" Nick complained, and then threw his head back and dramatically wailed, *"Why!"*

"Don't worry, Nicky." Antonio laughed. "They will one day."

Nick frowned and gave him a dirty glare. "I *hate* being called that."

Antonio gave him a sly grin in return. "I know."

Once everyone had taken their places and the announcements had been made, they watched as the gorgeous Luca Saint took to the stage with his guitar and backing band.

"Oh, my God, he's gorgeous!" Summer exclaimed, staring wide-eyed at the Italian crooner on stage. *"How did she score him?"*

"Don't know, but I completely agree," Angie murmured to Maggie. "How *did* she score him and holy Jesus he's gorgeous."

"Certainly is, and listen to that voice. So smooth." Maggie found herself closing her eyes and swaying to the music.

"Holy fuck, he's hot." Cabot gazed up at Luca.

Tony nodded. "I agree and perfect for your cousin."

"Who's talking about Alena? I was thinking about…" Cabot glanced at Tony and blushed. "Oh…"

Tony's left brow rose. "About what…?"

A girly giggle escaped Cabot and he covered his mouth. "Never you mind."

Tony leaned in close to his lover's ear. "What? A threesome?"

Cabot's eyes widened and his jaw dropped. "Tony! I thought I was the only one thinking that, you dirty boy." He playfully swatted him and went back to gazing adoringly at Luca.

Nick scanned the crowd behind them. "Mmm," he grumbled. "He's got them eating out of the palm of his hand. How the hell does he do that?"

"By looking like that." Danté pointed at the heartthrob on stage gyrating his hips as if he were Elvis. "And *sounding* like that."

"Yeah, yeah." Nick's grumbling continued, but even he had to admit the songs were good. Looking at his sisters and mother, he found all of the females in the family gazing up at Luca. "He's even sucked in our mothers and sisters. Look."

Danté glanced to his left and saw that even his grandmother, Viv, Diana and Deidre couldn't take their eyes off him. "Jesus! He's done a number, or three, on them."

*****

Backstage, where Alena was warming up her vocals for her performance, she stopped long enough to hear the crowd go nuts. "Mmm, the support act must be good. La la la la la la la laaaa, fa fa fa fa fa fa fa faaaa, ba ba ba ba ba ba ba baaaa…"

"Thank you, ladies and gentlemen, here's a little something I threw together this afternoon." Luca's voice wafted over the sound system and the strings of an acoustic guitar were sensually played.

"Mmm, so it's a guy…" Alena murmured. "Or a band?" She wished she could see from where she was.

"Why do I feel so lonely? Why do I feel so blue?
Is it because I miss you? Is it because of you?
I feel so lonely without you, feel so damn lonely over you."

"Hey!" Alena exclaimed and thrust her hands onto her hips. "He's singing my lyrics!"

"What do you mean *your* lyrics?" Maria stopped pacing and checking her phone long enough to glance at Alena.

"What I was singing this afternoon." Alena waved a hand towards the stage. "This afternoon when you asked me what the song was and I said it was just something I was singing. Well, now *he's* singing it."

"Did you write it? Is it an actual song? We could sue him for breach of copyright," Maria told her. "You didn't give him permission, did you?"

"No, of course not. It was just something that I was singing. But now he's taken that and turned it into something he claims he wrote."

"Well, that could be a breach of copyright, unless it's some other artist's song and you were singing it. Is it yours?"

"I guess." Alena frowned at the circular conversation and then fired up. "That bastard took my song and claimed it as his. How dare he!"

"You haven't seen him yet, have you?" Maria watched her pace.

"No, why? I don't even know who we hired for the tour, let alone have seen them." Alena's frown deepened and she bit her lip as she paced.

"Luca Saint."

"Who?" Alena faced Maria. "Who are they?"

"Not *they, he.* Gorgeous he is, too. Italian American, six-foot God knows what, dark hair and eyes, stunning. Sings, writes, plays. Top five hit for weeks, number one for half of it. The hottest thing out of Italy since…" Maria paused and thought about it. "Well…who and whatever last came out of Italy. Anyway, he's been busy in the lead-up to this tour and you've been with your family on Mykonos. It's no wonder you two haven't met, yet."

"Yeah, well, that doesn't give him the right to steal my song." Alena heard the thunderous applause for the song and stomped her foot. "Goddammit, he even got the bloody crowd on his side. With *my* song!" She heard him launch into an up-tempo number and say, "Ladies and gentlemen, this is my last song for the evening, very soon you'll have the gorgeous Alena on stage to entertain you, but before I go, this is my current smash hit number one single, *Blown Away By You.*"

"I was Blown Away By You…and every little thing you do,
From your wink and your smile, to your ocean blue eyes…
I was Blown Away By You…"

"Oi! Really?" Alena pulled a face. "Lyrics for toddlers. How childish are they?"

"No more childish than some of yours over the years," Maria muttered and then stopped Alena's tirade in the making. "Especially your early ones when you were still young. Thank *God* your parents can write a decent song, *they saved you,* they did, with their expertise in songwriting."

"Excuse me!" Alena's hands went back to her hips and her mouth and eyes grew wide.

"Excuse you?" Maria glared at her. "For what? Your childish behaviour today? No. I won't. For stating the truth? No. I won't. You're a grown-ass adult, Alena, act like one." She saw the astonishment come over her charge. "You're snippy over the fact he took something you were singing today. Well, tell him you don't appreciate it. You're depressed because you're single. Well, do something about it. Otherwise, shut up and get back to warming up, or go and get dressed." Staring at Alena's outfit, she added, "That's not a stage outfit, is it? Because it's hideous."

Stuttering, Alena managed, *"No, it isn't, Maria."* She stormed off to her dressing room where she slammed the door and let out an almighty growl, fists clenched by her side. She paced back and forth until her wardrobe stylist came in.

"Time to get ready…" Kafka, Alena's wildly dressed African American long-time stylist, stopped short. "You okay?"

Heaving a sigh from the pit of her diaphragm, Alena calmed her breathing. "No, Kafka, I'm not okay. Just had a spat with Maria, but she's right. I need to act like an adult and not a child. So, let's get ready."

Fifteen minutes later, she was ready to go on stage.

"Okay, here's your microphone, and your pack, let's put it on."

Rodney hastily buckled her sound pack around her. "Have you warmed up? Say something into the mic." He spun her around and listened to her say, "Me, me, me, meeee…" He nodded at the reply in his earpiece. "Good to go. *You* good to go?"

Alena's smile did not reach her eyes. "I'm fine, Rodney. I've done this thousands of times."

"I don't know about thousands, but stand by." He walked away to check on something, leaving her alone in her space.

"And here is the star of the evening now. I'm so glad I didn't miss you before you went on stage. I must thank you for hiring me as your support act. Even I can't get fifteen thousand screaming fans, just yet. But one day."

Alena heard the voice behind her, and her anger flared as she turned around ready to spit fire at the musical thief. "So, *you're* the beefcake who stole my song from today. How dare…" Her gaze travelled up and up and up over a hard muscular, masculine body encased in black leather pants and an open to the waist shirt into dark eyes that she drowned in.

"Oh…" he murmured, captivated by her beauty in person. "You *are* gorgeous."

"And you're…oh, you're…" She was falling, and she knew it.

"I wanted to tell you to break a leg," Luca managed while gazing into her ocean blue eyes.

"You're welcome," sighed out of her. The whole backstage area had disappeared. Everyone and everything. It was just them in the moment.

Luca's dazzling smile slid across his gorgeous Italian face. "For what?" He breathed her in. Her eyes, her flesh, her lips.

"I don't know," Alena murmured, mesmerised.

"Yes." Maria smirked from a few feet away. "I timed *that* right." She'd gone to Luca's dressing room to let him know if he wanted to wish Alena luck then he had a few moments before she went on stage. From the looks of it, it had been perfectly timed. And if all went to plan, Alena would shut up her whinging about being single and they could have a peaceful, calm tour.

"One minute before stage, Alena," Rodney called as he walked up to them. "Alena?" He noticed them staring into each other's eyes. "Alena?"

"Mmm?" Alena could barely tear her gaze away from the gorgeous stud before her. "What?"

"Thirty seconds till stage, let's go." Rodney clapped his hands and waved her on.

"Um, yeah, okay." Her eyes darted back to Luca. "Will you, um, watch, or um…"

"Oh…I'll be here," Luca told her. "I may even go out on the floor to watch."

"Oh, okay, I'll, um…" She was being pulled backwards by Rodney.

"Alena, come on, showtime."

"Um, bye…" She waved at Luca who wiggled his fingers in return.

Rodney spun her around and marched her to the stairs leading to the stage. "Ten seconds. Get ready, five, four, three, two, one, and go."

She marched up the stairs in her silver platform knee-high boots and stood on the platform at the back of the stage where she would make her grand entrance after the curtain fell. A guitar struck a chord, she struck a note, and the curtain fell to rapturous applause. She went on to sing three songs before stopping. "Hello, Athens." The screaming came at her like a freight train. "How are we tonight?" Gazing across the crowd, she wiped her forehead with the back of her hand. "Is it hot in here, or what? I am *so* hot, and not because of the summer heat, but because of the heat left behind by my support act." The crowd screamed louder. "*How hot was he?* Whew!" She fanned herself with her hand while walking back and forth across the stage. "Holy Jesus Christ on a unicycle, he's hot. Did you all see him? Distracting, wasn't he? So, if I *seem* a little distracted…" She laughed and looked down at her family. "You all did see him, right? I'm not seeing things? He *is* hot, right? My family, everybody." More screams. "The whole Stephanopoulos family is in the house tonight with some extras tagging along. My grandparents, my parents, my aunt and uncles, my siblings and cousins." She listened to the screams for her family and zeroed in on her mother. "You did see how hot he is, right?"

Angie nodded in return and waved her hand in her face to cool down much to Pedro's amusement.

"Yep, didn't think I was seeing things." Alena kept on walking. "Hey, cuzzes. Steele and Phoenix Stefan in the house, ladies and gentlemen."

Cabot turned around to the crowd and waved his arms madly back and forth.

"Bet you guys thought he was hot, huh?" She giggled and Cabot gave her two thumbs up. "If anyone knows how hot a guy is, it's my cousin, supermodel Cabot Stephanopoulos, a.k.a. Steele Stefan." She kept on walking. "Hello Athens, how are we over this side?" Stopping at the edge of the stage to look out over the crowd down the side of the arena as they screamed and waved back at her, she felt the thrill race up her spine. "Ready for some more music?" They continued going wild and she sang, "Hey…everybody… You sing."

"Hey…everybody…"

"Nice." She nodded and walked back across the stage to the crowd on the other side. "Hello over this side, how are we?" She waited for the screaming to die down before continuing. "You sing, hey…everybody…"

"Hey…everybody…"

"All right, good job." Walking back to the centre of the stage, she set the microphone in its stand and pointed both arms at the crowd. "Down the middle, I want to hear you all sing, hey…everybody…"

"Hey…everybody…"

"Nice, here we go…" Pulling the microphone from the stand she sang, "Hey, hey, hey, ow," and launched into her latest number one European hit, *Get On The Floor (Hey Everybody)*.

Three songs later, and a change of costume, she had the crowd on their feet for a medley of her old hits, and then slowed it down for a change of outfit and a medley of her ballads. "This is the acoustic part of the show. It's where we slow things down to give you all a breather, to give the band a rest." She giggled at her backing band sitting on the steps in front of the drum kit stage. "And where I get to rest my worn out tootsies." Sitting on a stool with her legs crossed, she pulled up her black, ankle-length satin evening dress to reveal her right foot ensconced in a diamanté slipper and showed it off to the crowd. "Nice, huh? *Haus of Stefan*, if anyone wants to know. Get them instore or on the website."

As she adjusted the dress back over her foot, the guitarist strummed the acoustic guitar and she moved her head in time. "I'm going to sing some of my favourite ballads from my career. Not that I've done many, but I usually include one or two on each album. And I did that ballad album about five years ago. Did you all buy it?" Screams. "Did you all love that?" Louder screams. "Good. Because a couple of those are about to be sung. *So red the rose*," she crooned softly. "*Save me, oh save me… so red the note, he wrote me, he showed me, come prick me with your thorn…yeah…*" The song went on and she sang four more before letting the band exit her off stage. She quickly changed and prepared for the home stretch.

"Fascinating conversation, earlier," Luca smoothly interrupted before she went back out. "I love the way you interact with the crowd and include your family."

"And which conversation would that be?" She raised a brow and looked him up and down with a critical eye. He may have been hot, but he'd still stolen her song.

"The one where you spoke about me being hot." He'd watched her performance intently, noticing what a firecracker she could be, and wondered if that fire and passion for music translated into the bedroom.

Alena tried to act nonchalant, so gave a one-shoulder shrug. "You are, and I bet you know it. A guy that looks like you…" She gave him a side-eye. "And I bet you think those looks can get you what you want. *Including* stealing someone's lyrics."

An expression of distaste and anger flickered across Luca's face. "I don't need to *steal* lyrics. I come up with my own."

"*Sure* you do." She nodded. "Which is why you stole my lyrics from this afternoon for one of your songs. "*Why do I feel so lonely? Why do I feel so blue? Is it because I miss you? Is it because of you? I feel so lonely without you, feel so damn lonely over you…* I sang that at rehearsal and I have my whole crew to say I did. And then all of a sudden, poof, you sing it on stage and claim *you* wrote it this afternoon. Pig-bloody-shit you did!" Hands on her hips, she turned away from him, fuming.

"Ah, that one." He gave a nod of his head in recognition. "Yes. You did inspire that song, which is why I gave you a songwriting credit on it."

"A songwriting credit!" she declared incredulously and turned to stare at him. "*You* steal *my* lyrics and put it in a song. *You're a thief,* and *you're* giving *me* songwriting credit. What a joke!"

"Are you always this much of a firecracker?" Luca inched closer to her. "I wrote it for a reason."

"*Stole it,* you mean!" she scoffed and looked away.

"I *wrote it* and gave *you* songwriting credits because I believe we could make beautiful music together."

"*That old chestnut.* I highly…doubt…" she trailed off and stared at him. "What?"

He leaned over her and gazed into her eyes. "I believe we could make beautiful music together. On *and off* stage."

"Oh…" Her lips grew fuller, and her pupils dilated with the sexual chemistry.

He went in for his final line. "And in *and out* of bed."

"Okay, Alena, back on in ten." Rodney pushed her toward the stairs leading up to the stage. "Get your mind on the show. One more set and then the encore. And whatever you do," he turned her to face him, "*stop* thinking about lover boy and concentrate on the damn show." Staring hard into her eyes, he shook her gently. "You got it?"

Distracted by Luca's words, Alena blinked a few times. "Ah… yeah…got it."

"Good, now get up there." Rodney pushed her up the stairs and she walked onto the raised platform waiting for her cue.

"Breathe, just breathe, and worry about him later. You've got a show to do, you know how to be professional. Put him out of your bed. I mean head. Oh, Jesus." She banged her palm against her forehead. "Get it together, girlie, you've got a show and your family's in the front row, not to mention your damn ex." That fired the fury in her, that her ex was still dating her sister, and with the beats of the next song, she went on to sing another four songs and the encore.

"Thank you, so much, ladies and gentlemen. Thank you for being here, thank you for buying my music and loving my songs. Thank you for coming to see me play, see my band play. Fantastic, aren't they?" She waved to the crowd and went on to speak in Greek, the language of her paternal side. While English was the main language spoken in the Stephanopoulos family, the kids had learned Greek in school, and Spiros and Tomas still spoke it when they were out and about traversing with the older townspeople who didn't speak English, so they had helped her dust off her language skills. "I love you, thank you for loving me back. Thank you for coming. I love you, Athens. Goodnight." She ran up the stairs to the back platform, still waving madly. "I love you, Athens, I love you, Greece, goodnight and safe travels."

The lights went out on stage and she disappeared from sight.

"Holy crap that was fun. I can't believe I forgot how much fun it is," she told Maria as she rushed down the backstage stairs. "But my feet are killing me."

"Then let's get you into a cool shower and the masseuse's hands, shall we?" Maria escorted her back to her dressing room where Alena dashed into the shower and the masseuse set up the table.

Luca knocked on the open door. "Oh, do we get a massage on tour? Excellent. Wish I had known." He eyed both ladies and saw no Alena. "Is the pop princess not available to visitors at the moment?"

"As you can full well hear, Alena's in the shower at the moment." Maria cocked her head towards the bathroom where Alena was singing. "And no, the masseuse is not for you. Just Alena." Eyeing his outfit of black leather pants and matching shirt, she wondered if he'd even bothered showering. "Didn't you wear that on stage?"

Luca's dazzling smile lit up the room. "No. But it is my favourite outfit to wear that I wear a lot. It suits me, no?" His ears picked up the sound of people coming. "I must go. Tell Alena I will see her on her tour bus." He nodded and quickly left the room, leaving her puzzled.

The family entered the room en masse.

"Did I just see the gorgeous Luca Saint leave?" Melody asked and her lips pouted. "Oh, I *so* wanted to meet him. He's so freakin' gorgeous it hurts."

"He is." Her twin sister, Summer, sighed. "And it does hurt. Right in here." She pointed to her heart. Both girls were still single even though they regularly dated.

"Ugh," grunted out of Alexis. "You two and your drooling. You didn't take your eyes off him the whole time he was on stage. Neither did your mother." She casually leaned into Lorenzo's arms; glad he was just as good looking as the Italian crooner.

"For *that* matter, neither did *your* mother," Summer retorted, crossing her arms and turning to her mother. "Aren't you and Aunt Angie *too old* to be perving at young men, *Mother!*"

"Don't *Mother* me, little girl," Maggie chastised, knowing full well she was only called that when her daughters wanted to take a dig at her. "*Unlike* you, I'm a woman who can perve at a man like that. And he's *definitely* a man."

"Argh." Mike rolled his eyes at Pedro. "Seriously?"

Pedro grinned at his best friend. "She's making up for all the time you spent pulling chicks behind the bar at *69*, and then *SB3*."

"So, all of this drooling over hot Italian men is payback for over thirty years ago?" Mike frowned in concentration, dragging the joke out.

"Oh, absolutely." Pedro nodded along. "You had hot Italian men throwing themselves at you left right and centre in *69*, she's just getting her own back."

"Oh, so funny, ha-ha." Maggie rolled her eyes at her husband.

"Point aside, where is he?" Angie asked. "Is he coming back?"

"Don't think so," Maria told her as Alena came out of the bathroom wrapped in towels. "He did say he'd see Alena on her tour bus, though."

"Who did?" Alena patted her still-damp skin. "Who's coming on my tour bus? Am I getting another bodyguard? We all know how *that* ended the last time I had one." She remembered back to her 2007 American tour where James Gardo had been chosen to be her personal bodyguard after an attempted shooting.

An uneasy silence rippled through the room before anyone spoke.

"Ah, no, no bodyguard, this time," Maria went on. "Luca Saint dropped by before your family, and said to tell you he'd see you on your tour bus."

Alena's brows furrowed. "But why? I have my own. I presume the support act has their own. Why would that pompous, two-bit, hustling lyric thief need to see me on my bus?" She hopped onto the massage table. "You know he admitted to stealing my lyrics. Claimed he's given me songwriting credit. *Me, me,*" she said incredulously. "When *I'm* the one who came up with the lyrics in the first damn place."

"What did he steal?" Pedro piped up. As the owner of *Sync,* the family's music studio, all copyright, trade marks and IP were important and he kept a tight rein on them.

"The song lyrics that I sang on stage today, Daddy." She towel-dried her hair. "It was just a little thing. Not even a verse during rehearsal, and then he gets on stage and says it's a little something *he* threw together this afternoon. The absolute *nerve* of that man. Stealing *my* damn song lyrics. And when I confronted him during the show, he claims I inspired it and he gave *me* songwriting credit. The *nerve.* The *absolute nerve.*" Tilting her head, she noticed Lorenzo. "But then, some men seem to have a lot of nerve."

Lorenzo flashed a cold glare back at her and tightened his arm around Alexis who hadn't noticed Alena's glare.

But most of the family had, and Jenny brought it to a halt. "Then, at some point, your parents can sit down with him and discuss copyright." She glanced from her son and daughter-in-law to Lorenzo and Alexis who snuggled in his arms. "But for now, we'll leave and let you finish up. The after-party is at *Stefan Productions,* correct?"

"Yep. The place is done up like a spring chicken ready to party," Carlos told her. "And we have the limos to take us, so let's go, everyone." *Stefan Productions* sat on a massive lot outside of the city with soundstages for *S'Reel,* his movie company, *Sync,* and had the main offices for *Villiers Inc* and *Haus of Stefan.* They had decorated a soundstage for the after-party.

"Okay, we'll let you have your massage now, sweetie." Angie kissed her daughter. "How long do you think you'll be?"

"Knowing her, hours," Diana muttered cheekily. "Will we even *see* you at the after-party, cuz?"

"Funny, *cuz.*" Alena eyeballed her. "I'll try to be there in an hour or two. It's going all night, isn't it, Daddy?"

"We're on a lot so the noise won't really travel." Pedro thought about it and shrugged. "However long we want it to go for."

"But she needs to be on the bus at some point." Maria started ushering everyone out. "No later than six tomorrow morning, as it's," she checked her watch, "nearly eleven now. "I'll try and have her at the party by midnight."

"Or she'll turn into a pumpkin," Cabot joked and looked over his cousin. "Although with all of that fake tan…"

"What, I'm *already* a pumpkin?" Alena raised a brow at him. "*My* tan's natural, *unlike* yours."

Cabot pursed his lips and feigned anger. "*How dare you!* This tan's as real as the hair colour Carlos gets out of a bottle."

"Hey!" Carlos pointed a finger at his son. "This hair colour's as real as my mother's, *not* out of a bottle."

"Oh, Carlos, calm down. Mine's not so real anymore, either." Jenny gently pushed him out the door and then glanced at Alena's manager. "Good to see you doing your job, Maria."

"That's what you pay me for, Jenny," Maria replied and finished corralling the family. "I'll have her there by twelve." She shut the door on them for privacy.

Cabot turned and pointed at the door. "Was Maria a bit…snippy?"

"Mmm…seems like it," Jenny murmured and looked at her grandson. "At least she has control of Alena. *Unlike* Matilda and you." She held her arm out for him to take, but he slipped his arm around her shoulders and she slid her arm around his waist instead.

"Yeah, well, Grandma. I was going through a phase," he acknowledged.

Guffaws followed them as they walked out of the arena and into the underground car park.

"Hey," Cabot cried and looked over his shoulder at his siblings and cousins. "I *was*. And *I* am the first to admit these days that I *was* a dickface, as Antonio used to call me." Guffaws turned to laughter. "But with a lot of help from the right people, namely Grandma," he kissed her temple, "and Xanthe, I came good."

Jenny smiled at her grandson. "And I am so proud of the young man you turned out to be." She kissed his cheek. "I'm so proud of you, Cabot."

"Naw, shucks, Grandma." The blush raced across his face. "I'm proud of me, too."

Antonio scoffed. He was walking behind Cabot and Jenny, with Tony beside him. "*Still* making it about you. *You're* proud of you? Good grief."

"Why shouldn't he be?" Jenny looked over her shoulder at him. "Aren't you?"

Sighing, Antonio came to a halt and stared at his twin while they waited for the limos. "I *suppose* I am. *Regardless* of everything he did, he *has* tried making up for it these last few years."

"Naw, Tonee, Tone, Tone, Antonio, thanks, bro!" Cabot blushed harder. His twin was the most important person in his life. Ever. But his grandma came a close second.

"And so there's nothing wrong with Cabot being proud of himself, too," Jenny told everyone before climbing into the limo. At eighty-two she was incredibly proud of all her children and grandchildren and the careers they had taken in life. While several of them had been problematic, and others had been dealt a rough blow, they had all come through their life lessons and out the other side as grown men and women. And she really couldn't be prouder.

"And that's fine when he's *not* acting like a dickface," Dom muttered and gave his cousin a dirty look. "When he's normal, he's fine." Unfortunately, Cabot's bad reputation still followed him three years on.

"I'm normal a lot these days, Dom. You know that," Cabot said. Even though he and Antonio were a year older than Dominic, they had grown up together as a threesome until he and Antonio moved to New York. But after he'd contracted HIV, a chasm appeared in their relationship and things hadn't quite gone back to the way they used to be.

"When you *want* to be, Cabot," Dom replied coolly. "You still let Steele Stefan take over when you shouldn't, and can still act like a dick when you want."

"Okay, that's enough," Pedro intervened, staring down his son and nephew. "I thought things had become cool between you two."

"They are." Dom glanced away and crossed his arms. "For the most part."

"Not the way it used to be," Cabot muttered. "Hasn't been the same since Antonio and I left and then *that year* happened." He darted around Tony and his brother and came up behind Dom, throwing his arms around his neck and shoulders. "I'm sorry, Dom. Sorry I was an absolute dickface to everyone. And I know we're still repairing our relationship, but I hope it continues and you don't still hate me. I'm sorry."

Scowling at being hugged, Dom glared at Cabot over his shoulder. His blue eyes glared into their mirror image as Cabot's chin rested on his left shoulder. "Get off me, Dickface," he said with a twinkle in his eye. "And no amount of apologising will ever be enough. You'll have to kiss my butt and lick my feet forever."

"That's just gross, Dom." Cabot's eyes closed and he shook his head. "So gross."

Glad to see his son and nephew back to normal, Pedro noticed the smirk on Antonio and Tony's faces. "Okay, let's get everyone into the car and get to Alena's after-party, shall we."

Dom moved for the limo, but Cabot hung on. "Ugh, get *off* me, Dickface."

"Nope, you're stuck with me until the end of time." Cabot dragged his feet, but didn't let go.

"*Get off me, Cabot.*" Dom pulled at his cousin's arms.

"Nope, you're stuck with ow—" Cabot had been spun around and trapped in a headlock. "How the hell'd you do that?"

Dom rubbed his knuckles into Cabot's head. "I've been doing martial arts for three years. So's Danté and Alexis. Even Antonio drops by occasionally."

"How ow…what ow…when ow…stop it!" Cabot clawed at his cousin's arms. "How did I not know that? Antonio!"

"Don't whine at me." Antonio entered the limo, leaving his brother to fend for himself.

Dom let go of Cabot with a final knuckle rub and rushed into the limo, slamming the door on his cousin.

"Argh. Dom, you get back here," Cabot demanded and opened the door.

"Enough, Cabot, just get in." Pedro rolled his eyes and shoved his nephew into the car. "Tony, try and control him."

Tony grinned. "Yes, Mr S." He climbed in after Cabot and settled in for the ride.

"Behave," Pedro warned them as they fought, and shut the door. He rushed to the other limo and took his seat. "Children! Who'd have them?"

"You did," Jenny retorted. "So did I. And I'm so glad I did."

"Naw, Mama," Pedro gushed. "So are we."

*****

They drove to *Stefan Productions* and got the party underway, with Alena arriving just after midnight. They partied until a quarter to six when Maria finally pulled her away to get on her tour bus for the next stop in Bulgaria.

"Bye everyone, bye." Alena waved madly from the bus steps. "I love you. See you in six weeks. Bye. I love you." The bus pulled away slowly, but she stayed where she was, waving, until the driver stopped at the road and finally shut the door.

"Time to go, miss," he said and locked the door tight. "Settle in for the ride. We've got a long trip ahead of us."

"Thank you. Get us there safely." Alena waved madly from the window.

"Will do, ma'am. You off to bed?"

She sighed as her family disappeared from sight. "Once the sun finishes rising, yes." Slumping back on the couch, she watched the new day start in Athens, blazing its way across the Acropolis and surrounding city. It was a beautiful sight and one she rarely saw. Even though the sunrises in Mykonos were stunning, and she'd seen many from around the world, there was something a little breathtaking about this one.

Yawning, she stretched her arms above her head and retired to the bedroom. Locking the door behind her, she pulled her mini dress over her head and managed to make her way into the bathroom for a quick cool shower. After drying off and hanging her towel on the rack to dry, she wandered back into the bedroom to find something to sleep in.

"Well…what do we have here?" a deep throaty voice asked from the bed.

She jumped back in alarm and covered herself with her hands, desperately looking for something to put on, and for who was talking.

He threw back the bed covers and stood up, proud and naked. "Don't be so shy, my little pop princess. Didn't you get naked for your thirtieth in that photo shoot? You *and* your gorgeous cousin."

"Who are you?" Alena cried out in alarm, seeing how gloriously fit he was. Blushing, she averted her gaze and tried to find her robe in the dim lamplight.

He came closer. "Don't you recognise me, Alena? We met last night. Backstage. You accused me of stealing your song and I told you I wanted to make sweet music with you." He sidled up to her, reaching his arm toward the wall she was backed up against and flicked the light switch on. "Hello, Alena."

She looked up into his dark eyes and gasped. "You! How dare you sneak onto my bus! You've got your own. Get off."

"Love to. But not the bus." Luca leaned closer. "On you." His lips met hers and fireworks exploded.

"No, what are you…" Alena twisted her head away. "How dare…"

He grabbed her hands from her body and pinned them to the wall, outstretched so she looked like Jesus on the cross. "So fucking beautiful."

"Ah," escaped her as she breathed in his scent. Warm, masculine, aroused. "Ah…" His lips landed on her cheek and made their way to the nape of her neck. "I…need…ah…" Struggling to keep her senses, Alena was naked in every way and on show for the Italian stud before her, and she knew she was being seduced. Her body knew it. And it ached for him, reacted to him. "Ah…"

Luca's hands released her arms and his fingers trailed along them as they came back to her body, caressing her sides, finding their way to her breasts, which they stroked.

"Ah…" Alena could barely stand upright, could barely keep her legs together even though they were fighting to move apart. Her body ached for the man before her, and her resolve was nearly gone. "Ah…"

His thumbs rubbed her nipples, finding them already rock-hard, but velvety to the touch. "You are so fucking beautiful, Alena Stephanopoulos," he breathed in her ear, pressing his whole body against hers.

"Ah…" she breathed and opened her legs, arched her back, and took his tongue into her mouth. "Ah…"

He lifted her onto him and she wrapped herself around him as he thrust into her, pushing her against the wall. But that wasn't enough.

He turned and threw them both onto the bed, making her cry out as he drove into her and thrust like a stallion, leaning on one arm with one leg bent to better enable his position of power.

She clung to him, kissed him, dug her nails into his buttocks, spread her legs wide and cried out as the orgasm hit in rolling waves of shock and awe. "Ah…oh…" Her breasts thrust up and her eyes squeezed shut as he rode her hard across the barren wasteland that had been her love life. Rode her like the man he was, rode her like the woman *she* was, and in one passionate mind-blowing moment, her drought came to an explosive end.

He slumped onto the bed beside her. "Holy fuck," he gasped, his chest heaving. "I've never fucked like that before."

"I've," gasp, "never been fucked like," gasp, "that before." Alena lay with her left leg under his and her left arm under his torso. "Oh, fuck?" She couldn't get air into her lungs fast enough and her whole body shook. "Fuck you, Luca Saint!"

"You just did, Alena Stephanopoulos." He got his breathing under control, rolled onto his side to face her, leaned up on his arm and rested his head in his hand. "*Now*, are you going to accuse me of stealing?"

"*You Italian bitch!*" Alena spat and heaved in air. "You steal my song; you steal my tour bus—"

"I steal your heart and your body." His left hand forcefully kneaded her right breast. "It's mine now. Both of them. All of you." His eyes burned into hers as his hand slid down her body and between her legs. "All of you is mine," he whispered before sliding his middle finger in.

"Argh." She arched, drew her legs up, and squeezed her eyes tight as the orgasm exploded through her.

His finger tormented her spot and she grabbed his hand with both of hers, curling upward as she flung his hand away from her, rolled him onto his back and slung her leg over. "You don't get to do that to me." She pinned his hands to the bed and mounted him, gasping at the intensity of the motion. "Argh!" Pleasure exploded through her and she jolted in a frenzied ride of exquisite pain.

Luca took her by the hips and bounced her, his knees bending as his body curled. He grunted, his head exploding with fireworks, and he lifted the maniacal woman from him and threw her onto the bed beside him. "No one gets the better of Luca Saint," he declared and kneeled between her legs. He lifted hers and placed one over each shoulder, making her body rise to meet his as he entered and thrust wildly.

"Ugh," she cried, her voluptuous breasts bouncing with every movement. All she could do was lie there, her arms spread out, her head rolling from side to side. She'd never been so thoroughly fucked in all of her life and couldn't get a grip on how to deal with it. Luca Saint was a man like no other. Definitely not like one she'd ever had. And there'd been a few that she'd had.

Luca took pleasure in seeing her lie there, helpless and unable to move, with a look of such delirium upon her face, he knew she'd have the inability to do anything. He thrust to ejaculation and slowed, head back, eyes closed. Dropping her legs, he slumped back. "Oh, that's so fucking good, so fucking powerful." Sliding his hands through his hair, Luca slicked it back and looked down at Alena in her blissful state, lying like a rag doll with no control over her body whatsoever. A slick smile curled his lips, and he shifted her legs apart so he could lie between them, his body full out on top of hers. He was a good five inches taller and easily covered her. "You are mine, Alena Stephanopoulos. Do you understand that?" He waited for her to open her eyes and focus on him.

"I'm not anybody's," she mumbled groggily, feeling every inch of him pressed against her flesh. Naked flesh on naked flesh burned and sizzled hotter than the sun.

"Yes, you are," he said in her ear, moving his pelvis against hers, lifting her, knowing she could feel his length against her.

"Argh..." she mewed, her mind thoroughly blown and her body thoroughly fucked by this man. A man like she'd never had before. A man whose body had taken ownership of hers in more ways than one. And he was a man she didn't want to let go of. "I love you..." breathed out of her.

He pulled his head back sharply to gaze down into her hooded eyes. "Did I hear you right? Did you say you love me?"

"Yes..." She still couldn't move, couldn't lift her arms or legs, but she knew full well what her heart was telling her. She'd fallen for him the moment they'd met, and knew that he was the man she'd been waiting for her entire adult life. Just like her mother had told her, just like her grandmother had told her. And if the stories were true, she wasn't the first in the family to fall in love at first sight. Or have sex on the night they met. And it wasn't as if she was a whore like Cabot, fucking every man that wanted her. But, by God, the sex had made her feel like one. And she *liked* it.

"Do you believe in love at first sight, Alena Stephanopoulos?" Luca was intrigued and excited at the prospect of owning such a famous acquisition. Because that's what he would do. Own her as no other man had.

"Yes," she murmured dreamily. "I do…and I fell for you the moment we met."

"Good." His slick smile slid across his lips. "Because I fell for you, too, and now I own you, Alena Stephanopoulos."

*****

Ten days later, when they arrived at the hotel in Italy, Alena had a package waiting for her.

"Mmm, what's this?" She ripped open the envelope and pulled out a folded newspaper. "A paper from New York?" A frown fled over her face. "Why would…" She unfolded the paper and saw a note written in black texta on the bottom half. "*Page 92. Enjoy, Alexis.* What the…"

"Is that your sister? Alexis?" Luca asked, casually sampling the fruit from the complimentary basket in her suite. They had been joined at the crotch since Greece and had barely surfaced each morning after torrid nights of passionate sex.

"Yes, my younger sister," she murmured absentmindedly and searched for page 92. "But why would she…oh…" Seeing the half-page photo, her brows rose and her mouth stayed in an o shape. "Oh…"

"What?" Luca was by her side before she could shut the paper. "What is it?"

"Oh…nothing…just the wedding section. Not sure why she sent it to me. Unless she's tormenting me about not being married yet." Alena tried to snatch the paper from his hands. "No need to worry."

"Why would I worry?" Luca glanced at each photo and landed on the largest. "He's very good-looking. Mmm…Detective James Gardo and Sarah Willmore married July 24th, 2010. But it's August 10th and this paper is dated," he looked at the cover for a date, "July 31st. Why would she send you one that's almost two weeks old?"

"We, ah, get them in. It takes time to get to Mykonos," she mumbled, staring at the photo. James's hair had grown back, covering any leftover sign of his scar, and he looked damn good. Just as good as he had when they met. "And then she sent it to me, so yeah…late…" Her brows slid down. "Why would Alexis think I want to see this? Is it some sort of joke? Not funny if it is."

Luca studied her face. "Do you know them?"

"No…" She turned away to stare out the floor-to-ceiling window and thought back to meeting him. Breathing out, a sigh left her. "Not the woman. But the man. The detective."

Luca looked up from the photo. "His eyes are a colour I cannot figure out. Blue?"

"Aqua." Alena crossed her arms. "So aqua blue they were like the ocean surrounding Mykonos."

"It sounds like you know him well." Luca's eyes darted back and forth between the paper and Alena. "You were born in New York, so you must know him."

"*Knew* him," she corrected. "For a few short months."

"How short?" Luca wandered over and a flash of jealousy fled through him.

"About two months, if that," she told him. "Look, I don't want to talk about it."

"But you must. It clearly still affects you, and if we are to be a couple and have a relationship then your exes, if he is one, should be discussed."

Alena riled up at that touch of sexist bullshit. "Will you tell me about all of yours?" She arched a brow in return.

"Well, I don't see the need…" Luca realised what he'd said and knew he needed to play it cool, so he gave a nod of his head. "I see that would make me a hypocrite. But the big difference is, my exes don't affect me the way he clearly still affects you."

Shaking her head, she stared out the window. "I toured America in 2007 and the first night, at Madison Square Gardens, there was a possible shooter. The police captain offered the police officer who'd knocked me out of harm's way to be my bodyguard for the rest of the tour. It was June and July, that's it. I fell into a crazy crush on him, but once he left the tour he was injured in a police pursuit and I left New York to go home to Mykonos with my family. Whatever relationship might have been, it wasn't *to be*, unfortunately. End of story."

"How was he injured? He looks perfectly normal in the photo." He studied the tall, good looking James Gardo with the aqua blue eyes, almost ex of his new lover, and detective of the NYPD.

"Shot in the left side of the head. He barely survived."

Luca's eyes darted from the paper to her. "You're kidding?" Lifting the paper closer, he tried to see any evidence of the incident. "Can't see anything."

"It *was* three years ago." Alena snatched the paper from his hands and studied the photo. "We talked via Skype for a few weeks, but both of us had other priorities. And Grandma invited him and his parents to Mykonos for Thanksgiving. We haven't seen him, or them, since." And in that moment she realised she felt nothing for him, or the situation, at all. Too much time had marched on.

"Why would you see his parents?" Luca knew there was something going on, and it was more than she was telling him.

Glancing up sharply, she said, "His father knew my father many a decade ago. That's it, end of story. I'm not discussing it anymore." She closed the paper and walked over to her stationery case for a Sharpie and business-sized envelope. She scribbled out Alexis's message and wrote on the top half of the paper, *NOT FUNNY, ALEXIS! I'M HAPPY FOR HIM, SO JUST CAN IT!* Sliding the paper into the envelope, she addressed it to her sister and rang down to the front desk to send a bellboy up. "Please have this sent off with express delivery," she told him and gave him a tip.

"Yes, ma'am." He nodded and scampered off.

Once the door was shut, Luca asked, "Did the two of you ever have sex?"

"What!" she exclaimed. "Why would you even ask that? Are you jealous?" Her instantaneous frown changed to amusement. "You're jealous," she sang and slid her arms around his waist.

"No…I'm not," Luca huffed and tried to remain resolute. But it was quickly dissipating. "I'm not…" As Alena planted kisses on his chest he tried to stop her. "And why are you…oh…stop kissing my chest." He hardened.

"It's hard not to when you wear your shirts open to the waist and I'm shorter than you. I come up to your chest." She slid her hands into his shirt and kissed the tanned skin in return.

He gave in. "Okay, so that's how you want to play it." He carried her into the bedroom and threw her on the bed. "You know better than to torment me, Alena Stephanopoulos." He unbuckled his belt and dropped his pants, setting his erection free.

Alena knelt in front of him and ripped his shirt open. "Fuck you, Luca Saint."

He pulled her against him. "Oh, you will, Alena Stephanopoulos, you will."

*****

The next night, at the first Italian concert during Luca's opening set, he introduced the song he'd written around Alena's lyrics. "It was inspired by the beautiful woman you're all here to see tonight. I heard her sing a few lines and completed the song. And tonight, she has agreed to come on stage and sing it with me. Please welcome to the stage, Alena." He sensually strummed his acoustic guitar and watched her walk out on stage in a tight black mini dress and high-heel ankle boots.

"Hello, Italia," she yelled and waved her arms. "Ciao."

Once the screaming had died down, Luca sang what had become the first verse and Alena the second. They sang the chorus together and a third and fourth verse each, before dividing the bridge line for line. Singing the chorus to the end, they gazed into each other's eyes and never once looked away. When the song was over, and the crowd screamed their acceptance, his slid his guitar around to his back, took her into his arms, dipped her, and gave her a very passionate kiss that made the crowd scream harder.

*****

Pedro and Angie burst through the door to his mother's house the next day. "Mama, did you see this? It's all over the papers and gossip sites online, not to mention the news and gossip shows on TV." He slammed down several papers on the table in front of her. "*What was she thinking?*"

There, on the cover, as front-page news, was a photo from the concert of Alena and Luca kissing.

Jenny moved the papers apart and gazed at each. "Well, she was thinking she was kissing a hot Italian stud. She *is* thirty-two, Pedro. She's a full-grown woman who can kiss any man she likes. Within reason."

"Yeah, but Mama…" He pulled out a chair and sat next to her. "It's the guy who's her support act. Talk about unprofessional. That's not how we do things in the company. It's in the contracts, we've warned all the kids. *Do not* become involved with the people you work with until the work and contract are over." Pedro looked to his brothers. "What do you guys think about this?"

Carlos shrugged from his seat opposite Pedro at the table. "I agree with Mama. Alena's an adult. The guy she's kissing is an adult. What do you *want* us to say?"

"She's an incredibly *stunning* adult," Tomas said. "And is old enough to kiss who she wants, Pedro. If the guy's single, and we know *she* is, where's the harm?" He went to pour them glasses of cool mint tea that he'd made earlier. "Is it actually *in* her contract for the tour that she can't date her support act *while* on tour?"

"Well…no…" Pedro frowned at the consequences it might cause the family. "But it's incredibly unprofessional and she knows better. She knows to leave it until the work is over and done, and then there can be no legal standing for any inappropriate behaviour that might happen *during* the contract. Whereas whatever happens *after* it, is up to both parties. Babe, what do you think? You haven't said much so far?" He turned to Angie for support.

"Sorry, babe." She shrugged. "I think he's gorgeous and they look incredible together. Plus, he's into music as much as she is. Maybe it's a match made in heaven. After all of her whinging and moaning and groaning about not being in a relationship, now she might actually be getting somewhere with one, and I'm all for it."

"Thanks for your support." A sigh blew out of him and he turned back to his mother. "What do you think? Is this okay?"

"Haven't we all just said that?" Jenny squeezed his hand. "Calm down, my baby. They're clearly attracted to each other. Let them have their fun. It's what comes *after* the tour that we need to worry about."

"What does that mean, Mrs S?" Roger asked and passed a plate of home-baked chocolate mint chip cookies across the table. "What will happen then?"

"We could very well be meeting him as her boyfriend." A smile lit up Jenny's face. "Look, the tour's six weeks long, it's barely been a week. In another five, or so, weeks she'll come home. If he's with her to meet all of us, we'll know it's serious. If not, then it was just a fling. Don't worry about it until then. Seriously, Pedro," she told her son. "There's no need to worry about any of it until then. Just wait and see."

"I hope you're right, Mama," he conceded, knowing full well his mother was *always* right.

*****

Six weeks later, at the end of the tour, Luca Saint did indeed go home to Mykonos with Alena to meet her family. He'd decided that being in the world's biggest musical family, one that had their own movie and music studios, plus the nightclub that had launched a thousand careers, was better than being in a family that didn't. So, thanking God that sex with Alena was the hottest he'd ever had, and that she was fairly easy on the eye, he'd made the decision to be with her after the tour. Because, after all, according to his narcissistic sensibilities, he owned her body and soul. And for now, she was a damn sight better looking than some of the women he'd bedded before meeting her.

"I'm going to tell you a little something about my family." Alena mounted him and slowly thrust up and down.

"What? Now?" Luca grasped her hips and tried not to explode inside of her.

"You'll be meeting all of them at lunch. It's Sunday, so you'll have Grandma's famous roast chicken, meet them, my parents, my siblings, my uncles and cousins, and in-laws."

"Ugh… So, what do you need to tell me?" He clenched his eyes shut as she clenched herself around him and held on. "Ugh."

"Well…" Her fingers moved through the trail of hair on his lower abdomen. "It's a large family. A passionate Greek, Australian, American family. A very close, tight-knit family who would do whatever it takes for each other." She slid down and clenched, taking joy in seeing the exquisite pain on his face. After weeks of claiming that he owned her, and her being a willing servant, she'd turned the tables and taken charge. "They will question you, asking a million and one of them, about your intentions, wanting to know what your future holds, where your career's going, what you plan on doing, etc," clench, "etc," clench. She flung her head back and came. "Etc…ugh." Collapsing onto him, she nestled in his chest. "I haven't had a relationship last this long in years. If it continues, you'll be an honorary member of the family for however long we're together. So that means everyone will be watching, *especially* my parents and Grandma."

"And if the relationship becomes long-term and serious?"

"Then you had better prove you're serious and *not* out to get your hands on whatever it is the family's got. Capeesh!"

"Capeesh," Luca muttered and let his fingers slide up and down her side. He'd hated losing control over her, but actually didn't mind her taking charge in bed. She just wasn't going to be doing it in *any other* aspect of his life.

Figuring it was best to arrive at her grandmother's early before the rest of the family; Alena led Luca up the stairs from her house at ten and into her grandparents'. They'd been there most of the week, hiding out and resting, unbeknownst to everyone else. "Grandma? Grandpa?

We're here." She wanted to introduce Luca to the adults first before being confronted by her siblings and cousins.

"We're here, darling." Jenny came down the hall from the laundry room where the spare fridges were. "Oh." She saw her granddaughter holding Luca Saint's hand and beaming a huge smile. "Hello there."

Alena clung to Luca's hand with both of hers. "Grandma, Grandpa, this is Luca. Luca Saint. He was my support act on tour." Looking from them to him, she added, "Luca, this is my grandmother, Jenny Stephanopoulos, and my grandfather, Spiros Stephanopoulos. The heads of our family."

"Hello there, Luca, it's nice to meet you." Jenny shook his hand and saw up close how criminally gorgeous he was. She watched him shake hands with Spiros.

"Mrs Stephanopoulos, Mr Stephanopoulos." Luca beamed his high-watt smile, pouring on the charm for both of them. "Such a pleasure to meet you both. Alena's told me so much these last two months. And, of course, everything I've read has done *nothing* but describe how wonderful this family is."

"Oh, why, thank you, Luca. Such kind words. And please, call us Spiros and Jenny." Her eyes darted to her granddaughter's face to see blissful happiness as she gazed up at the man beside her. "You seem to have made my granddaughter very happy."

Luca smiled down at Alena, removed his hand from hers, and slid his arm around her shoulders. "She makes *me* very happy, Mrs Steph, ah, Jenny," he corrected. "So incredibly happy. I believe it was love at first sight."

"Oh." Jenny's brows rose. "That old chestnut. Yes, it seems to happen a lot in this family. Alena, was it the same for you?"

"Yes, Grandma, it was." She excitedly gazed from her to Luca. "Very much so."

"Then I hope the two of you can spend some time getting to know each other away from the tour. Luca, I see your career is going well. Are you able to take time away from it?" Jenny studied the young man hoping to gain an insight to the type of person he was, and what potential harm he might do to her granddaughter.

"Ah, yes, Jenny. I have the rest of the month off. The single is still selling well and I'll be going back to work come October." He put his dazzling charm on high beam and hoped it did the job he needed it to do. Jenny Stephanopoulos, as the matriarch, would be a tough nut to crack. And no doubt he'd need *her* blessing as well.

"That's good to hear." Jenny saw Tomas and Roger in the doorway. "And here come some more family members now. Alena, do the introductions."

Alena rushed over to her uncle and flung her arms around him. "My prince has come," she whispered in his ear before pulling back. "Uncle Tomas, Roger, this is Luca Saint, my boyfriend." She giggled softly and grasped Luca's right arm. "These are my uncles, Tomas Stephanopoulos and his husband, Roger Dencott."

"Well…hello Luca Saint. Nice to meet you." Tomas shook his hand and saw how ecstatically happy his niece was. "You were the support act on Alena's tour, right?"

"Yes, Mr Stephanopoulos, I was." Luca shook hands with Roger. "Mr Dencott."

"Please, call us Tomas and Roger," Roger replied, noticing the smooth Italian genes.

"Ah, thank you, I will." Luca nodded and glanced at everyone. "Is lunch preparation starting soon? May I be of assistance? Do you need anything from the store? I'm afraid I didn't bring anything which is rude of me as a guest." His left hand went to his chest and he feigned over-politeness. He needed to make a good impression.

"Oh, no, Luca, that's fine," Jenny said. "We had no idea you were coming, so don't worry about not bringing anything. Would you like some iced tea?"

"Yes, thank you, Jenny. It's still quite warm here, isn't it?" He continued to make small talk as he followed her into the kitchen.

Tomas pulled Alena back. "Do your parents know he's here?"

She shook her head. "They'll know whenever they turn up."

"Maybe you should call them over, so they can meet him before everyone else. We just happen to be here early for lunch prep," Tomas murmured. "Then you won't have the whole family trying to talk to him at once."

"Maybe." She chewed on her lip. "But if I call, everyone in the house will come running."

"There's no one else *in* the house," Roger told her. "You know Dom lives with Antonio, and Danté stayed with Nick, and Alexis stayed with Lorenzo."

"Ugh." Alena briefly closed her eyes. "*That's* going to be a fun conversation."

"Then don't have it," Tomas whispered and squeezed her hand. "Call your parents."

She sighed. "Okay." Seeing that Luca was entertaining her grandparents, she pulled out her phone and dialled her mother's phone.

"Hey, sweetie. How are you? Are you back yet?"

"Yes, Mama. Can you come to Grandma's now?"

"Of course, is anything wrong?"

"No. Just want to talk and see you before the crowd gets in, that's all."

"Okay. We'll be over in a few. See you then."

Alena pocketed her phone and walked into the kitchen, sliding her hands over Luca's shoulders. He was sitting at the island bench and had been regaling her grandparents with stories from the tour. "So, the usual roast meal with all the trimmings today?"

"Of course," Jenny replied. "We'll have to prepare more, but Tomas is making up a list of those who'll be coming. We always make it work."

"Probably all of them," Alena murmured. "Knowing my luck."

"Probably." Jenny smiled at her granddaughter. "It will be fine, don't worry. You don't mind big families, do you, Luca?"

"Not at all, Jenny. My father is from a big Italian family, I'm used to it."

"Good." Jenny's head nodded slightly. "We're a big Greek, Australian, American family, so not much difference."

Pedro and Angie walked in and shut the door on the early fall heat. "Still warm out there, even at this time of the year."

"Mama, Daddy." Alena rushed over, hugging and kissing them both. "There's someone I want you to meet. Come and I'll introduce you. Come on." She pulled them into the kitchen where she introduced Luca who had stood to meet the two most important people that he needed to impress.

"Mr and Mrs Stephanopoulos, it's so nice to meet you both." He shook Pedro's hand and kissed Angie's, making her giggle. "Alena has told me so much about you both. About her whole family. I feel as if I've known you all of my life."

"Oh, well." Angie blushed as her hand lingered in his. "That's a very sweet thing to say, Luca. Thank you." She glanced at her star-struck daughter. "Have the two of you been chatting for the whole tour? It ended over a week ago. You must have been taking a week off to unwind?"

"Yes, we have." Luca finally released her hand. "Since the first night on tour in fact. We've been talking a lot. About music, careers, family, life, mi amore."

"Did you get that little songwriting issue sorted out?" Pedro asked. His hands on hips stance was meant to be intimidating, as was his frown. But it seemed to be having no effect on Luca.

"You mean with the song lyrics I heard her sing and then added to?" Luca glanced from Pedro to Alena. "We most certainly did. We are going halves in the songwriting credits and my music label wants us to release it as a duet."

"Well, as the *owner* of *Alena's* music label, I'll have to think about that and read over any contracts with a fine-tooth comb." Pedro stared him down, but Luca was unfazed.

"Of course, Mr Stephanopoulos, I wouldn't expect anything less."

Carlos and Vivian arrived and Alena dragged Luca over to introduce them.

Pedro glanced at his family and leaned closer to his mother. "What do you think? There's something about him I don't like."

"He's slick," Jenny murmured, looking past her son to see Luca charming Vivian. "And I'll have him checked out."

"Thanks, Mama." Pedro kissed her temple and grabbed a peeler to help with the vegetables.

Carlos wandered over and sat next to his mother. "So...they *are* a couple."

"So it seems." Jenny counted up the number of people coming for lunch. "Better put more food on, it looks as though everyone's going to be here."

"*Including* Lorenzo," Angie said from beside Jenny.

"Oh…" Jenny's brows rose. "That *will* be fun."

Tomas grinned at his mother. "That's what Alena said."

Slowly, everyone turned up for lunch. Dan and Derek came back from their morning out, Diana and Charles arrived with Adam, Simon and Deidre with Stella and Liam, Dom and Antonio walked through the door, and then Danté and Nick followed with the whole Gatos family, and finally, Cabot and Tony arrived and Cabot zeroed in on the newcomer.

"Oh, you *are* gorgeous, aren't you?" Cabot held on tight as he shook Luca's hand. "Quite the Mediterranean stud." He took in the lithe physique, jet-black hair, and dark eyes. "Absolutely gorgeous."

"So you said, Cab. You can let go of his hand now." Tony extracted Cabot's hands from Luca's. "Hello, I'm Tony DeLuca, Cabot's partner."

"Hello. DeLuca… Is that Mediterranean?" Luca narrowed his eyes in thought.

"Spanish." Tony nodded. "My father and grandfather, my grandmother was Colombian, my mother was English."

"Yes." Luca raised a brow and wondered how Tony had come to be a part of the family. "I can see that in you."

"And you seem Italian *all* the way through." Cabot openly gaped at him. "Is Luca Saint your real name, or a stage name?"

Luca's slick smile spread across his lips. "Both. I shortened Saintangelo to Saint when I turned twenty-one. I thought it sounded much better for when I was going to be famous."

"Did you always know?" Cabot asked and saw his twin and Dom pull faces over Luca's shoulder. "We've been famous forever as we started our careers early."

"Yes, I did," Luca replied with a single nod of his head. "I was already singing by the age of ten in the choir, and I picked up the guitar at twelve and knew it was what I wanted to do for the rest of my life. Everything else came naturally."

"Nice." Cabot glanced between Luca and his cousin. "Then you and Alena are well suited. In looks *and* career."

Luca smiled and slid an arm around Alena's shoulders and she beamed. "Yes, we are."

Cabot raised a brow at his brother and cousin. "I don't see Alexis and Lorenzo here yet. Are they coming, cuz?"

The smile quickly slid from Alena's face. "Apparently."

The corners of Cabot's lips curled up slightly. "Last to arrive then. You seem to have met everyone else, Luca, just one more family member to go."

"And I look forward to meeting Alexis *and* Lorenzo," Luca replied.

*****

Out on the street, in front of Jenny's door, Alexis was passionately kissing Lorenzo. But after a few minutes, she sighed and let him go. "If only we could have stayed in bed. I haven't seen you in days." Her hands slid through his hair and her lips left kisses over his face. "I've missed you. God, I wish I could fuck you right here I'm so horny." She pressed herself against him as hard as she could.

Lorenzo pulled out of her arms to breathe. "I wish we could too, Alexis. You're so hot right now and I'm so turned on."

"Maybe we could have a quickie in a back lane, or my room next door in my parents' house," Alexis suggested. "I need you inside me."

"And I need to be inside of you, but we are here at your grandmother's house for lunch." Lorenzo grasped her arms and held her away from him. "You have given me a hard-on and I don't want your family to see. Stop it."

"Then let's go next door." She reached for his erection. "I can make it go away."

Knowing it wasn't going away anytime soon, he groaned and relented with a nod.

She quickly led him next door and let them in. "Mama? Daddy? You home?" she called and hurried him into her bedroom, pushing him onto the bed. "Let's make this quick." Pulling his pants open and setting his erection free, she guided it inside of her and they quickly came to climax. "Ugh," she panted and spread her legs to settle on him. "A quickie's just as good."

"It is," he gasped. "And we better clean up, so we can get to your grandmother's. We're late."

Alexis looked at her watch and dismounted. "Not really. Grandma knows we all run late at times." Picking up her knickers from where they'd landed, she pulled them on. "Let's get you tucked in and presentable, shall we."

Chuckling, he zipped up and tucked his shirt back in. It was always best to look sharp and well-dressed in front of Jenny Stephanopoulos.

*****

Cabot quietly sidled up behind Tomas at the island bench and put his arms around his uncle's waist. "So…what do you think of Luca Saint, Uncle T? Fucking gor.ge.ous or what." He kept his voice low, so only the four of them could hear.

Tomas stopped chopping garlic to glance at Luca, then over his shoulder at his nephew. He grinned. "He is, but why are *you* noticing?"

"Can't help it." Cabot's eyes were wide to take in *all* of the Italian stallion. "Look at him. Who knew Alena could attract someone who looks like that?"

"Now, now," Roger said softly beside them. "Your cousin's stunning."

"I know. But fuck, if I were single *I'd* be trying to tap that," Cabot dreamily murmured.

"And what about me?" Tony asked, peering at Luca from between Roger and Tomas. "Forgotten about me already?"

"Of course not," Cabot whispered. "But *I* wasn't the only one thinking about a threesome at her concert, was I?"

"Cabot!" Tony's whispered exclamation drifted in the air. "I didn't think you'd mention that. It was a joke."

A little giggle came out of Cabot. "I know, just joking." He looked past Tony to see Alexis and Lorenzo arrive. "Hold on to your hats, kids, it's about to get bumpy."

Alena rushed over to Alexis and hugged her tightly. "Alexis," she squealed and dragged her towards the kitchen. "There's someone I want you to meet."

"Ugh, okay." Puzzled, Alexis glanced from her sister to Lorenzo and frowned.

"Luca, I want you to meet my baby sister, Alexis." She introduced them. "Alexis, this is Luca Saint, my boyfriend."

Alexis's eyes widened in surprised. "Jesus! You work fast," she told her sister and extended her hand. "Nice to meet you, Luca. Last time I saw you, you were on stage at Alena's concert. Guess *you* work fast, too."

The slick smile spread across Luca's lips and he laughed, deep and throaty, as he took in the gorgeous looks of Alexis. "Yes, when I want to. But it was fairly obvious from that night that your sister and I were meant to fall in love." His arm went around Alena's shoulders and he pulled her close for everyone's benefit. And as a form of ownership. "She is the most beautiful woman I've ever met and I believe that she is my soulmate." Having been told the basics of the story of Alena and Lorenzo, he was about to use it to his advantage.

"Oh, this is getting good," Cabot whispered and noticed everyone else was watching. "I need popcorn." He quietly, and very casually, walked into the living room, so he was within earshot of the conversation.

Luca finally looked up from Alena's smiling face. "And you, Alexis, is this your soulmate?" His gaze coolly turned to Lorenzo. "Luca Saint. Pleased to meet you."

"Um…" Alexis's eyes finally moved from Luca's face to her partner. "Not sure. But he is *my* boyfriend. Dr Lorenzo Gavalas."

"Ah, Lorenzo… Good, Greek name." Luca shook his hand and waited while Alena excitedly pulled Alexis away. He lowered his voice. "Alena has mentioned that the two of you dated, many a year ago. I'm glad it didn't work out because you put your career first. That's very noble."

"Why's that?" Lorenzo frowned, unsure of what game the new intruder was playing at, and what lies his former flame had been telling.

"Well, if it had," Luca murmured, "then she and I would not be together now."

"Yeah, well, don't hold your breath." Lorenzo crossed his arms and squared off against the Italian. "Men don't last long in Alena's life. She uses them and then discards them."

"Yes, it's no wonder *she* dumped *you*," Luca replied calmly, waiting for his final shot.

"What's that supposed to mean?" Lorenzo's arms unwound.

Luca arched a brow and cast a critical eye over the ex from head to toe. "Because I can *definitely* see why."

Cabot froze and his eyes and mouth went into wide circles.

"Jenny, Tomas…" Luca turned around and poured on the charm. "Is there anything I can do to help?" He walked over to them and left Lorenzo in shock.

Behind Lorenzo's back, Cabot mouthed *burn* to everyone before covering his mouth with both hands, unable to believe how much, how hard, and how hot Luca had just burnt Alena's ex. *Fuck!* he silently exclaimed and waved at the tears of shock filling his eyes.

Lorenzo, gathering his wits, walked over to Alexis and put on a 'fucked if I care about my ex's new cunt' smile for the family and Alena to see.

But unlike him, Alena could not have cared less about her ex. Her attention was all on the gorgeous Luca Saint.

*****

"Mama, did you have Luca checked out?" Pedro sat beside his mother on the couch in her lounge room at Thanksgiving. All of the family were there except for Alena who was with Luca in London promoting their duet. It was nearly two months since they'd met him and he and Alena became an official couple.

"I did. I had him investigated on all levels as usual." Jenny watched as Diana, Alexis, Cabot and Antonio helped Adam decorate the Christmas tree she always put up at this time of the year. "I had both our lawyer and private detective look into him and found nothing. No speeding ticket, no lawsuits, no illegitimate children."

"Thank God for that," Pedro muttered and accepted a glass of brandy from Tomas. "Thanks, T." The brown fluid slid down his throat, tingling his insides as it went, and he enjoyed the sensation for a moment. "I suppose all of that is a good thing. And we sorted out the copyright issue. I *hate* not having full ownership of our songs."

"That *was* unfortunate, the way he did that. But as long as Alena has her name on it and ownership as lyricist, then it worked out okay." Jenny's hand closed over his and squeezed gently. "Except for Alena, we're all here for Thanksgiving for another year." Her blue eyes sparkled and his matched hers in every way as he'd inherited her eyes and Spiros's black hair.

Pedro grinned in return. "We are. And I'm grateful that I get all of you for another year. That we're happy and healthy and still alive." He paused and glanced at Adam screaming at the tinsel being dangled over his head and trying to grab it. "Things could have been so different after 1980's Thanksgiving."

Both of them cast their eyes to Tomas, who was sitting on the arm of the chair Carlos was occupying and talking to him and Roger, knowing full well that 1980 could have been his last Thanksgiving with the family. But he'd kept struggling and had pulled through his illness to celebrate in 1981 and every year since. And they'd celebrated as much as they could as a family, depending on whether Diana and the twins were home, ever since.

"Do you think he's good for her, Mama?" Pedro's brows furrowed. "Angie told me Luca and Alena remind her of us and our origins." He watched his wife go up behind Alexis, who had slumped onto an ottoman, and lean over her shoulder to kiss her cheek before wrapping her arms around her for a hug.

"Considering your origins were shrouded in drama, kidnapping, mystery and death, probably not the best comparison." Jenny smiled at the memories. "But I get where she's coming from. The dark hair and features, the passion for music. So far, he seems to be good for Alena. She's in a relationship for the first time in years, in love, happy, and not whining about anything."

Pedro's grin reflected hers. "True. When she calls, all I hear out of her is Luca this and Luca that. She doesn't even seem annoyed at Lorenzo dating Alexis anymore, and doesn't even mention James."

"Which is a good thing," Jenny reminded him. "She doesn't need to keep going back to either of them. Even if her ex dating her sister *is* still weird." She watched Lorenzo push his way onto the ottoman and slip a protective arm around Alexis.

"Yeah," he murmured, watching his daughter canoodle with the doctor. "Weird."

"As long as Luca does right by Alena, then all's well." Jenny sipped her hot toddy and gazed into the crackling flames in the fireplace. Her house was warm and cosy on such a cold and blustery November day and, with everyone snuggled up and happy, it was a good place to be. And that was all that mattered.

*****

On Christmas Eve, Alena and Luca joined the family after a successful promotional tour for their duet that had taken them around the world. And as they all sat around the lounge room after stuffing themselves on Jenny and Tomas' succulent roast turkey and vegetables with a Christmas baklava and cookies, they regaled themselves with carols on Jenny's old piano that sat beside the fireplace. Alena pulled Alexis up for a couple of duets to entertain the family before they set the sound system up to play music for the rest of the night.

"I'm so glad you get to spend our first Christmas together with my family. They're awesome, aren't they?" Alena snuggled into Luca's chest and his arms tightened around her.

"They are," he agreed as they danced in the hallway leading to the bedrooms for some privacy. "Your parents seem very happy with us. Your grandparents and uncles, even your siblings and cousins are happy for us." He leant down and kissed her gently. "*I'm* happy for us."

A soft giggle escaped her. "So am I." Her lips sought out his for a deeper kiss and got it, and her body fell into his and let itself melt into the emotion of the moment.

Pulling back, Luca tried to catch his breath. "Maybe we should go back to your place. I need to get you naked."

The giggle gurgled in her throat and she tried not to let it out. "I guess we could. I need to get *you* naked, too. Let's say goodbye and grab our coats. We'll be home in no time." She led him back to the lounge room. "We're heading off now. We'll see you all tomorrow. Thank you for lunch and tea, Grandma and Uncle T." She kissed her way through the adults. "We'll see you sometime tomorrow. Bye, all." Quickly retrieving their coats from the closet, she kissed her parents and opened the door. "Bye."

Cabot watched them leave from his spot on an easy chair by the fire. "She just wants sex." He snickered. "They were pashing in the hallway."

Antonio threw a cushion at his twin. "Just because you, her, and Alexis are getting it, doesn't mean the rest of us want to hear about it."

Cabot pushed his golden-brown hair out of his face and threw the pillow back. "Naw, poor Tonee, Tone, Tone. Antonio's not getting any." He stuck his bottom lip out. "Naw, poor Tone."

"Can it, Dickface." Antonio bashed his brother in the head with the cushion.

"Hey!" Cabot cried and put his arms up to protect his head as the bashing continued. "Tonee…"

"Nope, not Tonee," Antonio said, and kept hitting him.

"Argh," Cabot growled and managed to get off the chair and grab the cushion he'd been leaning on. "This is war!"

"Oi, not in the lounge room," Carlos yelled. "Not near the bloody fire."

"And watch Mama's cushions," Tomas called, seeing Dom and Danté get their cushions and belt Cabot.

"Hey! Three against one ain't fair," Cabot yelled as he ducked and weaved.

"Get in the hallway," Carlos told them. "Nothing to break in there."

"Except two walls of photos," Jenny retorted. "Go to your father's old room, there's nothing breakable in there."

"Oh, boys, be careful." Viv scooped an excitable Adam out of harm's way.

"Why is it just the boys getting to have fun?" Alexis grabbed a cushion and bashed Dom over the head.

"Hey! What'd you do that for?" he demanded and hit her back.

"Because I can." She tried to hit him again, but he side-stepped and the cushion hit Antonio. "Woops, that was meant for Dom."

"Sure it was," Antonio huffed and copped one from Cabot who in turn copped one from Diana.

"Hey! Why are you hitting me?" he asked her.

"Because *you're my* brother and Alexis can deal with her two."

"Hey!" They turned around to see Nick had been blindsided by his sisters. Summer and Melody had hit him from both sides simultaneously.

Cabot took that moment to take off for his father's bedroom.

"Hey! Get back here, Dickface." Antonio chased after him with everyone else hot on his heels.

The adults heard shrieks of laughter for a good five minutes before it stopped and Danté came into the lounge room huffing.

"Dan, Derek, Cabot's cut himself and he's bleeding."

Dan and Derek rushed for their medical bags and essentials.

"What! Oh, no," Viv fretted and stopped bouncing Adam on her knee. "Is it bad?"

"A bad scratch, I think." Danté followed the doctors back to Carlos' old bedroom to see Cabot still curled up on the floor around his arm.

"Hey, boys." Cabot saw the doctors and unfurled. "I tried to keep it covered while they beat me, so no one would get it on them."

"What happened?" Dan pulled on surgical gloves and inspected the wound.

"I think there's an old nail sticking out of Papa's desk. I scratched my arm on it when I fell." Cabot shifted into a sitting position. "I kept it covered when I saw the blood."

"Anyone get it on them?" Derek asked the others and removed gauze and a bandage from his bag. "Even a spot?"

"No," came one by one as they examined themselves.

"He just lay there while we hit him, and when I asked why he wasn't fighting back, he mentioned cutting himself," Antonio told them. "We stopped and sent Danté out to get you."

Dan cleaned the wound and dried it. "From the look of it, you won't need a tetanus shot, but that nail will need to be removed and disposed of as hazardous waste, just like everything we're using here." He applied superglue over the cut to keep it together and then layered the gauze and bandage. "Can one of you get—"

"The hazardous waste bin." Tony came in and handed it over. "Figured if anyone's qualified to care for Cabot after you two, it's me since we're both positive."

"Thanks, Tony." Derek dumped gloves and gauze into the bin. "You couldn't grab us a hammer or pliers, could you?"

After taking care of Cabot, removing the nail, and making sure everything was cleared properly, they went back to the lounge room where they found everyone sitting sombrely in front of the fire. "Everything's taken care of and disposed of."

"Thank you, Dan, Derek. Cabot, how's the arm?" Jenny looked at her grandson.

Cabot held up his right arm. "Just a bad scratch, Grandma. It'll heal."

"Good, and since you're bound to get plenty of those, why don't you sit down and rest a bit before going home," Jenny suggested. "There's plenty of eggnog left."

"Ooohhh…" Cabot's spirits rose. "With alcohol?"

"No, but you can put some in yours. And put some in mine while you're at it."

The twinkle in his grandmother's eyes made him grin.

*****

Alena and Luca barely made it through the front door of her house before they ripped each other's clothes off. Coats lay where they fell, tops went flying, and shoes were kicked in different directions.

The lounge lights had been left on low and the Christmas tree twinkled in the corner of the lounge, and stumbling into the room, they were naked by the time they fell onto the fur rug in front of the fireplace. Under the lights of the Christmas tree, they mated like animals in a forest. Wild and free.

Alena gasped as Luca came to a stop. "Oh, God." Panting, she swallowed several times to quench her dry throat and watched him lay full out on top of her.

His hands grasped hers and reached out to the side. His head hovered over hers, and his dark eyes stared intently into her blue ones.

He was trying to project into her, over her, around her. His possessive nature still wanted to own her. Show her he was in charge, even if he was not. He wanted the illusion of being so, as the man. Even if he was not.

"God, I love the way you fuck me." As she wrapped her legs around his waist, her inner muscles clenched around him. "And I love your dick and the way it fucks me."

"It is impressive, isn't it," Luca agreed. "It's always done its job."

"It certainly does a number on me every time." She squeezed tight.

He gasped, momentarily closing his eyes. "Yes, and you know how to do a number on me, Alena Stephanopoulos." He thrust his hips forward, making her cry out. "But I am the one in charge and you'll do as I say."

"Is that so?" She managed to roll him over and straddle him. "Or maybe you'll do as *I* say because *I'm* the one in charge. After all," she pinned his arms by his side and clenched, "*I* am a Stephanopoulos. And just like my grandma, *I'm* in charge."

He deftly rolled her off him and stood up. "Is that so?"

"Hey!" She pouted. "No fair!"

"No, I suppose it wouldn't be for you." He plucked a large bauble from the tree and, kneeling next to her, held it out. "This goes to show who's *actually* in charge."

Puzzled, Alena took the bauble and tried to look inside, but couldn't see through the fake snow painted on it. She shook it, but could only hear a dull thudding. "What's in it?"

Luca rolled his eyes and leaned back against one of the sofas surrounding the fireplace. "Open it and find out."

She tried pulling it apart, but that didn't work, so twisted the two halves and out fell a small red velvet box. Ice water flowed through her veins from her heart to her fingers and toes. "Oh…" Looking into his eyes, trying to gauge his expression, which was extremely cool and unmoving, she wasn't sure if she should open it or not. After all, it could just be a pair of studs. Picking the box up, she slowly opened it and screamed. "Oh, my God, oh, my God, oh, my God. Yes, yes, I'll marry you. Oh, my God yes. Put it on me." Thrusting the box towards him, she shuffled over on her knees and watched as he placed the diamond ring on her finger.

"Alena Stephanopoulos, will you do me the honour of being my wife?" He knew he had her wrapped around his finger, just as she had the ring wrapped around hers.

"Yes, yes, oh, my God I love you." Smothering him in kisses, she stopped to glance at the ring and managed to say, "I love it," before kissing him again. "I love you," she murmured between bouts of lip smooching passion. "Yes, yes, I'll marry you and you'll sign the prenup, and we'll get married on the anniversary of when we met." Because it wasn't as though she *hadn't* been thinking of marrying Luca Saint and being his wife. It was *all* she'd been thinking about since they'd met.

"Wait…" He grasped her arms and pushed her back. "What do you mean, prenup?"

Alena's hands clasped his face and the glimmer of diamond brought a sparkle to her eye. "Everyone has to sign it. Well, I mean, everyone who marries into the family. As in, marries *us*. Charles signed it, you'll sign it, Tony will sign it when he and Cabot get married. Whoever marries Antonio, Dom, Danté and Alexis will sign it. God, I hope it's not Lorenzo." She finally stopped for a breath and sat on his legs. "You're okay with that, aren't you? It's a prerequisite for being in this family via marriage."

"And what is in this prenup?" Luca inquired, thoroughly annoyed that he didn't know about it and hadn't been told in the last two and a half months of them fucking.

"Just the usual." She kissed him. "What we come into the marriage with we leave with. Any property I own, or is given to me by my family, is mine. You get no money upon divorce, etc. You know, the usual." Her lips landed on his.

"Well, I don't know what the usual is because I've never been married before." Luca pushed her away. "So, because of who you are and what you have, you have a prenup."

"Of course…um…" Alena shook her head in confusion. "Are you okay with that? You seem annoyed that you'll have to sign it."

He thought quickly and considered his options. Sign the prenup and be a part of the biggest musical families on the planet, or, say no to signing it and get nothing. Including Alena. And because he seriously doubted the family would let it happen without his signature on it, he chose the former. "Of course not. It's perfectly understandable that your family would want to protect all of you in the event of a divorce. I think I was just a bit shocked that you brought it up right now and are already talking about it. I was hoping we could just enjoy the moment and not discuss unsavoury things until we were dressed and had not just fucked."

"Oh…" She blushed. "Sorry. Of course, I should be thinking of the moment and not the legalities." Sliding her hands down his torso, Alena adjusted herself onto him. "*Of course* I'm thinking of the moment. *That* moment and *this…*" she clenched, "moment."

He closed his eyes and groaned.

"And *this* moment…" clench, "and *this* one…"

*****

After a long night of passionate sex, they walked into Jenny's house at 12:30 p.m. on Christmas Day. "Hey, everyone, we have something to tell you all," Alena called and saw that the family were already gathered in the lounge room.

"Shoosh, sweetie, Diana has an announcement," Angie quietened her. "Go on, Diana."

Luca shut the door behind him and rested his hands on Alena's shoulders as they listened.

"It's about time you got here, cuz, because now I can tell all of you together." Diana excitedly stood in front of the family, holding a photo she wanted to share with everyone. "You all know that it's our third wedding anniversary this Christmas." She slid her arm around Charles's waist and gazed up at him. "And you know that we have Adam."

"Adam," Adam called from his grandmother's lap.

Viv hugged and kissed him and he giggled. "Yes, of course, you're Adam."

"Well," Diana smiled lovingly at her mother and son and turned the photo around. "He's getting a baby sister in five months' time."

The family stared at the ultrasound in Diana's hand.

"What!" Alena shrieked. "You're pregnant! Yay, another girl." She bounded over to her cousin to hug her and they bounced around in circles while the family gathered. "It's a girl. Give me a look." Taking the photo, she looked at the baby in her cousin's belly. "Naw, look at her. She's a teeny weeny Stephanopoulos."

Diana hugged her way through the family and made it back to her husband's arms. "I'm four months and everything's fine. We figured we'd wait until now to announce it, as I was having my first ultrasound the other day and wanted to make sure everything was fine before letting you all know. The doctor says she's perfect."

"Oh…" Viv's hand went to her heart at the maternal flutterings, remembering being pregnant with her baby girl. "I'm going to be a grandma again and have a baby girl. Oh, Carlos…" She moved into her husband's arms and gently wept tears of joy. "Our baby's having another baby."

Cabot rolled his eyes at his brother. "If she's like this when D gets pregnant, God help her *and* us when *we* have kids."

Antonio snorted and then laughter burst out of him. "*You! Have kids! That'll* be the day. *You're* still a kid yourself. *They'll* have to look after *you.*"

"Hardy har har, *Antonio,*" Cabot replied. "Can't wait to see *you* be a father."

"I'll be a damn sight better and more mature than you," Antonio snapped back and kept on laughing.

Seeing everyone in a festive mood, Alena called for attention. "While we're celebrating good news and announcements, I have one of my own."

Groans went through the room.

"Hey!" she demanded, gloved hands on hips. "Why does Diana get all the congratulations and I get groans? That's not fair."

"No, it isn't," Jenny agreed. "Quiet everyone, Alena has an announcement. Take your seats, or just calm down and let her speak. Don't be rude."

After the kids quietened down with their grumbling, attention started turning to Alena and Luca. "Go ahead, sweetie," Jenny encouraged.

Once all eyes were on her, Alena whipped off her left glove and held up her hand. "We're getting married."

"What!" Diana burst out and grabbed her cousin's hand. "Oh, my God, you're engaged. Oh, congratulations, you two." Hugging her cousin, she kissed Luca on the cheek.

"Fuck, he works fast," Cabot grumbled to Tony and his brother while watching Dom, Danté and Alexis congratulate their sister. But he also noticed the adults with raised brows or open mouths. "Some people aren't happy," he whispered, noting their expressions. They went over to congratulate their cousin and future in-law. "Well, cuz, I *am* jealous. He's gorgeous." He kissed her cheek. "You two are going to make beautiful babies that will continue the dark side of the family."

Alena giggled and beamed every ounce of happiness she felt. "I know. He is and we will." Clinging to Luca's arm, she added, "I'm so happy."

"You look it, my darling." Jenny stepped forward to congratulate them.

"Grandma." Alena hugged her tightly. "I love him so much," she whispered in her ear. "I know we're meant for each other."

"And that's obvious for all to see." Jenny moved her granddaughter's hair off her face and cupped it. "And we all love you and want to see you happy. Which you clearly are." Turning to Luca, she held out both of her hands and clasped one of his, gripping it tightly. "Luca. You are coming into this family as Alena's husband. Your role is to take care of her when we cannot, to provide for her as her husband and equal, as the father of her future children. You will provide for them all and be the man worthy of her and her hand in marriage. Has she informed you of the prenup you'll be signing?"

"Yes, Jenny," Luca replied smoothly. "While I expected one I was not expecting to discuss it so soon. We haven't even set the wedding date as I only just proposed last night."

"Um… I was thinking August 1st. The anniversary of when we met." Alena nervously played with her ring. "If you're not doing anything. I know *my* diary's free."

Luca's slick smile showed off his white teeth. "We'll have to check my diary, but if I have something planned I will move it for you, my love." He took Alena into his arms. "Anything for you, my love."

"Naw!" Angie couldn't hold back any longer and went over to her daughter and future son-in-law. "Congratulations, my darling." Hugging her daughter, she added, "Welcome to the family, Luca. I know you'll take care of my baby girl."

"Do we?" Pedro muttered loud enough for his brothers to hear. After exchanging glances with them, he walked over to offer his congratulations. "Luca." He shook his hand and slightly pulled him aside. "If *you* hurt my daughter, *I'll* hurt you. And her grandmother will kill you. We've done it before." Staring into his eyes he raised a brow and gave a slight nod. "Got it?"

Unaware of what had befallen Alexis' attacker, Luca took the threat to mean nothing. "Of course, Mr Stephanopoulos. Understood."

"It had better be," Pedro told him. "And you *will* be signing that prenup."

"Of course." Luca's grin never faltered. "Once my lawyer goes over it."

Irritated, Pedro's eyes narrowed and he turned his back to hug his daughter. "My little girl's getting married."

"Yes, Daddy. And you'll be walking me down the aisle, of course." She snuggled into his arms.

"I wouldn't have it any other way, Princess Alena." He kissed the top of her head and let go. "I think your uncles want to congratulate you." Nodding in their direction, he watched her fly into Tomas's arms.

"My princess has finally found her real-life prince," Tomas murmured. "And he *is* gorgeous. I'm just a *little* bit jealous that he's the new prince in your life."

Alena pulled out of his arms and stared earnestly at him. "Don't be like that, Prince Tomas. You'll *always* be my *first* prince."

A beaming smile lit up Tomas's face. "That's my little A-ena. I think everyone else wants a hug."

Smiling, Alena hugged her way through the rest of the adults. "I'm so glad all of you are here." Gazing at everyone, she linked her arm through Diana's. "The two eldest of the grandkids, with the exclusion of Simon," she waved a hand in his direction and received a nod in return, "have both made monumentous announcements and I'm so glad we could do it together, so we can celebrate together, and share it with everyone in the family who's here." Her eyes took in their beaming faces. "Because now we can talk about wedding dresses and christening gowns and oh…" Her eyes grew wide and she sucked in air. "Baby clothes. We can start doing christening gowns for *Baby Stefan*. And expand the wedding dress line."

"And here she goes again," Cabot called out. "Christmas may as well just stop right now, Alena's on a roll."

*****

"Will Uncle Tomas be back in time for the wedding?" Alena smoothed the French lace and silk of her soon-to-be wedding dress as it was being altered on her body. It was a month before her wedding and the dress needed much work, *and* she'd been dieting for two months already just to make sure she could fit into it come her wedding day, and damn she was hungry.

"He should be," Jenny informed her as they sat in the headquarters of *Haus of Stefan* in Athens. "You know he wouldn't miss your wedding for the world. And Simon and Deidre, and Cabot and Tony will be back as well. They all had so much work to do getting Marie Von Burstenstore's house ready. The legals needed completing for the handover, everything else needed updating, and they had Bertha's house to complete as well. It was so incredible that even after all these years those ladies still thought of Tomas and Roger and helping AIDS patients end their lives peacefully."

"So incredible," Angie agreed, watching her daughter spin around on the platform while the seamstress inserted pins and took measurements. "I can't believe the girls all considered them and willingly handed over their homes." Her eyes turned to the dress rack where her dress was hanging in a garment bag ready for her to try on. All of the women in the family were receiving dresses made for the wedding, while the men were receiving tailor-made suits.

"Yes," Viv murmured. "With everyone we lost in the '80s, we have no one left except for Mike and Maggie." She glanced at Maggie who was sitting beside Angie. "Everyone else is gone that we knew, and there's only a couple of girls Tomas and Roger are still in contact with."

"No…" Jenny frowned in thought. "I think Roger's friend, the lawyer, David Marks, is still alive and going well. But yes, all of their other friends are gone."

"And they're lucky that Simon and Deidre are willing to help out," Viv continued. "Cabot and Tony, too." She gently smoothed the fabric of her peach dress. "I'm glad Cabot's turned his life around."

"We all are." Jenny nodded and watched Alena carefully step off the platform to go and change. "All of the children are doing well."

Alexis came out of the change room wearing a blue silk dress with a bolero jacket which still needed decorating. Standing on the platform, she stood still while the seamstress examined the dress.

"Oh, Alexis, that blue is so pretty," Summer told her, eyeing her friend's svelte figure.

"And that style is definitely flattering," Melody added, wondering what sort of creation they'd be getting to wear.

"Mmm…" Alexis turned this way and that, admiring it in the mirror. "I do quite like it. Not an Alexis original, but it will do."

The seamstress nodded at her and Alexis stepped down to make way for Diana who stepped up.

"Oh, sweetie, you look beautiful," Viv said as her daughter twirled around. While made of the same blue material, Diana's dress was cinched at the waist and swirled around her shapely calves.

"Thank you, Mama. But I do feel fat." Diana patted her flat stomach. "I know I had Jaqueline two months ago, but I haven't really bounced back as quickly as I thought I would." She turned left and right, critically eyeing her slim figure in the mirror.

Jenny raised a brow at Viv who frowned in return. "You are *not* fat, Diana. You're as slim as you always were."

"I *know*, Grandma." Diana turned to her. "I said I *feel* fat. All the years of having to be skinny for modelling, and now, after two children, I just feel…" She struggled to find the right word, so shrugged and said, "Blah."

"You had a baby two months ago," Jenny said. "Not every woman bounces back so soon, and especially after the second baby. You'll feel fine by the wedding."

Diana sighed. "I hope so." Smoothing the waist of her dress she turned back to the mirror. "I hope so."

Alexis and Alena stepped out of the change room. "Looking good, D." Alena gave her two thumbs up and went over to her mother. "Yours and Aunt Viv's turn."

"Okay. I hope you designed something fabulous for me as mother of the bride." Angie kissed her cheek and hurried off with Viv.

"Oh…I have." Alena sat next to Jenny. "Grandma, your dress is waiting, too. I hope you love it as much as I do."

Jenny took her granddaughter's hand in hers and smiled. "I'm sure I will because you designed it." Brushing aside a tendril of her grand-daughter's hair, she added, "I see that you are so happy. And I hope that he makes you happy for the rest of your life."

The smile beamed across Alena's face. "I am, and he will."

"You think he's your soulmate?"

"Yes, Grandma. I know he is."

"Argh! Oh, my God, I love it!" Angie rushed out of the change room and stood on the platform. The black and silver silk clung to her sexy curves and swished to the ground around her ankles. Sequins and beads accented the shapes and swirls of the pattern, and the top was a flattering V-neck with floating sleeves down to her elbows. "I love it."

Alena grinned at her mother's enthusiasm. "I knew you would."

*****

On August 1st, 2011, the family gathered in *The Windmill Hotel* and prepared for Alena Jennifer Stephanopoulos's wedding day. The bride's room was aflutter with activity. Alena's personal hairstylist, and make-up artist, were in to do the honours. Alexis and Diana were there to help with the accessories, undergarments, and the dress itself. Angie, Viv, and Jenny were there in case anything, or anyone, was needed.

Some of Jenny's siblings and their families had flown in for the wedding, as had Luca's family who'd taken over half of the hotel. They were in awe of the Stephanopoulos family and had been shown around by Alena who'd proudly told them the story of Spiros and Jenny and how they'd built the family empire and fortune. How her sister and cousin had started the assault centre, how her parents had *Sync*, and her uncles had *S'Reel* and *In Shape*, and the family owned half the island.

Alena got along with Luca's parents. Italian born Gino Saintangelo, and American born Meredith Faulkner, who had welcomed her into the family. As had Luca's three brothers and two sisters who couldn't wait to see what freebies they could get out of *Haus of Stefan* and the rest of the family.

This was something that had always worried Jenny. That anyone who married her grandchildren would be in it for what they could get. But in this case, it was the family who were trying to wheedle their way in, much to Jenny's chagrin.

"Are you doing my hair right, Avalon?" Alena turned her head this way and that so she could see herself in the mirror. "It *will* work properly, won't it?"

"*Yes*, Alena." Avalon dug through her bag for the necessary tools. "We've tried this three times to make sure and the curlers have been in for fifteen minutes. Don't worry." She pulled out the wide-tooth comb and spray, completely used to Alena's frenzied worries over hair after all these years. "We've got this."

A sigh left Alena and she settled back into her seat. "I know. I'm just so nervous."

"*We know.*" Alexis rolled her eyes and leaned over her sister to check herself in the dressing table mirror. Her short hair was swept back and had tiny Swarovski crystal hairpins in it. "You're fine. Calm your farm."

"Get out of it, Alexis. You'll mess up my hair." Alena pushed her back and quickly inspected her hair for damage and saw her make-up was only half done. "Amira, can you finish my make-up, please. I'd like it done before my hair."

"Then we'll have to cover your face when your hair's sprayed." Amira looked through her kit for the right eyeshadow palette.

"That's fine. Let's just get this done." Alena crossed her legs and clasped her knee, her knuckles turning white with the pressure.

"Is there anything you need, sweetie?" Angie fussed around the room.

"No, Mama. Not unless you want to break open a bottle of champagne."

"Oh, I think we'll leave that for the reception." Jenny subtly placed a napkin over the bottle, so no one noticed it on the table. "Do you want anything to eat? It's warm outside and we won't be eating until later. We don't want you fainting on us."

"No, thanks, Grandma. If I eat dairy I'll be phlegmy. If I eat carbs I'll be bloated."

"What about some protein? It will keep your blood sugar steady," Jenny said, inspecting the table of food.

"No, thanks. I'm really not hungry." Alena looked up at the ceiling as Amira brushed on mascara. "My stomach's in knots I'm so nervous. If I eat, I'll be sick."

"If you *don't,* you'll be sick." Jenny nibbled on a piece of cheese from the fresh food platter the hotel had sent up.

"I'll just have some juice, or something." Alena studied herself in the hand mirror Amira gave her to look at her false eyelashes. "Nice. They have crystals on them."

"All the rage." Amira dabbed glitter on Alena's cheeks. "Do you want crystals around your eyes?"

"No. I'll have them in my hair and on my veil and dress. It will be too much."

Alexis grabbed Diana's arm in mock surprise. "Alena…refusing sparkle? Call Dan and Derek, there must be something wrong with her."

Diana giggled, and Alena gave them both a dirty look.

Amira finished off the make-up, and Avalon got to work on Alena's updo, a soft, sweptback French twist with crystal hair combs and clips that her veil would attach to.

"Oh, that style suits you." Angie appeared over her daughter's shoulder as Avalon put the finishing touches to her hair. "That's so pretty. You should wear your hair like that more often instead of dead straight all the time." She admired her own sweptback chignon.

"I only do it for special occasions and when I'm wearing evening wear." Alena admired her hair and make-up in the mirror and saw Alexis appear next to Angie. "Naw, look at us. The dark side of the family. And that dress looks spectacular on you, Mama."

"I should think so." Angie modelled it for her daughter to see. "It *is* an original one of a kind, made just for me." She gazed at her daughter's reflection, slid her right arm around Alexis, and rested her left hand on Alena's shoulder. "Look at us. Look at you. You're beautiful, my baby. My firstborn baby's getting married."

Diana, who was standing between Jenny and Vivian, moved to interrupt, but Jenny stopped her.

"Let them have a moment," she whispered, and Diana smiled in return.

They waited while Angie had her moment with her two daughters and finally turned around. "Okay, time to get you dressed."

Diana and Alexis helped Alena into the wedding gown. A stunning silk and lace concoction covered in Swarovski crystals, sequins, and beads, it hugged her curves and swept to the floor into a small train. The v-neck showed off her ample cleavage, and the lace sleeves dropped to the elbows.

Avalon attached the veil to her hair, and Alexis and Diana held up the hem of her dress while she stepped into her white satin platform stilettos. She added diamond earrings, a necklace, a bracelet to each wrist, and finally turned around.

"Oh, my baby." Angie's face crumpled and tears flowed.

"Oh, don't cry, Mama, you'll have to get your make-up redone," Alena said. "And we don't have time."

"I know, I know." Angie dabbed at her face. "But I can't help it. You're so beautiful."

"Naw, thanks, Mama. So are you." Alena carefully helped dab away the tears. "There. There we go. Now. I need to pee and then we can go."

"Alena!" Alexis threw her head back in exasperation. "Could you not have gone *before* we put you in your dress?"

"Sorry, sis. But I gotta pee, which means you and D will need to hold my dress up." She grabbed their hands and rushed into the bathroom where they held her dress and turned away while she did her business.

"Done." She finished and stood up carefully. And after she washed her hands, they settled the dress back around her ankles and collected their bouquets just as there was a knock at the door.

Knowing it would be Pedro, Jenny answered it and saw him standing there in his new *Haus of Stefan* suit. "She's ready, so we'll go and let you get her there." She kissed his cheek and stepped aside so he could see his daughter. "She really did turn into a princess." With a gentle touch to his arm, she and Viv left them to head to the church.

"Aw…my baby girl." Pedro's hand went to his heart and tears sprang to his eyes. "My baby's getting married and you are so beautiful."

"Thank you, Daddy." Alena clenched her bouquet with both hands, trying to quell her nerves. "Are we ready?"

"Are you?" Angie touched her arm. "It's *your* wedding day."

Beaming, Alena could only nod as she couldn't believe it was actually happening.

"Okay, then. The car is waiting, so let's get this show on the road." Pedro held out his arm for his daughter to take, and escorted her, Angie, Alexis and Diana downstairs and out to the car where they settled themselves in for the short ride to the church. It was the same church her parents, uncles, and Diana had married in.

"You're lucky you have a car to drive you to the church. You certainly wouldn't have been able to walk in those heels," Angie said, glancing at her daughter's feet. "I did. It was a ten-minute journey in freezing November. I wish we'd had a car back then."

"But you wouldn't change anything about it for the world," Pedro reminded her.

"Nope." Angie grinned. "Even if my feet *did* kill me and my stomach wouldn't calm down because I happened to be pregnant with a certain Princess Alena." Her grin grew ear to ear as she gazed at her daughter. "You're beautiful, my baby."

They pulled up to the church and Diana and Alexis alighted to give them a moment.

"Sweetie." Angie held her daughter's hand and gazed in wonder at the beautiful creature between her and Pedro. "We love you *so* much. We've *been* through so much. With you, and as a family. And for all of the celebrations, today is *your* day. *You* get to celebrate August first every year as your wedding anniversary. A special day, that with luck, you'll have only once in your life, like your father and me. We see that Luca makes you happy, and hope he will do that for the rest of your life. And we see that this is truly what you want and what makes you happy. Congratulations, my baby."

"Aw, Mama." Alena clasped Angie's hands and kissed her cheek. "I love you so much."

"We love you too, my baby." Angie dabbed at her tears and beamed happiness for her daughter.

"Alena."

She turned to her father. "Daddy."

"You were my little girl for nearly ten years." Pedro tried holding back his tears by breathing. "And then along came Alexis, so *both of you* will always be my little girls, and *you* will always be Princess Alena. Don't you ever forget that." He kissed her hand. "Whatever you need. Whatever you want, we will always be here. Do you understand?"

"Yes, Daddy." She nodded. "I love you."

"I love you, my baby." Pedro sniffed back his tears. "Okay, let's walk you down the aisle." He and Angie alighted and helped Alena step out of the car.

Diana and Alexis straightened the dress and lifted the veil over her face while Charles was snapping photos of every moment.

"Ready?" Pedro held out his arm.

Exhaling, Alena slid her hand into the crook of his elbow. "Ready."

Angie rushed inside to take her place, and Diana and Alexis followed the bride into the entrance hall, adjusting the train of the dress as they went. After taking their position in line with Luca's two groomsmen, they waited for the music before walking down the aisle.

Everyone in the church turned to watch and saw the breathtaking vision of Alena Jennifer Stephanopoulos walking down the aisle on her father's arm.

"Aw." Tomas's hands went to his mouth and his eyes filled with tears as she passed and smiled broadly at her family.

She gave her prince a special smile, as did Pedro, and they continued on.

Roger grinned and rubbed his husband's back to help calm him and Tomas glanced at him, tears in his eyes.

Pedro stopped at the altar, kissed her cheek, and joined his wife and parents in the front pew.

Even though they were in the Greek Orthodox Church, and Alena was Greek, with Luca being Italian American, they had included some of their family's traditions in the service, which the priest performed with the usual parts.

"Do you, Luca, take Alena, to be your lawful wedded wife, to have and to hold, for richer, for poorer, in sickness and in health, till death do you part?"

Luca's smile spread ear to ear, knowing that regardless of the prenup which he'd signed, that he would still be better off married into the family than not. And he planned on using every ounce of his connection to them. "I do."

"And do you, Alena, take Luca, to be your lawful wedded husband, to have and to hold, for richer, for poorer, in sickness and in health, till death do you part?"

Alena gazed up into Luca's dark eyes and gave her heart fully and unconditionally. "I do." In that moment, she knew that he was it. That *this* was it. *Her* forever.

"You may now exchange the rings."

Luca's best man placed the rings on the bible and stepped back in line.

"Luca, take Alena's ring and place it on her finger and repeat after me. With this ring, I thee wed for all eternity by the grace of God."

"With this ring, I thee wed for all eternity by the grace of God." Luca slid the gold, diamond-encrusted, wedding band onto Alena's finger.

"Alena, take Luca's ring, place it on his finger and repeat after me. With this ring, I thee wed for all eternity by the grace of God."

"With this ring, I thee wed for all eternity by the grace of God." With her smile beaming for the whole church to see, she slid the ring on Luca's finger and clasped his hand.

"I now pronounce you, husband and wife." The priest closed his bible and nodded. "You may kiss the bride."

Luca lifted the veil over Alena's head and knew he had to put on a show for his family as well as hers. It wasn't that he didn't love Alena, he did, but marriage wasn't going to constrain him. He wanted a lover, not a ball and chain, and God help him when kids came along. But then again, there were plenty of people to look after them while he continued being the rock star that he was. Gently cupping her face, he kissed her so passionately that it raised eyebrows in the audience.

"Holy hell," Cabot whispered. "He does realise we're watching, right?"

"I think that's *why* he's doing it," Antonio murmured. "He's an attention seeker and he has all of our attention." He noticed the murmurings and head shakes going through the family.

Finally letting go, Luca's smile matched hers. "Now, I really *do* own you, Alena Saint," he whispered.

Blushing at the attention the kiss had received; she leaned against him and giggled. "Not on your life, Luca Stephanopoulos."

Luca snorted, and led her down the aisle under a rainbow of confetti and rose petals.

When they reached the steps outside, Alena inhaled deeply. "Ah, smell that."

"What?" Luca tilted his head, but could only smell the sea.

"Love and happiness." Alena laughed and ran down the steps to the waiting car.

Once the families had migrated back to the hotel and into the reception hall, photos were taken with immediate family and friends out in the garden, and then the celebrations commenced.

"To my darling daughter, Alena." Pedro held his glass aloft at the family's table. "My firstborn, my first daughter, my first child to get married. We are your family, we bore you, we love you, we will protect you and honour you, and will always be here for you. Congratulations."

"Oh." Tears sprang to Alena's eyes and she dabbed at them as they fell.

Pedro pulled his mother's chair out so she could stand.

Jenny held her glass out. "My darling granddaughter, our secondborn grandchild, you are as precious to us now as you were the day you were born thirty-three years ago." A few snorts and chuckles went through the family, but Jenny ignored them. "And we love you even more *now* than we did then. You were honoured with your aunt's name as your own, and we were honoured and blessed to have you come into our lives as our daughter, niece, and granddaughter. We are here for you, we love you, and we will always cherish you. Congratulations."

Applause flew around the room and she waited for it to die down.

"Luca," she addressed him. "We know that your job now is to take care of our Alena. To honour her, cherish her, and forsake her above all else. To respect her, support her, and encourage her like no other. You have come into this family and won our Alena's heart above all others, and she has given it to you above all others. So respect it, cherish it, and encourage it like no other." Her eyes moved from glaring at him to lovingly gazing at her granddaughter. "Alena and Luca. We are here if you need us, when you want us, and will always help if you ask. We love you." She raised her glass. "Alena and Luca."

Diana and Alexis exchanged glances at the head table while the boys all traded knowing looks amongst themselves. Cabot raised a brow and grinned. All of the family knew their grandmother was warning Luca to never hurt Alena. Charles had received the same type of speech when he married Diana.

Pedro helped his mother sit, and watched his daughter and new son-in-law while Luca's family made their speeches. And then it was the bride and groom's turn.

"I want to thank all of our friends and family for being here today to share in this momentous occasion in both of our lives." Her gaze drifted back and forth across both families. "It means so much to both of us to have you all here, knowing that we are loved like we are fills my heart with such joy and happiness." Her knuckle nudged a tear aside. "To know that I," she glanced at Luca, "we, get to start our married life together with all of you here cheering us on. To my new in-laws, the Saintangelos," she raised her glass, "thank you for welcoming me into your family as your daughter and sister-in-law. You have shown tremendous love and respect for me, and us, and we thank you."

Gino and Meredith nodded their recognition and raised their glasses.

"And to *my* family, the Stephanopouloses, from Grandma and Grandpa to Mama and Daddy, Princes Tomas and Carlos," that scored a grin out of both of them, "Aunt Viv and Uncle Roger, my siblings and cousins, thank you for putting up with me for thirty-three years. For loving me even when I was throwing tantrums—"

"Baha," burst out of Cabot and he continued laughing when the others laughed with him.

"Hey, we loved you through yours, Cab," Alena reminded him and he blushed. "For respecting me as a human being and adult, and allowing me to make my own mistakes so I could learn from them. For guiding me through life with love fiercer than any other I've ever known." She raised her glass to her family. "And thank you for accepting my choice of life partner, husband, and lover, and for welcoming him into our family which grows bigger every year. Thank you, I love you, and I will always need you. Thank you all for being my family." A tug on her left hand made her look down to see Diana and Alexis holding it and smiling up at her.

"We love you, too," they both said.

"Time for the first dance," someone in the crowd called and the band started up.

"Oh." Alena glanced at everyone gathered and set her glass down. "Shall we?" She turned to Luca who smiled and took her hand.

He led her to the dance floor, his arm extended so she could show off her dress, and then twirled her into his arms. Once she was ensconced, he stared deeply into her ocean blue eyes. "We are now one, Alena Saint."

She smiled up at him and wrapped her arms around his waist as they slow danced. "We may be husband and wife now, but *I* will *always* be *Alena Stephanopoulos!*"

Antonio & Maria - 2012

"Mmm, this is the life." Antonio stretched luxuriously on his cabana bed in the poshest resort on Mykonos. It was the only beachside resort to have sectioned off an area of the beach's sand and sea with glass walls and ceiling, so the island's people could enjoy sunbaking all year round in the warmth without the chilly cold winter winds.

The sun gently beat down on his already tanned muscular torso and highlighted the soft golden hair on his body. At six feet, with golden-brown hair and emerald green eyes, his fabulous good looks had helped earn his way into the resort. So did having the surname of Stephanopoulos. As the Phoenix half of modelling duo, Steele and Phoenix Stefan, he and his brother's life had been good for the last twenty-nine and a half years, and come their thirtieth in July, they had plans to stop modelling altogether.

"It is, isn't it," Cabot replied and sipped his margarita. As twins, they had been together most of their lives. Lived together, worked together, breathed the same air together. But the last five years had seen him step away from full-time modelling into part-time. And with soon-to-be husband Tony DeLuca taking up his time, he didn't get to spend enough of it with his only brother anymore. "How did we get so lucky?"

"Well, we have the great supermodel Vivian Villiers as our mother, for a start." Antonio's eyes took in the guests wading in the aqua blue waters just metres from their chairs.

"But Carlo Stefan, the world's biggest manwhore porn star, for a father." Cabot finished his drink and set the glass on the table beside him. He stretched his arms above his head and lay back.

"Mmm," Antonio murmured, and slid his glasses down his nose to gaze upon a rather gorgeous woman doing the breaststroke back and forth in front of them. "Hasn't done us any harm, though. Especially in the *genetic* region of our DNA. Hell, you even take after him in the manwhore stakes."

"Not anymore." Cabot closed his eyes against the sun and shook his head. "I stopped doing all of that after the assault, you know that. And once I met Tony, it was all over. I became a one man, man."

"What? Instead of a one man woman? We do wonder sometimes; you act so girlishly silly." Antonio scored a filthy look for that, but continued. "How's the wedding going?" His gaze followed the woman in the water. She seemed vaguely familiar, but he couldn't place her.

"Pretty much done, thanks to Mama and Tony. Everyone RSVP'd by the end of last year, we have Tony's family home for the whole month of May to celebrate the wedding, Grandma's birthday, and hers and Grandpa's anniversary. We just need to be there on the first to get everything done in time for the fourteenth."

"I had my suit fitting yesterday." Antonio looked around for a waiter and signalled him over. "*Haus of Stefan*, of course. You want another drink?"

"Another margarita, thanks."

Antonio gave their order and went back to people watching. Even though it was Valentine's Day, they had spent lunch together with an afternoon of relaxing before their father's and uncles' birthday celebrations that night. "All of Tony's family coming? Did his friends RSVP? I know he hasn't seen them in a while."

"Yep, they're coming. We've filled up the house with my family and the hotels with his family and friends."

"Will it be hard for his grandparents and aunts? His parents were married there on that date, and that was the last time they were in Spain at the house." Antonio picked up both glasses from the waiter's tray and handed Cabot his drink. "Here. It can't be easy for them."

Cabot took a sip. "He had a long talk with them after we picked the date, and told them it meant a lot to him to marry on the same day they did. That it would bring him closer to them, *especially* his father since he's buried on the grounds. His parents joined in marriage in the pavilion while his mum was pregnant with him. In a way, he was already there back then, and now he'll be coming full circle kind of thing."

"Is that why they're staying in town?" Antonio's attention turned from the woman in the ocean to his brother on the bed beside him. "Too many memories if they stay in that house. They stayed there in '78 didn't they? For the wedding."

"Yes, they did, and yes, that's why. They agreed to stay in town, didn't want to be in that house if they didn't need to be, but are more than willing to be there for the wedding. Now..." Cabot set his glass down on the table between them. "I know *you* RSVP'd as a single, but if there's someone you meet in the next three months that you want to bring to the wedding, feel free. We kept extra spaces open in case you, Dom, or Danté, or any other guest, ends up hooking up before May."

"I seriously doubt *that* will be happening." Antonio breathed a deep sigh and thought about his non-existent love life. Even though he'd dated many a woman, had many a showmance, or fauxmance as he called them, and many a sexual partner, he was yet to find someone to have an *actual* long-term relationship with. Not that he had to rush; he was only thirty in July, and only Diana and Alena had been married off so far, with Cabot set to wed in a few months. "We *are* still retiring at thirty, aren't we?"

"Oh, God, absolutely." Cabot eyed all the men in tiny swim briefs, and his brows rose as one pulled his swim briefs down to adjust himself in full view of the beach and resort. "Jesus."

"Perving at other men?" Antonio teased. "How *dare you* cheat on Tony. Sick of him already?"

"No, but when you've got some dude pulling their junk out in front of everyone... Jesus!" Cabot rolled his eyes and turned to his brother. "You don't have a problem retiring, do you?" After his HIV diagnosis, they'd cut back on their modelling, deciding that they'd retire on their thirtieth birthday. "It'll be fifteen years in the industry since we started way back when we were just wee lads of fifteen."

Antonio snorted. "*Wee* lads. We were hardly *wee lads*. I think we'd already hit five-ten by fifteen, six feet by seventeen. But yeah, it has been a hell of a long time in the industry. And it hasn't all been good. It's actually been quite shit at times." He watched the woman who'd been swimming exit the water with grace, smoothing her hair and string bikini that barely covered anything at all. "Fuck!" murmured out of his mouth, jaw hanging. His eyes could not take themselves from her. But then, neither could any other straight man's eyes.

"She's hot." Cabot raised a brow at the scene. "Go meet her."

They watched her walk up to her cabana bed, pick up her towel, and dry herself off. She clearly knew she was being watched, and clearly knew how to deal with male attention. Not by ignoring it, but by using the attention to her advantage. By seductively patting the towel over her voluptuous breasts, her curvaceous hips, and down her long lean legs, bending over to give every man watching a hard-on, whether they were straight or gay.

"Wow." Cabot's eyes darted from the woman to his brother's slack jaw and glassy expression. "If I were straight," he murmured, and then noticed her glance their way as she slowly moved the towel back up her body. "Oh, she's eyeing you off." He watched her stand and glance away, but then flick her eyes back to Antonio. "Oh, bro, she's *definitely* looking at you."

The woman laid her towel over the foot of the bed and, in a very ladylike manner, sat, swung herself around, and with a last glance at Antonio as she sipped her drink, settled back to take in the rays of the sun.

"Oh, she was *definitely* checking you out." Cabot swung his foot over and poked at Antonio's leg. "It's you she was looking at. Did you *see* her checking you out?"

The motion of being poked at brought Antonio back from dreamland. "Huh?" His head swung around to his twin. "Huh?"

Laughter bubbled out of Cabot. "Oh, yeah, you were *definitely* checking her out. As was every other man here. But she only had eyes for you, bro."

Antonio cast another glance in her direction, but she was busy lying back in the sun, black shades on, fiery red-brown hair burning in the sun's rays. "No. No, she wasn't. She was just looking up."

"Oh, she was *definitely* looking up. *At you.*" Cabot nodded. "From the time she got here, to the time she swam back and forth in front of us, to the time she walked out of the water and dried herself off *just for you. All* just for you."

"Hardly!" Antonio scoffed and finished his drink. Signalling for another one, he stared at his brother. "I'm waiting for us to retire so I can get into other things. I'm planning a holiday to Aus to see some of the family and parts we've never explored. I'd like to travel more through Europe into the smaller towns and countries we've never been to, like Pompeii in Italy. The wine region in France, maybe even head up to the highlands of Scotland. I want to explore the world while I can, because even though we've only been working part-time these last five years, we've spent most of our time here in Greece. Alena's concert tour was last year—"

"And subsequent marriage to Luca Saint," Cabot butted in.

"Our nephew and niece being born and spending time with them as uncles—"

"And siblings and cousins, and children and grandchildren. It has been nice spending more time with the family," Cabot agreed.

"I'm not looking for someone right now," Antonio went on. "I'd like to get the next five months out of the way first and then be free to explore the world—"

"And *all* the women in it," Cabot said.

"Just as *you've* had all the *men* in it," Antonio continued. "I don't want to go actively searching for a mate, because as we all know—"

"*Especially* in this family—"

"Stop interrupting me," Antonio chastised. "As we *all know* in this family, true love and soulmates happen when we're not looking for them."

"Are you looking for it now?" Cabot watched the woman to see if she would do anything else to get his brother's attention.

Sighing, Antonio thought about it. "No, because we're still working. Today's busy with three birthdays, we've got birthdays for the next five months that we have to work around. You and Tony have the wedding in three months, you're working with Uncle T and Roger on those YouTube videos, or at the centres in Miami, or the centre here with Alexis. You're always busy when we're here."

"Is that why you've been spending more time with Dom, or at the club?"

"Not really *with* Dom. He still keeps himself to himself when he's not working, but the club's a good place to hang out and let loose."

"I thought you'd been getting him out and about more." Cabot swiped his hair out of his eyes and donned a pair of aviator sunglasses.

Antonio barely shrugged a shoulder. "We've seen a movie in the theatre, or watched DVDs at home. He talks a lot about making music for movies and stuff, and I talk a lot about making movies and stuff, or directing docos. *Someone* has to take over *S'Reel* after Papa, and it's obviously not going to be you."

"Is that what you'll get into after your world-wide holiday?" Cabot teased. "Because it's not like you'll be getting into any woman anytime soon."

"Ew, Cabot." Antonio screwed his face up and threw a disgusted look at his brother.

"What?" Cabot grinned. "It's not like you haven't had sex before."

"We're talking about careers, you dipshit." Antonio scowled. "I'm hardly going to be like Papa, though, which is why he's hiring other directors, so he's not always on his own and overworked. I might get into documentary making, screenplays, directing, producing. I don't know. We've done nothing *but* model for fifteen years and have never had any other career. And now I have no idea what I'm going to do."

"Keep modelling for *Haus of Stefan*," Cabot suggested. "We're not turning our backs on D and A. Maybe you could design for the men's line. Or we could go in a direction completely different and start producing our own product lines."

"Like what?" Antonio's brows furrowed in thought.

Cabot shrugged. "We're models. Skincare, haircare, clothing, accessories, pretty much everything we've modelled we could turn around and slap our names on. We'd make a fortune."

"Haven't we already?" A smirk slid across Antonio's lips. "But yeah, we could. If the Kardashians can do it with no talent, then *we* certainly can with *all* the talent."

"Exactly! And I once told Xanthe I could model anything. She dared me to model my paintings and I did. So we *can* model and promote anything. *That's our* talent."

"But as for love…" Antonio shrugged and glanced over at the woman who casually picked up her drink and took a sip, watching him from over the top of her black shades. She seductively licked her lips and went back to lying on the bed.

"Oh, yeah, she wants you." Cabot nodded. "Definitely. You may as well just go over there and bang her brains out now."

"Cabot!" Antonio threw him a look of disgust. "That's gross. Does she look familiar to you? I've been trying to place her."

"Mmm…" Cabot puckered up in concentration. "Not really, why? Where do you think she's from?" His gaze moved between the woman and his brother.

"Don't know, and that's what's annoying me." He heard the soft chime for four o'clock and sat up. "That's *our* time over. Dinner's at six at Grandma's."

"And then it's off to *SB3* for Valentine's Day. Yay!" Cabot lightly clapped his hands and checked to make sure he had everything before pulling a lightweight knit sweater top over his head. "I can't believe we have to go out in the cold. It's so nice in here."

"It is." Antonio stood to pull up a pair of cotton track pants and noticed the woman watching him as she smothered her white flesh in cream. His hands stopped and the pants hitched under his massive manhood that was actively seeking attention.

Her lips moved into an o shape and her hands slowly stopped, her eyes peering over the top of her shades as she took in the size of his package.

His eyes took in the hunger on her face as he pulled his pants up.

"Oh, yeah, she wants you." Cabot chuckled and slid his tote over his shoulder. He'd been watching them both. "If anything," he said as he stepped into his sandals, "I'd say she knows who you are and wants some of that *Stefan charm*." He walked around his brother's bed and waited while Antonio pulled on a matching tracksuit top.

"Hardly!" Antonio frowned and slid his feet into sneakers before picking up his bag. A glance at the woman told him she was clearly after something as she hadn't stopped staring. "I still say I've seen her somewhere."

"Well…" Cabot slung his arm around his brother's shoulders. "She's definitely seen *you* somewhere. Hard not to with all of the modelling we've done." He led Antonio out of the indoor beach, but they both had a quick look over their shoulder before leaving. "Oh, yeah, she *definitely* wants your Stefan charm." Cabot grinned at the woman and slapped his brother on the back. "And I'd say, from the movement in your pants, you want to give her some."

"Cabot!" Antonio complained and shoved his brother aside. "Why does your mentality *not* come with a mature English and conversation level? You still talk like a kid."

"I'm probably mentally stunted at fifteen," Cabot joked. "But then again, I *was* right." He flicked Antonio on the groin and ran off.

*****

"So, what are we having for dinner on this very prestigious occasion?" Carlos asked his mother when he kissed her on the cheek after arriving just before six.

"For a start, it should be me kissing *your* cheek," Jenny replied and hugged her eldest son. "I'm so glad I had you, my baby. I love you, happy birthday."

Carlos chuckled. "Not like you had much of a choice, Mama." He hugged her tightly in return. "You were having me whether you liked it or not."

"And I wouldn't have it any other way. Have you enjoyed your day with Viv?" She cupped his face. "Birthdays are about enjoying one's self."

"Oh, he certainly did that," Viv murmured and blushed at the memory of just an hour earlier.

Jenny's brows rose. "Well, then. Your favourite meal and birthday cake are coming up; since there's not much else I can do for you."

"Mama, Viv…" Carlos blushed. "It's been a good day so far."

"Good." Jenny let him go and turned to Pedro who'd come in with Angie at the same time as Carlos and Viv. "My baby boy. My little Pedro. Come here."

"Mama." He wrapped his arms around her and lifted her off her feet.

"Happy birthday, my baby. Fifty-five today. Have you enjoyed your day so far?"

Angie snorted. "Yeah, he has." Resting her right hand on her hip and leaning against the back of a kitchen chair, she added, "it was all about *him* this morning. Wouldn't let me get out of bed, and then cornered me in the shower, wouldn't leave me alone." Realising they were looking at her, she turned deep red. "Sorry. Guess I shouldn't be talking about that. Um…" She glanced away and saw Tomas and Roger come in. "Oh look, there's Tomas. Happy birthday," she called.

"Hey." Tomas's grin spread ear to ear and he enveloped his brothers into a hug. "It's our birthdays, yay." He kissed them both. "Happy birthday little brother, happy birthday big brother. Who knew I'd get to see this many?"

Gazing at his brother, Carlos said, "We hoped you would. Every year is a momentous occasion."

"Exactly. And we'll keep counting our blessings on this day every year," Pedro added. "We're brothers. Stephanopoulos brothers three. The whole reason for *SB3*."

Tomas's smile beamed across his face. "I love you two so much."

"And we love you," Carlos and Pedro replied and wrapped their arms around him.

"Now why can't we be like that?" Cabot asked Antonio as they stood in the doorway. They'd just arrived with Tony.

Antonio pulled a face. "We slept in the same bed for about twenty-five years of our lives, doesn't that count? And it's not like we've never hugged."

They left their jackets in the coat closet and gave everyone a hug. "Happy birthday, y'all."

"It's so good that you could both be here again," Carlos told Antonio as he wrapped his arms around his son. "We missed a lot of birthdays and anniversaries when you were both gone."

"I know, which is why I'm glad we're here now," Antonio replied. "Catching up on everything we missed out on."

Dom, Danté and Nick arrived. "Hey, happy birthday. When are we eating? We gotta get to *SB3* for our shifts," Dom said.

The door had barely shut when Diana and Charles lugged Adam, Jaqueline, and presents through the door.

"Gandpa, happy berfday." Adam ran for his grandfather and launched himself at Carlos's legs.

"Oh, hello, my boy." Carlos picked him up and flung him over his shoulder. "And how do you know it's my birthday?"

"Mama told me." Adam giggled at the tickling he received before Carlos swung him downward in his arms. "Happy berfday."

"Thank you, young Adam." Carlos nodded. "And do you know who else is having a birthday?"

"Unca Tomas and Unca Pedro." Adam's blue eyes sparkled with joy. "Happy berfday."

"Thank you, young Adam." Pedro kissed his cheek at the same time Tomas kissed the other one, making him burst into a new fit of giggles.

Antonio took nine-month-old Jaqueline from her pram and held her against his chest. "Hello, my precious. Hello, my beautiful niece. Hello, Jaqueline."

Big blue eyes twinkled up at him and her cherubic cheeks grew red as she smiled and showed off her two bottom teeth. Her golden hair sat in a halo around her, and the pink bow on her head sat at a jaunty angle on its pink frilly band.

"Oh, look at those two teeth," Antonio said softly, his brows raised, eyes wide. "Jaqueline's got two teef, look at those two teef."

She gurgled and laughed and grabbed at his face.

"Naw, would you look at that," Cabot said. "Antonio's in daddy training."

Rolling his eyes, Antonio arched a brow at Cabot. "Hardly. Just being a doting uncle to our first niece."

"Mmm, hmm." Cabot arched a brow back. "I have a feeling you're getting pretty clucky, especially after seeing that woman today."

Antonio sighed. "Don't go there, Cabot." He bounced Jaqueline and pulled faces at her, making her giggle.

"What's this? What woman?" Viv asked, ever-present in the knowledge that she was growing older and may not see grandchildren from her sons.

"Doesn't matter, Mama." Antonio put an end to it. "I don't know her, didn't talk to her, didn't bother with her."

"Your dick certainly did," Cabot retorted. "Got a hard-on over her, you did." He saw the frowns on everyone's faces and his eyes widened. "He did. She was hot and staring at him, and he was staring at her and got a hard-on." Shrugging, he added, "I wouldn't be surprised if she pops up at the club tonight."

"Wait." Tony put his hand up. "They were staring at each other the whole time, but he didn't make a move, talk, say hello, nothing?"

"Nope!" Cabot shook his head and stared at his brother. "She swam back and forth in front of us to get his attention, walked up to her bed and dried herself off, getting *every* straight man's attention—"

"And *yours*, apparently," Antonio butted in.

"But she only had eyes for my bro. She kept glancing over her glasses at him when she took a sip of her drink. She licked her lips at him and he stared the whole time."

"But you didn't go and say hello?" Tony incredulously asked Antonio. "Why the hell not?"

"Ah, for fu-ff's, sake," Antonio managed to correct himself, so he didn't swear in front of Adam and Jaqueline. "I'm not looking for anyone right now. We're too busy with celebrations or work. I want to wait until we retire to be able to take the time to settle into myself and a new life before actively looking."

"And as *I* reminded him," Cabot told the family as they had everyone's attention, "*none* of us were looking for love when it walked into our lives. Or in the case of our grandmother, *sailed* into her life."

A soft giggle came from Jenny. "Very true, Cabot, very true. Antonio, why don't you ask her out? Do you know where she's staying?"

"What? And look like a stalker?" Antonio frowned. "No, Grandma. She was just some woman at the resort today looking to catch some sun out of the cold the way we were. If anything, you should be more worried about Cabot looking at another man's junk."

"Ugh, don't remind me." Cabot shivered and screwed his nose up. He saw Tony's raised brow. "Don't worry. It was just some actor dude sorting out his junk by pulling his swim briefs down right in front of *every*one. Talk about rude." He crossed his arms and scoffed. "Like the women needed to see that."

"How do you know it was some actor dude?" Antonio asked. "I didn't recognise anyone."

"Antonio," Cabot reprimanded. "We were at the *private beach* at the resort. The one reserved for *celebrities* only. And besides, I recognised him from one of Carlos's movies. He was some two-bit small part actor who's *clearly* packed on the weight since the movie came out. And *not* in the junk department, if you catch my meaning."

"We get it, Cabot," Carlos cut him off and handed Adam over to him. "Say hello to your nephew."

"Ah, hello Adam." Cabot wrapped his arms around him. "God, you're big. And heavy."

"Unca Cabbie." Adam smacked him on the face, each hand hitting a cheek.

"Hey!" Cabot frowned. "No fair. No slapping or I'm gonna tickle you."

"So, sweetie…" Viv moved over to Antonio and tickled Jaqueline on the cheek. "*When* do you think you might find someone? I'm not getting any younger, you know."

"Mama!" Exasperated, Antonio handed Jaqueline to her. "Content yourself with your granddaughter and for the *love of God*, everyone, *stop* talking about my non-existent love life. It's not like Dom or Danté has hooked up, yet."

"Hey," Dom called out. "I'm too busy working. Don't bring me into this."

"And I'm too busy *not* looking," Danté added, getting a grin from his brother. He shrugged in return.

"And who knows how long Alexis will last with Lorenzo," Antonio went on. "Just leave it alone and let it happen when it's ready."

"Well your dick was certainly ready this afternoon," Cabot quipped.

Adam giggled. "Dick, dick, dick."

"*Cabot!* Now look what you've done," Diana complained. "He'll be saying that for weeks."

"Dick, dick, dick, dick, dick," Adam cried and threw his hands up in the air.

"Well, that's what it's called, D." Cabot handed her son to her. "And I have a feeling that if that woman shows up tonight, then she's gonna be getting some of Antonio's."

*****

After a delicious dinner and layered chocolate cake for dessert, the family headed off to *SB3* for the Valentine's celebrations. Couples and singles mingled over red and white cocktails, had their photos taken on a heart-shaped platform holding heart balloons while red and white confetti and rose petals fell on them, and ate heart-shaped raspberry-filled white chocolates.

The club was full and pounding to the beats that Danté was putting down on stage, and the scent of sex and sweat filled the air, soaking it in the tension of a fervoured desperation to mate with one's partner. A frenzy of passion and desire, as bodies joined in the tribal rhythm of dance.

"Thank God we have the air-conditioner on, or this place would be burning down with the heat everyone's giving off," Jenny said to Spiros as they sat upstairs in the office watching over everyone and everything. Crowds like that weren't their thing anymore, and they preferred to slow dance in relative quiet and watch over the family.

"Well, it *is* Valentine's Day. The day of love. The day I proposed." Spiros leant over and kissed her cheek, his moustache tickling her and making her giggle like a young woman in love.

"Spiros," she murmured, and gently kissed his lips. "We're not alone, you know."

"We can be if we lock the doors and close the curtains. The sofa folds out into a bed, doesn't it?" A twinkle lit up his brown eyes and a cheeky grin crossed his lips.

"Yes, it does. But are you saying you want to get frisky? Anyone could walk in." Normally, Jenny was up for a bit of romance, but not in the club's office, and certainly not while the family was around.

"I'm saying, my darling, that I want to make love to you and cannot wait to get home to do so." Spiros closed the balcony doors and pulled the curtains over, then strode over to the door and locked it. "Now…" He turned to his wife. "I want to make love to my wife on Valentine's Day. The day she bore me three healthy sons."

With the fires burning in her belly, Jenny quickly pulled the sofa out and set it up as a bed.

Spiros swung his wife into his arms and kissed her. "I love you, Jennifer Stephanopoulos." They fell onto the bed in a passionate embrace.

Down on the dance floor the family had partnered up except for the singles. Alena was setting fires with Luca, Diana with Charles, and Alexis with Lorenzo. Carlos was spinning Viv around, and Angie and Pedro, Tomas and Roger, Mike and Maggie, Dan and Derek, Cabot and Tony, plus Simon and Deidre were all getting into the swing of dirty dancing.

Dom was too busy worrying about his set at midnight to notice if every other single in the family were dancing. Nick had girls around him, his sisters were surrounded by cute guys wanting to dance, and Antonio was cutting loose on his own, dancing with whichever woman planted herself in front of him.

Having grown up in the club, and then being invited to every club in New York to promote it, Antonio knew how to dance, and he and Cabot knew how to move, either on their own, or in sync with each other. And since Cabot was dancing between his brother and partner, Antonio also had time to dance with any woman throwing themselves at him.

Turning away from his brother, Antonio saw her across the room. She was also dancing on her own, carefree, vivacious, sexy as hell. She was pushing away any man who tried to dance with her. Her fiery red-brown hair was piled high on her head, and the silky red spaghetti strap dress she wore was slick against her skin with sweat. Throwing her arms above her head, she glanced his way.

His eyes never left her, recognised her from the resort, noted the pert, full breasts unrestrained against the thin film of fabric covering them. Her nipples were hard against the material straining for release. His eyes moved lower, noting the lack of lines demonstrating undergarments didn't exist. The curve of her sensual hips and thighs titillated him, as did her breasts, as did her lips that were open and aimed at him. His gaze travelled up to see her eyes were watching him as he watched her, and he found himself dancing toward her, hypnotised by the beating of the music and the sexual heat on the floor. He gyrated his hips and swivelled his feet, moving one foot at a time toward the woman who was capturing his attention above all else. Thrusting his hips and swaying his body in time to the music, his eyes never left hers as she swayed and gyrated back, staying where she was while he came to her. It was as if she had an invisible lasso around him and was slowly pulling him in.

They were only metres from each other, still swaying, gyrating, stomping to the beat. The heat and sexual tension electrified the air as they moved closer, eyes only on each other. No one else existed in all of space and time. It was just them on the dance floor and no one else.

A metre away and the tension was palpable. So thick you could have slashed a knife between them and it still wouldn't've cut it. The world didn't exist, the club didn't exist, only them and the driving tribal beat that blasted around them did.

The metre disappeared and they were right in front of each other. Emerald eyes gazing into emerald eyes. Two bodies moving in sync with each other to a beat that was driving them insane. His hands reached for her hips and brought them to his. Her arms snaked their way around his neck. His crotch thrust against hers, her breasts pressed themselves to his muscular chest and their eyes continued to gaze into each other, setting the club ablaze.

"Whoo, hey, Antonio…" Cabot spun around to find his brother gone. "Hey! Where'd he go?"

"Dancing off by himself, I think," Tony replied, pulling Cabot back against him. He kissed his shoulder and added, "We don't need him, though."

"Tony!" Cabot grinned at his lover. "If he's disappeared, I want to know."

"Well, it's not like he went poof in a puff of smoke." Tony swayed side to side, moving Cabot with him. "He's probably getting a drink, or off dancing with someone. He could've even gone to take a leak. He'll be back."

Puzzled, Cabot gazed across the room trying to find his brother and found him dancing with a woman. "Whoa, go Antonio."

"What?" Tony's head popped up over Cabot's shoulder. "Where is he?"

"There." Cabot pointed. "Look at the way he's dancing with her. *Very* sexy, even for Antonio…hey…" His brow furrowed. "That's the woman from today."

"What woman?" Tony thrust his crotch at Cabot.

"Tony." Cabot shifted and playfully slapped his husband-to-be. "Stop it. The woman from the resort today who couldn't take her eyes off Antonio. *That's* her. I gotta tell the olds." He made his way through the crowd to his parents and pulled them out of each other's arms. "Hey, Mama, Antonio's dancing with that woman from the resort today." He pointed to his brother and his dance partner. "Woo, they're steaming up the place."

Peering through the crowd, Viv spotted the evocative dancing. "Oh, my, she's gorgeous. Are you sure she's the one?" Craning her neck for a better look, she noticed how close and unaware of everyone else they were. "She seems a little familiar."

"That's what Antonio kept saying, but he couldn't figure out who she was," Cabot said. "But she's *definitely* hot, and look at them go." They watched for a few moments.

"If he's finally getting lucky, good for him." Carlos went back to dancing. "He's nearly thirty, time to get himself a girl. Hell, I was your age when we had the two of you."

"Yeah, but it could just be a fling, not evolve into a relationship," Cabot replied.

"What's going on?" Diana asked. She and Charles had been dancing nearby and had seen them talking. "What are you looking at?"

Viv turned to her. "Antonio's dancing with the woman from the resort today. The one who was watching him. Cabot says it's her." She swung her head around to keep watching. "She looks familiar, but I can't place her."

"I'll go take a look," Diana told them. "I need a drink anyway. I'll go around them on my way to the bar. Back in a minute." She walked off in her brother's direction, skirting them on her way to the bar where the bartender gave her several bottles of drink.

On her way back, she studied them again and realised why the woman had been so familiar. "She's a model," Diana said when she got back to her family. "Which is why both you and Antonio thought you knew her, but couldn't figure it out." Handing out the drinks, she cracked hers open and sculled down the mineral water.

"From where?" Cabot asked. "I can't place her either."

"Can't remember." Diana shook her head. "France, Italy, one of those, I think. She's in a lot of magazines right now, and has done a car ad for TV. Star..." She racked her brain. "Van Star?" Clicking her fingers, she added, "Maria Van Star, French Italian, I think she is. Very hot right now in Europe."

"Are you sure?" Cabot asked. "I've never heard of her."

"I did, awhile back. An old client of mine mentioned her at a function I attended. But I haven't taken much notice in the last year since having Jaqueline," she conceded. "My attention isn't on the modelling world anymore."

"Well, whoever she is, she's hot and has Antonio's attention all to herself." Cabot cast a glance in his brother's direction and saw they were still physically entwined.

"They do seem very much into each other," Viv murmured, her eyes taking in the body language. "But is a model the best partner for him? Why not a normal girl who can give him all of her attention and isn't off flying around the world modelling."

"That's a bit biased and judgemental, Viv," Carlos said. "I was a normal guy who dated a model, and now look. Cabot was a model and is dating a normal guy, and Diana was a model and dated a normal guy.

None of us have ended up with bad lives because we dated models. And to say he needs a normal girl is rubbish. He'll end up with whoever he's meant to end up with—"

"Besides that," Cabot interrupted. "*He's* a model. He'll be understanding of her career and profession, even when he retires."

"Exactly!" Carlos agreed and waved his brothers over. "Antonio's met the woman from the resort today. The one that was eyeing him off. Turns out, she's a model like him. Check them out." He pointed in their direction and watched his brothers' brows rise.

"She's gorgeous," Pedro said. "And they look good together."

"They do," Tomas agreed. "Hope he gets some kind of relationship out of it and not just a one night stand."

"Not that that would be a bad thing," Roger told them. "Sometimes hot sex is better than getting involved."

"Not in this family," Tomas replied. "If you're like Mama and Papa, we marry the first person we fall in love with." He looked up at the balcony and saw closed curtains and doors. "Hey, where are they? Did they go home and not tell us?"

A strange sound came from Pedro's throat and he coughed. "Nope. Not home."

Everyone looked at him strangely. "What does *that* mean?" Tomas asked.

Pedro chuckled. "When the balcony doors are closed and the curtains drawn, it means someone's getting jiggy with it in the office."

"What do you mean? Oh…" Tomas's eyes grew wide. "Oh… Mama…"

"Yep." Pedro's chuckle turned to laughter at the expressions on their faces. "I doubt it's the first time for them, either."

"Definitely not for us." Angie grabbed his hand. "Let's get back to dancing like nobody's watching. In other words, like Antonio and that woman. It's *your* birthday, *not* his. He shouldn't get all the fun."

"Yes, ma'am." Pedro's grin slid ear to ear and he was led away to dance with his wife.

"Guess we should get back to dancing and let Antonio have his fun." Tomas slid his arms through Roger's and added, "I need a drink. Let's have a breather."

"Is that code for *you just want to check on your parents?*" Roger grinned and walked him to the bar. "They're fine, you know. Just like Antonio and that model."

"Maria," Tomas provided and gazed at his nephew. "They're very into each other. Look at the body language. Bodies pressed tight against one another, eyes laser beamed into the others, hands all over. I say they'll end up together tonight."

"For sex or a relationship?" Roger handed him a bottle of orange juice.

"Definitely sex." Tomas opened the bottle and paused. "There's no way sex *isn't* going to happen; the chemistry is explosive."

"It is." Roger gazed at their nephew. "A hundred bucks that sex tonight leads to marriage."

"What?" Tomas swung his head around. "You're putting a wager on it?"

"Yep." Roger nodded and took a sip of juice. "That body language is so explosive they won't be able to stop. My bet, it will lead to marriage, and possibly a quick one at that." He studied them for a few moments more before turning his eyes to Tomas's surprised face. "What? You can't have chemistry like *that* and *not* have it lead to marriage. A hundred bucks says they'll get married."

"You're on," Tomas agreed. "I think it will just be sex for a couple of weeks. She's a model, but so's Antonio, although he's retiring this year. Once she finds that out she'll pass on him because he won't be famous anymore."

"That's a cheap shot," Roger said. "I didn't take you for the judgemental kind."

Tomas shook his head. "I'm not. I just see chemistry that's white-hot and doubt it will last past a couple of months. If she's working full-time and he's retiring, it won't last."

"A hundred bucks says it will." Roger held out his hand. "Deal?"

"Roger!" Tomas's brow furrowed, but after a few moments, he shook. "Deal."

"Easiest hundred bucks I'll ever make." Roger finished off his drink.

"You could've charged more and I still would've shaken," Tomas replied.

"*Now* you tell me." Roger rolled his eyes and left their bottles on the bar. "Let's get back to dancing, so you can make up the extra money I *could've* charged."

Laughing, Tomas followed his husband back to the dance floor.

*****

Just before midnight, Danté thanked the crowd. "My shift is over for the night, everyone. Thanks for being here. Thanks for celebrating Valentine's Day, which also happens to be my father's and two uncles' birthdays." A loud cheer went through the crowd. "Let's lead a cheer of happy birthday for Pedro, Tomas and Carlos Stefan before I leave the stage to make way for my brother, Dom Stefan." He led them through a resounding rendition of the tune before waving goodnight and exiting stage left.

"Hello, Mykonos, how are we this morning?" Dom grabbed his headphones and introduced himself. "I'm Dom Stefan, he was Danté Stefan, and five minutes ago it was the end of my father's and uncles' birthdays. Let's get this place jumping for a Wednesday morning, shall we?" He hit the button on a '90s track and turned the mic down. He had six hours to go and had plenty of energy for it.

Antonio and Maria had slipped away while everyone's attention was on the birthday boys, and he'd led her into the back office and locked the door, shoving her against it and lifting the shift dress that barely covered her, while her hands dived into his pants to release the erection she wanted.

He lifted her leg and pushed inside of her, making her groan. Her legs wrapped around his waist, her arms around his neck.

His right hand gripped her ass tightly as he thrust, his left hand planted against the door and his heels digging into the floor for more power.

She cried out. "Oh God, oh God, oh God." Every sense was being blown by every millimetre of his body. Tall, hard, masculine. She dug her nails into his muscles and let her high-heeled sandals slip off. Her feet went to his bent legs and pushed against his thighs. Her hands pushed her dress up and fed him her breasts. "Oh…God, fuck me, fuck me. Oh…God." Her eyes lolled in her head. Her breath came in short gasps. Her fingers curled in his hair. She lost all sense of time.

Grunting, Antonio came to a stop, breathing hard against her neck. "Who the fuck are you?" he gasped.

"The woman you just fucked?" She gazed into his lust heavy eyes and slid her legs around him. "We need to do that again."

Antonio lifted her from him and deposited her on her own two feet. "I need a break. Ugh…" He stumbled back. "And a shower."

"How 'bout a swim?" she seductively purred and slid her dress down her body. "The resort is open 24/7 and I *am* a guest. We could get the cabana closest to the water and fuck all night."

Antonio leaned heavily against the desk and packed himself away. "Or we could just go to the beach."

"Won't that be too cold? It is still winter." Maria slid into her sandals and sidled over to him. "Won't that be an issue for you?"

"Considering my size, no," Antonio replied. "But it will make other things harder."

"Such as?" Her brow rose in anticipation.

His thumb flicked across her nipple. "Things. Let's go for a swim." Grabbing her hand, he led her down the hallway and out the back door. "Won't take long. We're not far from the cove."

The cool breeze from the Aegean swept across her bare arms and legs, making her shiver and her nipples harden. Making her stomach tighten in knots with anticipation of what was to come. She stumbled in her strappy heels, but Antonio caught her and easily swung her into his arms while hers went around his neck.

He stepped onto the sand in the cove, a favourite spot for his whole family, which was halfway between the club and their houses, and kept on walking until he reached the water. "Ready?"

She leaned into him and shivered. "No. Are we really going to do this?"

"You wanted a swim." He walked into the chilly water until it was thigh-high then let her legs go so she could stand.

"My heels," she squealed and quickly grabbed them from her feet.

"Oh, my God, it's cold. Let's go in, I don't want to swim after all." Running for the beach, she stumbled and fell onto the wet sand at the water's edge. "Oh."

Antonio was on her in an instant. Clasping her hands in his, his lips claiming hers as their own, his knee pushing her legs apart. With the water rushing in around their legs, they joined. Her dress pushed up around her neck as she arched into his hungry mouth and hands. He thrust into her with a fervour he'd never known with any other woman, and made her cry out into the night as the sea soaked more than just their rampant cries.

"Ugh," she groaned, fireworks exploding in her head. "Fuck me." His mouth covered hers and she clung to him like a life raft, clawing his shirt from his torso, pushing his pants from his taut ass to stake their claim. "Ugh."

He thrust until the end and lay panting on top of her. "Well, that was invigorating."

Gasping, she managed, "That was fucking hot, but this water is fucking cold. Get me out of it."

Grinning, he climbed to his feet and pulled her up. "How about we take a quick dip to get all of this sand off?"

"Not on your life. I need a hot shower. Now!" Maria rubbed her arms to keep away the chills. "Where's your place?"

"Not far. Come on." Taking her hand, he hurried them back to the house he shared with Dom, and locked the door behind them. "Your shower awaits, madam." He flung her over his shoulder and marched up the stairs to his room and into the bathroom. Without putting her down, he turned on the hot tap and waited until it steamed up. "Here we go." He set her on her feet, and they quickly undressed and stepped under the hot spray, washing the sand from their bodies.

Taking the nozzle hose from the wall, he sprayed her down from the top of her head to her bottom, sliding it between her legs and making her gasp.

"Hey." Her hands landed flat against the wall and she looked over her shoulder. "Do that again." She watched him grin and slowly slide the nozzle from her back to her front. Groaning, her eyes closed and she arched against him. "Ugh, that feels good."

Antonio pressed against her and moved the nozzle from the front to the back, repeating the motion until she collapsed against the wall.

"Who knew you could get off on a shower nozzle." She gasped in the thick air of the steamy heat. "Fuck me now while I'm good for it."

He replaced the nozzle with himself and pleasured both of them until they both climaxed, crying out against the explosion. They turned off the taps, dried themselves, and stumbled into bed.

"Is anyone else home?" she asked against his lips.

"Not now. Dom will be in around seven." Antonio's fingers tangled themselves in her damp curls. "Why?"

"Just wanted to know in case someone comes running in thinking you were murdering a woman instead of it being the throes of passion." She descended onto him and clenched. "Like this," clench, "and that," clench, "and—"

He rolled her over and had his way.

*****

At seven-thirty in the morning, Dom quietly walked through his door and closed it behind him. He didn't know if Antonio was home, but if he was, he didn't want to wake him. Yawning, after being awake for twenty-four hours, he quickly deposited his sweaty work clothes in the laundry at the back of the house and went into the kitchen for a bottle of water before hitting his bed for a good ten hours sleep. He'd showered and changed at the club to make it easier on Antonio as he always came home this time of the morning and figured stomping around the house having a shower would wake him. He stopped in the doorway, surprised to find a woman in his kitchen. "Ah…hello?"

Maria turned around. She was wearing one of Antonio's white shirts. It was only buttoned in one hole and showed off her ample cleavage with her dark nipples pushing against the fabric. And the fact she was a natural fiery red brunette.

Dom's brows rose as he eyed her up and down. "The model Antonio met. Right?"

She casually sipped the coffee she'd made and eyed him back. "You must be Dominic, Antonio's cousin. Apparently, the two of you share a house. Care to share more?" She seductively licked her lips and moved her legs slightly, so she showed off more.

Making note of her flawless body, Dom shook his head. "No, thanks. I don't share."

"Hey, Dom, you're home." Antonio slapped him on the back and walked into the kitchen wearing nothing but blue sweat pants slung so low on his hips, they may as well been hanging off his manhood. "Have you got that coffee?" he asked Maria. "Ooh, you have." He took the cup she handed him and sipped the hot brew. "You want one, Dom?"

"No, thanks, it will keep me awake. Just came in for a bottle of water." He watched them both and caught the bottle Antonio grabbed from the fridge and threw at him. "Thanks. I'll head upstairs and leave the two of you to it." Backing out of the kitchen, he nodded at the lack of response and knew what was about to happen was none of his business.

"Ah, right, yeah." Antonio remembered him. "We'll try not to wake you," he called and Maria took his cup and placed it on the kitchen counter. "What?"

She spread apart the shirt she was wearing to show nothing underneath and then her hands deep-dived into his pants to bring out his cock.

He lifted her and set her on it in seconds. Stumbling back into the table, he laid her down on it and thrust, eliciting grunts from both of them.

"You'd better not be doing it on the dining table," Dom yelled from the upstairs landing. "Don't be disgusting, Antonio."

"We'll clean it off…" Maria's voice lilted at the end as she came. "Ugh."

"Ugh, gross," Dom muttered and slammed his bedroom door behind him, thanking God for the thick walls between him and his cousin.

*****

Dom arrived at his grandparents' house just before six and saw that Antonio wasn't there.

"Where's Antonio?" Cabot asked and handed him a beer.

"Probably still in bed with that model he brought home." Dom cranked it open and took a swig. "She was standing in my kitchen this morning wearing nothing but a shirt and asked if I cared to share." He shuddered. "Then Antonio came in and they did it on the dining table. Gross."

"Ew." Cabot screwed his face up. "That *is* gross. But not the first time one of us has done that. Have you seen him since?"

"Nope." Dom turned to Tomas. "I've got the club at eight, Uncle T, is dinner nearly ready?"

"Just about to serve it up," Tomas replied. "I take it Antonio won't be coming?"

"Not to dinner, anyway," Dom muttered and heard Cabot's laughing snort. He turned to his cousin. "And even if he did, he'd probably bring her along."

"We always have more than enough," Jenny replied and counted those who were there. "Danté's with Nick, and Alexis is with Lorenzo. We have enough if she does turn up." She watched Alena snuggle into Luca's arms and a soft smile lit up her face. Her grandchildren were slowly falling in love and getting married. With Diana and Alena hitched, and Cabot about to be, she only had four more to worry about before she left this mortal coil. "Do you think they're serious?" she asked those there.

"Certainly seemed to be last night," Cabot told her. "They left before midnight and now we know she ended up at Antonio's. I think she's the first woman to stay the night in quite a while."

"When was the last time he even had a relationship?" Viv asked. "Not just one night stands."

Everyone in the room looked to Cabot who shrugged. "I don't know. I know he's had a couple of girls in the last five years, but nothing long-term. Work always got in the way, or he just didn't find anyone worth investing in. I think the last time he *did* have an actual long-term relationship was before we moved to New York."

"That long ago?" Viv wrung her hands and frowned. "That's not good. That's over ten years ago. To think my baby hasn't had a relationship in that long—"

"Mama, I said *long-term*, and it's not hard to see why it hasn't happened. Look at what *I* was doing. Antonio did it, too, just not as much. And after my diagnosis things calmed down for both of us and he took it easy. There's no need to worry." Cabot wrapped his arms around her and rested his chin on her shoulder. "He's a big boy, Mama. He'll have a relationship if and when he wants one."

*****

Maria rolled off Antonio and lay spread-eagled on the bed. "My God your cock is fantastic. I can't get enough of it."

"And it can't get enough of you." Antonio tried to breathe in through his nose and out through his mouth to regulate his breathing, but it just wasn't working. "Fuck, I love sex."

Maria's laughter fluttered around the bedroom and she curled up in his arms, her hand resting over his wildly beating heart. "And I love you."

Antonio, not catching what she'd said, stretched out and wrapped his arms around her. "Damn, sex is good. *Fucking* is good. Don't you just love it?"

"I do." Maria leaned up on her elbow. "I love sex and fucking and doing it with you. Don't you feel it, Antonio?" She watched him intently for a sign.

"Feel what?" He settled his head into the pillow and watched her watching him. "What?"

"The passion, the desire, the burning feeling inside?" she pushed.

"Sure that's not from too much sex? I'm not hurting you, am I?"

His concern touched her, and considering how big his cock was… "No." Maria shook her head and slid her hand up his chest to his heart where it rested. "I'm talking about here." She moved her hand to the spot just under his ribcage. "And here." Her hand went to his crotch. "Here, and finally…" Her hand moved to his temple and stroked his face. "Here… Don't you feel it, Antonio? The passion, the explosive desire and insatiable appetite. The desperate need to fuck and keep fucking. How many times have we done it now? Ten? Twenty? I lost count every time the passion kicked in. Oh, Antonio, don't you feel it?" She straddled him. "We literally explode when we fuck, and I've never experienced anything like that before with any other man. This is special, this is a once in a lifetime magnifique, bellisima, mi amore. Don't you *feel it*, Antonio?" She saw he was grinning up at her, his emerald eyes alive with excitement. "Don't you feel it?" Sliding down until she was face to face with him, she stared into his eyes. "Don't you feel it, Antonio? The passion, the excitement, the once in a lifetime wave of emotion that sweeps over you, mi amore. Tell me you're feeling it."

Watching her expressions, hearing the softness in her voice, and feeling every damn word she was saying in his gut, he knew exactly what she was talking about. He swept her hair back off her face and kissed her. Felt the explosion in his heart, the fire in his belly, and the movement in his crotch. He knew, in every fibre of his being, that this was the woman he wanted to be with. The woman he wanted in his life. The woman he wanted in his bed. She was in his heart for all eternity. The woman he'd been waiting for to come into his life. He gazed into her fiery green eyes and saw exactly what he was thinking and feeling reflecting back at him. Knew that she had found him, as he had found her. Sighing from the pit of his stomach, he allowed the release of all mental and emotional constraints and let the emotion from his heart, right in that moment, override everything else. "I love you."

The smile beamed across her face. "I love you, too. How is that possible after only one night together?"

"It's possible because love at first sight is possible. Because love and passion and desire take over when you find your soulmate and you just know." He brushed her hair back and a light laugh bubbled out of him. "This is love. Because it's meant to be. We were meant to meet in this time in this place exactly the way we did." He rolled and landed on top of her. "We're meant for each other, Maria Van Star. Do you understand that?"

"Yes, Antonio Stephanopoulos." She stroked his face. "I do. I love you, too, and am so desperately happy right now." She held onto his head as he kissed her and felt the passion rise when he pushed inside. They made love in a frenzy of rutting, and when they were done, Antonio leaned up on his elbows. "I know this was quick and all and I don't have anything to give you, but…" he took a breath, "will you marry me?"

"What?" Her brows rose in confusion. "What?"

"Will you marry me?" He repeated and ran his fingers through her hair, his face soft, his tone softer. "I love you, Maria Van Star. I want to spend the rest of my life with you. Will you marry me?"

"Ohhh, ah, where would we live? What would we do?" Incredulous, she actually considered the prospect.

"Here on Mykonos, when you're not working. Otherwise, I can travel the world with you when you *are* working. I retire from modelling in July. I'll be free to travel then. What do you say? Care to give this love and life a try?"

"Ah…" she pondered. "Would you consider yearly trips to Rome, Paris and London? They are *my* homes, after all."

"Of course," he replied smoothly. "My future brother-in-law is from London, so we're there a lot. And Paris is across the channel from there, and Rome is across the sea from here. We have our own private jets that we can take anytime, anywhere. Just say the word and we can go anywhere."

The prospect was looking better and better all the time. "And where would we marry?"

"Hadn't thought about it. But Cabot and Tony are getting married in May at Tony's family home, we could piggyback that if they'll let us. Everyone will be there. It will be catered; decorations will be up…"

"Not everyone," Maria said. "My family won't be, or my friends…"

"We can let them know, and if they can come we can book them into homes and towns nearby like Tony's family and friends. We'll get chauffeured vehicles for them as well."

"It actually sounds like you've thought about this a lot." A frown crossed Maria's brows. She'd never actually thought about where, or when, to get married. She'd figured she'd know, or work it out, once she'd been proposed to. And now that she had, she had no idea of where to choose, or when to choose it for.

Breathing deeply, Antonio considered the question. "No, but weirdly, the more we talk the more things seem to be falling into place and everything coming out of my mouth sounds right. Like the universe had planned it all along and I'm only just realising it." Rolling onto his side, he looked at her. "I have no idea where this is all coming from, but it sounds good. What do you think?"

Unnerved that she wasn't setting the rules, she shook her head. "I… don't really know. I hadn't planned on getting married so quickly, or at this point in time, so have no idea myself about preparing one, or when to have it. It's a great thought to piggyback off your brother if he'll let us. It means everything will be prepared as you said. But none of it will be ours. I might like certain decorations, music, food. I would want everything my way for my wedding, and I don't know what your brother has planned."

"Why don't we go and find out? Let's go upstairs and ask. And maybe make the announcement while we're at it." He arched a brow. "You haven't given me an answer yet."

Smiling, she leaned up on her elbow and kissed him. "*Of course* I'll marry you. But I expect you to take me shopping tomorrow for the biggest diamond ring ever."

Antonio scoffed in jest. "I'm not *that* rich."

They dressed quickly and ran up to his grandparents' house, knowing they'd still be home since most of them congregated there most nights. Antonio burst through the door pulling Maria behind him. "Hey everyone, oh, a lot of you are still here." His parents, uncles, Alena and Luca, Mike and Maggie, Dan, Derek, Diana, Charles, Cabot and Tony all looked at them. "Great, ah, pretty much everyone." He pulled Maria to his side. "This is Maria Van Star. My fiancée."

"What!" burst out of Viv.

"Fuck, dude!" Cabot chided. "You work *mega* fast. Faster than the rest of us put together."

"When it's amore, it's amore," Maria drawled, glancing at all of the people there. "But, apparently, this family knows all about love at first sight and soulmates." She gazed up at Antonio. "And I've found mine."

Everyone else in the room traded glances. Shock was the general consensus, with confusion running a close second.

"Told you!" Roger whispered in Tomas's ear. "You owe me a hundred bucks."

Tomas scowled and gave a flippant shrug of his shoulder. "You'll get it when I give it to you."

"Oh…you'll *definitely give it* to me," Roger gave him a cocky grin in return.

"Anyway," Antonio continued, watching their faces, especially his parents and grandparents. "I know it's what I want, even though we only met last night—"

"Does the resort yesterday not count?" Cabot asked from Tony's lap. They sat on the easy chair near the fire and he had his legs slung over an arm.

"Well, no, because we technically only met last night—" Antonio tried to continue.

"More like only just *fucked* last night." Cabot arched a brow.

"Do you always interrupt your brother when he's talking?" Maria asked Cabot and scored a shocked frown in return. "He's trying to tell you all something. Be quiet."

No one told Cabot off except for his parents, grandparents and brother. So the hussy telling him to be quiet scored a high brow of distaste, and narrowed eyes of dislike. "Well, how *do you do*," he replied sarcastically.

"Cabot stop," Antonio reprimanded and faced his still shocked family. "I know we just met last night, but with everything I feel, I know this is right. Just like with all of you and your partners." He looked from his grandparents to his parents, to uncles, cousins and siblings. "*You* all knew, so why can't I? Why can't *I* make it happen as fast as possible?" He turned to his brother and Tony. "And I had thought of asking you if you minded letting us get married the day after you guys. We could honour our father and uncles by getting married the day after like they did. But that may not be such a good idea, now." He watched Cabot's expression change.

"Naw, Tone." Cabot got to his feet and hugged his brother. "That's such a sweet idea and one I'd like to do…" He pulled away and checked with Tony. "Could we? I know everything's set for us and to our taste, but could we get everything set up for the next day a well?" He batted his lashes at his future husband. "Pretty please."

Grinning at his lover's antics, Tony nodded. "We can talk it over, the four of us, and if they still want to do it, then we can arrange it. It's not like we can't afford it."

"Yay." Cabot clapped excitedly and hugged his brother again. "We're getting married in May. Yay. You'll be my best man and I'll be yours."

"And that's something we'll talk about in the next few days." Antonio gazed into his twin's eyes. "You okay with this, Cab?"

Cabot rubbed his brother's cheeks with both hands. "Why wouldn't I be? You're my brother. I love you." He gave Maria a raised brow. "I expect *you* to make my brother happy. He deserves it."

"I don't care what you expect, Cabot, because I'll do what I need to do," Maria replied smoothly. "I'll make him happy the way he deserves to be happy."

Cabot's brow wasn't the only one in that room that was raised.

"*Excuse me*, Miss Hussy?" Cabot stared at her. "You don't talk to me that way; I won't tolerate your bullshit."

"I just did and I don't do bullshit. That's your forte, isn't it?" She was as feisty as she needed to be and knew brats like Cabot.

"Antonio!" Cabot frowned at his brother. "Is this the sort of woman you want to marry? One who comes into your *grandmother's* house and insults your brother?" His hands went to his hips. "Spreading *her* bullshit."

"We've had to put up with yours for a lot of years, Cabot," Antonio replied. "You'll get used to someone else's."

Alena and Diana traded amused glances.

"Now…" Antonio turned to his parents. "How do you guys feel about this? Grandma?"

Jenny rose from her chair and went to her grandson. "Is this what you want, Antonio?"

He nodded. "Yes, Grandma. It is."

She gave a sharp nod in return and gazed at Maria. "You're feisty, I'll give you that. But in this family, we show love and respect, *especially* in *this* household. Do you understand that? We may have tolerated Cabot's behaviour for years, but we won't tolerate anyone else's. *Least of all* from the in-laws. Do *you* understand *that?*"

Maria inhaled and noted the narrowed eyes and sharp, firm expression. "Yes, Jenny, I do. And I was raised to respect my elders and parents. So I will in this house and this family." She had taken a punt on using her fiancé's grandmother's name, but hoped it paid off. "I see that you're in charge of this family, and I respect a woman who's in charge."

Everyone held their breath, including Antonio.

With another nod, Jenny exhaled and relaxed somewhat. "Then welcome to the family, Maria."

Antonio let out an audible sigh and blushed when Jenny gave him an amused glance.

"That wasn't so bad, was it?" she asked him. "Now, for the rest of the family." She turned to introduce them. "My husband, Spiros, and our son, Antonio's father, Carlos, and his wife, Vivian. It's the two of them you need to try and impress next." Jenny stepped aside and watched Maria meet her future in-laws, Tomas and Pedro, Diana, Alena, and the rest of the family who were there. She took note of Luca's appreciation of the beautiful model, and the disdain on Cabot's face. Walking over to him, she pulled him aside. "Be happy for him."

"I am," he whispered, casting a glance over his shoulder. "But she's a bitch."

"So were *you* five years ago," Jenny reminded him and scored a shocked expression.

"Grandma!"

"Oh, don't feign indignant ignorance." She shushed him. "We tolerated a lot from you, Cabot. And someone new comes along and puts you in your place. It's quite refreshing."

"She called you Jenny without asking permission," he argued.

"So did *you* five years ago. And it *is* my name, so I can hardly complain. Charles and Luca call me by it, and so does your mother."

"But Roger and Tony call you Mrs S."

"Even though I told *them* to call me Jenny. It's *their* choice. I'm fine either way." She took his arm in hers. "And so should you be. Your brother's getting married."

Sighing, Cabot tried to let it go. "I know. I just hope she reins in the rudeness."

"I find her refreshing," Jenny said and turned him around to watch. "But I warned her. And if she doesn't rein it in, I'll have another chat."

"Wonder if she knows about the prenup," he murmured. "She may not be happy with that."

"Probably not. But she *is* a model, so she'd have her own money and won't need his."

"I don't think any of the in-laws are as rich as Tony," Cabot whispered. "He's loaded and had no issue signing it. But Luca did. Maria might, too."

Nodding, Jenny gazed at her family, and honorary members there, and saw their shock give way to happy smiles. Another of her grandbabies was getting married.

*****

On Thursday, Antonio took Maria to Athens to buy her engagement ring.

"This is the only store in town, in the whole of Greece, that sells diamonds over ten carats," Antonio told her and saw the manager walking over to them. "Aristotle, how are you?"

"Antonio, my boy." Aristotle captured Antonio's hand between both of his and shook it vigorously, his eyes taking in Maria. "Good to see you, good to see you. And who is this beautiful creature?"

"This is my fiancée, Maria," Antonio introduced them. "And that means we need engagement and wedding rings."

"Engagement! Fiancée!" Aristotle clapped his hands in joy. "Congratulations, Antonio. Come this way. The rings are over here." He led them to another room in the store that had no windows, and the cabinets were behind bullet-proof glass. "Come, come, gaze upon our specimens. Do you know what sort you want?"

"I don't, but Maria gets to choose," Antonio told him, and then suggested Maria have a look around the room. "Whichever one you want."

"That's a dangerous thing to say to a woman," she teased and went to work looking at each beautiful ring. She let out an occasional ooh and ahh, and finally decided. "This one."

Aristotle removed it from the cabinet and held the box out for Antonio. The sparkler was an emerald cut diamond, surrounded by smaller diamonds.

"Wow!" Antonio's brows rose. "That's huge."

"And I *love it!*" Maria gazed expectantly at him and held out her hand.

Nodding, Antonio removed the ring from the box and slid it onto her finger. "Fits perfectly." He turned her hand back and forth to see the fires burn brightly within the stone. "Fiery, like you."

"That's why I want it." She held her hand up to admire the ring. "I want it!"

"Then I guess I'd better buy it for you." Antonio handed the box back to Aristotle. "Got matching wedding bands?"

*****

On Sunday, Antonio finished introducing Maria to the rest of the family. They noted the size, and assumed cost, of the engagement ring, as well as her feistiness and Cabot's disdain.

"Don't like her, Cab?" Alexis asked as they stood in Jenny's lounge room. They watched Maria chat with other family members, but all Alexis heard was grumbling.

"No. I don't," Cabot muttered. "She was a right bitch on Wednesday. Called Grandma Jenny, thought she could have a go at me. What a cow." His face puckered up in distaste and he turned to look at the photos above the mantel, so he didn't have to look at her.

"Nasty little piece of work, aren't you?" Alexis grinned. "So, you don't like someone who put you in your place? Not the first time for you. You're used to getting your own way and being the centre of attention."

"Alexis!" Cabot rolled his eyes at her and kept his voice low. "That's the *old* me from five years ago. I've changed a lot since then and know full well the world does *not* revolve around me." He sneaked a glance over his shoulder and watched Maria charm his family. *Some* members of the family, anyway. His mother didn't look too happy and others had unreadable expressions. "I don't think anyone likes her. Look at their expressions."

"Well..." Alexis glanced at each one. "She's new, has come in quickly, and we're still shocked at the suddenness of it. But Antonio's clearly in love and we all know how *that* works in this family."

"Are you still in love with Lorenzo?" Cabot's grin was sly. "How's *that* going?"

"Ah..." Alexis let out a breath. "I don't know if it will last much longer." She saw his raised brow and shrugged. "I know he's not my soulmate. I don't want to marry him."

"Then why are you still with him?" Cabot crossed his arms and leant against the mantel.

Another shrug. "Sex, companionship."

"Is he coming today?"

Alexis glanced at the wall clock. "His shift finishes now, so he *might* be here in half an hour or so. If not..." A third shrug.

"Wonder what he'll make of Maria. Luca *loves* her." Cabot raised a brow and looked over at Luca and Maria conversing. Luca's body language showed he was *very* into Maria, especially when they were speaking Italian.

"Keep the conversation to English, please, so the rest of us can understand and join in," Jenny told them as she laid napkins on the tables. She'd seen Alena's puzzled expression and knew her granddaughter was put out by her husband's attention being distracted by the newcomer.

"Of course," Maria replied smoothly. "I forgot my manners. It's just when I'm with a fellow countryman it bursts out of me. The same with my French." Jenny was someone she wanted on her side and knew she needed to keep her placated.

"I fully understand." Jenny smiled at her. "But in this house, English is the main language, so it's spoken at all times. Remember that." Her gaze coolly turned to Luca. "*Both* of you. I believe your *wife* would like your attention for a few minutes."

Controlling his temper, Luca smiled coolly in return. "Of course, it was rude of me to take up so much of Maria's time. I'm sure Antonio would like her back." He nodded at both of them and walked over to Alena.

"Holy shit did you see that?" Cabot whispered to Alexis. "Grandma put them *both* in their place. She's definitely got *their* numbers."

Alexis shook her head. "Wow. Grandma only gets like that when she doesn't like someone. Or someone's marrying into the family." She shrugged. "Both cases, I guess."

"She's disrespecting Grandma, and we all know what happens when someone does that." He absentmindedly rubbed his cheek. Even though Jenny had slapped him for the first, and only, time five years ago, he'd never forgotten it.

"I doubt she'll slap Maria." Alexis watched Antonio slide his arm around his fiancée. "But she might slap Luca."

"Didn't she warn Lorenzo when you started dating?" Cabot saw how happy his brother was and his heart hurt. He wanted to be happy for him, but not for him to be married to a rude hussy like Maria Van Star. "She thinks her own shit don't stink," he muttered.

Alexis grinned. "She does, and yes, Grandma did. But he's been respectful to her and the family since."

"He *should* be. Grandma paid his way through med school on a scholarship," Cabot said and acknowledged Tony when he stopped beside them.

"Lunch is nearly ready," Tomas called. "About ten minutes."

"I hear it's the famous Sunday roast," Maria said as she and Antonio walked up to the island bench. "I do hope it's not fattening. I have to keep my figure for modelling."

Tomas and Roger froze in their spots. No one had ever said such a thing about Jenny's roast chicken. Tomas glanced at Antonio, but he didn't seem fazed by what she'd just said.

"Everything we cook is as healthy as we can make it," Jenny calmly told her. She walked around them to gather the plates. "That's how the boys are in such fabulous shape, and why our cookbooks are massive best sellers. But if you don't like chicken, or your food roasted, feel free to not eat any." Jenny remained calm and set the plates on the counter. "Feel free to go out and buy yourself something that would be more appropriate for your delicate tastebuds. The choice is yours. Everything is as healthy as can be. Do you have a problem with that?"

Maria's mouth dropped in shock. "Ah…no… No, I don't. I'm sorry." Her hand flew to her chest. "I didn't mean any offence. It's just these days modelling is harder than ever and we have to watch every little morsel we eat. I'm sorry if I offended. I've been told my manner is brusque, but I just see it as speaking my mind." She looked back and forth from Jenny to Tomas. "In this business, you have to speak your mind, otherwise you get eaten for breakfast, lunch, and dinner."

"Yes, you're brusque." Jenny nodded. "And we encourage speaking one's mind. We have no problem catering for food allergies, or dietary requirements, but since we were told nothing, we didn't prepare anything else. So, if roast chicken and vegetables are not to your liking, please, go and buy something that is, otherwise, roast chicken and vegetables are what you'll be eating. Understood?"

Maria nodded, thoroughly chastised. "Understood. Once again, I'm so sorry if my manner offended."

"I like feistiness," Jenny said. "But not to the point of rudeness. Lunch is ready."

"Holy fuck she's an arrogant bitch." Cabot shook his head. Everyone else had heard the conversation and didn't know what to think of the rude new member of the family. "And Antonio doesn't even seem to care."

"He's in love." Alexis grinned wryly. "Love makes you very blind indeed."

"Then *he'd* better start seeing the light, or *she'd* better get her shit together," Cabot mumbled as Jenny corralled the family.

"Of course, and I didn't mean to be rude. This is me; this is my manner. And now, suddenly, I'm in a new family, getting to know new people and finding my way around. I think my nerves are making me worse. I just want to make a good impression and I seem to be doing the opposite by sticking my feet in my mouth. I don't want to offend anyone."

"Then maybe if you listen to everyone and what they're saying, watch how they interact with each other and not talk yourself; you might learn how we cohabitate as a family," Jenny suggested and handed out plates of food.

"Yes, of course. Observe. Good idea." Maria glanced nervously at Antonio who offered her an encouraging smile.

"Maria, what would you like?" Tomas asked, dishing out chicken as he cut it up.

"Oh, just one piece of everything, thank you." She watched as one piece of chicken, one potato, one carrot, and a small scoop of peas and beans went onto the plate that was handed to her. "Thank you," she murmured, and carefully turned around in the crowd moving past her.

Antonio received his plate, and with a hand on her back, guided her to two chairs at the second table.

Everyone waited until the entire family was seated, and then commenced devouring the meal between conversations.

Maria did as she'd been told and didn't speak unless she was spoken to. She observed the different relationships between partners, siblings, and cousins, plus the other in-laws, and saw how everyone interacted. Between each bite of food, she sipped her mineral water to wash the saltiness down, and when the meal was over, she patted her lips and left her napkin beside her plate.

"What did you think?" Antonio asked as he helped gather the plates.

She tried to choose her words carefully. "A little too salty for my liking, but the taste was unusual. I've never tasted anything like it."

The clattering of dishes quietened as those who'd heard looked her way.

"There *is* no salt in Grandma's chicken," Cabot said over his beer glass. "They don't add any. It's in the ingredient used for the marinade and gravy. Which I see *you* didn't have." Even he could hear the snideness in his tone, but his anger was bubbling up inside of him.

Maria noted his cool expression and tried to remain calm. "You know what it's like as a model. We restrict calories and carbs and remove as much as possible from our diets. So, when we have something with salt or sugar in it, we can taste it very strongly. I'm sure that's all it is."

"Ah-huh," Cabot muttered, his eyes narrow and uncaring. "You won't want dessert then. Best if you go somewhere else in future to eat."

Antonio tilted his head at his brother and frowned. "Cabot," he warned. "Stop it."

"Just reiterating what Grandma said before," Cabot sweetly told his brother. "When you come to Grandma's you eat the food she and Uncle T make. It's all low calorie, low sugar, low salt, as healthy as they can make it. *You* know that."

"Doesn't mean you need to be rude," Antonio said and slid his arm around his fiancée who smiled brightly at him, ignoring Cabot.

"I'm not the one being rude," Cabot muttered under his breath and behind his beer glass. "Why can't you see that?"

*****

The next three months flew by quickly with Maria making inroads with the family. She tried to smooth the way with Cabot who still remained suspicious, appeased Jenny, and had Viv and Carlos on side. She even had Diana eating out of the palm of her hand. But they were the only people who mattered. The direct blood connection to Antonio. Dom and Danté weren't overly interested in her, and Alena was suspicious due to Luca's behaviour. She got along with Alexis, Simon and Deirdre, but had somehow put the rest of the adults offside.

Maria bit her tongue as much as she could, but burst out with her opinion on more than one occasion, receiving either a smile from Jenny who laughed with her, or put her in her place, but was someone she could sit down and have a decent conversation with. In fact, Jenny had warmed to her quite quickly.

And wedding preparations went more smoothly than she thought they would, noting that Cabot and Tony's wedding would be rather tasteful and it wouldn't take too much to add a few more things that she wanted. If she was getting married in Spain, then she was going to have what she wanted and no one would get in her way.

Her family could make it, even though it was short notice, and after many complaints, their frowns turned to smiles after hearing she was marrying one half of a world-famous modelling duo from one of Greece's richest families. *That* little tidbit of information they loved.

*****

Two days before Cabot and Tony's wedding, everyone went through the rehearsals so they knew their places. And once ceremony number one was rehearsed, the rehearsal for ceremony number two swung into motion.

"I will be walking up the path to here where Antonio will be waiting." Maria pointed in several directions. "My family and friends will be on this side, your family on that side, the priest here." She stood in the centre of the marble pavilion on the DeLuca estate. "We will face the priest, go through the ceremony, and then exit back down the path to the house. It should take about fifteen minutes in total."

"Fine by me." Antonio nodded and glanced over all of the family and people there. "Do we need an altar? A platform? Or will we just stand here on the marble?"

Maria looked up at the canopy of trees. "When is the sunlight brightest? And it's May, will it be hot? I don't want to have to put sunscreen on. It will make me sticky, and I don't want to be sticky in my wedding dress on my wedding day." Looking at everyone there, she went on. "Does anyone know what the weather will be?"

Cabot rolled his eyes at Tony and turned away. Even though Maria had smoothed things over with him for the most part, and liked most of their wedding decorations, she had still wanted something to call her own, and he'd had no problem with her doing that the morning of her wedding. However… She was becoming more annoying as the wedding grew closer.

Someone Googled it.

"It's supposed to be 23 Celsius. What's Celsius? Is it the same as Fahrenheit?" Atula, one of Maria's modelling friends, asked.

"About 73 Fahrenheit," Danté replied, sitting behind his grandmother on Antonio's side of the pavilion.

"Oh, that will be beautiful, then." Maria nodded. "Are we using the same photographer?"

"That's what *we* decided," Tony reminded her. "Charles and his assistant will be photographing and filming everything."

"Oh, right, Diana's husband," Maria informed her side of the pavilion. "Make sure you put your best faces on for his camera. He used to be a professional photographer in his previous life before joining the family."

Diana exchanged an amused glance with her husband who stood nearby taking photos of the rehearsal while his assistant took video footage.

"Okay. Since everyone's in place, let's rehearse me walking down the aisle, shall we." Maria hurried down the path with her father who was giving her away. A minute later, music wafted into the pavilion and everyone took their seats to watch Maria be escorted down the aisle by her father, Giovanni Van Star. Maria's smile beamed with the power of a thousand light bulbs and didn't stop, even at the altar when her father kissed her cheek and stepped aside. She turned to Antonio and grasped his hand.

"This is where I will start," the priest said. "We go through the readings, the vows, you'll kiss the bride, and then you'll walk down the aisle as husband and wife. Everyone will follow and the party will continue."

"That seems easy enough." Antonio nodded and smiled in return. "Is everything in place?"

"The decorations will be put up on the morning of the ceremony. You have your tux; I have my dress. Does everybody have everything they need?" Maria asked the crowd. "You have your wedding outfits, shoes, hats, etc?"

Yeses and nods went through her side of the crowd.

"Good. I don't want to hear on the morning of my wedding that some of you don't have what you need. I *won't* be interested and you can go without because you will *not* ruin my wedding day. Do you understand?"

"Yes, darling, geez, as if we'd ever do that to you." Escala, another model friend, rolled her eyes. "Calm *down*, Maria. We have everything. Almost…" She eyed Dom from across the aisle. "I wouldn't mind having Dom Stefan to myself."

Dom's eyes widened, he sucked in a sharp breath, shook his head and said, "No thanks, not interested." This was much to the amusement of his family who chuckled or elbowed his side.

"Pity," Escala replied and tossed her long, black glossy hair over her shoulder.

Dom studied her creamy skin, dark eyes, and sensual lips. She was hot and sexy, but for some reason, he just wasn't interested. "Not really." He looked away and muttered under his breath, "Jesus."

Danté snorted from beside him. "Maybe you should give it a shot. She's clearly into you."

Dom elbowed his brother. "Why don't you? You're old enough."

A frown crossed Danté's brows. "No, thanks. I'm not after a man-eater, and I don't want to be eaten by one."

That elicited snorts and laughs from those around him.

"If everything's ready for three days' time, then I guess we're set." Maria gave three short, sharp claps. "Dismissed, everyone."

"Dismissed?" Cabot inhaled and turned away from his brother and future sister-in-law to stare at his husband-to-be. "She dismissed us like kids in a classroom, for God's sake."

"Don't make a big deal out of it." Jenny laid a hand on his back. "Your wedding's first, so don't worry about theirs. I have a feeling it will turn out better than it looks."

Cabot frowned. "God, I hope so, Grandma. She hasn't been too bad the last three months, but the last two weeks she's been almost intolerable."

"And it will all be over in a few days. Now, walk me back so we can chat."

He escorted her, and Tony escorted his grandmother, back to the house where they were taking refreshments in the afternoon. The house and grounds were majestic in the lazy spring sunshine, and the view down to the lake was clear and unencumbered from the back terrace.

"It is nice here." Alice York, Tony's grandmother, gazed across the landscape. "Even if it does hold bittersweet memories."

"It is, and it does," Tony agreed and served both families drinks. His grandparents, aunts and uncles, siblings and cousins, along with his three best friends, were in attendance, staying at the hotel in town. "But we'll be okay, Grandma, won't we?" He gave her hand a quick squeeze and continued serving drinks.

"Of course, we will be." She sipped her chilled lemonade. "Regardless of the memories and tragedies that come with them. This is your ancestral home and we will never deny you that. We will always cherish the memories of your parents' wedding and those few moments of joy we spent celebrating. But after that, there is nothing for us here."

Sighing, Tony nodded. "I know. And I understand that."

Maria was on the other side of the terrace chatting to her model friends who were boldly watching Dom and Danté.

"Are they single?" Escala asked, provocatively rubbing the rim of her margarita glass as she made eyes at Dom across the terrace.

"He is." Maria noted his discomfort and watched him turn away. "So's Danté and his best friend Nick. You've met him, too."

Nick noticed Maria's gaze and nudged his best friend. "Those hot model friends of Maria are watching us."

Danté glanced over his shoulder and turned back. "I doubt they're interested in me. I'm too young for them. It'll be Dom they're after."

"Or me." Nick snickered and gave the models a nod of acknowledgement. "They're hot."

"And too old for you," Danté replied, watching everyone interact.

"We did," Chanel, an Italian model, told Maria. "And even though I love the fact Danté's rich, too, I prefer his brother. Would you get a look at that ass." She could not tear her eyes away from Dom. "They're like two voluptuous melons just ripe for the eating."

"*And* he's shredded," Fiera, a fiery French redhead, said. "You can see his six-pack through his t-shirt it's that tight."

"His t-shirt or his six-pack?" Chanel asked.

"Both." Fiera laughed.

"I wonder if he's up for sex?" Conturi, a Swiss model, mused. "A quick fuck in the forest, down by the lake, hell, even in that shed beyond the olive grove. I would do him anywhere, anytime, anyhow, anyway."

"Wouldn't you all?" Maria exchanged her empty glass for a full one from the passing waiter.

"Yes," all her friends replied and burst out laughing.

Danté wandered over to his brother. "You might end up mincemeat for some very hungry models."

"So I heard." Dom sighed. "Why is it, that women hate being objectified, but have absolutely no problem doing it to men?"

"Don't know, but since they're eyeing *you* off the most, and *you're* closer to their age, they're pretty much leaving me and Nick alone." Sipping his drink, Danté took a quick look over his shoulder at the group.

"Not that *I* want that," Nick grumbled. "I'll take one for the team if you're not interested, Dom."

Dom snorted. "Funny."

Nick shrugged a shoulder. "Not being funny. They're hot and you're not interested."

Shaking his head, Dom chuckled. "Then have at. You don't need my permission."

Escala drained her margarita glass. "I'm going to take a chance. Wish me luck." She sauntered over to Dom and stopped by his side. Breasts pressed against his muscular left arm. "Hello, Dom Stefan. I wasn't fooling around before. I *am* interested."

Dom stared into her doe-shaped eyes. "You're one hell of a stunning woman, but *I'm* not interested."

Her right hand rubbed itself over the round curves of his ass. "You sure, Dom? I could take you to heaven and back."

Hearing a guffaw out of Nick, Dom stepped away. "Don't do that," he warned and set his glass down on a waiter's tray. "I'm not interested." Shoving both hands into his jeans pockets, he tried to continue his conversation with a surprised Danté.

But Escala was having none of it. Moving closer, she purred, "Now, that's no way to talk to a woman that wants you, Dom." Her left hand made its move and latched on to his crotch.

"*What the fuck!*" Dom grabbed her hand and flung it away from him as he thrust backwards. "*How dare you do that to me!* I'm not some piece of meat you can assault. If a man did that to you you'd be screaming bloody murder."

Seeing his furious expression, she raised a brow. "*You're* lucky you *have me* hitting on you. You couldn't get any better."

"Are you saying *you're* the best that I can get," Dom scoffed. "I aim a hell of a lot higher than you, sweetheart."

Shocked that any man could *and* would speak to her that way, Escala raised her hand to slap him, but Tony's hand clamped around her wrist, making her wince and look at him.

"*Not* in *my* home," Tony murmured furiously in her ear. "If you weren't here for Maria's wedding, I'd throw you out now."

She tried pulling out of his grasp, but he pulled her back.

"You don't come into my home and assault my future cousin-in-law. Do you understand me? Now…" Tony peered into her eyes. "I suggest you leave and get a lot of coffee into you." He escorted her over to a shocked Maria and her friends. "I've told your friend it's time to go. You are in *my* home, and I will *not* tolerate behaviour like that. Do you understand me?"

"Yes, yes, of course, Tony. I'm so incredibly sorry. I didn't expect her to do something like that," Maria fretted. "She's clearly had too much to drink and not enough to eat." She took her friend's arm. "Come on, Escala, we'll get you a car back to your hotel. You've drunk too much."

"I've only had three margaritas," Escala argued and tried wrenching her arm from Maria. "I'm perfectly fine, but as for you…" She turned to Tony.

He cut her off by thrusting a warning finger into her face. "Don't you even dare, or you *will not* be here for the wedding." Moving his gaze to Maria, he added, "Control your friends or *none of them* are welcome." He turned on his heel and walked back to his family.

"Of course, Tony. I'm so sorry," Maria placated, and she and her friends hurried Escala into the house to hail one of the cars for the family. "*You stupid bitch! How could you?* I don't want *anybody* ruining my big day. *Why* would you hit on him and grab his cock? In front of the whole *fucking* family." Maria's hands slammed onto her hips and she stared Escala down. "*How could you be so fucking stupid?*"

"Hey, it's not my fault. Men normally fall all over me." Escala flung her hair over her shoulder. "He must be a fag, or something, if he's not interested in me."

"Or maybe he's just straight and just not interested in you." Chanel raised a brow in distaste.

"*Seriously*, Escala. *That* was *uncalled* for. Couldn't you have waited until you were alone with him?" Maria said.

"Ugh, what *is it* with you hoes?" Escala rolled her eyes. "I'm outta here."

"Make sure you sober up for my wedding, or *don't* bother coming." Maria watched her open the door and stop in the threshold to cast a withering look over her shoulder.

"I won't bother coming," Escala told her and pulled the door shut with a bang.

"*Jesus Christ!*" Maria growled in Italian before continuing in English. "How could she do this to me? *That bitch.*" Pacing, she thought about the ceremony. "At least she was only a guest and not in the bridal party, so she won't be missed. And it won't matter if she's not at the party afterwards. Okay…" She stopped and inhaled slowly. "One, two, three, out, two, three. Everything's going to be okay."

"What about Tony?" Fiera asked. "He was pretty pissed."

"Well, he's English, Colombian, Spanish. He's a hothead like me, and I'm marrying his future brother-in-law, so we'll both be in-laws marrying twins." Maria went back to pacing and played with her bottom lip. "But this wasn't *my* fault. Escala did it all on her own. So, I will go and apologise and smooth things over. It will all be fine."

Out on the terrace, Dom was thanking Tony.

"No need." Tony shook his head. "I'm about to be an in-law, like Maria. I don't have to tolerate her bullshit, or the bullshit of her friends. This is *my* home and *my* rules apply. Just like your grandma's house. I'm not about to have anyone assaulted on my property, or in my house. Least of all a future family member." He slapped Dom on the back. "But you clearly don't need my help."

"Hey, Dom," Pedro called from his spot next to his mother and saw his son turn their way. "You okay?"

Dom looked at all of his concerned family, gave an annoyed shrug, and sighed. "Yeah. We've had girls throw themselves at us for years, but unlike Cabot and Antonio," he glanced at his cousins, "we've never been into the physical smash and grab scenarios of it. We're always on stage, and I have absolutely no desire to have my crotch grabbed by some woman."

Cabot snorted. "Yeah, sure Dom. You will one day when you find the right one."

"Meh, doubt it," Dom disagreed.

"Well, it's not like you're the first one. Your father could tell you some stories from his days at *69*," Angie said, waving her wine glass around. When everyone looked at her, she bit her tongue. "But now's not the time for those." Glancing at Pedro, she burst out laughing at his expression.

"Don't you plan on getting married, Dom?" Cabot asked. "Coz that'll be the day. The only Stephanopoulos to never get married."

"Didn't say anything about not getting married," Dom said. "Just didn't plan on getting grabbed."

"Dom, Tony, Cabot, I am *so sorry* for Escala's behaviour before." Maria came to a stop beside them. "I had absolutely no idea what she was planning when she walked over to you, Dom. But I feel so awful that she treated you that way." Laying it on thick, she had to bite her tongue from saying what she really thought. Her hands went apologetically to her chest. "I am so sorry. I've told her if she can't sober up for the wedding, to not bother coming."

"Good." Tony gave a sharp nod. "I won't tolerate that behaviour in my home."

"Of course not," Maria agreed. "And I wouldn't either. Dom, I am so sorry."

"Not your fault, Maria," Dom replied. "At least, *her* actions aren't *your* fault. But from the comments being made before, you didn't do anything to stop them. You only encouraged them." He coolly stared at her hoping his expression told her what he really thought.

"Ah…" She relented, embarrassed because she knew everyone was watching and listening. "Yes, you are right. I was playing matchmaker with my single friends. I probably should have asked you beforehand if you'd be interested. My apologies." She put her hands up in defeat. "I will stay out of yours and my friends' love lives from now on."

"Apology accepted. Not that my love life is any of *your* business to be getting into in the first place. Don't do it again." Dom watched her eyes widen in surprise. "I don't need *you* setting me up. Least of all, with *your* friends."

"Oh." Maria gulped. "Of course. I didn't, oh…" Shaking her head in humiliation and embarrassment in front of not only her future husband's family, but her host's family and her own, she backed away. "I didn't mean to. I'm so sorry." Turning, she rushed over to her family, who Antonio was talking to, and sheltered in his arms.

"Interesting," Tony murmured as they watched her with them.

"What is?" Cabot asked.

Tony's head swivelled around to his lover. "When's her birthday?"

"Why?" Cabot's brow furrowed in curiosity.

"She's very much like a Gemini," Tony said. "One minute, feisty as hell, the next minute, apologetic as can be. Almost like two different personalities."

"Maybe she's hangry," Nick offered and looked at Cabot. "Don't you models refuse to eat, or something."

"Ha-ha." Cabot pulled a face. "More like good and evil," he muttered and looked at his cousin. "You okay, Dom? You look a little shaken."

"I'm fine." Dom glanced in Maria's direction. "But I definitely get what Tony's saying. One minute she doesn't care what she says to us, or how she treats us, but then she'll turn around and apologise profusely."

"Why do you think I haven't liked her from the day we met her?" Cabot slowly shook his head. "I wish Antonio had never met Maria bloody Van Star. You got in some good one-liners, though."

Dom chuckled. "Yeah, well, you can't hang around Grandma without learning a few things. You've had a few good ones yourself at times."

Cabot agreed. "Learnt from the best."

After most of the festivities had died down, and the families had been driven to their hotels and rented homes, the Stephanopoulos family lingered on the back terrace to take in the view of the lighted pool, gardens, and lake.

"This really is a beautiful home, Tony," Jenny told him. "The remodelling you did is perfect for the feel of the place."

"Thanks, Mrs S." Tony smiled his appreciation. "I tried to make it mine and not my grandfather's. Since the renovations were done it's just about been rented all year round."

"Yes, it is beautiful," Maria chimed in, trying to make peace once again. "Thank you so much for allowing Antonio and me to marry the day after you and Cabot. I know it means so much to him." Feeling his hand on her shoulder, she gazed up into his eyes. He was sitting on the arm of the wicker chair she was in, and she slid her hand over his.

"Thank you, Maria." Tony remained neutral. "I know that decision meant a lot to Antonio *and* Cabot."

Cabot's sly little smile grew bigger as he looked from his future sister-in-law to his lover. "It did, thank you."

"Anything for you, my love." Tony gave him a soft kiss on the lips.

"Everything is done then?" Alena casually crossed her legs and sipped her cocktail. She was in a two-seater chair with Luca.

Tony and Cabot exchanged a glance. "It is with us."

"And us, too." Antonio lovingly rubbed Maria's shoulder. "You don't have any last-minute thing to do, do you?"

"No, not me. Everything's catered for thanks to Tony and Cabot. My family will be chauffeured in, and my dress is done."

"A *Haus of Stefan* dress?" Alena inquired.

"No," Maria replied. "I found a dress by *Vera Wang* that I adore and had it altered to my taste."

"And what's that?" Alena went on. "Is it '80s? You always remind me of Sheena Easton when your hair is piled on top of your head like that." She noted the well-crafted curls pinned up on Maria's head.

Maria arched a brow. "I do love the '80s, and have been told I look like Sheena, but no, my dress is classic and well-made. Unlike *some* design houses."

Alena's brow arched higher than Maria's. "Meaning what?"

"Meaning, that some design houses put out very shoddy work, or simply steal designs and call them their own." Maria tried to remain calm while expressing her opinion, and without, she hoped, insulting anyone. But Alena was getting on her last nerve. "Vera is classic, clean, and beautiful."

"Unlike *Haus of Stefan*, you mean?" Alena's eyes narrowed. "Just come out and say it. You don't like our company, or what we make."

"Oi, Jesus, Alena," Alexis complained and swung her legs over the arm of her chair.

"What you make is fine for the people you make it for," Maria said.

"But *you* clearly don't wear it," Alena interrupted. "What? Too good for it?"

"Alena," Jenny warned. "Don't."

"No, Grandma. If she's insulting *HOS* then she's insulting *us* and that's not fair." Alena uncrossed her legs and set down her glass, ready for a fight. "So, what is it?"

"I'm insulting no one, Alena," Maria said. "Not everyone in this world wears *Haus of Stefan*. There are other designers and other clothes. What you make is fine for the people you make it for. But it's not for everyone, and certainly not for me. It's not my style or taste, and there's nothing wrong with that." She leaned back in her chair, mentally daring Alena to reply. "But *you* seem to have a problem with that. You get angry when people aren't wearing your label. That's *your* problem, no one else's. I can wear whatever labels I like and *you* have no say in the matter." She left the line hanging in the air and heard silence. Until Alena opened her mouth.

"I never said you *had* to wear *HOS*, Maria. I have *never* said everyone needs to wear it. I just happen to be proud of what Diana and I have achieved and the designs we've made, and promote it and put it out there at all times. So, to hear it insulted pisses me off," Alena finished through clenched teeth.

"I insulted no one," Maria repeated. "And I'll thank you kindly to stop repeating it."

"Thank me kindly," Alena spat, and thrust herself up. "You've done nothing but insult this family since you came into it, always getting your little digs in here and there. Hell, you didn't even have a problem with one of your friends assaulting my brother." She waved a hand at a surprised Dom. "And don't think apologising will get you out of it because I heard you egging your friends on. You may be marrying my cousin, but that doesn't give you the right to still be a bitch. I thought you had learnt your lesson in the last three months."

Maria's ears moved back like a cat's when it's about to strike, but she kept her cool. "I apologised to Dom and Tony for that. They accepted my apology. *Clearly,* you and I still have a ways to go in forging a friendship."

"A ways to go," Alena scoffed and stepped towards her. "A ways to go to something that will *never* happen. I'll tolerate you for my cousin's sake, but we will *never* be friends." She turned to her shocked and disappointed parents, uncles, and curious grandmother. "Excuse me, I need to freshen up."

Watching her walk into the house, Tony exchanged a glance with Cabot and Dom. After Maria's performance that afternoon, she was definitely not one to trust.

Cabot looked at his twin and wondered why he seemed completely oblivious to everything Maria was doing and showed no anger or offence to anyone except him when Maria riled people's ire. But then again, love *was* blissfully blind.

*****

On the day of the wedding, Maria lay back on her bed and thought about the biggest day of her life and the family she was marrying into. If she didn't love Antonio as much as she did, she wouldn't be anywhere near them.

"Thank God for Jenny," she murmured, staring at the ceiling of the room she had been sharing with Antonio until last night. "And ugh, why did I have to party so hard last night? I look awful." The knock at the door pulled her out of her mood. "Yes?"

The door opened and her mother came in. "Darling, your make-up and hair girls are here." She stepped aside for them to enter. "Do you want us to stay?" Her two other daughters, Tulu and Oriana, were behind her.

"Yes, Mother, please." Maria waved everyone in and slid off the bed to her feet. "I need all the support I can get."

Anais Van Star closed the door and went to her daughter's side. "It's not that bad. Jenny and Vivian seem very nice and supportive of your marriage to Antonio."

"*They* are, but his siblings and cousins are not." Maria quickly told everyone what had happened after they'd gone home from the rehearsal. "They just don't like me," she wailed.

"They don't know you, yet," Anais chastised. "You're nearly thirty-three, Maria. Be an adult and put on your best face." She critically examined her daughter. "Not that it's your best face today. Looks like you partied a little too hard last night. Did you wear that oil mask to bed to hydrate your skin?"

"Yes, Mother." Maria sat in the chair by the window for the work to be done. "And gave myself a facial this morning after my shower."

"Good." Anais nodded. As a high fashion model for many years, she had introduced her daughters to all manner of things to stay young.

An hour later her hair and make-up were done and she was being helped into her dress; the '80s inspired frilly Vera that hugged every curve on her body.

Tulu, her eldest sister, also a former model having retired a year ago, looked out the window at the approaching cars. "Your guests are arriving. Not long now."

Maria checked her bedside clock. "An hour to go. I can't wait that long. Do you see Escala? She'd better be sober."

Tulu looked again. "No. But she could already be here, or still coming."

"Oh, she can be a bitch," Maria growled. "I don't know why I invited her."

"Because she's your friend, darling," Anais quipped. "Models *are* bitches. We're hungry all the time; that's what makes us bitchy, and why we have bitches for friends."

*****

In the room Antonio had shared with Dom for the night, the men in the family were helping him get ready.

"Here are your cufflinks, bro." Cabot presented him with his own initialled white gold and black onyx cufflinks, a tradition their father and uncles had started back in 1977 and continued with their children. He set them in Antonio's shirt cuffs, adjusted the sleeves, and stood back. "You look like me yesterday."

Antonio's smile was wide and bright. "Well, we are twins, Cab."

"No." Cabot chuckled. "I mean, you look like me from yesterday all wrapped up in a tux ready to get married and nervous as hell." He brushed off the jacket shoulders, sighed, and said softly, "You're getting married, Tone."

"Yeah, Cab." Antonio pulled his brother into his arms. "Just like you did yesterday."

"Jesus." Dom shook his head. "Who figured you two would get married."

"Dom," Pedro chastised his son.

"No, I agree. I certainly didn't think they would. Especially Cabot." Carlos watched his only sons stand side by side, mirror images except for the eye colour. He exhaled. "Oh, you definitely take after your mother and me. I see both of you in us."

"And that's one thing we share with you, Carlos." Cabot arched a brow at his father. "We were both inside Mama."

"Ew, Cabot," everyone complained.

"Did you *have* to go and ruin the moment?" Antonio screwed his face up in disgust. "We were having a *nice* moment."

"What?" Cabot shrugged. "It's true. And he was in Mama the same time we were, so..."

"Enough, Cabot." Carlos held up a hand. "You really know how to ruin a moment."

Another shrug from Cabot was followed by remorse. "Sorry, can't help it. I'm funny and quick with the one-liners."

Choosing to ignore him, Carlos pulled Antonio into his arms. "Today, you are getting married, and just like with Cabot yesterday, we are about to impart on you the speech Papa gave me on my wedding day to your mother."

"Oh, God, not again." Cabot groaned and pulled a face. "He heard it yesterday."

"And he'll hear it again, now," Carlos told them and went on with the speech, but the knock at the door brought the moment to an end. "Yes."

Viv popped her head through the doorway. "Everyone's ready… oh…" Her face crumpled and she flew over to Antonio and encased him in her arms. "My baby's getting married. My baby boy's all grown up."

"Yes, Mama. I am." Antonio rolled his eyes at everyone and patted her back. "Don't cry, you'll ruin your make-up. There, there."

"Come on, Viv. Let's go downstairs and get ready." Carlos managed to untangle her from Antonio. "Let's give them a minute together. Come on, everyone." He waved the others out of the room to leave Cabot and Antonio to each other.

"Well," Cabot said when the door closed on everyone. He looked at his sibling and smoothed his jacket's lapels. "You're getting married, Tone."

"Yeah, Cab, I am." Antonio shook his head in amazement. "It's all happened so fast I haven't fully grabbed on to it and realised it, yet. But I know it's what I want." He smiled and stared at his mirror reflection. "Just like you did with Tony."

"Yeah, but that was a long time in the making," Cabot reminded him. "Five years, almost."

"But you knew. You knew and didn't let it go." Antonio breathed in to calm his nerves. "I don't know why I'm so nervous. We've been to plenty of weddings."

"Because it's different when it's your own." Cabot gently kissed his brother's cheek. "I've got your back, Tone. Always."

Antonio hugged him tightly. "I know, Cab. And I've got yours."

"I wouldn't be here if you didn't." Cabot blinked his tears away. "Literally."

Kissing his brother's cheek, Antonio straightened himself. "It's time."

"It is." Cabot slid his arm through his brother's. "Let's get you married off."

Minutes later, Antonio was standing in the middle of the marble pavilion surrounded by loved ones and the scent of spring blooms.

Maria's mother hurried away to inform her daughter that the ceremony was about to start, and found her waiting in the back room of the house. "Oh, my darling, you are stunning. But the ceremony's about to start."

"Thank you, Mother." Maria shifted her gigantic bouquet to her left hand and slid her right hand into the crook of her father's arm. "Go and tell them we're ready."

Anais hurried away and Maria and Giovanni walked out of the house and along the marble path to where the trees began. When they heard the music wafting on the breeze, they slowly made their way into the forest and to the pavilion where Antonio was waiting for her in the centre. Her lips curled up and the smile they turned into could have lit up the whole country. Coming to a stop in front of the priest, she directed that smile at her soon-to-be husband.

Her father kissed her on the cheek and gave her hand to a beaming Antonio. "Take care of my daughter."

"I will," Antonio assured him, never taking his eyes from Maria.

Giovanni hurried to take his seat, and Maria and Antonio turned to the priest for the ceremony to begin.

Alena, seated beside Diana, touched her arm to get her attention, and when she had it, mouthed, *the dress, bleh,* and screwed her nose up.

Be nice, Diana mouthed back and turned her attention to her brother.

"We have come here today for the wedding of Maria and Antonio, and if anyone objects to this marriage, please speak now, or forever hold your peace."

Alena snorted, and Cabot sneezed, both resulting in coughing fits.

"Sorry, sorry." Cabot sneezed again. "Can't help it. Spring flowers." He waved a hand for them to continue and saw them look back at the crowd.

Luca slapped Alena on the back, but it didn't help.

"Sorry, swallowed a fly, or something. Pollen…I don't know." She quickly took a sip of water from a bottle someone handed to her and said, "Continue." Seeing Maria's furious expression, she wiped her watery eyes to hide her smirk and heard soft snickers behind her. When

Maria and Antonio had turned back to the priest, she looked over her shoulder and saw her siblings smirk at her. Raising a brow, she settled back to watch the ceremony and saw her parents, uncles, and aunt's disappointed expressions which made her skin red with embarrassment.

"Do you, Antonio, take Maria, to be your lawful wedded wife. To have and to hold, for richer, for poorer, in sickness and health, till death do you part?"

"I do." Antonio gazed from the priest to his fiancée.

"And do you, Maria, take Antonio to be your lawful wedded husband. To have and to hold, for richer, for poorer, in sickness and health, till death do you part?"

"I do." Maria's happiness shone around the pavilion.

"Then do you have the rings?"

Cabot approached them and presented the rings to the priest, smiling at Antonio and rubbing his back before sitting beside his new husband and grasping his hand.

"We're going to read a passage before the placement of the rings." The priest read a passage from Corinthians, that was a favourite at every Stephanopoulos wedding, and then moved on. "And now, Antonio, place the ring on Maria's finger and repeat after me. With this ring, I thee wed, with my body I thee worship, and with all my worldly goods I thee endow. In the name of the Father, and of the Son, and of the Holy Ghost. Amen."

Gazing into Maria's eyes, Antonio slid the ring onto her finger and repeated the words.

"And now, Maria, place the ring on Antonio's finger and repeat after me. With this ring, I thee wed, with my body I thee worship, and with all my worldly goods I thee endow. In the name of the Father, and of the Son, and of the Holy Ghost. Amen."

Maria slid the ring onto Antonio's finger and repeated the words, never tearing her eyes away.

The priest closed his bible, gazed upon the couple before him, and the family and friends beyond them. "I now declare you, husband and wife. You may kiss the bride."

Maria's smile grew even more dazzling as Antonio gently cupped her hands and kissed her. But she wasn't about to tolerate gentle. Throwing her arms around his neck, she deepened the kiss.

"Oh, God," Alena muttered. "Like *that's* not attention-seeking."

"Yay." Cabot was on his feet applauding before the rest of the guests, and they all clapped for a good five minutes while they kissed.

Throwing her head back, Maria laughed, and Antonio lifted her and spun her around. "Woohoo, we're married." She threw her bouquet into the air as high as she could and laughed in the faces of her haters. There was no way she was going to let them get the best of Maria Van Star Stephanopoulos.

Dominic & Davina - 2016

"This is Davina Smythe reporting for *UKTV*. Back to you, John." Davina signed off from her story and received the *cut* hand gesture from her producer. "Are we done?" She pulled out her earplug and handed it, and her microphone, to the cameraman who dropped them into his bag.

"We're done. All we have to do is pack up and go." Miranda Garrison had barely finished the sentence when her phone rang. Checking to see who it was, she added, "Uh-oh, it's the boss. Hello."

"Miranda, I need Davina down at *The Go-Go Club* tonight to do the story on that DJ Dom Stefan. Laura *was* doing it, but she's had to pull out. Get down there and film it." Rob Henson, *UKTV* boss, hung up.

"Ugh," Miranda groaned and rolled her eyes. "Guys, we've got another gig."

"Oh, what!" Davina complained. "Now what? I wanted to get home and shower. I'm hot and sweaty." She slid off her blazer and wrinkled her nose at the sweat stains on its armpits, and on her cotton tank top.

"You still can." Miranda checked the time. "It's only six-thirty, we have to do the story on that DJ appearing at *The Go-Go Club*. Laura can't do it, so we don't need to be there until later."

"How much later?" Davina patted her neck and face with a damp towel she kept in her drink cooler bag. "Damn, it's hot."

Miranda searched *The Go-Go Club's* website on her phone and saw Dom was going to be playing from eight until four in the morning.

"Not until after dark. He's playing until well after midnight, so we'll head back to the studio and then home for a shower and change, and meet at the club at what…ten?" She looked from Davina to Paul the cameraman and saw their nods. "Great. Paul, pick me up at my place, it might be easier, and we'll meet Davina there."

"Do we have passes?" Davina grabbed her jacket and cooler bag from the back of the van, so Paul could shut the door.

"I'll pick them up at the station when we get back," Miranda told her.

They drove to the station where Davina retrieved her car and headed home to rest and shower. She hated being sticky in this ridiculous summer heat, but she knew the club wouldn't be any cooler, even after ten at night, *regardless* of who the DJ was. She racked her brain for info on Dom Stefan and if she'd heard the name, or come across it somewhere. But while it sounded vaguely familiar, she just couldn't place it. Having parked in her garage, she hurried inside, flicked on the air-conditioner and slipped her clothes off. A nice cold shower was what she needed, and once she was thoroughly cooled off, she wrapped a fluffy towel around her and wandered into the kitchen for a chilled bottle of wine and a TV dinner. It wasn't much, but then most of her money went into paying off the mortgage on her modest two-bedroom semi-detached cottage. While the meal was heating in the microwave, she turned on her laptop and went in search of Dom Stefan, finding his name on his own website, the *Sync* and *SB3* websites, and thousands of links to him, his siblings Alena, Alexis and Danté, his parents, grandparents, aunt, uncles and cousins. She clicked on one family photo to enlarge it and saw how good looking everyone was.

"Wow." Her left brow rose and stayed there. "Hello…" She peered at the screen to read the name. "Steph-an-op-oul-os family. Mmm…" Pulling up his website she saw the photo front and centre of his piercing blue eyes, dark brown, almost black, hair and his Greek Australian good looks. "Holy crap you're hot," murmured out from between her lips, and she found herself drowning in his eyes. "Fuck!" Breathing in, she scrolled down the main page to see sections on the club and his DJing, his songwriting at *Sync*, his bio, music credits, and photo gallery. Clicking on the gallery, she saw photo after photo of him on stage in the club and around the world at parties, making music at *Sync* with his brother and sister, or his parents, all busy working. And there were a few with other family members at what looked to be a birthday party.

She clicked on the first and read the caption underneath. "Celebrating his thirtieth birthday with the family on Mykonos. Mmm…" She saw his cousins, Cabot and Antonio. "Just as good looking," she murmured. There were pictures of him with Diana, Alena, Alexis and Danté, his parents, aunt and uncles, and she stopped on the one of Dom between an older couple. "Jenny and Spiros Stephanopoulos help their grandson celebrate his thirtieth birthday at *SB3* on Mykonos." She leaned closer for a better look and enlarged the photo. "He definitely gets the Greek side of things, but Jenny does *not* look Greek." Leaning back, Davina clicked through to his bio. "Dominic Stephanopoulos, better known by his stage name of Dom Stefan, has quite the musical heritage. His Greek mother, Angelina, is a Juilliard graduate in piano, violin, and songwriting, and his Greek Australian father DJd at America's most famous club, *Studio 69*, from its grand opening in 1977 until May 1981. Born and raised on Mykonos, his Greek grandfather, Spiros, and Australian grandmother, Jenny, raised the grandchildren the way they raised their three sons, with strength, honour, and core family values. With older sister, singing sensation Alena, younger sister Alexis, who co-owns *The Mykonos Assault and HIV/AIDS Support Centre* with their cousin Cabot, and younger brother Danté, the dark side of the family, as they're jokingly known, will no doubt hand down those family values and musical abilities to the next generation."

She went on to read his stats. Height, weight, eye and hair colour. "Fairly obvious, I'd say," she muttered. Parents, siblings, cousins, favourite colour, food, drink… "The usual idiotic statistics," she added before coming across his bio timeline. It bullet-pointed almost every year of his life, from being born to graduation, learning to write and play music, to the year he first scored a number one hit record. It also included when he'd played every club, gig, movie, concert, in his life.

She scrolled back up and checked his stats again. "Mmm, three years older than me and Greek Australian like me. Nice combination and something to talk about tonight." She skimmed back down the page to look for times he'd been in Australia and found many. "Nice. Also played in Sydney, Melbourne and Brisbane." Right-clicking the page, she printed it out to read while she ate. "Oh, bugger!" She hurried into the kitchen and opened the microwave door to see her meal still hot and steamy. "Nice!" Sliding it onto a tray and grabbing a spoon, she topped up her glass and walked back into the lounge room. The pages had finished printing out, so she read through them while eating, and by the time she'd finished, and topped up her glass again, she'd marked off many items of interest to chat about. Not knowing if she'd actually interview Dom, she wrote out two different spiels. One was the questions she'd ask, and the other was a straight to camera piece. She quickly looked up *The Go-Go Club's* website for more information and made mention in her notes of him being there for three nights before his next UK stop. It was his first time DJing in the UK, and he had quite a tour planned, as the front page of his own website attested.

Once she had what information she needed, she re-wrote her spiel and read it out loud, timing herself to see how long it would be. Usually, segments like these were two, maybe three minutes long, just fluff pieces to fill in empty spaces of air time. But just in case she had the extra time to talk to him, she wanted to be prepared.

Davina looked up from the papers and thoughtfully walked around her lounge room. "I'll just have to get that interview." Pursing her lips, she wondered what she should wear. "It'll have to be station worthy, but doesn't mean it can't be sexy, or rock chic. I *am* going to a club, after all." She hurried into her bedroom and flung open her closet doors, scouring her large selection of business suits that she could mix with a funky top that was a little bit off the Richter for TV. After trying this goes with that, she came up with her shortest presentable skirt, high heels, a rock god top, and an '80s style cotton blazer. She picked out earrings and make-up, and then saw that it was already heading for nine. "Oh, crap, I better get ready."

After freshening up, she twisted her shiny, dark brown shoulder-length hair up into a high ponytail which she teased and hairsprayed until she was happy with it. She reapplied her make-up, making her liner a little thicker, and her eyeshadow a little brighter, and at nine-thirty she slipped into her shoes and surveyed her reflection in the mirror, giving herself the nod of approval. "Nice!"

She grabbed her jacket, the papers from the living room, refilled her cooler bag with icy drinks, and ran out to her car. The heat was still stifling, but she cranked the air-con to keep cool, and fifteen minutes later she was driving down the street where *The Go-Go Club* was and trying to find a park. Unable to, she drove on, finding one in a car park halfway down the block. "Bugger! I'll have to walk."

Glancing around to see if anyone was lurking, she gathered her paperwork, blazer and cooler bag from the passenger seat and alighted. Knowing she was walking, the time called for the necessary equipment. In the boot of her car, she dug out her black flats from a huge tote bag and shoved in her cooler bag, heels, and paperwork. She locked the car and muttered, "Okay, here we go," and, checking the time, she saw she only had five minutes to get to the club. Walking at a moderate pace to keep from sweating, she was glad to see the *UKTV* van pull up just as she arrived. "Thank God. Glad I don't have to wait long. Got the passes?"

Miranda waved them and went to the back of the van to help Paul with the equipment. "I've already called the manager to let him know there's been a change of plan. He said he'd set us up on a balcony at the back of the club. We just gotta find him." They gathered their things and hurried to the door where she waved the passes. They were let in and found the manager waiting in the lobby.

"Ah, you're from *UKTV*." He nodded. "Come with me." Leading them into the club, he turned right up a small flight of stairs and hurried along a balcony until he reached a table and chairs. The whole section had been cordoned off. "This is for camera crews and reporters for magazines, and whatnot," he yelled over the music. "Let me know if you need anything else."

"Can we film from other places?" Miranda asked. "It might be a bit too loud here." She waved a hand at the club. "We may need somewhere quieter."

"Sure." The manager nodded again. "Just stay out of everyone's way." He walked off and left them to it.

"Okay." Miranda turned back to Paul and Davina. "We'll get footage of him doing his thing for about fifteen minutes and then go back out to the lobby to get some peace and quiet. We can film from the doorway and do the camera piece."

Davina nodded and took a step closer. "Are we doing the interview with Dom?"

Miranda frowned. "I haven't even set it up. I'll have to talk to the club manager, or find Dom's manager." She quickly looked at her paperwork. "Marta Trademan is his manager. She told Laura to come and find him during a break, but I want to use his break for the interview, so we have some time. Let's get the footage filmed now." She gave Paul a nod and touched his shoulder. "Get the crowd as well as Dom."

He gave her a thumbs up and hauled the camera to his shoulder.

Davina took the time to review her notes and watch him play, marvelling at the way he moved and controlled the crowd. It wasn't just about playing music for him; it was about making the music a performance.

Miranda tapped her on the shoulder and she saw they were ready to move on. They walked back to the lobby and set up for her piece.

Having set her bag on the floor next to Miranda, Davina donned her heels and blazer, and checked her face in the mirror she had in her travel make-up bag. "Okay. Good to go." She zipped up the purse and dumped it into her tote, then took the microphone and earpiece from Paul. "How do I look?" she asked, shoving the earbud into her right ear. Seeing their expressions, she wasn't sure and waited to hear the answer.

"You look like someone who stepped out of an '80s rock video." Miranda smirked. "Not sure it's suitable for the news bulletin on *UKTV*, though."

Davina shrugged a shoulder. "It's a music gig at a club. What else was I going to wear, a business suit? Are we ready?"

"Move to the right," Paul told her and saw her move left. "I meant *your* right."

"Then why didn't you say that?" Davina arched a brow at him. "You know you need to be specific."

He chuckled. "I know. A little more, so I can get him in the background and…perfect." Paul held his hand up to stop her and then gave a thumbs up.

"Okay, in three, two…" Miranda counted down, holding up her fingers. She mouthed the word *one* and waved her fingers at Davina.

"Dominic Stephanopoulos may be a name many people wouldn't know, but do you know the name, Dom Stefan? From a musical family pedigree which includes Juilliard trained mother Angelina, *Studio 69* DJ father Pedro, and mega-famous popstar older sister Alena, Dom has made quite a name for himself on the stage behind his DJ decks. Born and raised on the Greek island of Mykonos, he first made a name for himself in the family's club, *SB3*, with his younger brother and fellow DJ, Danté Stefan, following in his footsteps. But regardless of how well-known he is around the world, even here in London, this is actually his first time DJing in our great city. For the next two nights, Dom plays *The Go-Go Club* before moving on to other parts of the United Kingdom. So, if you want to see the great man in action, head on down to *The Go-Go Club*, or find out where else he's playing on his website at domstefan.com. Not only is he good at what he does, and knows the business inside out, but he looks hot doing it. This had been Davina Smythe for *UKTV*. And I plan on watching the rest of the show, which is why I came dressed for a good time."

Miranda counted her out and tapped Paul on the shoulder. "Well done. Now, we need to find his manager to get that interview." She saw a guard wave them over to a side door.

Davina slid her coat off and grabbed her bag. "Even in here, it's warm. Are the air-cons on?" She fanned herself as they were waved through the door and down a corridor to the back of the club. Another guard checked their passes and led them to an area backstage where they could wait.

"Ah, you must be Miranda." A woman came forward to shake her hand. "I'm Marta Trademan, Dom's manager. He's on a break in…" she looked at her watch, "fifteen minutes *for* fifteen minutes. You have five of those minutes for your interview, so make your questions short, sharp, and to the point." She nodded at Davina's outfit. "Appropriate. But if you need, or want, a longer interview, it won't happen tonight. We can arrange a time, though. He's here in the UK for another two weeks before going up to Scotland and then onto Wales and Ireland."

Davina turned to Miranda. "Do we need an interview past this? Or was this all we had to do?"

"This is the only interview we had planned," Miranda replied. "Let's make the most of it, so only ask pertinent questions."

"Got it." Davina quickly took a sip of chilled lemon-flavoured water and checked her make-up and teeth in her mirror. Slipping into her blazer, she held the microphone and was directed to the best place to stand. While waiting for Dom to come off stage, she mentally went over all of the details she'd read, the questions she'd written, and picked them one by one. Breathing calmly, she watched Dom on stage from their position and heard him talk to the crowd.

"Ladies and gentlemen, I'm off to take a fifteen-minute break, so I can eat, drink and cool down." The crowd screamed at that. "So, I'm putting on an extended version of *Solitare* that will get you through my absence. Anyone care to *join me* on my break?" He raised a brow and flashed a cocky grin, listening to the decibels of the crowd rise and waved them to go higher. "What's that?" More screams. "No? Oh, well, too bad. See you in fifteen." He strode off stage, down the stairs, and was handed a bottle of cold Gatorade, and had an ice-cold damp towel draped around his neck and shoulders. He drank and listened to Marta tell him the TV crew were there for an interview, and saw them, saw the hot woman in the wild get-up, ate a couple of burgers and downed the rest of his drink. "How long?" He wiped his face with the towel and eyed off the reporter.

"Five minutes, then you're back on stage. You ready?" Marta asked.

He grabbed another bottle of drink and said, "Ready," before striding over to the camera crew.

"Holy hell, Dom Stefan, you *are* hot," came out of Davina's mouth when the Greek Australian stud stopped before her.

Dom frowned. *It's gonna be one of those interviews.* He inwardly groaned before his next line of thought was cut off.

"The heat is absolutely *rising* from you and you've been sweating buckets. It must take so much out of you being on stage because you don't just stand there and DJ, you actually turn it into a live performance, just like any singer or band." Davina shoved the microphone at him and raised a brow, trying not to drown in his ocean blue eyes.

Surprised, Dom's jaw dropped open before he spoke. "Ugh, yeah. Yeah, it does. A lot of people do think that DJs just stand there and put records on, but it's a lot more physical than that. I make a performance out of it. I sing, dance, get the crowd going, and I'm doing that for anywhere up to ten hours."

"And the crowds clearly love it," Davina went on smoothly. "You have them eating out of your hand. But you're not new to this. You have quite the musical pedigree in your family that prepared you for your career choice." She moved the microphone back to him.

He nodded, seeing that her questions were going to be serious. "Absolutely. My mother excelled at piano and violin at Julliard, and I sat on her lap as a baby and watched her play. My father's been a DJ since he was eighteen and turned his love of music into one of the most successful music companies in the world. *Sync* on Mykonos. They raised my sisters, brother, and me with a love of music that has extended to the world with what we do. They trained us in all things musical, so we know what we're doing."

"Your elder sister is mega-famous popstar, Alena," Davina went on, "your younger sister, Alexis, sings, designs and models, and has a centre for assault victims in Mykonos, which I think is fantastic, and your brother Danté is a famous DJ himself. But the pedigree doesn't stop with just *your* immediate family. Your uncle is Carlos Stephanopoulos, world-famous movie writer, director and producer, his wife, your aunt, is Vivian Villiers, world-famous model, their children are famous models Diana Villiers, and Steele and Phoenix Stefan. Your Uncle Tomas and his husband Roger Dencott are AIDS activists and personal trainers. It's quite a family of celebrities you've got there." She held out the microphone.

He raised a brow. "You've done your homework, I see. Yes, we are a famous family thanks to the hard work of our parents and uncles—"

"But of course," Davina cut him off. "It really comes down to your grandparents, Australian-born Jenny Stephanopoulos and Greek-born Spiros Stephanopoulos, the absolute rocks of the family keeping it all together and encouraging everyone to pursue their passion." She watched his facial expressions the whole time. From annoyance to surprise back to annoyance. The flickers in his deep blue eyes told her he didn't know what to think of her and she'd planned it that way. You got more when you annoyed or surprised the interviewee.

Intrigued by her questions, Dom thought about it before answering. "*Of course.* They are the cornerstone of who and what we are, and what we all live by. The glue that holds us together. If it weren't for my grandmother pushing my father and uncles to pursue their dreams and supporting them while doing it, and being proud of it, they more than likely wouldn't have achieved what they have. It's something they, in turn, instilled in us and we will hopefully instil in our own children and families." He eyed her dark brown hairdo and sparkling green eyes. Her creamy skin was soft and smooth, and her killer curves were killing him.

"You toured Australia last year and live on Mykonos. How *are* my two homelands?" Davina asked. "My mother's Greek and my father's Australian. So, like you, I'm mixed, but have lived here for ten years and miss both places. How are they doing these days?"

Even more intrigued now he knew her heritage, Dom's lips curled into a megawatt smile. "Great. Australia's doing well and I, and my family, don't get back often enough. But many of them came with me last year and we saw the Aussie side of the family. And Mykonos is great all year round. You should come and visit more often." He raised the bottle to his lips and took a swig.

"Well, now that I know *you* live there I just might." Davina gave a cheeky brow raise, making him choke on his Gatorade. "What's next for Dom Stefan? Besides this tour."

Recovering, Dom wiped his mouth. "Once this tour is over I'll be back in Mykonos with the family and then a quick September or October trip to New York."

"Ohhh, gorgeous. New York's on my bucket list." Davina saw Marta check her watch.

"Then maybe I'll see you there," Dom said, noting her shapely legs in killer stilettoes.

"Maybe you will." Davina saw his attention and asked her last question. "Now that we have the intelligent questions out of the way, I've been told by the bosses I just *have* to ask the most inane, stupid one on the planet that every rock star, actor, famous person hates—"

"And what's that?" Dom cut in.

Davina sighed and looked at the camera. Her brows rose. "Are you single?"

"It depends." Dom glanced from her to the camera and gave a cheeky grin.

Surprised, Davina looked at him. "On what?"

"On whether you are." He gazed into her eyes for a second to see the look of incredulity come over her and her jaw drop before he winked at the camera and walked away. Once they were out of earshot, he told his manager, "Ask her to stay so I can see her after the show." Ditching the towel, he grabbed another bottle of Gatorade from the table and ran out on stage. "Hello again, *Go-Go Club.*"

The screams drowned out anything Davina might have said, but all she could do was look at the camera in complete shock. That was, until Miranda dived to the floor out of camera view and slapped her on the legs to get her talking.

"Um, this is Dom…" She shook her head and blushed. "Ah, *he* was Dom Stefan and I'm possibly going to be shagging him later. Oh, no." She pinched the bridge of her nose in embarrassment and gathered herself. Looking into the camera, as composed as she could make herself, she started again. "I'm Davina Smythe, and this is *UKTV.*"

Paul gave the thumbs up and lifted the camera from his shoulder. "You didn't need to sign off from that. We more than likely won't use it."

A gush of breath came out of Davina. *"What the fuck just happened?"*

"What just happened was, one of the world's biggest DJs hit on you and all but asked you out. Go for it." Miranda helped get the gear together. "You don't need to be in tomorrow. Stay and see him when he gets off."

"I can't do that," Davina protested. "What will it look like?"

"Who cares?" Miranda nodded at Marta as she approached. "We're just heading off now. Thanks so much for the interview."

"Thank *you* for not asking stupid questions he's had a million times,"

Marta replied and turned to Davina. "He wants to know if you can stay for the rest of the show. He won't be done until four, or so, and it's nearly eleven-thirty. You can stay in his dressing room, or watch the show."

"Oh." Davina's insides fluttered like a caged butterfly, and she felt the beads of sweat trickle down her back. With a glance at Miranda who was eagerly nodding, she decided to take a chance. "Sure, why not."

"We'll see you next week, then." Miranda hauled her bag over her shoulder and added, "Thanks so much for the interview. It'll be on the news all day tomorrow." She shook Marta's hand.

"Thank you. I'll let Dom know." Marta waited to escort Davina closer to the stage. "You can watch from backstage here, or wait in his dressing room. But it will be a while before he's done."

"I'll, ah, do both." Davina gazed up at the frenetic man on stage. He never stood still, was always moving, always cheering on the crowd, talking, singing, dancing.

Around one in the morning, she was taken to his dressing room where she rested her weary body on the couch, and sliding off her heels, she nibbled on food from several platters and poured herself a wine. Feeling her muscles relax, she massaged her ankles and lay down, asleep within seconds and dreaming of Dom Stefan.

At four, he finished his gig, waved goodbye, and walked off stage. A towel was draped around his neck and a burger placed in his hand which he scarfed down in seconds. "Where is she?"

"In your dressing room. More than likely asleep by now." Marta gave him a bottle of Gatorade. "Make sure you eat and drink more."

"I'm going to change. I may be a while." Dom walked off for his dressing room, and quietly opening the door, found Davina sleeping on the sofa. He closed the door and locked it.

This was a woman who stirred him inside and he wanted to know more. He pulled his soaking t-shirt off, dumped it on the coffee table, and unbuckled his belt and jeans, watching her the whole time.

Davina groaned, thrust her chest up, collapsed with a sigh, and then woke, groggy after dreaming of sex with Dom, to see him standing before her half undressed. "Oh…" She scampered up and away. "I didn't realise you'd finished. What's the time?" She landed against the wall and he approached.

"After four. What were you dreaming about? Sex? Me? Sex *with* me?" He was normally not so brazen with women he didn't know.

Oh, God…was she ever! She blushed and averted her eyes from his rock-hard abs and sweat-soaked fur-covered chest.

Stepping in front of her, he gazed into her eyes. "I'm going to be blatantly honest. I haven't fucked a lot of women in my life, but I want to fuck you right now. Do you feel the same?"

With hooded eyes, and a throbbing between her legs, she looked into his eyes and stated boldly, "Yes. I want to fuck you so badly."

His hands went up her short skirt and yanked down her panties, making her shudder. Then they went into his own pants and pulled out his manhood.

Her brows rose. "Holy hell, you're huge."

"Think you can handle me?" He grasped her hips and lifted her.

Gazing into his eyes, she hiked up her skirt and wrapped her legs around him. "Fuck me."

Placing her on him, he thrust her into the wall, making her cry out in delirious pleasure.

When he was done, he set her on her feet, but kept her pinned against the wall. "Come back to my hotel with me."

Glossy-eyed, she breathed in his sexual scent and nuzzled his chest. "Will we do that again?"

"We'll do it all night if you want." He nuzzled back. "I'll just take a quick shower and we can go. Unless you care to join me?"

She stared into his eyes, clinging to his arms as she wobbled on her feet. Rising to her tiptoes, she buried her nose in his neck. "Could you wait to get back to your hotel and I might. But not here. It's a bit too… public."

"Good point." He grinned and backed away. "Grab your things and let's go." He donned a dry t-shirt, tucked himself away, and loaded up his bag.

Davina slid into her knickers, glad she'd chosen black lace ones, put on her flats, and stored her heels in her bag before grabbing her blazer.

"Done. Let's go." Dom slung his bag over his shoulder and opened the door, holding out an arm for Davina to go first. "I have a car waiting to take us to the underground entrance of the hotel."

Davina moved past him into the hallway to see a guard standing by.

"Ricardo, we're going now," Dom told him and received a nod in return. "My bodyguard and chauffeur," he said to Davina as they walked along. "If Marta has left then he gets me to where I need to be. Jordan has more than likely left with her."

"Jordan?" Davina felt the electric touch of his hand on the small of her back.

"My assistant." Dom stopped her while Ricardo inspected the parking garage for fans before giving him the nod and escorting them to the car. "He takes care of what I need before, during, and after the show. Water, drinks, towels, food, anything. You would have seen him backstage with Marta. He also takes photos of all the shows, and uploads them to social media, which he keeps going, along with the website. The three of us deal with everything together. My brother, Danté, manages the safety of the site. You may have read that he and his best friend Nick have their own IT business, but they've been dealing with the family's websites for years." He stopped talking long enough to step aside for her to climb into the car before getting in behind her.

Once Ricardo was behind the wheel, they drove off for the hotel.

"I do recall reading that." Davina settled back for the ride. "I've read a lot of things today. Before that, I barely knew who you were. And for the record," she eyed him critically, "I normally don't fuck complete strangers after meeting them."

"Record noted." Dom grinned. "And *also* for the record, neither do I. But you're not just some stranger, I feel as if I know you. Have we met before?" His brows slid down in thought, but he couldn't come up with an answer.

"That's original," she muttered dryly. "No, I definitely would have remembered meeting you. Oh, crap! My car. I left it in the lot down the road from the club."

"Don't worry. We'll drop you off tomorrow." Dom saw them approach the hotel. "And if the car's been impounded or fined, I'll pay for it." He had a sudden thought. "Actually, you know what…?" Opening the door as they pulled up to the underground entrance of the hotel, he went on, "Ricardo can catch a cab and get your car." Alighting, he held out his hand for Davina and helped her from the car. "Got your keys?"

"Somewhere in my bag." She straightened up and started digging in her tote.

"Ricardo…" Dom leaned into the car. "I need you to take a taxi to get Ms Smythe's car."

"Sure thing. Give me a sec." Ricardo parked the car and came back for the keys. "Where is it?"

"In the lot down the road from the club. It's a blue Suzuki Grand Vitara." Davina finally found her keys and handed them over. "Please don't scratch it."

"Of course not, ma'am. Anything else, sir?" he asked Dom.

"No, Ricardo, thank you. Just leave the keys at the front desk to be brought up with the mail and papers in the morning, and I'll see you tomorrow for the show."

"Very good, sir. Goodnight." Ricardo nodded and set off for the parking lot.

"Shall we?" Dom hit the button for the lift and the doors slid open. "After you." He stepped in after her and hit the button for the penthouse. "Are you okay with this? I don't invite women back to my hotel rooms. I'm not that sort of guy. But for some reason…you're different. I want to get to know you and yes, I want to enjoy sex with you. Which I certainly did before." He watched the red blush rise up her neck to her face and her eyes avert themselves. "Did you? I didn't hurt you, did I?"

The lift doors whooshed open with a ding and he waited until she'd walked into the hall before following. "We're just here." He pointed to their right and led the way to the penthouse where he quickly opened the door and let her enter first. As he closed the door, he saw her eyes widen in surprise in the semi-darkness at the sight of London still aglow at five a.m. "Quite a view, isn't it?"

She breathed out. "Yeah…it is."

"Did I hurt you? You didn't answer before." Dom set his bag on the coffee table and moved to her side. "I happen to be longer than most men, runs in the family, can't be helped."

"No, you didn't," she murmured and blushed at the memory of his length inside her.

"Good." He watched her. "Care to make love in that shower we were going to have?"

Glancing at him under hooded eyes, she nodded and accepted his outstretched hand, holding it between both of hers as he led her into the expansive bathroom off the master bedroom. They undressed each other by city light, with no need for any other, and kissed and touched and soaped each other down, luxuriating in the heat and steam. He lifted her onto him and they rode the wave of delirium until they were done.

He dried her down gently and wrapped the towel around her, carrying her to the bed where they made love in the darkened room until they were spent and fell asleep.

*****

Davina breathed in and rolled over. She moaned and exhaled, and her eyes slowly opened to see daylight peeking around the edges of the curtain. "Mmm…" Stretching on the palatial king-size bed, she remembered Dom and lurched back. After a moment of shock, she calmed down and relived their lovemaking. Signing in contentment, she snuggled into his side and started thinking. There had never been a man like him in her life. Certainly not one with a massive appendage like that. It was a lethal missile, a weapon of mass destruction, and it had destroyed her body in every way known to man. And she was happy about it.

The Cheshire cat grin slid across her lips to her ears. She was happy all right. Happy to be so thoroughly fucked like never before in her entire life. And she wanted more of it. A man like Dom, not that she knew what he was like on a personal front, came along once in a lifetime. If that. And since she was single, and he was single, then why not? They were two consenting adults, practising safe sex…her eyes widened. Crap! *Did he wear condoms? Did I take my pill yesterday? Oh, crap!* Having no idea of the time, she slid out of bed and hurried into the bathroom where she found her clothes and a city still in the throes of broad daylight. "Crap! I hope they can't see me." Rushing into the toilet, she freshened up, pulled her knickers up, and snapped on her bra. "I don't even know what time it is," she mumbled and spun her bra around. *Thank God I chose the black lace set and not my daggy granny panties.* She finished dressing and carried her shoes into the lounge room where she found her bag and a tray of mail, her keys, and a note from Dom's driver that the car was in the underground car park.

Picking a grape from the bowl on the table, Davina threw it into her mouth, heard her stomach grumble from starvation, and wondered if she should grab a pizza on the way home.

"Hey."

"Oh." Springing around; the shock caused her to choke on the grape. "Oh," squeaked out and she coughed to try and dislodge it.

"Shit, sorry." Dom hurried around the sofa and patted her on the back. "You okay? I know first aid. I can probably give you the Heimlich."

Surprised, her wide eyes gazed up at him and she coughed down the remains of the grape. "No," cough, "I'm okay," cough. She wiped her teary eyes and face. Cough. "I'm okay." Inhaling slowly, she calmed down. "I'm okay. I didn't mean to wake you."

He grinned and kept rubbing her back. "You didn't. It's five. The time I get up and get ready for the show. Were you planning on sneaking out?" His blue eyes pierced into her green ones.

"Um…" She averted her eyes. "Kinda. I should go." Reaching for her bag, she stopped when he took it from her.

"Do you have to?" His fingers slid along her jaw and his thumb played with her lips. "Can you stay? Come tonight…" He watched her eyes widen. "To the show…*and* afterwards." He raised a brow. "I'm only here for another two nights before moving on. I'd love to see you again and do *that* again." His lips landed on hers and noted how full they were and how good they tasted.

A soft groan came from her and she kissed him back, her hands went to his chest, sliding over the six-pack and pecs and the hair spread across them.

His hands went to her skirt and pulled it up to push her knickers down.

Her hands slid around his neck as he picked her up and laid her on the couch, settled his body over hers, and made his way inside.

Fireworks exploded in her head, her right leg hitched over his arm, her nails dug into his muscular back and buttocks, holding him in place, and her tongue mated with his like wild animals until they were done.

"Ugh…" she groaned as he lay on her, relaxing after their session. "I've never had a man that can do that to me."

"What?" Dom leaned up on his elbow to stare into her eyes.

"Fuck me so soundly," she murmured and ran her fingers up and down his back. "I want more of that."

"Then you can *have* more of that. *Come* tonight." He pushed against her, eliciting a sharp intake of breath and closed eyes. "*Come* tonight…" Grinding against her, he made her come once more, leaving her breathing heavily underneath him. "Come."

"Dom, are you up?" Marta stopped short in the penthouse doorway.

"Fuck, Marta!" Dom exclaimed. "A little bit of privacy, please." Here he was buck naked on top of Davina on the couch with his arm hooked under her leg. He glared at Marta over his shoulder. "Get out."

"Right, sorry, didn't realise." Marta beat a hasty retreat. "I've ordered room service. You need to start getting ready," she said before closing the door.

"Fucking hell!" Davina pushed Dom away and scrambled for her knickers. Once they were on, she slid into her flats, grabbed her bag and blazer, and stared down at him as he sat spread-eagled on the couch staring up at her with a sly grin. She noted his size and shivered. "I guess I'd better take a taxi to the gig tonight."

"*We'll* see you tonight." He gave a small crotch thrust. "No need to bring anything."

"Oh, I'm bringing *every*thing," Davina quipped. Snatching her keys from the tray, she hurried from the room to see Marta waiting in the hallway. "He's all yours," she said and ran into the lift before the waiter could roll out the food cart.

She thought about nothing but Dom all the way home, while she showered and dressed, while she packed a bag for that night, and while she scoured every page of his and the family's websites. Not only did they have *Sync*, but they had *S'Reel*. And even though it was a massive production company, there was always a good bet they would produce more. Content was the way of the world, and if she could have the backing of a production house like *S'Reel*, then who knows where she could end up. Not just as a lowly reporter for *UKTV*. She had worked hard for the last ten years to get where she was, proving she was more than capable of earning her way up the ladder. But if having herself attached to the Stephanopoulos/Stefan name could help, then why the hell not.

*****

Over the next few days, they spent as much time as possible together before Dom had to leave London, but he made it easy on Davina by inviting her to spend each weekend with him no matter where he was, and said he'd send the jet to get her there. He also made her promise to take two weeks off for the end of July and beginning of August for family celebrations back on Mykonos. So, not only would he get to take her home, but she'd get to spend some time in her mother's country.

She agreed and used up her vacation days for the trip.

The day before Dom was set to pick her up for the ride home, she was busy packing and had called her best friend, Katie Roman, around to help out.

"How much are you taking?" Katie sat on the lid of the new suitcase filled with new clothing that Davina had splurged on, so it could be zipped up.

"Pretty much everything I bought." Davina set the airport lock and waved her off. "I'm going for two weeks, maybe more. We're spending our time in Mykonos and Athens. I need casual cool, casual smart, fancy. I'm meeting his family, his friends, probably seeing Mama's family, attending his cousins' and grandfather's birthday, and his sister's wedding anniversary. It will be a lot to pack in and a lot of outfits are needed." She set the case on the floor next to the smaller one which was packed with shoes, accessories, make-up, toiletries and the like. "I racked up credit card debt for this trip."

"Now why would you do that?" Katie brushed her flaming red, side-swept fringe out of her face. "Do you know *how stupid* that was? You're already in debt for this house."

"I know, I know." Davina spread out everything she'd be packing in her tote. "But even though I have clothes appropriate for London, they're not appropriate for Greece in summer. Nor for meeting his family, which consists of models and fashion designers, like his sister and cousin."

"*Haus of Stefan*, right?" Katie sat on the end of the bed and watched her sort through her tote. "Alena and Diana, gorgeous stuff, most of it on the too-high side. Don't the rest of the family model for it?"

"They do. His sister Alexis and brother Danté have, as well as his cousins, Steele and Phoenix Stefan, who are known as Cabot and Antonio at home." Davina threw some things into the bin beside her bed and sorted the rest.

"Hell of a well-known family," Katie murmured. "Did you buy any of their clothes?"

"A few pieces that were on sale. I'm not made of money like they are. But guess what?" Davina picked up her bag and looked at her best friend. "When I went searching through my wardrobe for items I could take, I found several pieces of their clothing from past collections. Completely forgot I had them. Anyway, I've sorted through it all, added all of the new pieces to some of the old, and organised outfits ready to go, so I know what to wear with what and made sure it will works together."

"You call that a wardrobe capsule and it's *supposed* to help you cut down on what you travel with." Katie grinned wryly. "You look like you've shoved it *all* in that case."

Davina finished packing her tote and chuckled. "Yeah, I kinda did. Lots of kaftans and kimonos, lightweight cool cotton, no need for heavy stuff in summer."

"Where will you be staying? With Dom? Does he have his own place?"

"He does." Davina sat her bag on her large case. "It's a house he used to share with his cousin Antonio until four years ago, and then his grandmother let him have it." She scanned her bedroom for anything she might have forgotten.

"What do you mean she let him have it?" Katie slid backwards on the bed until her feet dangled. "Did she buy it for him?"

"Not exactly. His grandma buys a lot of homes and property, and as they all get older and move out of home, they move into their own place, or share. Once his cousin got married in 2012 and moved into a new house with his wife, Dom got the house they'd been sharing. It's his. They all have a house bought by Jenny. That's his grandma. Even his younger siblings Alexis and Danté have their own homes now."

"You seem to know a lot about the family." Katie raised an inquisitive brow. "Been doing research?"

A sly grin slid across Davina's lips. "Well…if you call fucking Dom research…"

"You dirty hoe!" Katie exclaimed. "How big's his dick?"

"Huge!" Davina's eyes widened. "The biggest I've ever had, but by God does it do the job."

"How huge?" Katie pushed on and held her hands up a good foot apart. "This big?"

"About that." Davina nodded. "Haven't measured him, but he's definitely close to it."

"Holy, Jesus!" Katie flung herself back on the bed. "Maybe I need to get myself some of that. He up for a threesome? Or does he have any relatives that are still single? His cousins, his brother… I need sex. How did you score such a hot guy and I'm still waiting? You bitch!"

Laughter bubbled out of Davina. "His cousins are married and one's gay. Danté's only twenty-three if you're into young men, and *his* best friend, Nick, is twenty-four."

"What about Dom's friends?" Katie sat up and saw the furrowed brow. "What's wrong?"

"He said something to me last month…" Davina stopped in thought.

"Go on," Katie urged.

"We were talking about who I'd meet and he mentioned his family, but no friends. He said most of them don't really have any because of their life and work. Danté has Nick, Alexis has Nick's sisters, Summer and Melody, Cabot and Antonio have each other, and Alena and Diana have had each other all of their lives. But while he hung around the twins, once they'd moved to New York he had no one. He kinda hung around with people from school for a couple of years after leaving, but he hasn't seen them since 2007." She sat beside Katie. "So, no *real* close friends. I found it kinda sad that he doesn't have any guys to hang out with, or a best friend like I have in you." She flung her arm around Katie's shoulders. "You've been my best friend since we were five and met the first year of school. You even moved over here with me ten years ago. Dom doesn't have anyone like that."

"Not all people are meant to." Katie hugged her. "Some of us are just lucky, and others don't want friends. They like being alone."

"I think Dom's a bit of both. He loves being alone to work, which he does a lot. But that's because he also has no friends, which I think he might miss. He became really lonely looking when he was talking about it. I felt sad for him."

"Maybe you can make some friends for the both of you. You've got me." Katie brushed a strand of Davina's hair aside. "We have plenty of people we hang out with. Maybe you can introduce Dom to them, hang out in London for a while. Are you two dating? In a relationship?"

Davina shrugged. "Don't really know. Dating this last month, yes. Fucking, definitely. But what happens once I finish my holiday? Do I come back here to work? Move to Mykonos to be with him? Will he move here for me? His cousin is married to an Englishman and they're here a lot."

"Which one?"

"Cabot. He's married to Tony DeLuca, some rich Colombian, Spanish, English dude. They're having a baby via surrogate this year. And then Cabot's brother Antonio is here a lot with his model wife Maria Van Star. He's a house husband these days and looks after their daughter Izabella."

"Do you know about *every* person in that family?" Katie watched her friend blush.

"I've seen the websites and follow them on social media." Davina hastily went through her closet to see if there was anything else to pack.

"Ah-huh." Katie's brows rose in amusement. "And *when* did you start doing that? *Before* you met him? Or *after* you fucked him?"

"Katie!" Davina spun around to face her friend. "I'm a TV reporter, I follow all manner of celebrity and personality. It gives us something to do stories on."

"Ah-huh, pull the other one." Crossing her arms, Katie grinned. "It was *after* you fucked. Right?"

"Ugh, if you weren't my best friend…" Davina growled in exasperation.

"Oh, I'm right." Katie excitedly put her hands up in the air. "I *am* right. You only followed them *after* you fucked the great stud himself."

"Ugh, Katie!" Davina's hands moved to her hips. "*He* also told me a lot about the family. *We do converse, you know.*"

"Before or after fucking?" Katie innocently asked.

Davina's eyes widened. "*What is wrong with you today?* We happen to have very lengthy discussions about all sorts of things when we're together."

"But if he's working from eight till all hours of the morning, and then you fuck all day long, and then he gets up to work…" Katie calculated on her fingers. "Exactly *when* do you have these conversations?"

"*Would you stop.*" Davina jokingly slapped her arm. "Now, I think I'm all done." She waved a hand at her two cases and bag. "Clothes and accessories are packed, toiletries and make-up. The food is eaten, and you'll take the rest today. Oh, my laptop." After digging her laptop bag out from the closet, she and Katie wheeled her cases into the lounge room where she packed her computer and made sure she had all of the cords and batteries. She also had phone chargers and her camera to pack.

"That makes two cases and two bags." Katie nodded at the luggage. "Will they let you take that much on a commercial? It's been a while since I've flown."

Davina's grin appeared. "Oh, *we're* not flying commercial. Dom's flying us home on one of the family's private jets. They have a small fleet of them now."

"What!" Katie's brows hit her hairline in shock. "What do you call a *small fleet?*"

"Six, I think Dom said. The family travels a lot, and with several away at once, they need them."

"Holy hell!" Katie shook her head at the extravagance of it all. "They certainly are filthy rich, aren't they? The stories are clearly all true."

"I don't know about that," Davina replied. "But they *would* be worth tens of millions each."

"And you've scored yourself one of them." Katie snickered. "Don't forget me when you get married and move to Mykonos. Little old Katie from Australia. I've got first dibs on being bridesmaid. And invite me to Greece soon, I want to meet the family for myself."

"Oh, hardy har har," Davina grumbled. "Like *that's* gonna happen."

*****

Dom picked Davina up the next day. "Are you ready for your holiday to your homeland?"

She grinned and wheeled her cases through the doorway. "Absolutely. I've got everything locked up, just gotta set the alarm."

"You do that and I'll take your bags." Dom wheeled them over to the car and loaded them into the boot.

Davina locked her door and ran after him. "All set."

"You plan on staying longer than two weeks?" Dom opened the car door for her.

"No, why?" Davina stopped short. "Is two cases too many? I know I packed a lot of stuff, but I figured we'd be doing so much that I'd need a lot of clothing. Casual, smart, islander."

"I'm joking," Dom calmed her. "Hell, my whole family packs a lot more than two cases for a two week holiday."

"Oh," she sighed. "Good. Good to know I'm not the only one."

They drove to the airport and settled into the plane where she saw Marta, Jordan, and Ricardo. "Are we all flying to Greece?"

"Yes," Marta told her. "Most Stephanopoulos staff live on Mykonos or in Athens. It makes it easier to work with our clients."

"And our managers only have us for clients, so it's easier," Dom added and buckled himself next to Davina. "Easier for staff meetings, easier to deal with issues if you're a hop, skip, and a jump from each other. Same with assistants and bodyguards."

"Mmm, I guess," Davina murmured. "You have a very strange working relationship. I know many rich families hire their assistants and guards, and whatnot, but most managers are from big agencies. You hire them to work solely for you."

"That's the way Grandma and our fathers and uncles set it up. So, we'd all have the best looking out for us." Dom held her hand as they prepared to take flight. "We either have our own manager, or share one these days because we do so much. Alena and I have one each, Danté shares one with Nick for all of their music and IT business dealings, whereas Alexis doesn't have one these days; she's a free agent working for *Haus of Stefan* and her centre. And then Cabot and Tony share one because they're doing so much health and advocacy work now. Antonio and Diana share one even though they don't model as much anymore, but they do other work for *Haus of Stefan*, etc."

"It's quite a family you've got, Dom Stefan." Davina grinned at him as they took to the skies.

*****

After an uneventful flight to Mykonos, they landed and went their separate ways. Except for Ricardo, who drove them to Dom's house and then left.

"Here we are. Home sweet home." Dom unlocked the door and swung it open. "After you, madam." He carried Davina's bags in after her and hit the alarm code. Once it had beeped green, he wheeled his four cases in and locked the door. "How do you like it?" He watched her walk around looking at everything.

"It's…" She paused and looked at the artwork on the walls. "They're beautiful."

"My uncles, Tomas and Roger, painted those. You'll find their paintings in all of our homes."

"Your uncles?" She swivelled her head towards him. "They're *good!*"

He grinned. "Yeah. They've been doing it, oh…" he calculated back, "thirty-something years, now."

"Wow." Her brows rose and she gazed at the furnishings. "It's very…bachelor, masculine, but with soft feminine touches. You can tell a woman doesn't live here."

"That's because one doesn't. I asked my family to help when Antonio moved out and Mama and Aunt Viv did most of it, with some help from Uncle T and Roger. So, you're right. Masculine with soft feminine touches." He looked at the blue and soft peach pink tones through the lounge into the dining kitchen. Across the hall was the office, with the laundry and bathroom at the back. Two masters and two smaller bedrooms were upstairs. "Come on. I'll get you upstairs and you can unpack and shower."

"Is that a shared shower?" Davina watched him pick up both of her cases.

"If you want." He gave her a jaunty brow and walked upstairs to his room where he left the bags at the end of the bed. "There's a walk-in closet through there," he pointed to the door on their right, "with the bathroom just past that. You go and freshen up and I'll drag my stuff up." He hurried downstairs and hauled his cases up two at a time, and set them on the bed where he unzipped them and flung open the lids. Two cases of clothes, one full of shoes, and one filled with his computer and electronic equipment. It was his office on wheels.

"I didn't think a DJ would need two cases of clothes," Davina teased and stared down at the luggage set on the bed.

He chuckled. "One case for normal wear and one for stage wear."

"And what's all this?" She pointed to his office on wheels.

"My laptop, portable mixing desk, recording equipment. I can work on the plane, in a hotel room…"

"Handy." She nodded. "And here I was thinking *I'd* overpacked."

His chuckling continued. "You should see Alena's luggage. She takes everything but the kitchen sink when she's on holidays, or touring. Although, we've often joked that she takes the kitchen sink as well." Closing the lid on his office, he zipped it up. "It can stay that way until I need it. Now…" He held his hands together, prayer style. "I told my family I'd see them for my cousins' birthday on the 27th, but I thought we could play tourist first. We can spend some time together before you meet the family, and then it's my grandfather's birthday, my sister's anniversary, and then we head off to Athens. I wanted us to be alone for a bit to just relax, because once you meet them, it will start. They'll ask you a million and one questions that you may or may not have the answers to, because we've only been together just over a month and we're still easing into this and don't really know what to call it yet." He took her hands in his. "I guess we're dating. Would you say that?" He searched her face for some kind of clue to what she was thinking.

"Well…" She stared into his eyes. "I guess. Although, *fucking* is more of a precise term for it."

Laughter burst out of him. "Yes, I guess that would be the better term, but not one we'll say in front of my family. Although, we're quite well-known for it."

"Oh…" Her brows rose in surprise at secrets she was not yet aware of. "*Are you* now?"

"Ah…" He scratched his head and momentarily closed his eyes while thinking of a way to cover up his mistake. *No one* needed to know about his father's and uncles' pasts. "Anyway, I thought that we would arrange a dinner with my parents first, or maybe with my siblings as well. Just so you can get to know them before the rest of the family. *Or,* we could just turn up at my cousins' birthday at the club and let it be a surprise, and you can meet everyone then."

"Mmm…" Her brows furrowed and she pouted in thought. "I'm a reporter; I *ask* the questions, not answer them. *But…*I'm also used to meeting and being in large crowds of people. So, while I'll be nervous either way, it doesn't matter how I meet them. What *does* matter is how you'll introduce me. Do you introduce lovers to your family as 'this is my lover'? Or is it boyfriend, girlfriend, *friend?*" she asked. "Maybe we should sort that out first."

"Ah, yes, well…" Dom stared at the ceiling trying to work it out. "The way I see it, is that I don't want anyone else." His gaze dropped to her. "I only want to date you, be with you, love you, fuck you, be a couple with you. I guess we'll have to figure out how that's going to work and how we make a relationship out of it." Noting her shocked expression, he quickly added, "That's *if* you want a relationship with me."

Her mouth moved up and down as she went over the words he'd spoken. "Love…" she managed; not even sure she'd heard it. "Love…" Her heart pounded and her knees became weak.

Dom breathed in and exhaled slowly. "Yes. I've fallen in love with you, Davina. I love you."

"Oh…" she breathed and slumped onto the bed. "Oh…"

"It's not exactly the way I planned on telling you." Dom hastily sat beside her and studied her shocked face. "I was going to set up a nice meal, lights, wine, the ocean. I see I surprised you. Sorry."

"Oh…" She gasped in air as she'd been holding her breath. "I…" Her eyes darted around the room. "I…" A million thoughts went through her mind. "I…" But her heart knew only one thing. "I…love you, too." Hearing the words come out of her mouth solidified them in her mind, and turning her face to him, she smiled. "I love you, too."

Dom's lips turned into the largest grin and he kissed her rather forcefully.

She responded in kind and moved into him as he laid her down on the bed.

"Ow," she muttered around his mouth. "Ow, what's that, Dom. Something's in my back."

"Huh?" He saw the suitcases and pushed them off the bed, his clothes and shoes tumbling across the floor. But he didn't care as he slid Davina up higher and undressed them both.

Hours later, they lay under the sheet watching the sunset through the window.

"It is beautiful," Davina murmured lazily from his fur-covered chest. She stretched her lithe body and curled back into his arms. "I haven't been here since I was a teenager when we came for a month. Before that, it was just a couple of weeks here and there."

"It's funny…" Dom's fingers slid up and down her arm. "You grew up in Aus and have barely been here, and I grew up here and barely get to Aus. We're opposite."

"And I've worked in London for ten years and that was your first time DJing there." She kissed his chest and snuggled into it. "Weird."

"First time DJing, yes. Not first time there, though. Maybe I saw you on TV, and that's how I know you."

"Or maybe we met in another life and know each other that way." Her fingers trailed down the centre of his torso and over his abs. "I definitely would've loved to've known this body in another lifetime."

"Do you believe in soulmates?"

She cocked her head back to look at him. "Seriously?"

"Yes." He gazed back.

"Ah…" She thought about it. "I guess."

"Would you say we are?"

"Um…" Knowing she was in love with him, she also knew what she was feeling for him certainly wasn't like anything else she'd ever experienced with any other man. "We could be."

"But you're not certain?" he persisted.

"Well…" She blushed. "You're the first man I've fucked straight after I met him. You're the first man I've carried on an affair with, without dating. You're the first man I've become a groupie of—"

"Groupie!" burst out of Dom followed by deep laughter. "Groupie?"

Davina giggled. "Well, what? I've basically become one. I've been to multiple gigs in the UK, followed you to Wales, Scotland, and Ireland, and now I've followed you back to Mykonos. I'd say I'm a groupie."

His laughter slowed to a chuckle. "And why have you done that if you're not sure we're soulmates?"

Becoming serious, Davina avoided his eyes. "Because I never believed I'd meet mine."

He gently lifted her chin so her gaze met his. "You have now. Whether you want to believe it or not. Because *I* do. It's been instilled in me since birth that our soulmate is out there somewhere. The greatest love story ever told is of my grandparents Spiros and Jenny, followed by my parents and uncles. They all found their soulmates and are still married and wildly in love nearly thirty-nine years later. My grandparents celebrated sixty-four years together back in May. They believe in it. My parents believe in it. *We* believe in it. *I* believe in it." His lips touched themselves to hers for a moment. "Do you feel it? The fireworks, the earthshaking, ground-breaking, glass shattering effects?"

"Yes," she breathed. "I do."

"Good. Then I guess I'd better introduce you to my family as my soulmate."

Her lips turned into a smile and a giggle bubbled out from between them. "Maybe you'd better, coz it's not like we figured out what else to call me."

*****

After two days of playing tourist, enjoying the island's cuisine and beaches, Dom led Davina through the doors of *SB3* at eight-thirty for his cousins' birthday. He was wearing a casual, short-sleeved, white cotton shirt and matching pants, and held her hand as he slapped the bouncers on the back in greeting.

The music was blaring through the club, bouncing off the walls and flying around the room making a cacophony of sound. He nodded to people he knew, and saw his cousins and siblings on the dance floor. Not seeing his parents or grandparents, though, he looked up at the office above the bar and saw the lights on. "They're upstairs," he yelled over the noise and pointed up.

Davina glanced at the office and nodded. Holding his hand between both of hers, she felt the butterflies start flying around her stomach. She hoped to make a good impression on his family by wearing a colourful, lightweight cotton kaftan dress that stopped at her knees, and gold strappy high-heeled sandals. Her hair was swept up into a bun to ward off the heat, and gold glittered at her wrists and in her ears, matching her small gold clutch bag.

He took her into the back hallway and up the stairs to the family's office, where it was much quieter, and opened the door. "Knock, knock." He saw his grandparents, parents, aunt and uncles, Dan, Derek, Mike and Maggie, all who were looking after his nieces Ava and Harper, and their cousins Jaqueline, Carys, and Izabella. "Adam not here?"

"Downstairs with Stella and Liam," Jenny said and noted the beauty at his side. "Hello."

"Hey, Grandma, Grandpa." He let go of Davina long enough to kiss them both before kissing his parents.

"Hey, sweetie. We didn't know you were back." Angie sent a pointed look at Davina. "Or bringing someone."

He slid his arm around Davina's shoulders. "Everyone, this is Davina Smythe. She's a reporter for *UKTV*. Born and raised in Australia to an Aussie father and Greek mother, and she's also my girlfriend." He raised his brows at her and turned to his stunned family. "These are my grandparents, Jenny and Spiros," he introduced them.

"Well…hello, Davina, nice to meet you. Excuse me if I don't get up, but these bones of mine are getting old." Jenny held out her hand to shake. "And how long have the two of you known each other?"

"Oh, since mid-June when I had to do a news story on him." Davina kept her cool as she shook hands. "I was a last-minute fill-in for the reporter who couldn't make it."

"And I'm glad you were, because otherwise we wouldn't have met." Dom kissed her temple. "And my parents, Angelina and Pedro." He watched them shake her hand and glance at him, but he continued. "My aunt and uncle, Carlos and Vivian, and my uncles Tomas and Roger. That's Mike and Maggie, Mama's and Papa's best friends, and Dan and Derek our resident family doctors."

Davina shook hands with all of them and turned her attention to the girls tugging on her dress. "Well, hello, gorgeous girls." She carefully knelt onto one knee in front of them. "And who are all of you?"

"This one is Ava, my niece." Dom picked her up and kissed her cheek. "Hello, my girl."

"Unca Dommy." Ava grabbed both of his ears. "Pwesent?"

"Pwesent," Dom repeated. "It's not *your* birthday." He sat her on his hip and tickled her. "Ava is Alena's daughter along with the one crawling toward you. Harper. She's what…ten months now." He watched Davina pick her up and sit her on her hip. "And then you have Jaqueline and Carys in front of you, they're Diana's daughters. And Antonio's daughter, Izabella, who's hanging on to your dress, at…seventeen months."

"Oh, you're *all* gorgeous girls," Davina gushed. "And all have big blue eyes, and look at you, Harper, with your halo of dark curls." She tickled her cheek and got a smile.

"Huh-oh." Carys clung to Davina's knee. "Who you?"

Davina turned her attention to them. "Hello, Carys, Jaqueline, Izabella. I'm Davina. Dom's girlfriend. And the three of you are gorgeous. Look at those curls."

Dom knelt beside her and placed Ava on her feet. "They're all close in age like Alena and Diana were. I just hope we don't get the same attitude my sister let rip on this family with. We do *not* need round two with their children."

The family chuckled and exchanged glances and raised brows.

"Have you two have been dating since you met?" Angie inquired. It was a well-known fact that Dom rarely dated, and when he did it never lasted long because his career was in the way, or the girl's greed for expensive things was.

"Ah…" Dom looked up from his nieces and Davina. "I guess you could say that. We've pretty much been together since then. Davina came to the gigs she could and we've spent our free time together. And now she's taken two weeks off for the trip, so yeah." He gave a nonchalant shrug to let her know he wasn't fussed about details, but knew they were all itching to know every little detail.

"And what part of Australia were you raised, Davina?" Jenny asked. "My family's from Armidale in New South Wales."

"Oh, that's interesting," Davina looked up in surprise. "My family's from Armadale in Victoria. My father's descended from English Scottish genes, but Mama's family came over from Greece in the '70s. She met my father in 1980, married, had my brother, then me, then my sister."

"Oh, that *is* interesting." Jenny arched a brow at Dom who blushed. "What are your plans for your stay here?" She noted how well Davina was coping with the children all picking at the sparkles on her dress, and how she silently stopped their hands without telling them no, or chastising them.

"Except for some fun and sun, I have no idea what our plans are. Dom's organised everything, apparently." She looked at her boyfriend. "It's all a secret."

He grinned and stood up. "It is. But for now, we're going to dance, so this one," he lifted Harper from Davina's hip, gave her a kiss on her chubby cheek, and handed her to his mother, "can go to Grandma, and this one," he held his hand out to pull Davina up, "can come downstairs with me to dance. I take it the cutting of the c.a.k.e hasn't happened yet, otherwise, the kids would be hyper."

"Not yet," Jenny replied, glad that her grandson had found someone. "About ten."

"Okay, we'll see you then. Bye." He waved his fingers at the girls and escorted Davina from the room.

"Bye." She waved over her shoulder. "It was nice meeting all of you."

"Shut the door behind you," Jenny called and saw Davina grab the handle and close it after them.

"So…what do we think of that?" Angie asked, gently bouncing Harper on her lap. "I'm still in shock."

Pedro shrugged and watched Ava crawl up next to Jenny and snuggle under her arm. "He's an adult. He can date who he wants."

"Exactly. What does it matter?" Carlos said, picking Jaqueline up and putting her on Viv's lap. "You complain when he doesn't have a girlfriend, now you're complaining when he does."

"She's very stylish." Viv wrapped her arms around her granddaughter. "That was a *Buccini* kaftan."

"She's gorgeous," Tomas replied, watching Izabella and Carys cling to his mother's knee as they tried climbing onto the couch. "Definitely. Mama?" He looked to his mother and they all waited for her to speak.

Jenny had been nodding at every comment and now eyed each of her children. "She *is* gorgeous and stylish. Australian Greek, like Dom. I think she'll fit right into the family."

*****

At the bottom of the stairs, Davina stopped, and tugged Dom back. "How do you think that went?"

He took both of her hands in his and smiled. "I think it went incredibly well, especially when all of the girls gravitated around you."

"Your grandmother seemed pleased with my heritage and the fact my family's from Armadale."

Dom shrugged a shoulder. "Grandma's into things like that. Numbers, star signs, true love. She probably thinks it's a good sign."

"And your mother," Davina persisted. "Do you think she's okay with this? Us? Me?"

"I think the whole family will love you." His lips gently kissed hers. "But, since it's my cousins' birthday party, and you're yet to meet them *and* my siblings, let's dance until you do because I am *not* working tonight." He started walking backwards towards the club, but she stopped him.

"Then when *will* I meet them?"

"Probably when the music's turned down and they cut the cake."

She glanced at her watch. "An hour and a half. Okay, then." Inhaling deeply, she let it out in a gush. "Let's go dance."

He grinned and led her out to the dance floor, twirling her around before twirling her into his arms, holding her close and breathing in her perfume.

"Oh…hello…" Cabot flung his arms around his brother's neck and spoke into his ear. "And who might Dom be dancing with?"

Antonio stared across the room to his cousin and noticed the body language. "Dom's got himself a girl," he crowed. "Look how close they are."

The twins watched Dom slide his hands over the woman's behind and grind against her, while her hands slid over his shoulders and into his hair. Dom nudged one leg between hers and held her close while they danced.

"Holy hell! She's *more* than just a friend," Cabot said. "*Definitely* more. Look at the way they're touching. You know who she is?"

Antonio shook his head. "No. Never seen her before. Wonder if he picked her up on his tour of the UK."

"Oh, *he picked her up,* all right." Cabot's grin was ear to ear. "From the way he's grinding on her, he picked her up the moment they met. His pants are exploding in the crotch. Look."

Antonio's grin matched his brother's and both went back to dancing with their partners.

At ten, when the music was turned down and they cut the cake, they were finally introduced to Dom's new squeeze.

"Well…hello…and who are you?" Cabot asked point-blank as he stood before the woman under Dom's arm. "You're gorgeous. Where'd you pick her up, Dom?"

"Cabot." Dom frowned at his overeager cousin, but saw Antonio's grin as well. "Not *you, too?*"

Antonio shrugged. "We're curious, considering the way you were dancing. And considering the fact you rarely date, and considering the fact we *rarely* see you with *any* woman."

"Yeah, Dom. You don't dance like that with me." Cabot batted his lashes and placed another forkful of cake in his mouth.

"Fun-nee!" Dom rolled his eyes at the twins.

"Davina Smythe? In person? Oh, wow. I see you every time we're in London." Tony stopped beside his husband. "We watch you on *UKTV*. What are you doing here?"

"They're dating," Antonio said as Maria slid her hand over his shoulder.

"No, they're *fucking*," Cabot said with an authoritative nod. "Most definitely."

"Cabot!" Dom's annoyance grew. "*Yes*, this is Davina Smythe. Davina, these are my idiot twin cousins. Antonio and his wife Maria Van Star, and Cabot and his husband Tony DeLuca."

"Nice to meet you. I've heard a lot about you." Davina shook their hands. "Quite a family you've all got." She saw how identical the twins were except for their eye colour.

Cabot couldn't help himself. "Are you joining it? Coz if you are—"

"Cabot, enough." Tony put his hand on his husband's arm. "Cabot gets excited about a lot of things, like a little puppy dog," he told Davina, making her giggle. "But there are other members of the family to meet, so I'll take him off your hands."

"Hey!" Cabot protested. "I just want to know."

"It's *none* of your business." Tony pushed him over to the family and Antonio and Maria followed.

"Who are you? We saw you two having sex on the dance floor." Alena stood in front of her brother with her hands on her hips, and boldly staring at Davina.

Luca, Alexis, Danté, Nick, Summer and Melody were around her.

Sighing, Dom introduced them all. "And everyone, this is Davina Smythe."

"Girlfriend? Lover? Fiancée?" Alena continued, giving her brother the evil eye.

"*None* of your business," Dom told her. "Davina is a reporter for *UKTV*, but she grew up in Australia like Papa did."

"Oooh, where in Aus?" Alexis asked, excited to see her brother dating such a gorgeous woman already famous and on TV.

"Armadale, Victoria." Davina watched their reactions. "Apparently your grandmother, father, and uncles are from Armidale, New South Wales."

"Well, that *is* a coincidence." Alexis nodded her approval and took in her stylish kaftan and gold accessories. "And probably approved by Grandma. Do the olds know, Dom?"

"Saw them when we got here," he replied and noticed a pair of twins talking to his cousins. "Who are they?" He nodded in the direction of the enthusiastically animated duo.

Alexis glanced over and rolled her eyes. "Uncle Carlos's new find. Action star wannabes Richard and Thomas Morrow who absolutely *adore* our cousins and want to be *just like them*. So, they created the stage names of To and Ro Morrow." She shuddered. "They're making a movie in Athens and met Summer and Melody at the studio one day. They've all fallen hard for each other."

They all watched To and Ro notice Summer and Melody and wave.

The girls waved their fingers and wandered over to the boys.

"God help us if they get together and have twins," Dom muttered. "Okay, who haven't you met?" He saw Diana and Charles chatting with Simon and Deidre. "Four for the price of one. Excuse us." He walked Davina over to meet them and they chatted for a few minutes while the rest of the family chatted about them.

"So...?" Cabot asked the family around him as he studied Davina. "Serious or what? They're *definitely* doing the wild thing."

Alena snorted. "Aren't we all?" She saw Alexis glare at her and Danté shake his head. "Okay, *not all*. But you know what I mean."

"I think she seems very nice." Jenny watched her grandson laughingly put his arm around Davina. "He treats her like the gentlemen he was raised to be. She's polite, friendly, gorgeous, and Greek Australian."

"Is that all that matters, Grandma?" Cabot crossed his arms and looked from Dom to Jenny. "That she's Greek Australian?"

"Of course not, but it helps," Jenny replied. "They look good together. But at the end of the day, we don't know what this will turn into. She has a job and profession, and is already on TV, so she won't need him to achieve that like other fame-hungry people these days. And she seems to be getting along with all of you."

"For the time we chatted to her, yes." Alena critically eyed Davina's outfit. "*Buccini* is *no Haus of Stefan*. Maybe we can style her. Get her into *HOS*."

"Why do you want to get everyone we meet into *HOS*?" Alexis asked. "Learn to stop harassing people." She saw Maria raise her brow, more than likely remembering the argument she and Alena had gotten into over that exact thing before she married Antonio.

"Alexis." Alena frowned. "I happen to be very proud of *Haus of Stefan* and think anyone who comes into this family should wear it. There's nothing wrong with that."

"Just because *we* do, doesn't mean *she* has to," Alexis argued back.

"Enough about *HOS*, for God's sake," Cabot cut them off. "It's *our* birthday, and Dom's *'I'm introducing my new squeeze to the family'* day. Let *us* have *our* fun. It's not about *you*, Alena. Jesus!"

Alena opened her mouth to argue, but Cabot waved a finger in her face.

"No," he warned. "Today is *not* about you. You had your birthday last month and your anniversary is in five days."

She grumbled and sullenly crossed her arms, watching Dom and his new girl, and saw how well she was getting along with Diana and Deidre. "Bugger it!"

Cabot rolled his eyes at his cousin, sighed, and kissed his brother's cheek. "Happy thirty-fourth birthday, Tonee, Tone, Tone. How did we make it this far?"

"With a lot of help from me, Dickface." Antonio grinned. "Otherwise, *you* wouldn't be here."

"No, no I wouldn't," Cabot conceded and hugged his twin. "I love you, Antonio DeLuca Stephanopoulos."

Antonio embraced his brother. "And I love you, Cabot Dickface Stephanopoulos."

Cabot's laughter was filled with snorts. "And we're both married, with our first kids." His blue eyes gazed into green ones. "Who the hell knew that would happen?"

"Definitely not the family," Antonio replied wryly. "Happy birthday, Cab."

"Happy birthday, Tone."

*****

Six days later, Dom and Davina touched down in Athens and drove to the small gated housing lot they owned next to *Stefan Productions* where the family stayed when in town. Consisting of five houses, they had a fleet of golf buggies out the back to get them around and to the studio via a back road joining both properties. Each home was luxurious and well-kept thanks to the small team of staff they had on hand.

"Here we are." Dom set Davina's luggage in the front entrance. "Home sweet home for the next week." He sighed and pulled her into his arms. "I think last week went well, don't you? You met all of the family, got along with them, survived birthdays and anniversaries, and my sister…"

Davina's lips curled up. "Alena is a handful, isn't she? The rest of the family are very sweet and kind, but the in-laws…" Her brows rose. "Mmm…"

"Ugh," he groaned and flung his head back in exasperation. "Which ones?"

"Charles, Tony and Deidre are wonderful beyond measure, don't get me wrong, but Maria and Luca…are just a bit…" She tried to find the right words.

"Arrogant?" Dom supplied.

"Yes." She nodded. "Luca thinks he's the bee's knees and Maria likes to think she's above everyone else. She pulled me aside one day and gave me the rundown of the family."

"What?" Dom was shocked. "She did *what?* What did she say? And *when* did she do it?"

"At your grandfather's party down at the beach of all days. She pulled me aside at one point and started asking me what I thought of everyone. I'd barely started saying how nice everyone was before she gave me the rundown on what *she* thought. She's really not a fan of most of you. Likes your grandparents, think's Alexis is okay, your aunt has had her day, and that Diana gave up modelling just in time before she ruined her looks and body by having babies. Alena she hates, and everyone else she has no need for."

"Fucking hell!" Dom's hands went to his hips. "You're clearly not kidding. Although, considering what she did at the twins' weddings a couple of years back." He told her the story of Maria and Antonio's wedding rehearsal and how her friend Escala had assaulted him. "Most of us have never liked her. Cabot, Tony and I are wary of her. Alena *hated* her and caused arguments. Danté didn't care either way. Alexis thinks she's great."

"And your grandparents?"

He sighed and thought about it. "Grandma definitely warned her after Antonio proposed. And while she likes her feistiness, she *won't* accept her rudeness. Aunt Viv and Uncle Carlos are happy that *Antonio's* happy. Everyone else is…" He shook his head and shrugged. "Getting along with her for Antonio's sake. And now they have Izabella, and Antonio's a house husband and dad, and he's around more than Maria. Although, she does seem to demand a fair bit of his time, and likes to keep him in London, Paris or Rome a lot. But thanks to the family values Grandma instilled in all of us, Antonio's here for a lot of the celebrations whether she likes it or not."

"She definitely *didn't* like it," Davina said. "Did you see her face at Alena and Luca's wedding anniversary? She *hated* being there."

"That's because there's no love lost between them." Dom ran his hand through his hair and thought back. "Jesus. I thought she'd calmed down, but then, I don't spend a lot of time with her."

"Well, if Luca was as grabby with her as he was with me, I can see why she hated being there. He's quite obnoxiously narcissistic, isn't he?"

Dom's brows furrowed and he looked at her intently. "What do you *mean* grabby?"

Davina blushed a little. "Oh, Luca thought he could hit on me at his anniversary. But I soon set him straight."

"What! He touched my woman. That fucking dog. How fucking dare he!" exploded out of him.

"It's okay." She put her hands up to placate him. "I slapped him."

"What?" Dom calmed down long enough for the incredulity to set in. "What?"

"I slapped him." She giggled. "He got touchy and I slapped him for it. Said I was going to tell you, and he begged me not to since it was *your* sister's anniversary and he didn't want it ruined. I warned him that if he ever did it again, I'd rip his balls off and tell the whole damn family."

"Bloody hell!" Dom's hand swiped the hair out of his face. "Good for you. But I'll do more than that." He pulled her into his arms. "You're okay, though? He didn't hurt you?"

"No, I'm fine." She slid her arms around his waist. "It wasn't inappropriate touching, but touching, nonetheless. I set him straight."

"Good. Because if he *does* do it again, I'm going to kill him."

She took note of how serious he was. "Oh, don't worry. I don't think he will."

*****

They spent the rest of the week touring Athens, seeing the sights, dining on fine cuisine, and visiting the maternal side of Davina's family. And come Saturday, Dom told her he had a special surprise planned to end their holiday.

"And what would that be?" Davina hooked her gold hoop earring through her ear and clicked it shut. Looking at herself in the mirror, she turned left and right, making sure her hair was pinned in place, and her sequined kaftan dress didn't show off what she had on underneath.

"You look incredible," he told her. "And so I'm taking you to an incredible place for dinner."

She spun around to face him. "And *where* would that be? You've already taken me to some amazing restaurants this week. For breakfast, lunch *and* dinner. I don't think I've eaten so well in my entire life, and I'm *definitely* getting fat on all of this Greek food." She touched her flat stomach and grimaced. "Yep, definitely getting fat."

"Hardly." Dom grinned. "We've been burning it off all night." He watched the blush rise to her face and continued. "This is somewhere majorly special. Since it's our last night here and we're back on Mykonos for the family meal tomorrow, and back to London on Monday, I have planned somewhere *very* special indeed."

"Ah-huh," she murmured and kissed his cheek. "And *where* are you taking me? It had better be somewhere fancy to be ready so early."

Dom checked his watch. "It's only a quarter past six. Dinner will be from six-thirty until eight-thirty, so we can watch the sunset. And since it's nearly time, we need to go."

They walked outside to the chauffeured car waiting for them and were driven to their destination.

"The Acropolis?" Davina's expression was quizzical. "How are we having dinner here?"

"Technically, we're not." Dom alighted and held out his hand. She accepted it, and when she was standing beside him, he added, "We need to walk."

"What?" Puzzled, Davina kept a hold of his hand and allowed him to lead her upstairs and along the ruins to the Parthenon where she saw a fully equipped dining table and portable kitchen for the chefs. "What! Oh, my God." To say she was shocked was an understatement. "Wait, we can't do this. How can we do this? The Parthenon is closed to tourists in the evening." Her eyes took in every aspect of the view. The sand-coloured ruins of the Parthenon, to the blazing oranges and pinks of the sunset, the square table covered in crisp white cloth, Dom in his black suit and matching shirt.

He took her into his arms. "I love you, and wanted to make our last night here in Athens special. Shall we?" With a hand on her back, he guided her over to their table where the waiter supplied them with champagne.

"Oh, this is too much." Davina sipped her drink as music wafted along on the summer breeze. "Way too much. The Parthenon, champagne, music. How did you make this happen?"

"A healthy donation to the restoration fund for this place." Dom gestured at the ruins. "They were most thankful for it."

"Does your money get you everything?" Davina asked, having a conflicting moment inside. On one hand, she loved having a rich man love her, on the other, it bothered her that so many things could be bought and paid for that only the rich could afford.

Seeing the conflict on her face, Dom chose his words carefully. "No. We have worked hard for our money, and fame has come *with* that work. We learned early on that just because we have both fame and fortune, it doesn't always get us what we want. But..." He kissed her hand and held it to his lips. "We ask the right people if we can do things, and if we can, for a donation to a fund, then we do it. Besides..." His grin was soft. "They're in need of funds to keep this place maintained, and my team and I promised to be respectful and clean up any mess we may leave. We'll leave it exactly how we found it."

The heady Greek summer atmosphere and the champagne made her lightheaded and agreeable. "That's so sweet of you. I'm always a bit testy around rich people who flaunt their wealth by getting to do things others can't."

"I may be rich, but I do use my powers for good, *not* greed," Dom quipped and saw their entrée being placed on the table. "And so dinner is served." He held out her chair while she seated herself and then took his place.

They dined on succulent prawn salad for an entrée, and freshly caught and cooked fish with Greek salad vegetables for dinner. Dessert was a raspberry chiffon cheesecake he'd asked Tomas to fly over for him.

"Oh, this is way too much." Davina patted the napkin to her lips and took a sip of her fourth champagne. "I've never dined in any place so spectacular. The food's been exquisite, the champagne bubbly, and the dessert incredible. The view, this place, the company, it's all been so…" She hiccupped and broke into giggles. "Spectacular! Sorry."

Dom's laughter was deep. "That's okay. Sounds like you've had a very merry time and I'm glad I could make our last night so special."

The sun finally slid past the horizon in a blaze of red, orange, pink and purple as it prepared to wake up the other side of the planet.

"Oh, you definitely have, Dom Stefan," she murmured. A giggle bubbled out of her and she covered her mouth. "Sorry. I think I've had too much to drink."

"Either that, or you're just in a *very* good mood. Let's dance." He escorted her to the small area in front of their table and held her in his arms. The music stayed in the soft pop and ballad zones and they watched the night sky change through all of the glorious colours while the lights slowly came on throughout the city and around the Parthenon and Acropolis.

"Oh, this is beautiful." Snuggled against his chest, Davina gazed out over the city to the sea. "And so romantic. Thank you for doing this."

"You're very welcome." Dom kissed the top of her head and checked his watch. "But you know…" He gently cupped her face so he could gaze into her eyes. "The night's not over just because we've eaten the food and the sun's gone down. It's still early and we still have *so* much to do."

"Like what?" Davina's brows rose in wonder. "What *else* do you have planned, Dom Stefan?"

"Oh, just a little something like this…" He held up his left arm and clicked his fingers.

Fireworks exploded into the air in a rush of reds and whites, followed by all the colours of the rainbow.

"Oh, my God! You set up fireworks," Davina gushed and spun around to see them go off from every side. "Oh, my God you set up fireworks." Gazing upwards, she didn't even notice Dom lower himself to one knee.

"Davina."

"Yes." Her gaze didn't move from the sky.

"I love you, and I want to spend the rest of my life with you."

She registered what he was saying. "I love you, too." After a few moments, she tore her gaze away from the sky to look at him, and then looked down to see him on his knee and holding out his hand. "Oh, my God!" Her hands flew to her mouth and she stumbled back, gaping at the cushion-cut emerald ring nestled in the open velvet box in his hand. "Oh, my God, Dom."

"Will you marry me, Davina? I want to spend the rest of my life with you." It was the most serious decision that he'd ever had to make in his life and he hadn't made it lightly. At thirty-three, he knew she was the one for him. The one he wanted in his life for the *rest* of his life. "Will you do me the honour of being my wife?"

A gurgling sound came from the back of her throat as she looked from the ring to the very serious expression on his face, and back to the ring, contemplating a million thoughts about her life, her love, the future she wanted for herself, and knew that regardless of how many roads her brain detoured down, they all came back to the man kneeling before her. "Yes…of course, I will. I love you, too. Oh, my God." She watched him pull the ring from the box, hold out his hand for hers, and pause.

"Um…" He gazed up at her in confusion. "Which finger do you want it on?"

"What?" She gazed back in just as much confusion.

"Greeks wear it on their right hand, Aussies on their left. Which one do you prefer?"

"Oh." Her nervous giggling continued. "Left is fine. Left, left." She thrust her hand forward and watched the ring slide onto her finger. "Oh, my God, it's huge."

He grinned and kissed her hand before rising. "Not really. But I wanted something different from all the other rings in the family. You like?"

Falling in love with her ring every second that she gazed at it, she finally managed, "I love it. And I love you and want to spend the rest of my life with you." Kissing him, she added, "This night has been the most romantic, spectacular night of my life."

"Good, I'm glad." He kissed her back. "Because there are many, many more to come."

*****

On Sunday morning, they flew back to Mykonos and walked into Jenny's house at midday.

"Hey, everyone, we're back." He saw that all were accounted for.

"Hey, sweetie. Have fun in Athens?" Angie called from the kitchen.

"Ah, we did." Dom glanced down at Davina who was snuggled under his right arm. "I have something to tell you all. I ah…" He saw everyone turn to face him and blinked at the sudden attention. "I've… made decisions about a few things lately, about my life and how I run it, and made a very big decision that came to fruition last night." He felt Davina's hand on his chest and grasped it. His eyes stared into hers and saw the encouragement. "I proposed last night and Davina said yes."

"Holy hell! I knew it!" Cabot rushed over to them. "Let's see the ring." Davina excitedly held out her hand to him. "Holy hell, an emerald! It's huge!" Cabot turned her hand this way and that to see the light reflecting off it. "Congrats, both of you." He enveloped them into a hug and then stood aside for the rest of the family.

"Welcome to the family, Davina." Jenny kissed her cheek. "Dom has picked well."

"Grandma." He blushed and hugged his mother. "Mama. Papa."

Pedro had to embrace both his son and Angie because she wouldn't let go. "Congrats, Dom. You chose well."

"Thanks." Grinning, he hugged his way through his grandparents, aunt and uncles, watching them embrace his new fiancée and welcome her to the family.

"An emerald, huh!" Alena grumbled when she hugged him. "You sod! Had to be different, didn't you? I'm surprised you didn't give her a music ring." She grabbed his hands and looked at the various rings he wore including a huge silver treble clef. "Could've just given her that as a sign of your love instead of a whopping big emerald."

"I could have." His grin was still beaming. "But I also couldn't give her a boring old diamond like yours, now, could I." He hugged and kissed cousins and siblings and came to Luca. Gripping his hand tightly, he leaned in to Luca's right ear. "If you ever touch her again, I'll do more than rip your balls off. Do you understand me?" He slowly retreated, eyeing Luca directly. Even though they were roughly the same height, Dom clearly had more muscular power and strength than Luca.

"Yes," Luca murmured through clenched teeth and a tight smile, realising Davina had told him. "Congratulations."

Dom let go and moved on to his brother, grasping him by both arms. "I want you to be my best man."

"What?" Surprise rolled over Danté. *"Why?"*

"What do you *mean* why?" Dom asked. "You're my brother, my best friend. Because in case you hadn't noticed, I don't have many of those."

"Well, that's true." Danté nodded in agreement. "In fact, you have none," he teased. "So I guess I'd better do it."

Dom's lips curled ear to ear and he hugged his brother tightly. "Thanks, Danté. This means to world to me."

Tears sprang to Danté's eyes. It had taken Dom fourteen years to accept him as his brother, or include him into his life and not treat him like a leper. But since his shark attack, things had changed and they'd bonded the last nine years.

"Aw, look at them," Angie murmured to her husband as they watched their sons. "As tight as brothers should be."

"Good to see them that way, finally." Tomas stood behind Pedro and squeezed his shoulder. "We grew up like that, the twins did, and they should have, too."

"Tell us about the proposal." Cabot excitedly clapped his hands. "Was it romantic? Spectacular? Beautiful? Small?"

Dom let go of his brother and told his family all about it. "I went all out with the proposal. I knew she was absolutely worth it and made sure it was spectacular." He moved to Davina's side and wrapped his arms around her. "But then again, why shouldn't I go all out for the woman I love."

"Jesus, Dom," Cabot complained. "None of us got proposed to like that. Fireworks! Pft! I got flowers."

"Hey, we were in my family's garden," Tony reminded him. "It's a sacred place."

"I know, sweetie." Cabot slid his arm through his husband's. "But they ain't fireworks, now are they."

"And I didn't even get dinner." Maria had to get her two cents in. "He proposed in bed."

"But you got a massive rock out of it," Alena muttered under her breath, arms crossed and a scowl on her face. "When's the wedding?"

"Ah, we haven't gotten that far," Dom said. "We need to get back to London tomorrow, so Davina can get back to work, and we'll take some time to figure it out, and when and where it will be, and what we'll do in the meantime."

"You know you'll have to make sure there's absolutely *nothing* else on that week. Right?" Alexis said. "With everything we've got going on, our years are booked out in advance."

Dom chuckled. "I know. We'll spend some time going over our diaries and make sure no one has anything else on."

"Wait, did you say you're going back to London tomorrow?" Tony asked. "We're leaving, too. May as well share the ride."

"Fine by me," Dom said. "When's lunch ready?"

*****

They chatted on the plane on Monday and then went their separate ways when they reached London. Cabot and Tony were staying at his house and preparing for the arrival of their first child via surrogate, and Dom moved into Davina's house.

"Home, sweet home," she said and wearily closed the door after him. "I finally have you all to myself again." Her arms went around his neck and his around her torso. Their lips found each other's and they woke up two hours later naked and in bed. "How the hell did that happen?" she murmured.

A chuckled rippled deep in his throat. "Don't you know? Once a Stephanopoulos starts, we can't stop. We can find our way into a bed with our eyes closed."

"Like a moth to a flame, eh?" Davina's hand made its way across his chest and back before following the trail of hair that led to the Stefan family jewels.

"So…" He put his hand under his head. "Do you have a date in mind? And what will you do about work?"

"Well…" She lazily slid her leg up his. "I think I might work until we're married. Which I know could be a year away. But, depending on where we live—"

"I was hoping Mykonos," Dom cut in. "But we can come back a lot."

"Then I would need to quit anyway and get myself a job on Mykonos, or in Athens. I speak Greek, have a Greek mother, and could fit right in. Or, who knows…maybe your Uncle Carlos could start up a TV show just for me." Her fingers walked across his chest. "The whole family could get into TV."

"Maybe." Dom shifted his leg to get comfortable. "I have a list of birthdays and anniversaries in my phone. Do you want a summer wedding? Do you want it in Mykonos?"

"I want a garden wedding," Davina said. "It doesn't matter if it's Greece or Australia. Maybe we could have two."

"Or; we'll just fly your whole family out," Dom suggested. "We own *The Windmill Hotel* and can book it out a year in advance. We could make it June or July. There's only a couple of birthdays in those months, or…" he twisted his head to look at her, "we could do what Alena did and get married on the anniversary of when we first met."

Davina thought about it. "That's an idea. Then we'd never forget it. When was it?"

Dom's laughter rang out across the room. "You *do realise* what you just said?"

"What? Oh…" She giggled. "It's just the day my whole life changed. June ninth."

"It certainly did. So did mine." He kissed her forehead. "For better, for worse."

"I guess we could pick that date. It's the second week of June, early summer, not too hot. I can finish work by the end of May."

"Maybe before that. Grandma's birthday is the twenty-first, and her and Grandpa's anniversary is on the twenty-third, but we celebrate both on the day between. I want to be home for that if possible. And Jaqueline's birthday is early May as well, plus Cabot and Antonio's wedding anniversaries."

"Okay, I can finish at the end of April and then take all of May to prepare." She calculated on her fingers. "That's eight months."

"Except," Dom dragged the word out. *"My* birthday's in April along with Roger, Alexis, Mama and Adam."

"Oi, Jesus!" Davina pinched the bridge of her nose. "March?"

"Aunt Viv and Danté's birthdays."

"Feb?"

"Papa, and Uncles Carlos and Tomas's birthdays."

"July?"

"The twins and Grandpa, as you know. You went to their birthdays."

"August?"

"Alena's wedding anniversary and Tony's birthday."

"September?"

"Is it too cold for a wedding? But it's also Ava's, Harper's and Carys's birthdays."

"Oi, double Jesus." Davina sat up against the headboard. "Okay. I'll need to know the *exact* dates of everything, so we can find the time to set the *actual* wedding date. And then we'll work backwards to see when I can stop working. But then we'll also have to figure out how we'll live. If I move to Mykonos then we'll live in your home. But in the meantime, as long as I keep working here, and you're working there, when will we see each other? It's only August."

"Well," Dom drawled and sat up beside her. "I have the feeling that once you announce your nuptials to your boss that they'll be more than happy to have you come to Mykonos or Athens a lot as a roving reporter. Pitch that to them. Because once you leave, they won't have the inside scoop."

She thought about it and nodded. "Very good idea. I like the way you think, husband-to-be."

*****

The next day, Davina headed into work and straight up to her boss's office where she told him of her upcoming nuptials and the plan she'd figured out.

Once he heard the bridegroom was Dominic Stephanopoulos, and that Davina would be moving to Greece next summer, he jumped at the chance to boost ratings. "We'll make a five or ten-minute segment every week out of your arrangements and make a big deal of it. You'll be the in-studio entertainment reporter until you leave, and we'll want to know every little detail." He sat back in his chair and puffed on his expensive cigar even though it was a non-smoking building and workplace.

"Okay, then." She placed her hands on her lap and stood. "You have me until next year. Not sure what date. It'll all depend."

That night, on the six o'clock news, the two hosts announced that Davina would now be seen weekly on everyone's screens.

"And welcome to the studio, Davina Smythe, who's been on our screens for ten years now. For the next eight months, or so, she'll be our in-studio entertainment reporter because after that she'll be leaving us," Gareth Mant said. "Care to tell us why you're leaving, Davina? Greener pastures somewhere else?"

"Yes, actually. My husband-to-be's pastures. I'm getting married in June next year." She blushed and smiled brightly at the camera.

"Oh, fantastic. When did you get engaged?" Olivia Tyson, the blonde thirty-two-year-old co-host, asked. "I didn't even know you were seeing someone."

Davina raised a brow. "Why would you? It's not as if we hang out after work. *And* I've kept him all to myself."

The producer controlled the cameras from the booth upstairs and flicked back and forth between Olivia and Davina to get their expressions.

Gareth just looked at the camera in amusement. "So, tell us, who's the lucky fella?"

"Dominic Stephanopoulos," Davina gushed. "Also known as DJ Dom Stefan. He did his first tour back in June and July, and when I filled in for Laura, that's when we met."

"And you've been together ever since?" Gareth asked.

"We have. We just came back from two weeks in Greece where I met his family who are *all* incredibly famous, and they welcomed me with open arms. And then he proposed in front of the Parthenon under the fireworks he had set up."

"Oh, it all sounds so *terribly* romantic," Olivia drawled, looking more than unimpressed. "We'll have to get regular updates on how the wedding plans are going."

"That's the plan," Davina replied and held up her hand for everyone at home to see the massive rock on her finger. "Cushion-cut emerald. It's a stunner, and so is he."

Olivia's eyes flared with jealousy. "How lucky are you that you managed to snag a rich man who could buy you a rock the size of Gibraltar. Congratulations. Again. We'll see you next Thursday." Turning to the camera, she added, "That's all we have time for. Thanks for watching."

Gareth gave his trademark salute and Davina waved happily.

"And...we're out," the producer yelled through his microphone. "Fantastic show, everyone. Davina, congratulations on behalf of the studio. Olivia, stop looking like the green-eyed monster. It's unbecoming for the six o'clock news. See you all tomorrow."

*****

The next nine months went smoothly, with Dom flying back and forth between London and Mykonos. The wedding plans were well ahead of schedule, the flowers, the priest, and the hotel were all booked. The wedding was taking place in the garden at *The Windmill Hotel* on Friday the ninth of June; the first anniversary of when they'd met.

Davina's family, and best friend Katie, were all booked in, the dresses were done, and she had ten minutes every week talking about it on the news so *UKTV* could get higher ratings than they'd ever had in their life.

She'd also made multiple trips to Mykonos to interview Alena, Luca and Danté on their music careers, Alexis and Cabot on their centre, Cabot and Tony on their surrogacy, Maria on her modelling, Alena and Diana on *Haus of Stefan*, as well as Carlos, Vivian, Tomas, Roger, Angelina, and Pedro on their respective careers. She even did a story on

Jenny and Spiros about running an empire, and Jenny writing romance novels. She filmed an in depth interview with herself and Dom, as part of the agreement with her boss, and come May, they were wrapping things up…

"So, Davina this is your last week with us," Gareth said into the camera. "We're sad to see you go, but you're off to greener pastures in Mykonos, Greece. We've loved seeing all of the stories you've brought us these last nine months, and now this is your last."

"Yes, Gareth. My last day here at *UKTV* after nearly eleven years." Davina swept her long glossy brown hair aside with her left hand to show off the ring. "I've covered all kinds of stories and topics as I worked my way up the ladder these last ten and a half years. And who knew that on that fateful day I had to fill in for Laura that I'd meet the man I'd fall in love with and marry." She smiled brightly for the camera.

"And we've loved seeing every minute of your journey, Davina," Olivia told her. "How are the wedding preparations? Are you all done?"

"Yes, Olivia, I am. Everything's booked. Everything's catered. Everything is ahead of schedule." Davina's radiant smile encompassed the whole studio. "It's all done and dusted and we're getting married in three weeks."

"Oh, that's fantastic. We do hope you'll give us an exclusive. We expect photos and videos of the wedding," Olivia went on.

"Yes, that's all planned. As I've mentioned before, *UKTV* are the only ones getting them other than our own websites. It's all so exciting." Davina gazed at her co-hosts and then across everyone else in the studio. "I'm so excited and can't believe how much my life has changed."

"When are you off?" Gareth shuffled some papers and leant on the desk. "Will you be leaving London first thing?"

"We're leaving on Saturday and heading off to Mykonos in time for Dom's grandmother's birthday and wedding anniversary."

"Oh, how lovely," Olivia managed through clenched teeth. Having been envious for the last nine months, because she was still single in her thirties, she'd barely contained it for TV. "The Stephanopouloses are such a large and varied family, and we've all seen that this last year with your stories on them. And now the matriarch and patriarch are celebrating *how many* years together?"

"It will be their sixty-fifth wedding anniversary, and in November Dom's parents and aunt and uncles will be celebrating *their* fortieth wedding anniversaries." Davina nodded her head and looked at both Olivia and Gareth. "If Dom and I last that long we'll be incredibly lucky."

"Well, you'll have to check in with us from time to time to let us know how you're doing." Gareth touched his hand to his ear and put on his game face. Facing the camera, he went on. "Ladies and gentlemen we're breaking into this segment with news to hand; there has been an explosion in the north of London. We don't have anyone down there at the moment, but we do have amateur video from social media of smoke and flames. Let's cut to it now…"

The producer cut to the footage which showed firsthand the thick acrid smoke, broken glass, bricks, and store signage lying in the footpaths and street, and the terrified screams of people hurt or running away. The person recording it was coughing and unable to speak properly, and with shaking hands, slowly panned to the left and right to show a scene right out of a war zone. Except it wasn't a war zone, it was London.

The producer crossed back to Gareth while keeping the footage in the corner of the screen so everyone could still watch.

"So far," Gareth had taken notes during the few moments off air. "We know it's situated in north London. We have no idea what caused it, whether a gas leak, electrical equipment, or…" he paused and looked dead straight into the camera, "something more sinister. We have no idea until someone steps forward with more information, or we find another camera angle. What we *can* tell you, is the street was crowded with everyone headed home, or shopping. It's a very commercial street in the area, and would have been incredibly busy." He touched his ear again and nodded. "We have more footage and a street name. Plus our chopper is in the air. Let's look at the video now."

They cut to the new footage and he spoke over it. "It's Chaplain Street, a very busy part of town that has many shops, restaurants and businesses."

Davina heard that and frowned. Where has she heard Chaplain Street recently? Picking up her phone from the desk in front of her, she scrolled through the messages to find the last one from Dom. *'Off to see a guy about setting up a Sync office and studio here in London. Says there's a studio space in Chaplain Street, north London. I'll call when we're done'.* "Oh, my God." She dropped the phone and covered her mouth with both hands. "Dom's there."

Gareth and Olivia turned to her, both on high alert. "Did you say Dom's there?" Gareth asked. "We've been intricately tied to this disaster, ladies and gentlemen, with the fiancé of one of our own caught up in what's unfolding before our very eyes. Davina?" He zeroed in on her. "What can you tell us?"

Regaining her composure, she held her hands together, prayer style, but continued to gaze at her phone, willing it to ring, to be from Dom, telling her he was all right. "My last text message from him…" her shaky voice paused. "Said…he was going to Chaplain Street in north London to look at studio spaces and that he'd call me when he was done."

Gareth was struck by the shocked horror on her face and the camera zoomed in on her. "We are so sorry, Davina. You're in our thoughts and prayers, along with everyone else involved in this tragedy. And we hope Dom is found safe and sound, along with everyone else caught up in it." Turning back to the camera, he shakily went on, but Davina heard none of it.

She grasped her phone in a daze and slipped from her stool, walked past the cameramen and crew, and out of the studio. She'd barely heard anything from the moment she'd realised, but now it all came rushing back. Dialling his number, she waited.

"This service could not be connected, please try again later."

"No, Dom, come on, call me," she muttered, her tears falling freely down her cheeks. She tried again.

"This service could not be connected, please try again later."

"Argh," she growled and burst into sobs, falling against the wall that barely held her up.

"Come on, luv, let's get you to the staff room." Ken, the producer, led her to the staff lounge and sat her down. "Is there anything we can do?"

"Find Dom," she stuttered through her tears. "Find my Dom. I have to find him."

"We can't do much with that," Ken said. "But I can send you home to wait for him. If he's not headed for the hospital he'll head home to you. Right? So let's get you out of here, come on." Escorting her out of the building, he put her in a cab and told her to go home. "I know it doesn't seem like you're doing much by being at home, but he'd think to look there. Right? And there's no point you running all over the place getting in the way of the first responders. They need to get everyone out of there." He closed the door and slapped his hand on the roof twice to let the driver know to take off.

She arrived at their two-storey luxurious home fifteen minutes later. Located in one of the richest areas of London, it was just a suburb away from Cabot and Tony. Dom had bought it for them as a wedding present, somewhere private to stay when in London, and within walking distance of many main thoroughfares. He'd spent a fortune decorating it to the standards he wanted, with a recording studio, bowling alley, and gym in the basement. The ground floor featured a media room, offices, library, a formal dining room, massive kitchen and butler's pantry, and entertainment area. The upstairs was all bedrooms including a fabulous master with closets the size of bedrooms.

She wearily let herself in the front door and immediately called Dom's phone again, but heard the same recorded message. "Jesus, Dom. Where are you?" she whispered. It was an hour after the news had first broken and there was nothing from him. Wanting desperately to go in search of him, she knew that she'd either get in the way, or, if more explosions happened, she'd more than likely end up in trouble herself. Unable to control her emotions any longer, she collapsed against the door and slid to the floor.

Davina had no idea how long she'd been there, but her phone ringing in her clenched hand brought her back to reality. Recognising the number from work, she answered. "Have you heard anything about Dom? Is he alive? Is he okay?"

"Davina, Ken. Dom just called to talk to you. When he found out you were home he said he'd catch a taxi. He's on his way."

"Oh, thank God." Her tears poured forth. "Thank you. Thank you for calling." She disconnected, climbed to her feet, and checked her reflection in the entrance hall mirror. "Oh, God. Look at you. Wipe those tears and get yourself together. Your fiancé's coming home." She looked at her phone for the time and found it was hours after the initial explosion.

Car headlights beamed through the leadlight windows either side of the front door, and she pulled it open to see a taxi pulling up in the circular driveway. Rushing to the car, she flung her arms around Dom when he alighted and sobbed on his shoulder. "Don't ever do that to me again. Don't ever scare me like that again, Dominic Stephanopoulos."

He hugged her fiercely and kissed the top of her head. "Sorry, Davina. Couldn't help it. Had no idea that was going to happen."

Davina pulled out of his arms and checked him from head to toe. "Are you okay? Oh, you're covered in dust and crap and God, you're bleeding." Her hand went to his forehead. "What happened?" She brushed some of the dust from him. "Are you hurt?"

"A little banged up, but I'll be fine." Dom grinned wryly. "Stephanopouloses are tough, you know. Just need a shower and a good sleep." He winced and grabbed his ribs. "Or maybe not."

"Not," Davina told him. "I'm getting you to the hospital." She gently sat him back in the taxi and told the driver, "Please wait a moment while I get my bag. We're going to the hospital." She closed the door and ran back in for her bag and phone, set the alarm, and locked the door behind her. An hour later, they were finally seeing a doctor in the local private hospital.

"We'll send you for x-rays, a cat scan, and get you cleaned up," the doctor said and sent him off. Two hours after that, he was discharged and they took another taxi home.

"Ugh, I can't wait for a hot steamy shower and our nice comfy bed." Dom groaned as they climbed the stairs to their room. His arm was around Davina's shoulders and he leaned heavily on her. It had been a hell of a day.

"But you won't be fit to fly home tomorrow. We'll have to wait until Sunday at the latest." She helped him into their bathroom where they undressed and stepped under the hot spray of water. She soaped him down and noted the bruises on his torso becoming more prominent. "No broken bones, fortunately. No blood clots that we know of. Your lungs are clear. Just a concussion and superficial wounds. You're incredibly lucky, Dominic."

"I know." He rested his hands on her shoulders. "Believe me, I know."

*****

They didn't fly out until early Sunday morning, to give Dom time to rest, but still made it home to Mykonos just before a late lunch. After depositing their bags at Dom's house, they went upstairs to Jenny's and walked through the door to mayhem.

"Oh, my God, you're alive," Angie screamed and ran at her son, throwing her arms around him and making him wince. "You're alive. Why haven't you answered your damn phone?"

"Mama." He trapped her in his embrace and was engulfed by his father.

"You're okay. Oh, thank God, you're okay." Pedro held his son and wife and let his tears fall.

The last few days had been torture, hearing nothing from Dom *or* Davina. He saw his future daughter-in-law being hugged by his parents. "You're okay."

Dom pulled out of his mother's arms and looked at his father, tears in his eyes. "I'm okay." He nodded.

Pedro saw the fresh cuts and scrapes. "Oh, God, you were caught up in it, Dom. Oh, God." He touched a gentle finger to the abrasion on his son's temple.

"But I'm okay, miraculously," Dom told the family. "Nothing major, just a slight concussion and bruises and cuts."

"Jesus, Dominic!" Alexis flung herself at him. "Don't ever do that to us ever again."

"I second that." Alena hugged them both. "We don't want to lose you."

Dom grinned and let them go. "I'm fine. But I really need to hug the birthday girl." Wrapping his arms around his grandmother he wished her happy birthday.

"Thank you, my darling. I'm just glad you're okay." Jenny rubbed his back. "But we expect the full story and *why* you didn't let us know."

"Ah…" Dom held out an arm to his grandfather and hugged him as well. "Long story."

"We've got all day," Angelina said, arms crossed and staring down her son. "We need to know, Dom."

The door opened. "Hey, I see the jet's back, does that mean…" Danté stopped short and inhaled sharply when he saw his brother. He'd been watching the news online non-stop and knew that no one had been able to get in contact with his brother. Not even Davina had answered the hundreds of calls they'd made.

"Hey, little brother, you can't get rid of me that easily." Dom strode over and engulfed his brother in his arms and let his tears fall.

Danté's arms went around his brother's neck and he burst into silent tears. He hadn't realised how much stress had been building in him because he refused to believe his brother could be dead.

The family gave them a moment before speaking.

"Can we get one of those?"

Dom looked over his shoulder to see Diana, Cabot and Antonio. "Get in here." He wrapped his arms around all three of them.

"Glad you're safe, Dom." Diana kissed his cheek. "The reports were conflicting."

"Yeah, sorry about all that. Just a lot happening at once." Dom finally made his way through the rest of the family, hugging and kissing his nieces and their cousins, plus his aunt and uncles.

"Glad to see you're safe, Dom." Tomas held tight to his nephew. "Gave your mother a heart attack when you didn't answer your phone."

"That's because it's busted," he told them. "I haven't replaced it."

"Davina could have answered *her* phone." Angie sent a pointed look at her future daughter-in-law and received an arched brow in return.

"Don't blame her, Mama. I told her to turn her phone off so I could rest. Marta called you, didn't she?"

"She only said you were alive and would tell us all about it," Angie shot back.

"Well, there you go. And I'll tell you all about it after lunch because I'm starving. I want to enjoy Grandma's roast, not be talking. I've barely eaten these last couple of days, and I'm hanging out for it. Is it ready?"

He inhaled the aromas wafting around the house.

"We're ready to plate up, so get in line." Tomas hurried to pull the pans from the ovens and they started dishing out Jenny's Sunday roast.

Dom carried his and Davina's plates over to the second table which had been expanded considerably. "Isn't it time to get another table?"

"I've been thinking the same thing." Jenny seated herself at the end of the adults' table. "We definitely need ones that expand more than these do. And we'll need to turn them in the other direction."

After a hearty meal, followed by delicious berry pies and apple ice cream, they settled the children into their grandfathers' old bedrooms for their naps, and then gathered in the lounge room for the full story.

"I was in the studio with Jackson, the realtor, checking the place out. It's a great spot for *Sync*, had a basement and three floors above it…well, it *did*." Shaking his head at the memories floating through his mind, he pushed them aside and went on. "We were in the basement when the explosion happened. I have no idea how long we were unconscious, but when I came to, I was under a layer of rubble. The staircase to the ground floor was blocked off by debris, and the room was full of dust. I helped Jackson from under the bricks and rubbish, and we tried to clear the stairs, but couldn't. He finally remembered there was a back way in and led me through a door to the hallway that led upstairs and out the back entrance. We were in the alley behind the street and there was a lot of rubble to our right from where the explosion had been. So, we headed left and found other people exiting their buildings as well. We made it the end of the street and saw roadblocks, paramedics, cops, fireys, the works." He was sitting on the arm of the easy chair Davina occupied, gazing down at her while retelling the story, and rubbing her back more to ease himself than her.

"My phone had smashed in the rubble and didn't work, but I managed to find a phone booth to call Davina, but *that* wasn't working. I stumbled my way into a store and asked to use their phone. I called the station and they said she'd been sent home, so I managed to grab a taxi and went there." He raised her hand to his lips and kissed it. "But; one look at me and she jumped in the taxi and rushed me to the hospital. I had the full scans, no broken bones, no dust in my lungs, just a lot of scrapes, cuts, and bruises."

"Why didn't you call us to let us know you were okay?" Angie asked. "We didn't know if you'd been caught up in it, or not, but still wanted to know if you were okay."

"As I said," Dom stared her down, "my phone was smashed and I haven't had time to replace it yet. I also told Davina to turn hers off, so I could rest. I have a mild concussion and just wanted to sleep. I knew Marta was calling to let you know, I didn't think anything else of it."

"She didn't say much," Angie grumbled and crossed her arms. "It would have been nice to have heard it from *my own son*."

"I understand that, Mama. But all I wanted to do was rest and be with my wife-to-be. Cut me some slack. I didn't do anything wrong and neither did Davina." His mother's attitude was grating on his nerves, but he remained calm. "I'm a bit beaten around, but I'll heal. I'm fine."

"I take it we're not setting up London *Sync* in that studio, or neighbourhood, then," Danté joked lightly and received groans in return.

Dom grinned at his little brother. "I think a lot of those buildings will need major refurbishment, or a complete demolition. Which sucks, coz it was a *great* building."

*****

The ninth of June finally rolled around, and Davina's family, and best friend Katie, had flown in, the dress rehearsal was done, and everyone gathered at *The Windmill Hotel* for the grand occasion.

Davina was in the bride's room getting dressed with Katie, her sister Olympia, and her mother Maria. Jenny and Angelina were also in attendance.

"Oh, you look lovely, my darling." Maria fussed around her daughter, straightening out the diamanté covered train and veil.

"Thank you, Mother." Davina gazed at her reflection. She wore a pale blue silk creation that clung to every curve, and showed off her ample cleavage and creamy Mediterranean complexion. Diamantés detailed everything including her hair which was swept back and pinned up. Her eyes sparkled like the emerald on her finger, and her bouquet smelled heavenly. "Okay. I think I'm ready."

"Only think?" Olympia eyed her sister in the mirror. "Think?"

"Well, I've got the whole somethings borrowed, blue, old and new, etc, the garter on my leg, my make-up's done. Yes. I think I'm ready."

"I'll go and let the boys know, then." Angie smiled and left the room, calling Pedro on her phone. "She's ready. How's Dom?"

"Nervous." Pedro watched Danté brush down his brother's suit. "But ready."

"Great. Get him downstairs and let me know when he's ready at the altar and everyone's seated."

Pedro tucked his phone into the inside pocket of his jacket. "Davina's ready. Are you?"

Breathing in to calm his nerves, Dom slowly exhaled and gave his suit the once over in the mirror. "I think so."

"Only think?" Danté eyed his brother in the mirror. "Think?"

"Well, I've got the tux, got everything on, got my cufflinks, and *you've* got the rings." He saw his brother's surprised reaction. "You *do* have the rings, don't you? You *better have the rings, Danté*, or so help you."

"I've got them, calm down. I was pulling your leg." Danté patted his breast pocket. "Seriously, calm down. You're about to get married, you don't need to have a heart attack."

"Yes, and that means I have to give you the same speech Papa gave us, and Carlos gave the twins." Pedro took his son by the arms.

"Oh, God, really?" Dom groaned and saw his uncles and cousins grin.

"Hey, we all have to get it." Cabot shrugged. "Just like the cufflinks." He pointed to Dom's wrists.

"Yeah, yeah. I know." Dom adjusted his cuffs and listened to his father, saw his uncles nod in agreement, and received a hug from them and his father.

"You're my first son, Dominic Spiros Stephanopoulos. My firstborn son, first to get married son, and even though I gave Alena away six years ago, today I am a proud father once again. Congratulations, my son."

"Thanks, Papa." Dom felt the love flow through him as the twins and Danté got in on the hug.

"Okay. Now that you're ready, as is Davina, let's get you downstairs and outside." Pedro smoothed his son's jacket and led them downstairs and out into the garden where an altar had been set up. Chairs either side accommodated both families, and everyone was ready to get the ceremony underway.

Pedro called Angie. "He's at the altar and everyone's seated."

"Great, let's get this started." Angie told everyone Dom was downstairs and escorted Jenny, while Maria, Olympia, and Katie escorted Davina.

Her father, Declan, was in the lobby ready to walk her down the aisle, and they waited while the rest went ahead, except for Katie who would follow.

"You look beautiful, my darling girl." Declan's strong accent came through. He'd been enjoying himself conversing with the Stephanopoulos family about all things Australia for the last few days, and got along famously with all of the adults, as did his wife Maria, who was quite shocked that an Australian woman had married a Greek and moved to Mykonos with him. But, as Jenny countered, Maria's family had moved to Australia, as Spiros had, and Maria had married an English Scot, so it wasn't much different.

"Thank you." Davina beamed into his green eyes that matched hers and took his arm.

Once they heard the music, they set off, out onto the terrace and down the stairs, along the path that led to the garden which stood guard upon Mykonos and its sea. The air was warm and scented with all of the blooms and touches of Aegean spice. Every person in attendance was beaming with their love and support, and watched as she walked up and stopped beside Dom.

Facing him, she smiled and held out her right hand.

He placed it between both of his and kissed it, his gaze never leaving hers.

Declan kissed his daughter's cheek and left her to sit with his wife, daughter, and son Conall.

"We are gathered here today before God to join together Dominic and Davina in holy matrimony. We'll start with a prayer." The priest continued and led them through the vows.

"I, Dominic, take you, Davina, to be my lawful wedded wife. For better, for worse, for richer, for poorer, in sickness and in health, till death do us part."

"I, Davina, take you, Dominic, to be my lawful wedded husband. For better, for worse, for richer, for poorer, in sickness and in health, till death do us part."

"Do you have the rings?" the priest asked Danté who handed them over.

Davina handed her bouquet to Katie and placed Dom's ring on his finger. "With this ring, I thee wed, with my body I thee worship, and with all my worldly goods I thee endow."

Dom placed the emerald encrusted wedding band on Davina's finger and repeated the vow. "With this ring, I thee wed, with my body I thee worship, and with all my worldly goods I thee endow."

"And so, by the power vested in me, I now pronounce you, husband and wife. You may kiss the bride."

To thunderous applause, Dom swept his new wife into his arms and kissed her passionately.

Breaking free, Davina threw her head back and laughed as she was spun around before landing back on her feet. They walked up the aisle to a cascade of rose petals with Katie and Danté following, and all of the family and friends behind them.

Champagne was poured, and they celebrated on the terrace before the official wedding photos were taken by Charles and his assistant, and then they made their way into the reception hall for the party.

"Okay, everyone, please take your seats. I want to get started with the thankyous," Dom told them and waited for them to settle. "Thank you all for coming and being here to support us on the biggest day of our lives." He reached for Davina's hand and she wove her fingers through his. "We appreciate this so much. Thank you, to both of our families, for accepting the other into it. My family's been so kind and generous accepting Davina into it, and likewise for the Smythe family accepting me."

Oh, the Smythe family had no problem whatsoever accepting a Stephanopoulos into the family. Maria had been thrilled to know her daughter was marrying a Greek Australian, and a rich, well-bred one, at that.

"Thank you, to all of you, who'll be staying to party the whole weekend away with us, we plan on making this a three-day celebration. And thank you, to all of you, for loving us the way we do you." He gazed across both families on the beautiful June day he would remember for the rest of his life and his heart overflowed. "Thank you, so, so much, and please, enjoy the festivities."

The crowd applauded, and Summer, who was between her sister and Alexis, nudged her best friend. "It's your turn next."

"What?" Alexis frowned and pushed her chair back because her dress was caught on it. "What are you talking about?" She tugged at the fabric.

"You're the next to get married in the family," Summer said. "Because it's not like it'll be Danté. What *are* you doing?"

"My dress is stuck." Alexis finally pulled it free, but found a hole near the hem. "Oh well." She shrugged. "It's just a dress. Now, what were you saying?"

"When Davina throws her bouquet be sure to grab it." Summer watched Dom lift Davina high in his arms and spin around. "You'll be next to get married."

"Hardly!" Alexis turned to see what she'd been looking at and saw Davina spinning in the air. She lost her grip on her bouquet and watched its trajectory in shock over Dom's shoulder.

Alexis watched it flying towards her and land squarely in her lap. "Oh, crap," she muttered, staring at it while the family around them teased her.

"Sorry," Davina called and Dom set her on her feet to see what had happened. "Sorry everyone, I lost my grip on the bouquet and Alexis has caught it. She's next to get married. Let's celebrate."

Alexis & Marcus - 2017

Alexis stared at Davina's bouquet.

A bouquet she had caught three weeks earlier at her brother's wedding. Somehow, it was still fairly fresh and being kept alive by sitting in a vase of water and getting a little sun each day on her windowsill.

A sigh escaped her. "Who'd've thunk it?" she murmured, touching a finger to the delicate white petals. *Of course, that doesn't mean I'm next to get married. I didn't even stand in line for it, since Davina technically didn't throw it. It just landed in my lap by accident after slipping out of Davina's hand as she was being spun around by Dom.*

But, it landed in her lap, nonetheless, and the whole family had teased her about it since. *'When are you getting married, Alexis', 'when's the date?', 'found a man to marry, yet?'.*

Oi! She was over it.

Heaving another sigh, she grabbed her handbag and headed off for her shift at the centre. She was so damn proud of how it had turned out, and with the money from her family, her own trust fund, and her mother's fortune from *her* father, the centre was well-equipped for the people of Mykonos. In fact, it had become so well-known, and had grown in popularity in the last ten years, that people from the other islands came in for help and counselling. And the centre had grown *physically*, too, with the two floors above them being renovated, decorated, and open for use.

Slinging her bag over her shoulder, she strode over the famous cobblestones of Mykonos as she made her way through the main streets. It was only a brisk ten-minute walk from home, and unless it was pouring rain, you didn't require a car to get there.

Feeling the heat of the day seep through her flesh into her bones, it warmed her and gave her the sun-kissed look of summer. The light golden tan made her look a little more Mediterranean than she already did.

Reaching the centre, she stepped through the door and removed her dark sunglasses, stopping momentarily for her eyes to adjust to the cool, dark interior. "Hey, Aleni. How are things?" she asked the receptionist behind the counter. They had a full-time staff of sixteen, five days a week, and a part-time staff of eight for the weekends, which meant two shifts each day from seven in the morning until eleven at night.

"Good," Aleni replied, glancing up from her computer. "The docs are currently in session, the others are taking a lunch break, and Cabot's showing some hot new doc around."

"Cab's on shift today?" Alexis slid her glasses into her bag and frowned. "I didn't think he was."

"Changed his day last week because he had something on. Been here since nine." She checked the windmill clock on the wall. "It's only one and he's got another hour. Been entertaining the doc for an hour, too."

"What have they been doing for that long? There's not much to look at." Puzzled, Alexis glanced into both main rooms off the reception area. "Can't see them."

"Probably out back or upstairs." Aleni removed her bag from the cupboard next to her desk. "Mind if I take my break now?"

"What? No, that's fine. Enjoy your lunch." Alexis watched her go and was all set to walk into the manager's office when she heard Cabot's voice approaching and waited for him.

"And here we are back in the reception area," Cabot told the man with him. "Ah, and here's the girl of the decade, my cuz, Alexis. Alexis, meet Doctor Marcus Wellcroft from Washington in America." He watched his cousin stand straight and tall as her eyes took in the hot doctor.

"Hello." She shook hands with Marcus, noting his tall, muscular stature, brown hair, and eyes which lit up when he saw her. "Cabot's been showing you around?" The tingle from his touch meandered like a slow-moving river up her arm, through her veins, and into her body. Her hand melted into his and she couldn't let go. Didn't want to.

"Yes," Marcus's voice rumbled deeply and he didn't release Alexis's hand. Her beautiful looks captivated him and he didn't want to let go. He watched her lips slowly rise into a smile, her brown eyes sparkle like chocolate-covered diamonds, and he was drawn to the creature before him. "Hello."

"Hello," Alexis murmured. "You're a doctor?"

"Yes, from Washington."

Cabot rolled his eyes and grinned, slipping behind the reception desk to take a seat and watch it all unfold in front of him.

"American. State or capital?"

"State." Marcus nodded and noticed she was the only one in the room. The only one in the world. That no one else mattered in that moment.

"Nice. What are you doing here?" Alexis had forgotten about everyone else; they just didn't matter.

"Well, I'm looking for a sea change," Marcus said, not letting go. "I was in New York a while back at a conference and met Dan Ardent and Derek Blaine. They suggested coming to see how the centre was running and what everyone did. And seeing if I was interested in a change of pace and lifestyle. It's definitely that."

"Yes, it is. New York is hectic and fast-paced, and everything here is slow and meandering." Alexis wondered if he'd moved over already. "Have you moved here yet, or are you just looking about? I can show you around. The centre, and the island." She hardly noticed the blush creeping over her face as she stared into nothing but his eyes.

"I'd love that," Marcus replied and saw the blush spread across her charming face. "Do you have time now? You could show me around."

"But I already..." Cabot let the sentence drift off as he watched Alexis lead Marcus off on a tour. "Mmm..." His left brow rose in amusement. "I gotta tell someone about this." He quickly facetimed his brother who answered on the fourth ring. "Guess what! You'll never believe what I just witnessed."

"Unca Cabby, dat u?" Izabella pulled her daddy's hand down to look at her favourite uncle. "Huh-oh, Unca Cabby."

"Hello, Izzy, you gorgeous girl. Is your daddy looking after you today?"

"Ah-huh. Dada ook affah Izzy ever day." She was wearing a bluish-green swimsuit and sitting on her daddy's lap under a sun tent on the beach.

"Can I have the phone back now, Izzy?" Antonio gently took the phone from her and held it up out of her reach. "What's going on, Cab?"

"You'll never guess what I just witnessed here at the centre. Alexis has found a man." Cabot excitedly squirmed in his seat. "And he's hot as hell."

"Why are you telling me? It's not the first time she's met a man." Antonio kept one arm securely around his squirming daughter. Maria was resting at home, being seven months pregnant, and he'd brought Izabella out to give her some peace and quiet.

"Well, I needed to tell *someone*, and *you're* my twin *and* Alexis's cousin. The hot doc's name is Marcus Wellcroft. He's from Washington State in America, and met Dan and Derek in New York a couple of months ago. He's tall, brown hair and eyes, is well-built, and did I mention that he's hot. Anyway, I gave him a tour of the place for an hour and had just finished when Alexis arrived and they met. I'd say love at first sight occurred and off they went on a tour of the place as if I hadn't even taken him. I say we're going to be seeing a lot of the hot doc."

"So, she's scored herself another one," Antonio said. "At least she's not back with Lorenzo."

"Ugh, don't even say that dude's name." Cabot groaned. "He was a dick and a half. Thought he could infiltrate the family a second time. I'm glad he's been gone for five years and Alexis is free to meet someone better than him."

"Is he nice?"

"Seems so. I think he's older than Alexis. I'd even guess that he's older than us."

"How old?"

"Don't know, but I'd hazard a guess at forty. *At least.* He has an older, mature look about him." He waved to Lani, the manager, as she headed out to a late lunch and watched Aleni walk back through the door. He slid from her seat, but she pointed to the manager's office which had a private bathroom. He nodded and sat back down.

"Well, let's hope she can have a productive relationship and he's a gentleman about it." Antonio dropped the phone while trying to catch his daughter as she slid off his lap.

"Antonio?" Cabot called, seeing nothing but black. "Antonio?"

The phone jumbled and finally made it back to Antonio. "Gotta go, wormy squirmy Izzy's ready for a swim. We'll see you later. Say bye, Izzy." He held the phone in front of her.

"Bye, Unca Cabby," she yelled and took off running.

"Izzy! Bugger! Gotta go." The phone went dead.

Cabot grinned. Izabella was a year older than his son, Antonio III, and he knew he and Tony were going to have a live one on their hands, just as his brother did.

"And this is the reception area," Alexis told Marcus as they walked through the door.

"The whole centre is very nice. Well laid out, well-planned. You must be very proud of yourself." Marcus didn't take his eyes off her as they came to a stop.

"I am, but not of myself." Alexis returned his gaze. "I'm so proud of the centre and how well it's done. I'm proud of the staff and how they give their all working here."

Marcus's head nodded along with her words. "But all that comes back to you. Your family must be very proud of you."

"We are." Cabot watched their interaction.

"They are," Alexis replied as if Cabot had never spoken.

Cabot chuckled and snapped a quick photo of them.

"They should be," Marcus continued. "You've done extraordinary work here on your own."

"Oh, I'm hardly on my own." Alexis blushed. "We have many staff members and volunteers. Including my family."

"Like me," Cabot piped up.

"Like my parents and grandparents, and my uncles. They all volunteer."

Alexis was completely oblivious to those around her. Except for Marcus.

Aleni came out of the office and took her seat behind the counter watching the scene before her. Alexis falling in love, Marcus falling head over heels in love, and Cabot sitting on the counter swinging his legs and taking photos of them.

"That's just so wonderful that they support you the way they do. As I was saying earlier, Dan and Derek suggested I come here because I was looking for a change of lifestyle. I don't want the big heavy city life anymore."

"Mykonos is definitely worthy of a sea change," Alexis said. "And we'd love you to come to work for us. We're nearly July. Our staff will be rotated for their yearly summer holidays and we'll have to get more volunteers in for the summer. Some paid staff, too. So, if you're interested, we have the room."

"Oh…I'm *definitely* interested." Marcus gave a slight nod. "Currently just here for a holiday and a look around to see if it would be viable. But my things are packed up and in storage back home. I can have them sent over if I choose to stay."

"Oh, I hope you do," Alexis murmured. "Stay, I mean." She was feeling quite lightheaded and warm, even though the air-conditioner was on and it was quite cool in the centre.

"It looks like it's heading that way." Marcus's watch alarm went off, but he barely glanced at it. "I gotta go," he said reluctantly. "I'm having lunch with Dan and Derek. But I hope I'll see you again." He slowly inched towards the door, unable to take his eyes off Alexis.

"Drop by any time, or just tag along with Dan and Derek, they're always at my grandmother's house," Alexis told him. "They're the family physicians."

"Yes, they told me." Marcus walked backwards. "I'll uh…" He nearly tripped on the doorstep, but righted himself. "I'll ah, I'm okay, I'll go." He pointed down the street, smiled and waved. "Bye."

"Bye." Alexis waved back and hurried over to the door to watch him walk down the street. A sigh, full of longing and wonder, left her.

"Well…" Cabot snapped a photo and watched her closely. "Someone's in love."

Her smile was soft and her cheeks rosy. "Am I? Hardly. But he is nice, isn't he?"

"Nice!" Aleni exclaimed. "He's smokin' hot."

Cabot's head bounced up and down vigorously. "I agree, he is. And what are you gonna do about it, cuz? Date him? Hire him? Fuck him? Wait, can you fuck and date a doctor who works for you? Isn't there some kind of morals or ethics or code?"

"*No*, Cabot." Alexis rolled her eyes at him. "I dated Lorenzo when he worked here."

"And I bet you're glad he's gone, otherwise you wouldn't be able to date Dr McDreamy."

"McSteamy," Aleni offered.

"McHottie!" Cabot decided.

Laughter bubbled out of Alexis. "McDreamy? This isn't *Grey's Anatomy*, Cabot. This is *real* life. We're not about to date everyone who works here."

"Just sayin'." Cabot put his hands up in defence and slid off the counter. "But I *definitely* say you're in love, and if you aren't, then you definitely *will* be. He is H.O.T. HOT!"

"*Get out*, Cabot." Alexis playfully punched her cousin's arm. "Isn't your shift over?"

Cabot glanced at the wall clock. "It is. And now I'm off to tell the rest of the fam Alexis is falling in love with another doctor. Bye." He scampered out the door before he was hit by the stack of brochures Alexis threw at him.

*****

Marcus met Dan and Derek at their favourite restaurant on the beach. "Hello to both of you. How are you?"

"Hey, Marcus. Good to see you." They both stood to shake his hand.

"Glad you could make it to Greece, finally." Dan waved a waiter over and they settled into their seats. "Ready to eat?"

"Absolutely. I'm starving. Hope the food's good here." Marcus ordered a beer and checked his watch. "I didn't realise how late it was. I haven't eaten since breakfast."

"When did you arrive?" Derek asked and sipped his cocktail.

"Day before yesterday." Marcus nodded at the waiter who delivered his beer. "Wanted to have a look around myself before catching up, get the feel of the place, and the lie of the land."

"And? How do you like it?" Dan asked. "Pretty easy to get used to, huh?"

A grin slid across Marcus's lips. "Just a bit. Especially when the weather's incredible, the food's incredible, the people are incredible, and the whole island's pretty incredible."

Dan and Derek chuckled. "You don't know the half of it. Have you met any Stephanopouloses yet? There's quite a few around."

"Oh…" Marcus casually glanced away. "I met two today, actually."

"Oh…" Dan and Derek traded knowing glances. "Had to be Alexis. You went to the centre, didn't you?"

"And how would you know that?" Marcus took a sip of beer and avoided their gaze.

"Because that's the whole reason you came," Derek teased. "You met Alexis, obviously. But who else?"

"A *Cabot* Stephanopoulos," Marcus told them. "Is that the model with HIV?"

"Yes, he's been an activist and advocate since contracting it," Dan informed him. "He and his husband, Tony DeLuca, who also has it because they were assaulted by the same man a year apart, is as well. And they help out at the centre which Cabot set up with Alexis. Their uncles, Tomas Stephanopoulos and Roger Dencott used to rally and march for the cause back in the '80s. Tomas's mother Jenny used to go out with them. We marched on New York, San Francisco and Washington together."

Marcus nodded. "Yes, I remember reading about that, I was a bit young at the time it happened, but read about it through high school and into med school. You guys really helped pave the way for HIV sufferers."

"We did, all thanks to Jenny. So…what did you think?" Dan watched him closely.

"Well…" Marcus thought a moment and listened to the waves gently lap the sand. "The centre's fabulous and has come a long way in the ten years they've been open. Cabot took me on a tour when I got there and I was quite impressed. And, of course, the hospital is just up the hill, maybe I could volunteer there as well. Islands like these always need doctors, and maybe I can help."

Dan glanced at his husband with a cheeky grin. "Good to know you like the centre, but we were talking about Cabot and Alexis. What did you think?"

"Oh…well…" Marcus said slowly. "Cabot seems very well put together, knowledgeable about the centre, and treatment, and is proud of his cousin."

"And…" Derek pushed.

"And what?" Marcus shrugged. "I really don't know what you're trying to get out of me."

"What did you think of Alexis?" Dan asked. "She *runs* the place, *owns* it with Cabot. Her family's pretty tough on newcomers, but *very* accepting. They like to hire people who have the same allegiances they do. Do you think you'd be a good fit there? Did you get along with Alexis? Did you get along with Cabot?"

"Yes, yes I did. But I didn't know I'd have to take the Spanish Inquisition just to work at an assault centre. Aren't my medical qualifications enough?" Marcus looked from Dan to Derek and back. "Am I not qualified enough?"

"Oh, you're qualified plenty," Derek assured him. "But you need to get along with the family for the most part. Not all people do." He raised a brow at Dan.

"What does *that* mean?" Marcus asked. "The two of them seem nice enough. Will I not be hired for my difference of opinion or belief system?"

"No, it's not that," Dan hastened to say. "It's just…Antonio's wife, Maria, Antonio is Cabot's twin with the green eyes while Cabot has blue, anyway, Maria gave the family a run for their money when she joined. Got Alena's back up, made others wary of her, and got off on the wrong foot in general. Things have calmed a little these last couple of years, only because Maria's not here often enough, and Antonio's looking after their daughter, Izabella."

"The whole family's in love with her," Derek interjected. "Izabella, that is."

"Yes," Dan went on. "Things can still be a little salty at family gatherings when Maria's around, which she currently is because she's about to give birth to their second child, another girl. But…" he raised a brow, "*so's* Alena. She's due with *her* third child in September, so there's been a lot of competition between those two."

"And Cabot and Alexis?" Marcus tried to keep things casual while finding out about the beautiful woman he knew he was falling for. "Do *they* get along?"

"With each other and everyone else." Derek sipped his drink. "At least the last ten years."

"What does *that* mean?" Marcus asked, his curiosity rising. He didn't know how anyone would not get along with Alexis.

"Well…" Dan rolled his eyes. "Alena caused all sorts of drama when Alexis was born as she was no longer the only girl of the family. But after Alexis was assaulted in 2007 they made up and have been tight ever since. Alexis always got along well with the rest of her family; it was just Alena."

"Assaulted?" A frown crossed Marcus's brows. "What sort? Was she okay? She clearly is now."

Dan exchanged a glance with Derek. "Don't mention it to anyone, least of all Alexis, but she was sexually assaulted, and that's all I'll say on the matter because the details are not my business to tell. But after that, Alena made up with her and they've gotten along like a house on fire ever since. And then *their brothers*, Dominic and Danté, didn't get along and had the same issues as the girls. Then Danté was bitten by a shark in 2007 and Dom saved his life and made up with him. And Danté was Dom's best man at his wedding earlier this month."

"They're now on a Mediterranean cruise for summer," Derek jumped in. "Dom's taking Davina, that's his wife, off for an extended honeymoon around Greece, Italy and onto Monte Carlo on the family yacht."

"And *then* there's Cabot. He caused *all manner* of grief for years for the family, especially his poor brother, Antonio. But after *his* assault and contracting HIV in 2007, plus being brought back here by Jenny and receiving a tonne of help from us and Xanthe, he's actually come better than good," Dan finished off the story.

"Jesus Christ!" Marcus exclaimed. "This family's been through almost as much as the Kennedys. Is it cursed? Do I have anything to worry about, or was it all back in 2007?"

"Pretty much," Dan said. "Besides '81 and '82, when I was Tomas and Roger's doctor, first in New York and then here, the family didn't really have problems again until 2007. That year was a turning point for many family members—"

"Especially when James Gardo popped up claiming to be Luiz Manning," Derek butted in dramatically and sipped his drink.

"Who's—?" Marcus started.

"Don't worry about that." Dan waved a hand. "But 2007 wasn't just about the kids. Hell, Diana even had her issues, and Roger scored himself an unexpected Christmas present when his illegitimate son, Simon, popped up, but once it was over, 2008 came and so did Adam, he's Diana son with her husband, photographer, Charles Kensington, and Tony resolved a lot of issues with *his* family, and all became right with the world. And pretty much has been ever since."

"Yes. All but Alexis and Danté are married off now, but they're both in their twenties, so who knows what will happen next." Derek set his drink aside as the waiter placed his food on the table, and he smiled up at him. "Yum. This looks divine, thank you."

Marcus's brows furrowed. "Wait…are you telling me…that if I start work at the centre, then I'll be involved in all of the family's business and problems? I'm not coming here for that." He set his beer down and inhaled the scent of his food. "I don't need anyone else's problems in my life. How large *is* this family? And how involved will I be just working at the centre?"

"Oh, you won't be, if you don't want to be," Dan rushed to reassure him. He'd read up on Marcus's credentials after meeting him and knew he'd be perfect for the family in some medical capacity. Either at the centre, or their HIV clinic in New York. "If you get a job at the centre, that's it. It's just a job. But you'll get to know the family because many volunteer there, and staff are invited to celebrations and given bonuses, etc, so, you'll see them around, *and* they own a lot of property and businesses on the island." He pulled a face. "Regardless of where you go, you'll run into one, or more, of them."

"It sounds like a *huge* family." Marcus was astounded by the family's grip on the community. "Do they have a say in the local government, too? The council? Or do they mind their own business and keep to themselves?

"Pretty much." Derek wiped his mouth with his napkin. "They help a lot of people, and a lot of businesses. Jenny sets up scholarships for children, buys up property and then lets families set up businesses and pay little rent. They donate to those less fortunate and the needy. All of the businesses in the family make a tonne of money, so a lot of profit helps out the island. All counselling is free at the centre, and her money set up the clinic at the hospital for those who can't afford it. They don't pay if they can't afford to. And *Stephanopoulos Meats* gives meat to the same people. Jenny's *very* wary of being more fortunate than most, so she makes sure the family gives back in as many ways as possible."

"Sounds like quite an extraordinary family." Marcus finished off his meal. "Sounds like a family I wouldn't mind working for after all."

"You'll get all sorts of benefits, a decent pay, and yes," Dan nodded, "they are quite an extraordinary family. The stories I could tell you from '81 and '82…wow…" He shook his head at the memories. "Jenny *really is* an incredible woman who's raised three sons, and helped raise seven grandchildren, to be the best they can be. I've seen her go through absolute hell and come out the other side. They're quite a family to know, and incredibly strong, resilient people."

"You really *are* trying to sell me on them." Marcus laughed and drained his beer.

"Are you sold?" Dan asked in return. "You can't ask for a better family, *or* business, to work for, and you *have* the qualifications. I've seen them."

Marcus raised a brow, half in amusement, half in curiosity. "You checked into me?"

"Of course. After we met and you said you were looking for a sea change. Look," Dan leant forward, "Derek and I aren't getting any younger. We need someone who'll become a trusted part of the family and possibly take over our clinic in New York. But you may, or may not, be that person. We don't know. But if you *do* move here and start work at the centre, then you need to know about the family in preparation."

"Sounds like I have a lot to think about." Marcus glanced around at his surroundings. "It's definitely beautiful. What's it like in winter? What's there to do every day?"

"Chilly, but warmer than New York." Dan waved the waiter over for a drink top up. "There's plenty of clubs and restaurants, and shops in the summer. And they're also open in winter, so, pretty much all year round."

"And Alexis is a good boss to work for?" Marcus pressed on.

"Fantastic," Dan told him. "Sweet, kind, caring. She's a standout in the family."

"Anyone in her life that will cause trouble?" Marcus pulled out his wallet to pay, but they waved him away and he stood.

"What sort of trouble?" Derek asked.

"I don't know. A boyfriend that might be jealous of her working with another man, or an ex that I need to look out for. I don't need trouble if I move here."

"Nothing like that." Dan shook his head. "No boyfriend, partner, or jealous ex."

"Good. I don't need trouble, but what I *do* need is a good holiday before considering taking a job. So, I'm off to take in more of the island. Thanks for the meal, boys, *and* the job interview." He grinned and left them to it.

Derek looked at Dan in confusion. "Job interview?"

"Mmm…" Dan murmured in thought. "And here *I* was thinking *he* was interviewing *us* about the family."

Derek's confusion turned to knowing. "Ah…*not* the family…"

Dan's brows furrowed. "What do you mean?"

"He's met Alexis and Cabot and what were his last questions about? Whether or not she had a *boyfriend,* or someone in her life."

"Ah…" Dan realised where he was going. "It *was* an interview. But *not* about the family, about *Alexis*…ah…" They broke into chuckles. "Guess she caught Davina's bouquet for a reason."

*****

"Alexis, Cabot says you have a new hot doctor working for you," Jenny teased her granddaughter at dinner that night.

Alexis frowned at her cousin. "Thanks for lying, Cab. *No*, Grandma, he's not working there, he was just looking into it. We haven't hired him." She took her place at the table next to Deidre. With Dom and Davina on their honeymoon, and Diana, Alena and Antonio staying in with their own families, the house was less crowded, and baby Antonio was the only child there, besides Cabot, so there was less noise as well.

"But he *is* hot, though." Cabot took his place beside his son with Tony on the other side trying to feed him, but not having much luck. "He should *so* work for you and then the two of you will fall in love…"

"Cabot!" Alexis complained and kicked him under the table.

"Hey!" Cabot kicked back. "*You're* the one who caught Davina's bouquet at the wedding, *no one else*, so, *you're* next to get married. We'll be hearing church bells in no time." He scored another kick for that and his expression became stony. "That's not polite, Alexis."

"Yeah," she scoffed. "Like *you* were being, lying to everyone."

"What did you lie about, Cabot?" Jenny asked. "That he was working there? Okay, he's not, but is he hot? Single? Interested in Alexis?" All eyes turned to Jenny.

"Grandma!" Alexis frowned at her. *"That's not funny."*

"Grandma!" Cabot exclaimed with raised brows. "You saucy minx."

Jenny's laughter tinkled around the room. "*Hardly*, Cabot. *You're* the one who raced in here telling us all how hot the new doctor is, and how he and Alexis couldn't take their eyes off one another." She turned to Dan and Derek. "Is he? Hot, I mean."

They chuckled and Dan set down his beer. "He's *very* qualified, *very* nice, and, if I do say so myself, *very* attractive. He'd be an asset to the centre."

"Well then, we'd better have him investigated before hiring him," Jenny continued. "Alexis, you didn't hire him, but are you thinking about it?"

Sighing, Alexis rolled her eyes. "Grandma, not a lot of doctors want to work in the centre in summer. If he checks out, we'd better take him, especially since the others are getting ready for their summer break."

"Oh, you'll take him all right," Cabot said. "You'll take him in the office, take him on the counter, take him any—"

"Cabot! Why do you *always* make everything about sex!" Alexis scowled.

*****

After having an island holiday and deciding he'd work at the centre, Marcus was investigated by Jenny's people and deemed fit and qualified for work, had his belongings shipped over, found a small apartment, received a visa to stay, and had met Angie and Pedro, Tomas, Roger and Tony, and the heads of the family themselves, Jenny and Spiros.

His first official day of work was July 27th. The twins' birthday.

"You know where everything is, you have the schedule; you know how it works." Alexis led him through it at seven a.m. "You're on until three this afternoon, along with the rest of the medical staff, and then shift two starts and goes until eleven."

"I'm very impressed." Marcus leaned against the counter. "And I'll reiterate that you have done an amazing job here."

She blushed. "Thank you. I am proud of the fact I have a legacy to leave to my children if I ever have them, otherwise, it will go to Cabot's children and stay in the family."

"You're still young," Marcus said. "Plenty of time for you to bring beautiful babies into the world. I'm sure you'll have many to hand the centre down to."

The blush deepened. "Ah...thank you," she stammered, unsure of what to say, and looking everywhere but at him for a way out of the conversation. "I guess I'd better let you get on with it."

"And how long will *you* be working today?" He took a step closer.

"Oh, until five today and then off tomorrow." She slowly moved towards the manager's office behind the reception counter. "Aleni is in at nine to man the desk, and then off at five, like me." She kept inching away and he kept following.

"And tonight? I've either been holidaying, or getting everything set up to live here and start work. I don't really know what happens after a workday."

"Anything you want." Alexis stopped moving and gazed into his chocolate brown eyes. "Your workday ends at three and the island's still open. Go to a restaurant, the beach, rest, relax, pop over to another island. Have you been to Santorini, or Naxos, or Delos, yet?"

He nodded, not tearing his eyes away, and delighting in the fact she would be there all day. "Yes. Spent a couple of days here and there. I much prefer Mykonos, though."

A couple of people walked through the door, interrupting them.

"Ah, here are the first group ready for their session." Alexis waved them into the large room on the right. "In you go, I think Nela's already in there." She watched them hurry in as others arrived. "And so the day begins, Dr Wellcroft."

"Haven't I told you to call me Marcus?" He kept his smile casual and friendly. "Otherwise, I'll have to call you Ms Stephanopoulos and *that* is a mouthful."

Alexis heard his words and blushed, wondering what it would be like to kiss his mouth and oh… The blush deepened further and she glanced away. "Alexis is fine… Marcus."

"There you go. Wasn't so hard, was it?" His smile hadn't wavered, but he did find himself wondering what she'd been thinking about to make her blush so.

"Mmm, guess we'd better get to work then. Your lunch hour is ten-thirty to eleven-thirty." She clasped her hands together in front of her and slowly backed away.

"And when is yours?" Marcus inched closer.

"My what?" She backed up, feeling the heat on her face and the throb between her legs.

"Your lunch hour?"

"Oh…" She reached the office door. "After yours. Time to get to work." She shut the door on him and sighed in relief. Oi! Did she really want to get involved with another doctor? After five years with Lorenzo, and a five-year gap since, she hadn't really been looking for a relationship and had thrown all of her time and energy into the centre, her nieces, her cousins' children, not to mention her family, and Summer and Melody, until they had buggered off with To and Ro Morrow.

Sighing, she sat heavily in the chair behind the desk and got to work, not looking up until there was a knock at the door. "Come in," she called and saw the door open to reveal Marcus. "Knock off time already?"

"Yes. *Your* knock off time. I finished two hours ago, but stayed behind to watch and learn. It's five p.m. Care to grab something to eat?"

Alexis gazed at him. "What do you mean it's five p.m.?" Her eyes moved to the clock on the wall to see it was indeed time to leave. "Jesus. I worked through lunch."

"I'll buy you dinner then. I'm starving. What do you recommend?"

"Um…" She fumbled around on the desk tidying up before grabbing her bag. "I can't. I'm actually having dinner at my grandparents' house for my cousins' birthday. I need to get home and change for it." She went to walk through the doorway, but he didn't move. "I um, sorry."

"It's okay. Do you mean the twins, Cabot and Antonio? How old?"

"Um…" She gazed into his eyes and started drowning. "Ah…thirty-five. Dinner's at six, so I…um…" Unable to tear her gaze away from his, she was grateful for Aleni's interruption.

"I'm off now. Everything's ready for tomorrow and I'll see you at the club for the big birthday bash." She flung her bag over her shoulder and stared from one to the other. "Bye."

"Ah, yeah, I'll walk you out." Alexis pushed past Marcus and walked with her. "Maybe you could suggest a place to eat for Marcus, or take him somewhere for dinner."

"Sure." Aleni glanced over her shoulder to see him following behind like an adoring puppy. "I'll take you to the most popular restaurant in Mykonos Town. You up for it?"

"Sure. Lead the way. Alexis, wish your cousins a happy birthday for me, and I will see you when I see you."

"Ah…sure. Thanks." Alexis hurried off in a different direction and soon made it home, bypassing her sister and her family in the street on the way to Jenny's. "Hey, I'll be there in a half hour or so." She kissed the cheeks of Ava and Harper and rubbed Alena's belly. "Not long now."

"Ugh," Alena groaned. "I just wish it were over and he was already here. One of the hottest months of the year and I had to be pregnant during bikini season."

"Oh, don't worry, another month, or so, and he'll be here and you can get back to dieting. I'll be there soon. Get yourself and the girls inside." She rushed off home, had a quick shower, and dressed up for the celebrations and club afterwards, arriving at Jenny's just before six.

"Oh, *here* she is," Cabot regaled the crowd. "Got waylaid by the hot doc, did we?"

Blushing, Alexis closed the door and saw the entire family look at her, including her brother. "Hey, you're back." She hurried over to hug and kiss Dom and Davina. "Aren't you supposed to be gone longer? Sailing around the Mediterranean, or Italy, or some such beautiful place?"

"We are, but had to come back for all of the celebrations happening," Dom said. "Between today's birthdays, Grandpa's in a couple of days, and then Alena's anniversary, you know how Princess Alena gets when people forget about her."

"I heard that, Dominic," Alena said acidly from her chair. "You don't need to be here for my anniversary *every* year."

"Good. I'll remember that for next year, and we'll leave straight after Grandpa's birthday," he quipped and gave her a side-eye.

"Considering the way she's been, can we *all* leave after Grandpa's birthday and forget about her anniversary?" Danté muttered loud enough for everyone to hear.

"Oi! You little sod." Alena threw a cushion at him and tried to get up. But being seven and a half months pregnant, and huge, made it difficult. "Oh, for God's sake, get me out of here?" She held a hand out to Luca who helped her stand.

In the dining room, Maria rolled her eyes and muttered, "Today is *not* about *you.*"

Antonio grinned beside her. "No, it's about *me*, so let's get *you* seated." He helped her into a dining chair and sat their daughter in her high chair.

"No, Dada," Izabella whined. "I sit wiv Harpa an' Cawys." She flung her curly head left and right and back again. Her hair was a mix of golden-brown with reddish tints, and her big green eyes were from both of her parents.

"We'll take her, Antonio," Diana offered and made space between Carys and Harper on the other side of the table. "Thank God you bought new tables, Grandma, and changed the layout. We have more room for everyone now." She helped her brother set Izzy's chair between her cousins and snapped on the brakes. "There. You go sit."

"Thanks, D." Antonio kissed her cheek and went back to his pregnant wife.

Diana looked around to make sure all of the girls were seated, and found Cabot taking his place beside his brother. They were grinning at each other. "Thirty-five, who'd have thunk it."

They turned their grins to her. "Not us."

Once everyone was settled, they went through the usual celebratory rounds and finally made their way to the club around eight-thirty.

Standing at the bar for a drink, Alexis saw Aleni and Marcus walk in and waved. Aleni waved back and made her way to the dance floor, while Marcus made a beeline for her. "Hey," she said when he stopped beside her. "How was dinner?"

"Nice." Marcus gave his order to the bartender. "Aleni told me a lot."

"About?" Alexis sipped her cocktail and tried to act nonchalant.

"Oh...this and that." Marcus put his back against the bar to watch the crowd. "The island, the people, the way of life..."

"Uh-huh," Alexis muttered. "And I'm sure the centre came up as well."

"Oh..." He turned to face her. "It did. And so did *you.*"

Her hand paused at her mouth; her drink left unsipped.

Noises emanated from Cabot's throat and he grabbed his brother. "There's the hot doc that works at the centre. Dr Wellcroft MD."

"Where?" Antonio peered through the crowd.

Cabot flung his arms around Antonio's neck and spoke in his ear. "At the bar talking to Alexis."

Antonio noticed and his brows rose. "Ah…he *is*. And clearly got the hots for our cuz."

Cabot saw Dom and Davina dancing nearby and dragged his brother over to them. "Remember this time last year when you brought Davi here and we all wondered who she was?" He scored an arched brow at his nickname for her which she hated.

Dom sighed and put his hands on his hips. "Yes, and don't call her Davi."

Cabot grinned at her. "Just teasing. But Antonio and I were left wondering who you were. Anyhoodle, this year it's Alexis's turn to bring someone. Look." He pointed and they saw them talking. "Hot Doc MD, now working at the centre. He arrived last month."

"Ooohhh, he *is* hot, but older. How old?" Scoring a dirty look from Dom, Davina stood on her tiptoes, leaned on his shoulder, and craned her neck to see.

"Don't know, but my guess is about forty," Cabot told them and watched Alexis and Marcus chat. "But this is getting to be a habit with your family."

"Oi!" Dom's brows furrowed. "What do you mean *my* family? *We* are family."

Cabot shrugged a shoulder and pulled a face. "Well, last year's birthday *you* show up with Davina who no one knew about, this year Alexis is getting hot and heavy with the hot doc. Who knows, maybe they'll get married and this time next year we'll be chatting to them about *Danté* bringing some chick to our birthday. It's all *your* family."

All three boys traded glances and burst out laughing.

"Yeah, right. Coz *that's* really gonna happen," Dom gasped. "Let's get back to dancing."

*****

In August, Maria gave birth to a baby girl she and Antonio named Valentina, and Alexis couldn't wait to tell the staff all about it.

"Oh, my God, she's so beautiful," Alexis all but squealed. "But then all of their children are." She passed around photos for everyone to see.

"How's that?" Marcus asked, gazing at a photo. "Aren't all of your nieces and cousins' children beautiful?"

"*Of course,*" Alexis replied. "But for *some* reason, Diana and Antonio's girls are just beautiful, while my nieces have their parents' dark hair and Alena's blue eyes."

"What makes them different?" Marcus pushed on. "She's beautiful." He handed the photo back.

"Don't know." Alexis took the photo and shrugged. "Maybe because they all have blue eyes and golden-brown hair from Aunt Viv and Uncle Carlos, or green eyes in Izzy's case. But somehow, it just makes them beautiful…ethereal. I don't know." She stared at the photos. "Alena's girls are gorgeous, but the golden side of the family is beautiful."

"Golden side?" Marcus was perplexed. He'd met Cabot with his golden hair, and had seen Antonio with his, but the others he'd met were dark.

"Thanks to Uncle Carlos taking after Grandma, who you've met, and marrying Aunt Viv, and Daddy taking after Grandpa and marrying Mama, all of us kids have ended up the complete opposite. We're the dark side of the family, and they're the golden side. We all have dark browny black hair and blue or brown eyes. They're golden-brown with blue or green eyes. Opposite."

"Oh…" Marcus nodded thoughtfully. "I've only met Cabot, but did see his twin, Antonio, at the club the night of their birthday, and your grandmother definitely does have golden-brown hair, while your grandfather is dark. But I haven't met your aunt and uncle yet."

"You've only met the dark Greek side." Alexis grinned. "Uncle T and Daddy take after Grandpa with their dark hair. It's where we get it from."

"I guess I'll just have to meet more of the family, then. I didn't meet any at your cousins' birthday." He'd talked to Alexis for about an hour before asking her out to dinner sometime. She'd politely declined, telling him they'd just met and were working together, and she didn't want to rush into anything. He'd accepted that and left, making sure to give her space at work while still getting to know her.

"Well…" She thoughtfully gazed at him. "At some point, they'll all come through the door to help, but most of them are busy, or not home."

"Are Dom and Davina still on their honeymoon?" Aleni asked and finally handed back the photos.

"Until September, lucky ducks." Alexis put the photos into their envelope. "It's the first summer he's had off in ten years, and he made sure to coincide it with their honeymoon. The Greek islands, the Mediterranean, Italy, and then up to Monte Carlo on the French Riviera."

"I'm *so* jealous," Aleni declared. "I wish a man would do that for me."

"Don't we all," Alexis agreed. "In the meantime, I gotta get home to celebrate more birthdays. Bye, all."

Marcus watched her go, wondering if he'd ever be able to take Alexis on such an extravagant holiday, or if something else would make her life more complete.

*****

In September, Alena gave birth to her and Luca's third child. This was their first son who they named Hunter Alexander Stephanopoulos Saint, and Alena stayed a full week in hospital just to get a break from her two girls who'd been bickering over who was going to look after the new baby.

Alexis took photos into the centre to show around. "I have my first nephew, yay!"

"Aw, he's adorbs," Aleni cooed over the photos. "First grandson on the dark side."

"Yep." Alexis's grin was ear to ear. "We're catching up."

"I guess Dom's next to produce then." Aleni giggled. "He was Mykonos's most eligible bachelor until this year. I think every woman was lining up to reproduce with him, I certainly wanted to. And I doubt Maria will be having any more. She bitches about her figure now."

Alexis laughed at her comment about Dom. "Yeah, I doubt she will.

But Cab's got another on the way. Their surrogate is expecting their second child next year."

"Aw, that's so cool." Aleni handed the photos back. "But they'll still be ahead."

Alexis snorted. "By the time Dom, Danté, and I have kids, we'll far outdo them." She collected the photos, holding out her hand to Marcus.

"I see what you mean." He handed over the photo. "There *is* a difference."

"Told you." She packed the photos away and shooed everyone else out of the office.

Marcus hovered in the hallway a moment and sighed. "Alexis."

"Mmm?" She looked up from what she was doing to see him standing in the doorway. "What?"

"We are…" He took a step closer. "We've been working together for a few months now, and I know I asked you in July, so I thought I'd ask again. If you're ready."

A frown lit up her pretty face. "What are you talking about?"

"At your cousins' birthday when I asked you to dinner." He inched closer, never taking his eyes from her face and saw it dawn on her. "When you politely declined and said because we work together it's best that we don't. Well…we've gotten to know each other, and while we *still* work together, you know me now, and I'll ask you again. Would you like to go to dinner with me?"

Surprised, she gulped and turned away to give her time to think about it. It wasn't as though she *hadn't* been thinking about the hot, good looking doctor, but he was a staff member. Not that *that* had stopped her dreaming about him all night and then thinking about him all day. She'd tried to keep her feelings at bay and not give in to them. "Um…how about lunch instead?"

"I can do that." The grin lit up his ruggedly handsome face. "So, let's go and get to know each other some more over lunch."

One look at that smile and Alexis knew she was coming dangerously close to giving in to her feelings.

*****

In October, they celebrated Halloween at the centre, putting up decorations and wearing costumes. Alexis set up a table of goodies in the reception area for any child that wanted some, and passed them out continually to all those who came in.

"Do you do this every year?" Marcus asked during a lull. He pulled off his Zorro mask and wiped his brow. "I didn't think Greeks celebrated American traditions."

"They don't, but we do. As in, my family do. Have been since the late '70s when they lived in New York, and continued it when they came back. We've done it ever since." She smiled at a boy of about ten in a zombie mask who hovered in the doorway, unsure if he wanted to actually enter. He eyed off the table of goodies and she handed a bag of candy to him. "A lot of locals have followed our lead over the years and will celebrate some of the traditions we do. They put up decorations and hand out candy, or attend the parties we throw for Halloween, Thanksgiving, Fourth of July, Valentine's Day, Australia Day, etc."

"Your family's been here for a long time. They've done so much for the community." Marcus handed a can of soda to the boy who grabbed it and took off. "It's a wonderful thing."

Alexis beamed in happiness at talk of her family. "Yes. We have. And I hope to continue that with this centre." She saw a group of children huddle together outside the door, giggling and looking inside. "Come on in. You can have a bag of candy and a can of drink."

They slowly inched their way inside, eyes wide at everything on the table.

"Here you go." Alexis handed them each a bag. "Would you like a candy apple as well?" She pulled five from the tray and handed them out. "And who knows, if you pull any teeth out, the tooth fairy might come."

The children accepted the sweet treat and took off out the door.

"Will you pay their dental bills as well?" Marcus joked.

"Probably." Alexis grinned and admired the way he filled out the Zorro costume. "We help the needy pay for health and dental at the hospital, or by paying their bills at the dentist of their choice. It helps them by getting new teeth and the dentists stay in business. And my cousin-in-law's a dental technician, so she helps, too."

"Cousin-in-law…" Marcus mentally scrolled through the list of family members. "Deidre?"

"Yes, that's right. She helps HIV patients with their dental health for free, making dentures for them, and whatnot, here on Mykonos, and in Miami at our centres."

"Your uncles' centres that his older lady friends left him?"

"That's right. The AIDS Care Homes. We have three now, and Uncle T and Roger do an absolutely fantastic job of running them. Roger's son, Simon, Deidre's his wife, and Cabot and Tony help out a lot." She reorganised the table and reached underneath for a box of candy bags to top up the trays.

"There's a lot going on in your family, isn't there." He watched her in her Elvira costume, noting the way it dipped into her cleavage and caressed the curves of her waist and hips. It clung to her in ways he wanted to unfold, undress, and ravish.

"There is." She straightened the table cloth and then her wig. Its bouffant style was making it hard to keep on every time she bent over. "Grandma has a list of everything. Every property, every business, who owns what, runs what, has what." Her wig slipped forward, so she pulled it off and flung it onto the reception counter. Running her hands through her short hair, she tried to create some height to look like a mini bouffant. "It's quite a detailed, extensive list. We have so many now after all these years. Grandma tries to help out not only the island, but the people, and tries to give back as much as she possibly can. We all do because that's the way she and Grandpa raised us all."

"You have quite an extensive family," Marcus remarked. "And I still haven't met most of them." He handed out sodas to kids that popped in for candy bags.

"I do. And with seven blood grandchildren, and one non-blood grandchild, and then the in-laws, and now great-grandchildren, it's ever-growing."

"And you'll add to it one day." Marcus watched her heave a sigh and lean against the counter, puzzlement on her made-up face. They had been having lunch and dinner together a lot in the last month, getting to know each other on a personal front instead of being all about business all of the time.

"So will Dom and Danté. And *who knows* if Alena has stopped. I'm sure there's many more children to come. Once we're done, they'll grow up and have children of *their* own, and *they'll* grow up and have children of *their* own…"

"And so on and so forth as the world turns and the human race moves on. Alexis…" He moved over to her. "Have you thought about who *you're* going to have children with? Because I'd *really* like it to be me."

Alexis was stunned beyond belief. "What?" Her gaze bored into his and the world ground to a halt. "What?"

"I know you don't want to rush into anything, and I'm *not* rushing you." He held his hands up. "I'm *not* rushing you, but *I* know *you're* the woman I want to have children with, and I know that I've fallen in love with you." His gaze never left hers. "I *love you*, Alexis, and I'd like this burgeoning relationship we have to go further. Hell…" He ran a hand through his hair. "I haven't even kissed you yet to give you time and space, for us to get used to, and get to know, each other, and for you to feel comfortable with me." His hands fell to his sides. "I love you, Alexis. I'm *in* love with you."

Her eyes widened and her jaw dropped. "Oh…" breathed out of her. "I… I…" All of her feelings surged forth and she could no longer remember why she hadn't wanted to rush into anything in the first place. "I…" Unable to control herself, she flung her arms around his neck and kissed him. Fireworks, bells, chimes, whistles, an earth-shattering cacophony rang out in her head as his arms went around her and his tongue melded with its mate.

Cabot and Antonio walked up the street towards the centre, their last stop after taking their children trick or treating. Baby Valentina was wrapped up in the pram, while Izabella was sitting in the attached chair in front of her daddy. One-year-old Antonio was in his pram, leaning forward and clapping his hands at the sights and sounds of the world around him. He was dressed up as little Eddie Munster from the TV show, *The Munsters*, while Izabella was dressed as a princess and munching on caramel corn. Maria and Tony were both at home having some time to themselves and getting ready for the Halloween party at the club.

"I hope still she's got candy. Cousin Alexis has candy, Tonio," Cabot said, using the family's nickname for his son, so he wasn't confused with his Uncle Antonio, or his father.

"Candy!" Izabella held up her bag. "More, Dada."

"More!" Antonio exclaimed, gazing down at his rambunctious daughter dressed in her pink dress, with curls in her hair that her plastic tiara was attached to. "You couldn't have eaten everything already."

Izabella's laughter carried on the wind. "Yes, Dada. I ate it." Big emerald eyes twinkled up at him. "I want more. Cousin Lexi have more?"

"Cousin Alexis *does* have more," Antonio replied and they pulled up to the centre's door to see Elvira in a steamy clinch with Zorro.

"Oh…" Cabot's eyes grew to the size of saucers and his lips formed an o shape. "Oh… Alexis and Marcus sitting in a tree, k.i.double s.i.n.g," he whispered.

A deep laugh rumbled out of Antonio and they stood watching as Alexis pulled drunkenly away from Marcus.

Izabella squirmed around in her chair and saw two people inside. "Cousin Lexi, you got candy?" she yelled.

Alexis's head spun around to see the twins grinning like idiots, and Cabot filming them with his phone. "Aw, fuck!"

*****

Alexis avoided her family like the plague that Sunday. She knew that the minute she set foot in her grandmother's house the questions would not stop. Nor would the teasing. So, she was thankful when they were finally gone and she could sneak in after them to visit with her grandparents. "I don't need crap from Cabot, or Alena, about the hot doc at the centre. And Marcus certainly doesn't need that."

"That doesn't mean you can't drop by to see us," Jenny said, and patted her hand. "It's really just Sundays that all of you kids come around now. You all have lives, and most of you have children of your own. It's just us adults who congregate here when we're not working, or doing anything else. Which, for your grandfather and me, isn't much these days."

"Yeah, I know. But I don't really need rubbish from Mama, either. I'm dating a guy after five years. Why is it such a big deal? Hell, *Danté's* not dating *at all*." She snuggled into Jenny's side as she sat between her grandparents on the couch, her arms linked with both of theirs. "I don't want to be teased or tortured. It's childish and stupid."

"They're just looking out for you, and want you to find someone like they did. They want you to be happy. We *all* do. Lorenzo was only your second boyfriend."

"Just because I've been single for five years, doesn't mean I can be teased about it. *Especially* by Cabot who's had four thousand two hundred times more partners than the rest of us combined. I don't need no guff from him, Grandma." She relished the quiet moments with her grandparents when the rest of the family weren't around to be loud and precious about being the centre of attention. Sometimes, quiet visits like these breathed life back into her soul, and she loved spending one on one time with them as she'd done as a child.

"Is it serious with Marcus? They couldn't wait to tell us all about it at the club on Halloween." Jenny breathed in the scent of fall that lingered in her home; roast chicken mixed with crisp fall leaves and spicy aromas from the logs burning in the fire grate.

"And *that's* the reason why I didn't end up going," Alexis replied. "I didn't want to cop it *then*, either. It's not the first time I've kissed a guy, and Cabot filmed it, for God's sake. What a dickface."

Jenny giggled at the nickname Antonio had given his twin. "He still can be, but he's just teasing you and thinks you'll end up with Marcus. He wants you to be happy."

"Then he needs to shut up because he's making me very *un*happy," she complained, and stared into the fireplace.

"Will you be coming to lunch this Sunday?" Spiros asked his grand-daughter.

Alexis rolled her eyes. "No. God, no! No offence, Grandpa, but I need a break from Cabot. I even changed my shifts, so I'm not working when he is. Hell, I even changed them from when Mama's on."

"Will you be coming to *Thanksgiving* in a couple of weeks?" Jenny watched her granddaughter's face and caught a glimpse of Spiros's amused expression from the other side of Alexis.

Alexis sighed and gazed around her grandparents' house. A house she'd grown up in. A house that was just as much home as her parents' house was. "I don't know. I suppose I can't miss out on trimming the tree, now can I. Not to mention your famous Greek-style roast turkey, and your famous Thanksgiving baklava. Can't miss out on that."

"Good. Now, since you and Marcus are dating, you can invite him, too."

"Oh, hell no!" Alexis's eyes grew wide. "There's *no way* I'm putting him through that torture." She blushed at Jenny's arched brow. "Sorry, Grandma. I meant my siblings and cousins' torture."

"*Are* the two of you dating?" Jenny saw the emotions fly over her Alexis's face.

"Yes." Alexis's eyes shifted away and down. "But we're *not* rushing into anything and before you ask, *no*, we haven't slept together."

"Why not?"

"Grandma!" Alexis's gaze flew to her grandmother's face. *"Why should we?"*

Jenny conceded. "Fair enough. But I'd say the only ones in this family who waited were your grandfather and I. Your parents, aunt, uncles, siblings and cousins didn't. Well, no…" She thought about it. "Cabot and Tony waited because Cabot was receiving treatment."

"Yeah, but I think that was only a two-month wait. The same with me and Lorenzo. Look…" Alexis brushed a wayward strand of hair from her eyes. "He only started work in July, and we've gotten to know each other since. Kinda started dating in September, and *only* at Halloween did he declare his love for me. We're settling into that at the moment."

"Did he now?" Jenny's brows rose in amusement. "And what about *you?* Is *that* why you kissed him?"

Cabot couldn't wait to show the whole family the footage he'd taken of Marcus and Alexis kissing in the centre at Halloween.

Alexis sighed and felt her body deflate. "Yes, I love him. Yes, I kissed him, because I love him. But… I just…" She struggled to find the words. "I didn't want to rush into anything with *another* doctor, you know. I've been working hard these last few years, enjoying life, family as they come along, Mykonos, travelling, having fun. I didn't want to jump into another relationship and figured that if someone was meant to come along, then he would."

"And has he?"

Alexis came to the answer in less than a second. "Yes, Grandma. He has."

"Fireworks?"

The grin lit up Alexis's face. "Yep. Choirs, bells, whistles, the lot."

"Mmm," Jenny mused. "Well then, I'd say it's clearly time for the rest of the family to meet him."

Alexis's face fell. "Ugh, not all together. That's always a disaster."

"Not so," Jenny disagreed. "We met Tony, okay, that didn't go so well. Davina, Charles, oh, no, that was staggered. Maria, well that was interesting, and Luca… Okay," Jenny waved a hand, "not the best examples. But Marcus has already met half of us. Why don't I send the rest in and stagger it, so he isn't overwhelmed? And I'll warn Cabot to keep his pie hole shut, or I'll shut it for him."

Alexis burst out laughing. "His pie hole! Oh, Grandma, that's hilarious."

"But true." Jenny giggled. "Since *he's* the one who's been spreading the gossip, I'll tell him to stop."

*****

Over the next two weeks, the members of the family who had not met Marcus because they were too busy minding their own business, dropped by the centre to see what the fuss was about. Carlos and Vivian dropped by with some of their grandchildren to look in on Cabot's legacy, and to see if anything else needed to be done. Diana and Charles brought last season's *HOS* stock in for those in need. Simon and Deidre took Stella and Liam in to see whether her dental skills were required and to check up on those she'd worked on. Dom and Davina stopped by to take Alexis and Marcus to lunch, and Danté and Nick dropped off food from the club and *Stephanopoulos Meats* for the needy.

The day before Thanksgiving, Marcus and Alexis were in the centre on their lunch break kissing and canoodling in the office.

"So…*what* are we doing tomorrow?" Marcus murmured into her neck. "More of this, I hope."

Alexis giggled at the tickling and planted a kiss on his mouth. "It's Thanksgiving." The light dawned and she closed her eyes in shock. "Oh, crap! It's *Thanksgiving.*" Her face fell and she leant against the desk. "I completely forgot."

"What?" Marcus became alarmed. "Don't we have the day off tomorrow? You mean we have to work on Thanksgiving?"

"Ah, yeah…that and ah…" She felt the blush rise to her face. "I was meant to ask you to come to Thanksgiving. Grandma said you're invited if you want."

"Ah…" His brows rose. "And *when* did she say that?"

"Um…" She cringed. "Two weeks ago."

"And you're just telling me now! Alexis, that is *so* rude. I could have RSVP'd your grandmother. Hell, I don't even know if I *am* working tomorrow."

"You are and I forgot to ask you," Alexis hastened to add. "I just wasn't sure if I even wanted you there. You'll be seeing all of the family, and Cabot was teasing me mercilessly and made me not even want to *go* to Grandma's on Sundays. I didn't want to take you there until I was ready."

"Alexis," he said calmly. "I was joking."

"Oh." She collapsed into his arms. "Don't do that to me."

Laughing, he kissed her soundly. "Sorry, couldn't help it. *But,* it's true. I *don't know* if I'm working tomorrow, and even then, what time am I supposed to show up? Also, I haven't let your grandmother know, so that *is* rude of me. And what do I bring?"

"Flowers, wine, beer." She shrugged. "It's all catered for."

"Well, I've met most of your family these last few months. Most have come once and not returned.

"Because they have respect, *unlike* Cabot," Alexis retorted and slid her arms around his neck. "Do you think you can handle all of my family in one room? All of the kids will be there, the in-laws, the parents." She rolled her eyes to the ceiling. "You haven't met Alena and Maria yet."

"Will *they* be a problem?"

"God, I hope not." She gave him a quick rundown of the relationship between her sister and cousin-in-law. "They *try* and stay on different sides of the room these days. *And* different ends of the table."

Marcus chuckled. "Then I am forewarned. Now." He pulled her in close for a kiss. "Am I working tomorrow or not?"

"Mmm…" Alexis kissed him back. "We'd better check." Looking through the schedule, she said, "Oh, you are, *but* that means you won't have to put up with my family for that long. However…" She turned back to him. "They'll be coming here about seven-thirty to hand out meals to the needy and feed them. You're off at three, we'll get to Grandma's about three-thirty, they leave at seven or seven-thirty to come here. That's only three and a half hours, or so, that we'll have to put up with them tomorrow night."

"Will *we* be coming back with them?"

"Normally I would, but I organised to work tomorrow, so I could be with you. I think they can do without us for a few hours. But, neither of us is working Friday, *so* we can take a *long* weekend."

"I finally get to sleep in, do I?" He pulled her into his arms and she wound her arms around him.

"You do. Which is just as well considering how chilly it's becoming."

"Mmm…" he mused. "Maybe you could sleep in with me."

"Ah," gurgled in her throat. "What?" She gazed into his big brown eyes and could barely breathe. "What?"

"Maybe we could sleep in together?" His eyes never left hers. "If… you're ready. Considering all we've done for three weeks is kiss, and it's pretty damn evident we both want to rip each other's clothes off."

The laughter started deep in her throat and rose quickly. "Is it *that* evident, Dr Wellcroft? And here *I* thought we were being chaste."

"Well, *I* don't want to be chaste with you anymore, Alexis Stephanopoulos. I want to rip your clothes off and make passionate love to you all night, and all day Friday, and Friday night, and all day Saturday—"

"Okay, okay, I get it." She nuzzled into his neck. "I want that, too."

"Well, then. Does Thanksgiving mark the start of our relationship moving to a more *intimate* level?" He breathed in her scent and found himself in a field of wildflowers.

"Yes, Dr Wellcroft. I guess it does," she murmured and kissed him passionately.

*****

At three on Thanksgiving afternoon, Alexis and Marcus left the centre in the hands of the next shift and walked hand in hand down to her house, where they freshened up, and then walked up the hill to Jenny's house.

"Now..." Alexis straightened his shirt collar. "Grandma told everyone lunch was at three-thirty, so the tree trimming has probably happened already, as I'm sure *a lot* of gossip has, so be prepared. Also, the flowers are a nice touch." She looked at the bouquets in his arms, trimmed in turkey printed paper with little turkeys bouncing on springs in the floral arrangement. "Grandma loves cutesy things like that."

"Good." He nodded. "Let's get this show on the road. I'm starving."

She grumbled and pulled a face. "Let's go." Heaving a deep breath, she opened the door and stepped through. Seeing all heads turn her way, she turned her back on them to close the door after Marcus. "Oi," she whispered, and briefly closed her eyes.

"Mrs Stephanopoulos." Marcus homed in on Jenny. "Happy Thanksgiving, thank you for allowing me to come. These are for you." He handed her one of the bouquets.

"Thank you, Marcus. And as I told you when we met, please, call me Jenny." She accepted the flowers and saw the bobbing turkeys. "Oh, how cute. I haven't seen these before. Please, do come in, we were waiting on you both to serve lunch." She wandered off for the kitchen, so Alexis could introduce him to the family members he hadn't met.

"Aunty Lexi." Ava and Harper rushed over to her for hugs and kisses, making the other girls follow suit.

"Cousin Lexi," Izabella yelled, and not wanting to miss out, ran over for her hug, shoving in front of her cousins, Jaqueline and Carys.

"Izzy B." Alexis leant down and kissed her cheek. "Carys, Jaqueline, Ava, Harper." She wrapped her arms around them. "Hello, my girls."

Baby Antonio had also toddled over. "Tonio." She mooshed his cheeks and made him giggle, and then quickly hugged Adam, Stella and Liam.

Angie inserted herself into the scenario. "Dr Wellcroft, welcome, I haven't seen you in a few months. Not since we met at the centre."

"That's right." Marcus nodded and handed her a bouquet. "Mrs Stephanopoulos, these are for you. Happy Thanksgiving. And please, call me Marcus."

"Oh." Angie looked at the flowers in surprise before accepting them. "Thank you, Marcus. Please, call me Angie. Alexis, take his coat, Marcus, warm yourself in front of the fire before lunch." She smiled and followed Jenny into the kitchen.

Marcus spied Vivian and walked over to her. "And Mrs Stephan-opoulos, happy Thanksgiving. These are for you."

"Oh." Viv flew into momentary shock. "Thank you, Marcus. I'll just set these in the kitchen." She followed Jenny's lead and gathered with the others.

"And Mr Dencott…" Marcus zeroed in on Roger with a well-planned line he'd come up with. "These are for you." He handed a bunch of flowers to a stunned Roger. "Apparently, you're always missing out on flowers from the newcomers to the family, so I thought I'd be diligent with my duty and bring you a bouquet."

Stunned, Roger laughed and received a teasing from Tomas, and guffaws from his brothers-in-law. "Thank you, Marcus, for considering me. You're right, no one else has ever given me one; it's the first time."

"I figured it was only fair. Thank you for inviting me," Marcus replied and turned to Alexis.

"And now that you're done using Tony's playbook of how to charm your potential in-laws, I'll introduce you to the rest of the family," Alexis murmured in his ear and pulled him over to Alena. "This is my sister Alena, and her husband Luca Saint. They had Hunter two months ago." She reached down and tickled his cheek and he smiled back.

"Hello, nice to finally meet you both." He shook their hands. "Congratulations on a healthy baby boy."

"Thank you." Alena raised both brows at Alexis and a sly smile slid across her lips. "So, are you dating my little sister or not?"

"Alena," Alexis grumbled. "You're as bloody bad as Cabot." She spied him over Marcus's shoulder with a wild grin on his face.

"Hardly, sis, but except for Danté, it's only you to marry off."

"Argh," Alexis growled and grabbed Marcus's arm to drag him away.

"You know she dated a doctor before you. My ex. Do you know about that?" Alena asked coyly.

The family around her went quiet, listening in for what was said next.

Marcus didn't move, just stared down at Alena. "Yes. It lasted five years, unlike *your* three months with him. But then, really, *their* relationship is neither of *our* business. Is it?" He left her hanging and followed Alexis over to the couch, leaving Alena's mouth hanging open and her siblings and cousins giggling at the whip-smart comeback.

"And this is Antonio's wife, Maria, who had Valentina back in August. Naw, she's so cute." She touched her fingertip to Valentina's as she lay in her mother's arms.

"Hello, Maria, nice to finally meet you." Marcus shook her hand. "Another beautiful addition to the Stephanopoulos family this year. Congratulations. You too, Antonio."

"Thank you, Marcus." Antonio shook his outstretched hand and glanced from Alexis to Alena to Cabot and Tony with a raised brow. He'd only met Marcus at Halloween, but had heard a lot from Cabot going on about him non-stop since that first day.

Alexis pulled her coat off. "I'll just hang these and we'll grab a seat."

"Marcus, happy Thanksgiving. You might need this." Simon handed him a beer and lowered his voice. "You may want to drink half now."

"Um…" Marcus took the glass, but had no idea if he was meant to do it or not.

"Just kidding," Simon said. "I came crashing into this family ten years ago on Thanksgiving. I kinda know how you're feeling."

Marcus sipped the beer. "Mmm, Greek?"

"Australian," Simon replied. "Nice touch with the bouquet to my old man. Dad's never received flowers." He laughed lightly. "Just stay relaxed and don't let any of them get to you. Once you get to know them, they're okay people."

Cabot physically leaned into the conversation, butting in with his big head. "Well, *we* took *you* in, so we must be." He leaned out with a comical grin on his face.

Simon shook his head and smiled. "See what I mean. They're okay people."

"I can see that." Marcus nodded and looked at Alexis as she stood beside him.

"Let's get seated. There will be a rush in a minute." She had already strategically chosen seats at the adults' table next to her grandmother and led Marcus over to them. They had the seating arrangement of having their backs to the second table, so she didn't have to look at the gawking from her siblings and cousins. "Just gotta wait for the food to be put out and I'll go for our plates." She watched him set his beer down and smile at her.

"I'm fine, Alexis. *This* will be fine." He gently took her by the arms. *"We will survive."*

Her smile may have lit up the room, but she quickly guffawed. "Funny."

Jenny stopped beside her granddaughter and rubbed her back. "It will be fine. You chose your seating well."

"Figured you'd protect us," Alexis murmured. "And we don't have to watch the others watching us."

"Good point." Jenny took her place at the end of the table.

"So, Marcus, what made you want to come to Mykonos?" Angie asked from behind him. She was going to get to know the man dating her daughter, and after seeing where they were sitting, made a beeline for the chair next to them.

"Ah, Mama!" Alexis's smile was replaced with a furrowed brow and a worried glance at Jenny who reassured her granddaughter with a squeeze to the arm. "I'm going to grab our plates," she told Marcus and hurried over to the island bench where Tomas and Roger were ready to dole out the meal.

Marcus pulled out Angie's chair for her. "Well, it's a bit of a long story."

"Oh." Surprised for a second time, Angie sat and thanked him. "We have time. Babe," she called out to Pedro. "Can you get my meal for me?"

Pedro scoffed. "What am I, your waiter now?" Rolling his eyes, he took two plates from his brother. "Personal service, geez."

The boys chuckled and kept filling plates. They had forty people to feed and all were hungry.

Alexis set their plates down and took her seat when Marcus pulled it out. Smiling at him, she waited for him to sit while inhaling the aromas wafting up from the plate. Greek-style roast turkey and roasted veggies covered in thick rich gravy. "Mmm, glad I didn't miss this."

"We're glad you didn't, too," Jenny told her. "Although it means we're running late with the food for tonight. But we'll make it. We made the pies yesterday, as well as the baklava. All the rolls are done, the veggies peeled. Having so many grandchildren comes in handy."

"Slave labour." Alexis grinned and watched while everyone was slowly seated, or ran around setting their children up in high chairs.

Adam and Jaqueline wanted to be next to Carlos and Vivian, Harper wanted to be next to Carys and Izabella, Ava wanted to sit with Angie and Pedro, and Alena and Maria took opposite ends of the table because they used the prams for the babies. It also meant they could shoot daggers at each other for the whole meal.

"Will you be going back to the centre tonight, Alexis?" Jenny asked as everyone finally sat in their places. "I don't expect you to, since you both worked today."

"We thought we'd give it a miss." Alexis took a sip of wine and savoured the flavour. "Been there since six-thirty this morning. Thank God for heating."

"What will you be doing, then?" Angie asked, glancing from Ava on her left to Marcus on her right. "Will you be taking my daughter out for dinner, Marcus?"

"After this meal, Mama!" Alexis exclaimed. "I hardly think so. It's freezing cold and we'll be full. Is there enough for seconds, Grandma? I haven't eaten all day."

"There's enough for everyone to have seconds." Jenny sliced through her turkey roll and watched the juices slither to the plate. "Eat up, otherwise the fridge will be full of leftovers tomorrow."

"Apparently, we're not going out to dinner," Marcus said to Angie. "I'll probably head home and get a good night's sleep. Or maybe watch a movie first, have a couple of wines, and snuggle down for a long weekend in bed."

Alexis choked on her turkey and started coughing.

"Alexis." Marcus quickly slapped her on the back. "You okay? Is it stuck?"

She shook her head and sucked in air, giving a hard cough into her napkin. "I'm okay."

"Have a sip of wine to wash it down." Jenny handed her glass to her and watched her sip. "You okay, my baby."

Inhaling shakily, Alexis nodded. "Went down the wrong way when I breathed."

"*Sure*, it did," Cabot drawled and turned back to the table, raising a brow at everyone. "Didn't have anything to do with Marcus saying he was snuggling down for a long weekend *in bed*, did it?" He sniggered and laughter went around the table, making Alexis turn bright red.

Marcus saw her embarrassment and looked over his shoulder. "Ah, Cabot, how old are you again?"

Cabot turned around in his seat and leaned over the back with a smile, ready for a conversation. "Thirty-five. Why?"

"Because even your one-year-old son is behaving more maturely than you." Marcus gave baby Antonio a glance to see him quietly eating his food, and then gave Cabot a sharp nod. "That's enough, now." He turned his attention back to Alexis. "You okay?"

Cabot's head retreated like a turtle's, his left brow arched, and he opened his mouth to say something, but when he saw both his father and grandmother silently shake their heads at him, his brow lowered and he went back to his food. Seeing silent sniggers from his siblings, cousins, and in-laws, he glared silent daggers at them in return. He *hated* being told off. But damn, Marcus was good at it, and he had to hand it to him for that.

"You okay, sweetie?" Angie leant past Marcus to check on her daughter.

"I'm fine. Just eat." Alexis sped through her food and went for seconds, trying to fill up as much as possible, so she wasn't snacking all night. The rest of the afternoon flew by quickly with her finishing off the Christmas tree with its last tinsel strand and baubles, and she and Marcus chatted to the family while the second round of food was finished in the oven and wrapped up ready for delivery to the centre.

Tony pulled Marcus aside for a moment. "I see you came armed. Well done on the flowers."

"Thanks for the advice," Marcus replied. "I'd already met them, but since it was my first time in the family home, I figured I'd better make an impression."

"That's the food packed up," Jenny called. "Alexis, I've called the centre and told them we'd be a bit late. They're making sure everyone has coffee and tea until the food arrives. Spiros and I will be staying here for the night. It's too cold for our bones."

"You sure, Mama?" Tomas took his coat from Roger. "Need us to stay?"

"No. I need you to go and feed the hungry and homeless with your brothers and half your children and in-laws. I think you can manage without some of us." She kissed his cheek. "We'll stay here with the grandkids that aren't going."

"Okay." Tomas zipped up his coat. "We're taking the cars, so the food won't get cold on the way. Everyone ready to go?" He led them outside and they filled two cars with food, drinks, and coats they were donating.

Once she shut the door, Jenny turned to those who were left. Marcus and Alexis, Alena, Luca and their children, Antonio and Maria with their girls and baby Antonio who they were looking after for a few hours, plus Jaqueline and Carys. Dan, Derek, Mike, Maggie and Nick had gone with the family, so it was a lot of people to help those less fortunate. "Right, who's next to leave?"

"We are, Grandma. Sorry, I know it's still early, but I'm buggered and want a hot shower and my bed." Alexis kissed them both and then all of the children. "Bye, my babies."

"Bye Aunty Lexi," Ava and Harper sleepily murmured and rubbed their eyes.

"By Cousin Lexi." Izabella jumped up and down, still full of pep, while Carys and Jaqueline were quietly flagging in energy.

The girls and baby Antonio crowded around for more hugs while Marcus retrieved their coats from the closet.

"Mr and Mrs Stephanopoulos, thank you for your hospitality. It meant a lot."

"Thank you for coming, Marcus. And please, do call us Spiros and Jenny." She handed Alexis a huge white container with the lid snapped tight. "Leftovers." She leaned in close and whispered, "Enough for *two* meals."

Alexis's eyes grew wide, and the blush rose up her neck to her face as she took the container. "Thanks, Grandma. Bye, everyone."

"Are the two of you coming on Sunday?" Alena asked, watching Marcus open the door for her sister. She was still smarting at his comment when they'd been introduced.

Alexis didn't even bother looking at her sister. "Don't know. We'll let you know, Grandma. Bye."

They left, and Marcus walked her home before kissing her goodnight and leaving for his apartment up the hill.

"Ah," Alena gurgled. "He's *not* staying there." She was standing in the doorway to see if Marcus stayed the night.

Antonio leaned out beside her, peering down the street towards Alexis's house. "You're as bad as Cabot. And Marcus put *you* in *your* place, too. Two peas in a pod, you and Cab."

"And yet he's *your* twin." Alena pushed him inside and closed the door on the November cold.

Alexis had rushed to freshen up and collect the overnight bag she'd packed the night before. There was no way she was letting Marcus stay over because they'd all want to know, so they'd planned for her to go to his place. Swinging her bag over her shoulder, along with her handbag, she carefully balanced the food container in one hand while locking her door with the other. Looking up and down the street, she rushed off down the road, glad his apartment was in the opposite direction to her family and the centre, and arrived in ten minutes.

He opened the door, looked up and down the street, and waved her in. After locking the door he said, "I opened the wine, got the bed ready and all we—"

Alexis had cut him off by launching herself into his arms and passionately kissing him. When she finally stopped, she was breathing heavily. "I've waited for so long to do that."

Marcus lifted her into his arms. "Then what are we wasting time for?" Carrying her into the bedroom, he kicked the door shut on the world.

*****

Christmas Eve came, and after spending the day between the centre and various charities, delivering to those in need, and the Stephanopoulos household for the great-grandchildren to open their presents from Jenny and Spiros, plus their own grandparents, Marcus and Alexis retired to her house for the rest of the night.

She'd decorated the bedroom with Christmas lights and tinsel, and they lay in each other's arms after sating themselves with their lovemaking.

"Today was an interesting day," Marcus murmured. "Quite a full day it was, too."

"Always is at Christmas." Alexis ran her hand over his chest and it tangled itself in the dark hair spread across it.

"I gotta say, I don't think I've ever seen such a rowdy Christmas Eve. But then, I shouldn't be surprised after spending pretty much every Sunday since Thanksgiving at your grandmother's house. I should be used to it now." His hand lazily slid up and down her arm. "But somehow…" A frown flickered across his face. "This was different."

Alexis chuckled. "It's because presents were involved. The family does their charitable thing on Christmas Eve by giving out to those in need, and then the kids get to open their presents from Great-Grandma and Great-Grandpa, and their own grandparents, to make things easier on Christmas day. What kid would pass on multiple sets of presents at Christmas? And the girls are all spoilt rotten; so's Tonio. And now with the two new babies in the family, there's even more to go around." She rubbed her face against his chest and inhaled his manly scent. "I'm just glad we only had dinner there and got to deal with all of the kids at once. They're like a pack of seagulls homing in on food."

Marcus grinned softly at the description. "They are, and just as noisy. Especially when one received something another wanted but didn't get. What a racket."

"Just like Uncle Carlos way back when he was five, or so," Alexis replied. "Let me tell you a little story." She went on for five minutes regaling him about Christmas 1958. "Unfortunately, it was when Grandma had lost her baby, so not a great Christmas for anyone," she finished off the story. "My sister's named in honour of her."

"That's so sad." Marcus slid his arms around her and held her tightly. "It's always awful when a woman loses a child before she's due. The heartbreak is unbearable."

Alexis shifted her head to look at him. "Have you ever had to tell a woman…or deliver…" Letting the sentence go, she watched the changing reactions on his face.

"Yes," came out softly. "It's one of the worst things you can say to someone."

"And the other?"

"That they, or their loved one, are dying." Inhaling deeply, he exhaled slowly to calm his emotions. "It's *never* easy."

"No. I'm sure it wouldn't be." Resting her head on his shoulder, she listened to his heartbeat slow to a steady pace.

"It's one of the reasons I didn't go into paediatrics. As much as I want to help all people, I just couldn't deal with babies and children. It hurt too much."

"Is that why you haven't married, or had children, yet?"

Taking a moment to think about it, he swallowed. "Partly why I didn't want to be a father yet. Until I could be, or *was*, mature enough to raise children, and because I just didn't want to lose them if I did. It must be heartbreaking bringing children into the world, and then you can't save them, so you lose them. I wasn't mature enough to deal with that. Not after what I've experienced as a doctor. But the other reason was I just hadn't found the person I wanted to have children with. Until I met you." He shifted onto his side to face her and gently stroked her cheek. "I love you, Alexis Fallon Stephanopoulos. Until I met you, I hadn't found the person I wanted as the mother of my children. The person I wanted for a wife, a life mate, a partner in all things big and small. But once I did meet you, I knew there was no stopping it. I couldn't stop my heart, my soul, my mind, from falling in love with you no matter how hard I tried. Not that I really tried." He chuckled. "I love you Alexis, and I want to make babies with you. I turn forty next year, and I know you turn thirty, and I think that would be a good age for us to copulate and procreate, don't you?"

Laughter burst out of her. "Oh, my God, did you *really* just use those words?"

He laughed along with her. "Yes, I did. I think we should help populate the family, the island, *and* the planet."

"Oh, so now it's copulate, procreate, *and* populate." The laughter continued. "Any other word you want to use?"

"How about conjugate?"

The laughter died down and the smile left her face. "What?"

"How about we conjugate?" he repeated, watching her expression. "Will you marry me, Alexis?" He cupped her face and his thumbs gently rubbed against her bottom lip. "Marry me."

"What?" She barely breathed. "I…" Gazing into his eyes in the semi-darkness, her fingers ran over his face. "Yes…yes I'll marry you." Her lips planted themselves on his and didn't let go until they'd both ridden the wave of pleasure to the end result. "Ah," she gasped and collapsed in his arms. "Yes, I'll marry you, Marcus Wellcroft. Yes, I'll marry you."

"Good. Because I have a ring in my jacket pocket."

Her head flew up and she stared at him. "What?"

His brows rose in amusement. "Your ring is in my jacket pocket."

Bolting out of bed and into the lounge room, she found his jacket slung over the back of an easy chair and rifled through the pockets. Finding the box, she opened it to reveal a triple sapphire stone engagement ring.

"You like?" Marcus walked up behind her and slid his arms around her waist. "I didn't take you for the ostentatious type, so bought you something similar to your grandmother's ring." He rested his chin on her right shoulder. "I think it's perfect."

"So do I." She turned around in his arms. "Put it on me."

He removed the ring and slid it onto her outstretched left hand. "Will you, Alexis Stephanopoulos, marry me?"

Mesmerised by the glow in the soft light of the fire and lounge room downlights, she smiled softly. "Yes. Yes, I'll marry you, Marcus Wellcroft." Finally turning her eyes to him, she wrapped herself around him and kissed her fiancé until they were done making love on the sofa.

"Mmm, God, I love how we end up making love every time we kiss," she murmured, her body covered by his strong and virile one. "I also love your body."

He snorted. "One part, in particular, I take it."

"Not just that," she protested through her laughter. "But that part has certainly done its job, and done it well."

"And how's that?" he asked, his cheek against hers as he gazed into the small fire still burning in the fireplace grate. "It clearly pleases you."

"Yes, yes it does." Her fingers ran up and down his sides. "It definitely does *that* job well. But I was talking about its other job. The one pertaining to copulation, procreation and population." She waited to see if he got her meaning and was surprised by how fast he did.

He pushed himself up and stared down at her. "You're pregnant?"

She nodded, unable to say it out loud, because it would make it all too real.

"How, when, wait…" He shook his head. "I know the how. When?"

"Thanksgiving…" she said unsurely. "I took a test a week later and it was positive."

"Well…" Pause. "That obviously means you aren't on the pill, and because I didn't wear a condom…oh, Jesus." The realisation came over him. "You're pregnant. I'm a doctor, and I should've known better than to go without protection." He smacked himself on the forehead. "And I call myself a professional."

"Um…" A frown slid across Alexis's face. "Aren't *you* the one who told me he wanted to be the one I have children with back on Halloween?

And aren't *you* the one who's been talking about having a relationship?"

"I know," he conceded, "but I should've known better, and shouldn't've put you in that situation without us talking about it. It's happened faster than I expected."

"Which was?" She watched his face intently and all of the reactions flitting over it.

"Well…I wanted to propose first, *then* get married, *then* have kids. Turns out, that Marcus junior got in first." He shook his head and grinned wryly.

Alexis arched a brow. "Marcus junior? Let me tell you something. He ain't no junior, and at the end of the day, I forgot that I wasn't on the pill and didn't realise you hadn't worn protection. But as a believer in everything happening for a reason, clearly *all of this* has happened for a reason. At this point, I'm only four weeks. Anything could happen, as we both know. And for now, I'll be keeping it a big fat secret from my family until it's safe to tell them." She gently turned his face to hers. "I love you. I want to marry you, and yes, I'm currently pregnant. Let's just live with both of those things for now and not tell anyone until new year's when we've had a chance to get used to them and think things through. Okay?" Kissing him lightly, she clenched her inner self around him, arousing him. "But until then, let's just enjoy the week off, shall we?"

*****

On New Year's Eve, they arrived at Jenny's for dinner before the family headed off to the club for the big party they had every year. Once all of the family were present, Alexis and Marcus made the big announcement that they'd been keeping secret all week.

"We're getting married."

"Oh, my baby." Angie dashed over to her daughter with open arms. "Oh, my baby's getting married. Oh, congratulations."

"Thanks, Mama." Alexis received a kiss from her father before letting go to hug the rest of the family.

"I knew it the day he walked into the centre," Cabot declared. "And I told the rest of the family that he was the one, didn't I?" He looked to his siblings and cousins to corroborate his story, but they just rolled their eyes.

"*Sure*, Cab. Whatever." Alexis moved on.

"Marcus, I expect you to take care of my daughter." Pedro shook his hand.

"I will, Mr Stephanopoulos, I will." Marcus accepted congratulations from everyone while Alexis showed off her ring, noting everyone's surprise at the small size.

"Oh, it looks very similar to mine," Jenny held her granddaughter's hand next to hers. "Almost identical, I'd say. Except for the choice of stones."

"Good to know I've chosen wisely." Marcus watched the two of them. "I've noticed how close Alexis is to you and took note of her distinct lack of jewellery. If she was going to like *any* style, I was positive it would be one like her grandmother's."

"And I love it." Alexis happily stared at it before turning her attention to her fiancé. "And I love you."

"And that's a very thoughtful thing to do, Marcus." Jenny nodded at him. "It's very much to her style and taste."

"I thought so." Marcus smiled at his bride-to-be.

"There's also one other thing I want to say." Alexis waited for the crowd to become quiet. "Mama, do you still have your wedding dress?"

Surprised by the question, Angie replied, "Yes. Yes, I do. Why?"

"Because I want to wear it." Alexis waited for her mother's reaction. "We'll need to add something to the length, but it shouldn't take too much. If that's okay."

Surprise turned to shock, and Angie didn't know what to say until her brain kicked into gear and Pedro nudged her. "Of course, my baby. Of course. *Anything*. I'll be so honoured for you to wear my wedding dress. Of course." She took her daughter into her arms. "My baby's getting married. My baby's getting married."

"You do realise that technically your baby's Danté, right?" Alexis replied.

"Oh, hush, all of my children are my babies," Angie told her.

"Oi!" Danté rolled his eyes. "Mama's turned into Grandma."

"And there's nothing wrong with that!" Jenny exclaimed.

*****

After all of the New Year's festivities were over, and everyone returned to work, Alexis had her first dress fitting at Jenny's house.

"I just thank God it fits." Angie cast a critical eye over the dress as her daughter turned around in the middle of the lounge room. "I didn't really expect that any of my daughters would ever wear it when I bought it. I just bought what I liked and it fitted like a glove. And Alena didn't want to wear it when *she* married."

"That's because she couldn't fit into it." Alexis chuckled and looked down at how the dress skimmed her slim frame to finish mid-calf. "She was too fat."

"Now, now," Jenny said. "What do you plan on doing about the length?"

"I thought we'd add a section of lace. Something that matches the lace already on it, and then I'd wear a coat, or cape, over it since we're winter."

"Are you getting married that soon?" Angie asked. "Not waiting for spring or summer? You'll need a good foot or two added to the length. Unless you *wear it* at that length."

"I don't want to wait." Alexis turned left then right to check the dress in the mirror. "Antonio certainly didn't, and I don't want to starve myself for months like Alena did." She slid her hands over her flat stomach and cupped her belly. "The dress fits perfectly now, why wait until it doesn't and I get fat with old age."

Jenny noticed her granddaughter's whimsy and cupped hands. "Hardly *old age*, Alexis. You're not thirty, yet. When were you planning?"

"Well…" Alexis sighed. "We have birthdays on Valentine's, in March, April, May, June and July, wedding anniversaries, thank God we've just celebrated Diana's at Christmas. I don't know…" She turned to her grandmother and noticed her gaze.

Jenny was staring at Alexis's stomach before moving her gaze up to her eyes and raising a silent brow.

No one else had noticed, especially Angie who was busy going through the samples of lace that had been sent over from *HOS* in Athens.

Alexis moved her hands and glanced away, thankful when Jenny said nothing. "Maybe late January, or early Feb. Maybe late Feb, not sure."

"Will Marcus's family be coming?" Maggie asked. She was sitting on the couch filming the event for her girls. Summer and Melody were currently visiting her and Mike's families in America.

"He has a small family, so I hope they can make it. But until we set a date we don't know." Alexis picked up a roll of lace and held it to the dress to compare it. "I guess we'd better set a date."

"How about February first?" Jenny suggested, her finger resting under her bottom lip in thought. "That will be about two and a half months since you and Marcus got together. A month and a bit since he proposed, and then you'll still be able to fit into the dress and the two of you will have the chance to *grow* together." She glanced at her granddaughter's face. "As a married couple, that is. Until you're ready for children."

Alexis blushed, but didn't look at her grandmother. "Sounds good. I'll talk to Marcus tonight and we'll contact his family. If they can come, we'll let you all know." She chose another roll of lace. "This is nice."

"Mmm, mmm," Jenny mused. "I'm sure we'll be able to fit in another wedding at this late a date. You're very lucky that you haven't gained any winter weight. Still tall and svelte for now. Once you're a married woman your body will change. And who knows, maybe we'll be organising another baby shower by the end of the year."

Alexis's head shot around and she saw Jenny's raised brows. "Grandma! One step at a time, shall we."

"Uh-huh," Jenny muttered and winked in return.

*****

Alexis spoke to Marcus that night and they rang his family. Luckily, they could come, and the Stephanopoulos jet would be dispatched to pick them up at the end of the month. The hotel was booked for the guests and wedding reception, and the next day Alexis visited the church to make the plans. They were able to book it for the date they wanted and she informed her family. The date was set in everyone's diary, calendar, or electronic device.

*****

On the first of February 2018, Alexis Fallon Stephanopoulos stood in her grandmother's house admiring herself in the mirror. The dress now gently swept the floor with its added length of lace, and was topped by a white, faux fur, full-length cape tied at the waist to keep her warm. Her short hair was artfully twisted and curled and held back with Swarovski crystal hair clips. She was forgoing a veil and garish jewellery such as her sister had worn, instead, settling for a pair of diamond studs, and borrowed diamond bracelets from her mother and grandmother. The only other piece of jewellery was her engagement ring which was currently sitting on her right-hand ring finger.

"Oh, my baby." Angie dabbed her teary eyes. "You're so beautiful."

Alexis's lips curled into a sentimental smile. "Thanks, Mama. I hope I'm doing you proud by wearing your dress?"

"Of course, you are, my baby." Angie took her daughter into her arms. "I'm just glad *one* of my daughters wanted to wear it." She sent a scathing look at Alena who was dressed to the nines.

Alena shrugged. "Sorry, Mama. I run a fashion empire; I wanted my own dress."

"That's because you couldn't fit into your mother's," Diana joked lightly before turning the conversation back to the bride. "You look beautiful, Alexis."

Alena arched a sour brow at her cousin. "*You* didn't wear *your* mother's pantsuit at *your* wedding, so don't chastise me."

Diana bushed delicately. "*Besides* the fact I was five months pregnant and it didn't fit, the colour and style didn't suit me."

"And that's okay, sweetie, you made it new again in one of your collections." Viv admired Alexis's dress, remembering back to the day in October 1977 when they'd gone shopping in Athens for their wedding outfits. "It looks good after all these years. Just as fresh as when you bought it, Angie. You've kept it well."

"In its box with lots of acid-free tissue paper," Angie replied, and straightened her daughter's train and cape. "Maybe if you have daughters, Alexis, one of them might wear it too." She finished adjusting the cape's hem. "It can be worn again and again."

Alexis blushed and glanced at Jenny. She knew her grandmother had guessed, and thanked God she hadn't said anything in the last three weeks. "Maybe, Mama. Or maybe we can put it into a *HOS* collection. Everything old is new again. Like Alena."

"Hey!" Alena protested. "*I'm not old.* And I'm *always* releasing new music."

Summer handed Alexis her bouquet; a simple collection of pale pink peonies and white stephanotis. "I'm still pissed that you didn't ask us to be your bridesmaids."

Melody nodded in agreement. "Right! How dare you! We've been best friends since we were born."

Alexis shrugged. "Sorry girls. I didn't want bridesmaids *or* a maid of honour. So no," she stopped Alena's complaints with a pointed finger, "*you* don't get a say in this either."

"Mmm…" Alena grumbled and crossed her bejewelled arms.

A knock on the door ended the conversation and Pedro walked in. "Are we ready? Aw, Alexis, my baby girl, you're beautiful." He teared up and took her hand in his. "It's your wedding day."

"Yes, Daddy. And you're walking me down the aisle, so it's time to go."

With many tears and smiles, they collected their coats and bags and helped Alexis into the main car with Pedro and Angie, then climbed into the second car and followed behind. Arriving to find Spiros, Carlos, Tomas, Mike, and Charles with his camera waiting for them on the steps to escort their ladies into the church, they helped Alexis out of the car and up the steps into the entrance hall, and left her with Pedro for their walk down the aisle.

"We are so proud of you, Alexis," Pedro told her. "So proud of everything you've done, everything you've achieved, everything you are. We love you."

Tears sprang to her eyes. "I love you too, Daddy."

"And Marcus is a bloody good man; you've got one of the best."

Her smile lit up her face. "I know."

They heard the music start, took deep breaths, and proceeded down the aisle where Pedro left her at the altar with Marcus whose smile was as wide and bright as hers. Once everyone was seated, the ceremony began, and ten minutes later it was over with the announcement of, "I now pronounce you husband and wife; you may kiss the bride."

To confetti and rose petals, they walked down the aisle and out to the car which would take them to *The Windmill Hotel* for the reception. When everyone arrived, photos were taken and the celebrations began.

"Oh, my God, I am *so* happy that this day finally arrived," Alexis told everyone. "And I am *so* happy that all of my family and my two best friends could be here. We all have such busy schedules and lives, but when it comes to weddings, we all pull together and wouldn't miss them for the world. My nieces and nephews and baby cousins are here." She beamed her happiness at them and they beamed theirs back. "I am *so* grateful that you're all here for this momentous occasion in my life. Hopefully, it's the only time I marry." She turned to Marcus on her right. "I love you. And I want to be your wife for the rest of my life, and have babies and grow old, and celebrate all of the anniversaries my parents and grandparents have enjoyed. I get to live on one of the most beautiful islands in the world, I get to live in one of the best families in the world, and I get to do it with the best doctor in the world."

"Hey!" Dan protested, and received laughter in return. "*We are here,* you know."

"Sorry, Dan," Alexis called. "But he *is* better." She gazed across the tables of family, friends, and her new family, the Wellcrofts. In their early seventies, Bernard and Cassandra Wellcroft had long retired from their jobs as doctors and loved the fact their new daughter-in-law owned and ran an assault centre, while Marcus's brother, Levi, was a well-known trial lawyer and had already offered his services to Alexis and her family.

"None of us knows how long we're here for, and so much has

happened in my family." Her gaze encompassed all of them and she smiled softly. "But we've come through it, as we do, as a family unit. We were raised to love, protect and defend, till our dying breath, because that's how we get through it. As a family unit. And *without* that unit, some of us wouldn't have made it." Her eyes landed on Cabot and Danté. "*Without* that family unit, we wouldn't receive all the love and support that we do."

"Cousin Lexi, are we having cake now?" Izabella yelled out from beside her daddy.

Everyone laughed and Antonio shushed her.

"Yes, Izzy B, we're having cake a little bit later, and you'll get the biggest piece. But until then, I'll wrap this up. Thank you, to all of you, for being here and sharing in this special day in my life. For showing me, and now Marcus, your love and support by sitting in the church and being here now. I love you all, and appreciate you all, so much, especially Grandma who figured out my secret and didn't tell anyone, and I didn't even have to say anything."

Puzzled expressions and frowns crossed faces and all looked at Jenny who had a secretive smile on her face.

"I figured if Mama could be pregnant on her wedding day, then so could I," Alexis yelled out, and waved her bouquet in the air.

"Argh!" Angie screamed, and rushed over to her daughter. "My baby's having a baby."

Alexis hugged her fiercely. "Yes, Mama, I am." She saw the families start rising from their chairs to congratulate them. "Let's get this party started, we've got a marriage to celebrate."

Danté & Micheline - 2033

"Ain't this just swell," Nick groaned to Danté. They were standing in the entrance hall of the house belonging to their good friend, Jasmine Wetherill, for a Valentine's party.

"What is?" Danté asked, hands in pockets, his chocolatey brown eyes scanning the crowd. And quite a crowd it was.

Every celebrity they knew, or had heard of, seemed to be in the luxurious entertainment living area in front of them, and the crowd expanded out through the French doors onto the terrace, spilling into the elaborate pool and outdoor entertainment area. He waved a hand at Bruno Nochea, an up-and-coming singer-musician he'd worked with and produced at *Sync*.

Going by his last name, Nochea was a hot Italian hunk that all the ladies were hovering around, and his vocal ability had even blown Danté away and he didn't sing. With three top twenty hits, he was definitely on the rise in the music scene.

Waving to a few more people before sliding his hand back into his pocket, Danté turned to Nick. "What were you complaining about?"

At almost forty-one, Nick was a five foot ten hunk in his own right, with brown hair that waved across his forehead, and forest green eyes that always took an interest in the women he was looking at. No shrinking violet, Nick always had the balls to make the first move, and he was eyeing off a few lucky ladies right now.

"Who's complaining?" Nick's gaze drifted from the girls to Danté and back. "It's Valentine's Day, we're at a party hosted by one of the hottest actresses in the world right now, in her incredibly palatial home…" He glanced around at the wealth on display. "What's there to complain about?" Lifting a glass of champagne from a passing waiter's tray, he continued to eye the celebrities. He'd been accustomed to parties like this since he was a kid. That was the good thing about being the best friend of a world-class DJ, music writer, producer, and IT specialist, he attended everything Danté did thanks to their parents being best friends for the last fifty-six years.

The Gatoses had been honorary members of the world-famous Stephanopoulos family since 1977 and had been included in many, if not all, of the family gatherings since. The Stephanopoulos lifestyle had carried over to *all* of the honorary family members, something Jenny had insisted on. It included Danté's half-uncle Alfonso and his family, Dan and Derek, and all of the in-laws, even if they left the family via divorce, as Marcus had a few years previous. As far as Jenny was concerned, if you married into the family, or made children with a member of it, you were family, full stop. It was a family network of stability, support, and love for all in it to depend on when needed.

"Then why did you groan? And why are we here?" Valentine's parties weren't really Danté's kind of parties. Sure, he liked to mingle with the celebs he knew, produced, or whose IT he looked after, a by-product of running an IT business and having famous parents and uncles who'd also dealt with celebrities these last five decades. His and Nick's company had become well-known among the rich and famous for their high tech, up-to-date safety and speed. Any celebrity could rest assured their websites and socials were unhackable, and he was paid well for it. But partying was something he didn't do as often anymore. Not these days.

Or maybe it was the fact it was Valentine's Day.

Normally, on every Valentine's Day, they'd celebrate his father and uncles' birthdays as well as the day of love. But the last four years, and especially this year, were different. Carlos was still in mourning after the death of Vivian last November, just after their fifty-sixth wedding anniversary, and her passing came eight months after the death of their daughter-in-law, Maria, making 2032 a hard year on the family. And *that* was only three years after the death of their beloved matriarch Jenny, in 2029, and *that* was a year after the death of their patriarch Spiros, in 2028, leaving the family rocked to the core for quite a few years. While everyone was hoping 2033 was going to be better, it wasn't shaping up to be, especially on this day, and probably never would be again. Especially for Carlos, Tomas and Pedro Stephanopoulos, who would more than likely never celebrate a birthday, or Valentine's Day, again.

He sighed. Valentine's was also a day he despised due to the fact he'd never had a girlfriend at that time of the year. He'd dated in his almost forty years, but they always seemed to want the same things. His money, his status, and his dick. His money they wanted spent on them, and he'd occasionally oblige, buying them a nice birthday or Christmas present, or taking them on a nice holiday somewhere special. His status they wanted to be a part of for all the celebrities they would meet and hang out with, or the social positons it would get them. And, of course, his world-famous genetics, his dick, made them want sex like nobody's business. At ten inches, and from the gossip Cabot had told him, he was the same size as his Uncle Carlos, but not as big as his father, his Uncle Tomas, his cousins, or even his brother. Not that he'd asked Dom how big his dick was to compare. He screwed his face up and laughed while tiredly rubbing his eyes.

"What are you laughing at? This is no laughing matter, Danté," Nick scolded. "I'm single and there are too many women here to choose from."

"I'm laughing because of the reasons why women want me, and yet I never seem to be able to make them last to Valentine's Day. I always break up with them after Christmas or New Year's." At six one, Danté was in his prime. He'd physically matured into a man at twenty-five, but was peaking as he prepared to enter his forties. He worked out in his uncles' gym and ate well, lived well, and looked after himself. And, in his black pants and matching shirt with the sleeves rolled up and the buttons undone revealing his dark chest hair, he knew he looked damn good. But he just couldn't find a decent woman.

"You do. Why is that?" Nick raised a brow at a hot young thing and acknowledged her with a nod of his head. He wanted to get to partying, but knew the last few months had been hard on Danté's family, and his sex drive could wait a few minutes more.

"I think I realise by then what they're actually after and it's not my mind or my heart." Danté shrugged a shoulder and nodded at Chance Money, a hot, new, sinfully gorgeous actor on the scene that his cousin Adam had produced a young adult movie for. He and Dom had written and produced the musical score, and had met Chance during the filming.

"Nope. Just want your money and your dick, you lucky bastard." Nick gave him a dirty side-eye. "I hate you!"

Danté chuckled. "No, you don't. You've had plenty of women over the years, even a couple of long-term relationships, so you've done better than me." He scanned the crowd. "Come on, let's go mingle." He strode down the five steps into the large living area and continued until they stepped through the open French doors onto the terrace. The view of Los Angeles was spectacular and one he never tired of seeing whenever he came to town. That was only once a year unless he was making the score of a movie and then he came more often. But his home was Mykonos and he rarely strayed from it these days, especially after the deaths of his grandparents. That's the way it had been for all of the Stephanopoulos grandchildren. They all lived on Mykonos in the houses surrounding their grandparents' home which Carlos now owned, and his uncles Tomas and Roger still lived in, long after moving in to care for Spiros and Jenny in their old age. And they would more than likely stay there until their own final days.

"Hell of a view isn't it." Jasmine sidled up behind them. "I *do* love the fact your uncle made me famous enough to afford it." Flashing a grin at Danté, she added softly, "I heard about your cousin's wife and your aunt. The family must be devastated."

"We are, but we're dealing with it as we Stephanopouloses do." Danté nodded his thanks. "We pull together, love, protect and defend. No matter what."

"As much as I love your uncle for being the best director and producer I've ever worked with, I loved your aunt and cousins even more. How's everyone holding up?" At thirty-five, Jasmine had had a stellar career for the last twenty years. The films Carlos had directed and produced earned her multiple Oscars and golden globes for her performances, and they sat in the locked glass cabinet in the living room along with multiple other awards. Framed photos and magazine covers lined every wall and hallway. Carlos had made her a star all right.

"We're holding up," Danté said, noticing the skimpy red slip of a dress that showed off the fact she wasn't wearing anything underneath. "But it wasn't a good year."

"No, let's hope this one's a better one, hey." She touched her hand to his cheek. "You still single, Danté?"

"You offering, Jasmine?" he replied, used to being hit on by the opposite sex.

"Jesus, why doesn't she ask me that?" Nick muttered behind his back.

Jasmine tilted her head in his direction. "Because every time I see you, Nicholas, you have a girlfriend. But every time I see this one here," she playfully punched Danté's arm, "he's single. *Especially* on Valentine's."

"It's a bad habit of his, apparently." Nick finished off his champagne and swapped his empty glass for a beer from a passing waiter. "We were just talking about how he dumps girls after New Year's because all they want—"

"Is the world-famous Stefan cock!" Jasmine finished. Her fingers slid down Danté's arm. "Well, if it's anything like his cousin's and brother's, then it's no wonder. Either way, there's plenty of girls here, so go and have some fun. Toodles." She waved her fingers and sashayed off with a dirty grin.

"Wait," Danté called. "What did you mean by that, you dirty hussy?"

Jasmine laughed at him over her shoulder and disappeared into the crowd.

"Did she just…?" Nick pulled a face at the realisation. "Ew!"

"Ew is definitely *not* the word for it if she slept with Antonio *and* my brother. Fucking gross." Grabbing a beer from a waiter, Danté sculled it down and wiped the bad taste from his mouth. "*Fucking* gross."

"Wait…your brother is ten years older than you and Jasmine's five years younger. That means she went for dudes fifteen and sixteen years older and she's known the family how long?"

"Twenty years. Since she was fifteen. God, I hope she was legal when it happened." Danté leaned on the marble railing and gazed into the distance. "That's…ugh, so gross."

"But understandable," Nick said. "*They're* hot, *she's* hot, you're all famous. Hey, maybe you should have slept with her to complete it."

Danté's face screwed up. "Ugh, dude! What? What the fuck's wrong with you?"

A snigger passed from between Nick's lips. "Gotchya. Just kidding. But who knows, you're not going to find someone if you don't go and mingle." He turned towards the party and leaned against the railing. "You *do see* all of those beautiful people, right? Men, women, young, old, hot, hotter. I mean, *seriously,* all of your family got married way before forty. You're the standout. Why?" He studied his best friend's face. "You're not gay, are you?"

"What!" Danté's head shot around and he glared at him. "Are you fucking kidding me? *Of course,* I'm fucking not. *You know* that."

"Do I?" Nick casually crossed his ankles and grinned. "The girls never seem to last long and Cabot went that way. Maybe you're into men and don't realise it, or you're just in denial."

"Stop being a bloody dickwank." Danté scowled and turned to the party. "Just because *you* go through women. Why are you worried about me? If there's meant to be someone then there will be. I just haven't met her yet."

"*Or* you could be single the rest of your life," Nick suggested and eyed off a Brazilian beauty giving him the eye.

"What! Like you." Danté caught sight of an old friend and walked off, leaving Nick on his own. Although, not for long as the Brazilian beauty sidled over.

Making his way through the crowd, Danté found himself by the side of Scout Banning, the friend he'd seen from across the room. "Scout, how ya doin'?"

"Danté, my man. Good to see ya." They shook hands and he introduced Danté to the crowd he'd been talking to. "Everyone, IT specialist and music writer producer, plus Mykonos's biggest DJ behind his father and brother, and probably Mykonos's most current eligible bachelor, Danté Stephanopoulos. Also known as Danté Stefan." He waved his hand at the crowd. "Danté, everyone."

"Hello." Danté nodded and shook hands with up-and-coming actors and musicians. "How y'all doin'?"

"Danté here is from a *very* famous family." Scout regaled the crowd which was growing as people came over to see what the fuss was about. "His father and mother, Pedro and Angelina, are music producers and writers. His father was a DJ way back in the days of *Studio 69* in New York which most of you wouldn't know about since you were born *way* too late to appreciate such good times. His Uncle Carlos produces and directs movies, but *his* grandson is taking over. His other uncles are famous health and exercise gurus, and his siblings and cousins are famous in their own right."

"Why is it, that every time we meet at a party you end up regaling the crowd with my credentials?" Danté was slightly amused by all of the looks he was receiving from the women *and* men.

"Because we've known each other how long…?" Scout tried to think back. "Twenty years, is it? No… It can't be!" He lightly smacked his forehead with the palm of his hand. "It *cannot* be twenty years. That makes us old and I'm only twenty-one."

Polite laughter twittered through the crowd.

Scout looked more than his forty years. His hard excessive living made him look sixty, regardless of being six foot, blond, and still in good shape. His drinking and drug use, along with the years of sunbaking, had taken its toll.

"Scout, you will *always* be twenty-one," Danté replied. "Even when you're dead."

"Dead! Who's got time for being dead?" Scout quipped, grabbing two beers from a waiter. Handing one to Danté, he held his own aloft. "This man has made over a hundred number one singles, just like his brother and parents, he has the world's famous in the palm of his hands on the internet, and ladies…" he glanced around at the onlookers, "and gents, if so inclined… He's still single. So, have at him, boys and girls."

A few woos went through the crowd and Danté couldn't help but blush. It wasn't just Nick who got on his case about being single at his age. It seemed to be everyone else as well. From co-workers to people he worked with, even his family occasionally got on his back about getting married. Or made jokes of *'well, when you're married you can have a say'*, or, *'you'll know what it's like when you get married, but until then'*, and he was sick of it. The two people who had never been on his case were his grandparents. Jenny had always told him the woman for him would come along when she was meant to, and then it would be on like Donkey Kong.

He smiled at the memory of the first time she'd told him that. 2018 at Tomas and Roger's legal wedding in Armidale, New South Wales. The whole family had planned for a year to be there and managed it, but at twenty-five, he'd been the only one in his family without a partner and realised that by the time he married and had kids, she and Spiros would more than likely be gone. He'd had a panic attack at that thought and needed help getting off stage, just to collapse in his grandmother's lap and sob all of his feelings to her. She'd soothed him, telling him if she was gone, then it would be her sending the right one along. And here he was, all these years later, almost forty, and still waiting for Ms Right. In the meantime, he needed to extricate himself from everyone's clutches.

"Thanks for the build-up, Scout, but I can hold my own. Right now, though, I need some air." He left them wanting more and managed to get back to the terrace where he could breathe. It was always tough, having people try and set you up, and he'd tried to hold on to the thought of the one walking into his life one day. But as the years had drifted by in a sea of work and nothing *but* work, regardless of all the people he'd meet in a year, there was just never…*the one*, the spark, the light, the fireworks in the night. He wanted what his grandparents, his parents, his uncles had, and he was tired of waiting for it.

Sighing, he straddled the terrace railing and looked up at the sky. *Maybe, if I get a shooting star, I'll get lucky*, he thought, and wondered if it was the same sky his Uncle Carlos had looked up to when he lived there in the '70s.

"Hello, Danté, I haven't had the chance to chat yet, my darling. How are you?" Aleesha Moore slid her hand across Danté's leg onto his crotch, desperate for the treasure she knew she'd find there.

"Aleesha." Danté picked up her hand and returned it to her. "How are you? Still hitting on me, I see. Even though you know I'm not interested."

"Because I'm a woman, or because I used to have a penis?" In one deft move, Aleesha swung her leg over both of Danté's and straddled him. "Hello, big boy."

Dante grabbed her hips and deposited her onto the railing. "I'm *not interested*, Aleesha." He swung his right leg over and sat facing the view, his back to the house. "How've you been?"

"Fantastically awesome." Aleesha slid closer. "You know I had a number one hit single from my blockbuster movie, right?"

"I heard, congratulations." Danté nodded and kept his hands on his legs, making sure his crotch was covered.

"It was all thanks to you and your brother and the fantastic work you both do." She leaned close to his ear. "How *is* Dominic?" seductively slipped out from between her lips.

"Still happily married with four children." Danté glanced her way. "But then, you *know* that."

"Yes, yes, he's married." She flapped a hand and huffed. "And so's your cousin, Cabot, that hot piece of golden-brown, blue-eyed ass. But not Antonio." Her voice softened. "How is he? We all heard here in L.A., New York, too. Oh, the poor thing. He must have been devastated. To lose a wife and then his mother. Oh, the poor boy."

"He was, it was, we're dealing," was all Danté said.

"Well, let's move on to better things. Have you heard the latest gossip?" Aleesha went on to talk about the latest scandals on the Hollywood scene. "Rumour has it, that model, Rumor Vormoor, is screwing hot doc to the fake plastic stars, Maddox Everton, who's *still* screwing that singing witch, Quinn Gatlin, who's *actually* married to producer Emmett Sanford, who's in a *gay relationship* with actor Blaze Stryker. And then you have that old fart studio head, Harrison York, sticking his withered old dick into hot young model slash actor slash singer Melisandre Knight, who's *also* screwing that up-and-coming actor Channing Ashton. I don't know whether she knows *he's* also screwing the lead singer of *King's Alliance*, Zayn Mace, but Zayn is *also* screwing *me*." Aleesha stopped to inhale.

"It sounds as complicated as it was back in the '70s and '80s," Danté told her. "Be careful you don't contract a disease that will become the next HIV." He spied Nick in the garden making out with two girls. "You don't happen to know the women with Nick, do you?" Nodding in their direction, he looked at Aleesha. "There are some people here I don't seem to know."

"Nicholas is here? I didn't see him. Where?" She squinted in their direction. "Oh…those two hussies. He better watch out. They've also been hitting on his two hot to trot brothers-in-law. Mmm, mmm, mmm…" Aleesha swung her legs over the railing and stood. "Those trollops are out for every man in L.A."

"Wait… What do you mean they're after his brothers-in-law?"

"As I said." Aleesha straightened her dress. "They've been hitting on every man in the state of California that can get them into movies, music, fame and fortune. They'll stop at nothing, and sometimes, a man will stop at nothing to get some action in return. Even a wife and kids. Be warned, my beautiful Danté." She slid her hands over his shoulders. "You'd better warn him and his sisters about those two. They're well-known amongst the crowd. Probably the ones spreading the STDs around, they've been with so many." Her hands moved down his back and around his waist to his crotch where he caught them. She sighed. "At least I tried."

"Bye, Aleesha." He released her and watched her walk back to the party, sashaying her hips as she went. Releasing a deep breath, he swung his legs around, grabbed a beer from a waiter, and walked off for the garden. It wasn't Nick he was heading for, but some peace and quiet.

The garden was as elaborate and decorative as the house, with marble statues and columns that framed a pool that was even more so. Marble mermaid and dolphin fountains sprayed water into the blue lake in arcs of colours, there was a spa to one side, and an in-pool bar and seating. The view of L.A. was spectacular, and he stood for a moment to take it all in; the bright lights and city view. He wondered if his uncle had ever been to that house, or whether it had even been around then. Wondered what it looked like back in the '70s and marvelled at how different it was today. He knew they still had Viv's house under the property portfolio, but Carlos' apartment had made way for a new beachside multiplex some years ago.

He also knew that his half-uncle, Alfonso DeVille, was still running the DeVille Empire and lived nearby with his family. "Maybe I should drop by and see Uncle Alfonso. Mama would love that." He chuckled at the still cool relationship his mother had with her half-brother after all these years, and continued on through the garden, thinking about how his grandmother had tried to patch the rift between the two by making Alfonso and his family honorary members. While Alfonso had bonded with everyone else, especially his nephews and nieces, it was Angie he still needed to connect on a deeper familial level with.

Finding his way back to the terrace, he heard the melodic singing coming from the living room, and since everyone was crowded in the house, or on the terrace, he sat on the railing to listen. With a musical ear, it was easy for him to know when a singer was off. But this one never missed a beat, and she had no music, just sang it purely on her own.

"I don't gamble… But I'm willing to roll the dice,
I don't want to walk… Down the painful road not to you,
In the mirror… Only a reflection of my pain,
Do I give in… Do I go on… I don't know if I can."

"Oooh, nice," Danté murmured, eyes closed, ears open and concentrating. He heard the perfect pitch and longevity on a note. "Very nice." Trying to recognise the voice, he found he couldn't. *Must be someone new on the scene and we haven't heard of them yet,* he thought.

"Shall I give in to the pain? Shall I give in to the ache?
Of lovin' not returned, Of lovin' not replaced,
Can I make it through the night? Can I get over the way,
You make me feel inside, I want lovin' through the night."

His head moved with the words flowing from her lips, like a conductor's baton as it waved in the air. *Perfect. Beautiful. Crystal clear. I wonder who it is.*

Needing to see who it was, he made his way through the enraptured crowd trying to catch a glimpse of the singer. She hit a high note and held it, sending murmurs speeding through the onlookers who quietly applauded. Danté stood stunned. *Not too many can hit a note that high; she must be operatically trained and that takes time.* He saw Nick with a woman attached to his waist watching in fascination, and fought his way to the spot everyone was looking. As he moved closer, people he knew parted for him, knowing he'd want to see for himself.

Scout saw him, nodded, and stepped aside so he had a view.

Standing in front of the fireplace, without microphone or spotlight, stood the most beautiful woman Danté had ever laid his eyes on.

Golden blonde hair framed delicate features and big blue eyes like a halo. Plump lips formed words as the voice of an angel sang them, and her gentle soft hands were clasped in front of her. Her eyes caught Danté's and she sang directly to him. *At* him. Her voice enveloped him and only him. No other sound existed except for her voice and a billion fireworks going off.

Dante was falling…

He listened to the ethereal angel in front of him and no one else. *Nothing* else. All he heard was her voice and fireworks.

The lighting from the fireplace and downlights framed her in an aura and she glowed with softness and purity. He couldn't take his eyes from her, couldn't if he wanted to. Wouldn't because he didn't want to.

"So here I am, A Lonely Conversation to this photograph of you,

And I'm wonderin' if ever, my dreams will come true,

I pray and hope and cry myself to sleep every night,

My Lonely Conversation, will it ever be right?"

She sang on until her voice drifted off with the last note, but her gaze did not break his until she moved. Seeing the rapturous attention, she blushed as thunderous applause flew around the room.

"Oh, thank you, thank you so much. But really, no need, thank you." Embarrassed, the young woman shyly glanced at Danté and moved off into the crowd.

"Well…what did you think of that, then?" Scout slapped him on the back as he looked from the woman's disappearing back to Danté's lovesick expression. "Captured your attention, I see. Figured she would. Maybe she'll be the next Stephanopoulos acquisition." Everyone who knew the family knew what tycoons they were. Whether property, IP, copyright, trade marks, they owned what they had and never sold it off. And sometimes, that included staff and celebrities who came to work with them. Once someone new went to Mykonos to meet the family, they were contracted for life.

"Funny, Scout. Who is she?" Danté murmured, his eyes trying to find her in the crowd.

"That's for you to find out, Danté." Scout pushed him in the general direction of the woman and grinned as a lovesick Danté kept on walking. "Ah, what a sucker," he muttered to those still standing around him.

Danté shuffled through the crowd, craning his neck to find her. He caught a glimpse of her blonde hair here and there and moved in that direction. Arriving at the spot, he found her gone and spun around to find her, catching her golden halo making its way to the terrace. He hurried through the crowd trying to keep her in sight, and finally made it through the French doors where he saw her standing at the railing by the side of the grand staircase leading down to the pool. He watched her for a moment.

Her hair shone in the moonlight, and her tiny frame barely came up to his nose in her stilettoes. She sipped delicately from her glass and glanced over her shoulder to see him. Ignoring him, she turned and slowly walked along the terrace.

Danté hurried after her. "Ah…hello…" was all he could manage.

She stopped a moment to coolly gaze up and down at him and then finally said, "Hello," before she continued, ignoring him once more.

"I…um…" Danté moved with her. "I heard you sing."

"Everyone in the house did," she replied, not bothering to look at him.

"Yeah, ah," he mumbled, embarrassed and as shy as a schoolboy. "I guess everyone did, but ah, how many would know you have perfect pitch and can hit a G10." He watched her stop, casually turn her head to him, and raise a brow.

"You clearly know something about music to know such things," she murmured, knowing full well who he was. Not that she was about to give that tidbit of information away.

"Yes, you could say I do." He walked with her as she moved on. "And you're clearly operatically trained, perfect, beautiful. You sing like an angel."

"Don't tell me." She stopped him by putting her hand in front of him. "I look like one too. Yeah, heard *that* pick-up line before." She knocked back her drink and gave the glass to a passing waiter. "I'm not interested in come-ons," she told Danté. "So take those back to where you came from." Continuing along the terrace, she was enjoying the repartee and hoped it continued.

Danté wasn't to be put off, especially when fireworks kept going off in his head, so he followed. "Do you have a label? Have you been contracted by anyone? Who wrote that song? I've never heard it before. You're new on the scene, so new no one's ever heard your voice before."

She turned to him. "Huh! You *do know* a little something about music. No, no one's ever heard my voice before. Yes, I've been contracted by a label. No, no one's heard that song before because I wrote it, lyrics and melody anyway as I don't play any instruments, but can write a tune. So, it's new."

"Are you recording, yet?" Danté noticed her eyes glittered like aquamarines in the soft lighting. "Do you have a producer?"

"Yes, I'm recording," she said almost defiantly. "And my producer is Scott Barrowman. I suppose you're going to tell me you know *him*, too." Crossing her arms, she waited with an arched brow.

"Ah…Scott…yes…he's…*good.*" Danté shrugged nonchalantly, hands in pockets to keep them from wandering.

The blonde raised her other brow. "Only good?"

"Scott…" Danté tried to gather the right words. "Scott's good at what he does. He can write lyrics, write music, play instruments, record, produce, he's *very* good at producing. But he *makes* music. He doesn't *create* it."

"There's a difference?" she asked. "As if *you'd* know." Walking on, she knew he'd follow. And he did.

"Yes, there's a difference." Danté fell into step beside her. "The difference is the emotion, the feelings, the power behind the lyrics, the music, the production. Scott bangs them out on a daily basis, but it's his business, so he doesn't take the time to put the emotion into it. When you write lyrics and come up with the music for it, you create something." He stopped and used his hands to demonstrate. "You write lyrics from your soul, your heart, your experiences, heartache and heartbreak, loneliness and happiness, sadness and fear and desperation. And when you add the melody and harmonies and varying parts, you have to feel that, too. If the music itself doesn't emote in the same way the lyrics do, then all you've got is a song. Not a piece of emotion. That's why *he* makes and *we* create. My parents taught me to play music, but *their* love for it made *me* love it, too. It's in my soul, in my *family's* soul, and that's why every piece we write has those emotions." His hands went to his heart. "You have to feel it in here to *create* it on paper and in sound. That's why we throw every ounce of emotion we have into what we create. And Scott just does it to make a buck and make a record label happy. We don't have those confines and it's worked out very well for us."

"Yes," the blonde murmured. "I see that. I said something similar to Scott last month. That I wanted my songs to have heart and soul and every ounce of emotion I could put into it. He laughed and told me he wasn't paid to feel, just paid to write hits." A small frowned crossed her face. "It saddened me because that's what the label told me they wanted for me. My heart and soul when I sang. But they actually just want me popping out hits as soon as possible." A sigh left her. "So far, in this business, I haven't found anyone who thinks the way I do." Gazing up into the dark pools that were his eyes, she found herself drowning. "It's good to know someone does. Considering this is Los Angeles, Hollywood. The place where dreams are made. But then, so many people here are all after the same dream."

"It's not the only place where dreams are made," Danté told her. "There's New York, London, Mykonos. It hasn't *just* been L.A. in a good couple of decades."

"Maybe, but I'm lucky." She walked on; her arms crossed to ward off the chill drifting across her breasts. "I spent ten years training with my singing, learning every technique and trick I could. I looked after myself, kept myself thin, blonde, beautiful, and finally, someone saw me and took a chance on me. Which is surprising." She stopped again. "But it's not surprising that they want me to lie about my age because *apparently,*

I'm over the hill already."

"What are you? Twenty-five, twenty-eight?" Danté studied her features the best he could in the moonlight.

"Why, aren't you sweet," she drawled. "They want me to say twenty-five, but I'm actually thirty."

"Nothing wrong with that. My sister was still singing and touring at thirty, even at forty she was still singing."

"Does she still?"

"No, not professionally." Danté watched her rosebud lips. "Stopped at forty-five, so she could take on more of the business side of things. Her daughters are getting into singing, fashion, too. I think her boys will be into music as well."

"And…*your*…children?" the blonde murmured seductively, hoping he was going to say what she wanted to hear. Even though all reports had Danté as single, she didn't want to take any chances.

Danté's eyes slowly blinked, realising she must know who he was. "I'm yet to be a father." Watching her closely, he waited.

"But when you do, they will no doubt take after you and go into the business as well."

"Well, since *you* know my business, you know what we do. We are a family, after all." Considering that Scout had all but shouted his presence at the party, it was a safe bet she knew who he was. His lips smiled slightly. "It seems I'm at a disadvantage. You know who I am, but I have no idea who you are." Extending a hand for her to shake, he added, "Danté Stephanopoulos."

With a smile of her own, she said, "I know who you are. Everyone at the party already did the introduction." She was interrupted by her phone buzzing, and pulling it out of her clutch, she checked to see what it was. "I need to go. It was nice talking to you." Hurrying back to the party, she made her way through the house and out the front door.

Stunned, Danté took a moment to realise she'd left him and rushed after her.

"What's the rush? You leaving?" Nick stopped him with a hand on his chest.

"Did you see the blonde who sang before? Where'd she go?" Danté quickly scanned the room.

"I think she was headed for the door…hey!" Nick watched his friend race off and frowned. "Wonder what's gotten inta him?"

Danté made it to the entrance and down the steps in time to see her preparing to step into a 1963 silver Chevrolet Corvette Stingray. "Hey, we didn't finish our conversation."

Glancing up at his voice, she grinned. "Sorry, I have to go. If I'm not home by midnight I turn into a scullery maid." She slid into her car, and the attendant shut the door.

Danté raced over and planted both hands on the door. "And does your car turn into a pumpkin?"

Her grin grew larger. "It might." Gunning the engine, she let it roll forward.

"Wait." Danté grabbed the door. "You didn't tell me your name."

"Why do you need to know?" She watched him hurry alongside the car.

"Because I do." Danté held onto the car and tried to stop it, his feet skidding on the gravel. "Please."

"How badly do you want it?" She stepped on the gas a little and the car moved faster.

"Very." Danté ran for the front of the car and threw himself on the hood. He didn't know why, had never done anything like it in his life, but he also knew he couldn't let this woman drive out of it.

"Oh, my God." She hit the brake.

He slid off and the car stopped on top of him.

"Oh, no." She pulled the handbrake, put it in park, and ran around to the front of her car to find Danté lying flat on his back with the lower half of his body underneath. "Oh, my God, are you okay? You're not dead, are you? Oh, no. I've killed a Stefan, the family's going to kill me. You guys are like Greek royalty or something. Oh, my God, I can't believe I just did that. Say something. Are you dead?" She slapped his face until his eyes opened.

"I've never been slapped by a woman before," Danté murmured drowsily. He'd hit his head on the driveway and was a bit dazed. "Or been run over."

"You wouldn't've been if you hadn't jumped on my hood." She

helped him from under the vehicle. "Are you okay? You're not hurt, are you? I suppose I'll be in big trouble if you are." Brushing him down for a few moments, she stopped in surprise at her actions and backed up a couple of steps.

"Why would you be in trouble?" he asked, watching her closely. "I was the stupid one. And…you know…we're *not* Greek royalty." He saw her blush and become embarrassed. "You definitely know more about me and my family than I do about you." Rubbing the back of his head and feeling bits of gravel, he brushed it out. "*But* I'd like to know about *you.*" God, he found it so hard to hit on a woman.

"Like what?" she asked nervously.

"Like your *name*, for a start." He grinned to soften the moment.

"Oh, *that.*" She managed a grin in return and felt her nerves ease a little. "It's Michelline. Michelline Volmeyer."

Extending his hand, he took a step forward. "Hello, Michelline, I'm Danté."

She took a step forward and shook his hand. A million bolts of electricity fled through her, leaving her breathless. "Hello…"

"Hello…" Danté breathed in shakily. His stomach clenched and unclenched, knotting itself into a mess before releasing. "Hello…"

"Um…" She pulled her hand away and looked everywhere but at him. "I gotta go. I'm glad you're okay." Hurrying back to the driver's side, she slid in behind the wheel and shut her door.

Not to be left behind a second time, Danté did another thing he'd never done before. He jumped into the passenger seat. "Where are we going?"

"What!" Surprised, Michelline could only stare at him. "But you, but I—"

"Are going to finish telling me what you were going to tell me before," he replied.

"But I…need to…get home." Michelline had never experienced a guy jumping on her hood, or into her car before. Sure, plenty of guys had hit on her and tried to get it on, just not in these ways.

"Or you'll turn into a scullery maid, right?" Danté laughed. "I'd like to see that. You'd make a beautiful scullery maid."

"Ah…" Blushing, Michelline gripped the steering wheel. "No, I won't, but I *do* have to be at the studio tomorrow and need a good night's rest."

"What time do you need to be there?" Danté saw that seatbelts were installed in the car and strapped his on.

"Not until one or so." She put the car in drive, released the handbrake and let it roll.

"Good. We still have a good couple of hours," he replied.

"For what?" Stepping on the accelerator, she headed off down the driveway.

"For talking." He checked his watch. It was only ten p.m.

"Oh…*talking.*" She smirked. "Is that what *you* call it?"

"Don't you?" Danté watched her as she drove. "You know what it is, don't you? The exact thing we're doing now. Talking."

A giggle escaped her. "Yeah, *talking.* I get it now." She drove on in silence, winding her way down mountain roads and through the city until she reached the beach. Driving along her street, she turned into the driveway of a house and rolled to a stop. "I think the car's about to turn into a pumpkin. I, ah, suppose I'm supposed to invite you in." She couldn't look at him because it made her heart do flips flops, something it had already been doing the whole car ride. And it wasn't as if she hadn't had boyfriends, but Danté Stephanopoulos was an entirely different breed of man. As in a *man, not* a boy.

"Please do." Danté laughed and ran around to open her door. "I recognize this street and house number, funnily enough. I'm a bit shocked that you live here."

"Oh, I don't live here, the studio is renting it for me. It's not like I could afford something so nice." She daintily slid out of the car and stood. "Well, I guess I *do* live here, but it's not mine. Definitely not mine." She nervously fumbled for the house key. "Why do you recognize the street name and number?"

"Because that duplex there…" Danté pointed to the building next door. "Used to be a smaller apartment building my uncle had a place in. Owned it since the late '70s. Sold it off about ten, or so, years ago."

"Oh, really." She started for the front door. "And which uncle is that?"

"Carlos." Danté stopped behind her as she tried to unlock the door, and when she dropped the keys, he quickly bent down to retrieve them. "Let me," he breathed in her right ear and inserted the key into the lock. She came up to his nose in her heels, but he didn't mind the height difference. He quite liked the fact she was smaller in stature.

"Oh…thank you," she barely managed through the heady, giddy feelings and opened the door. Flicking on the lights, she deposited her bag and shoes by the table beside the door and hurried into the kitchen where she poured herself a stiff vodka, knocking it back in record time.

Danté locked the door and followed, noticing the elegant furnishings and wall art. "Nice. The label's paying for this?"

"Yes," she gasped and paused before pouring herself another drink. "Want one?"

"No, thanks. Unless you got beer." He watched her dig through the fridge for one and hand it over. "Do you have decent outside lights? The beach view must be spectacular."

"Um, yeah. Yeah, I do." At five-one in bare feet, she padded her way to the French doors, flicked a few buttons on the wall beside them, and not only did they open, but the backyard lights came on showing off a rectangular pool with waterfall, and a barbecue area with patio seating.

"Nice." Danté followed her out and breathed in the air. "Very nice. So…Michelline, what's your contract like?" He watched her swig back half the bottle she'd brought out with her.

"My contract?" she spluttered on the vodka.

"Your recording contract," Danté smoothly replied. "How many are you signed up for? What genre? What's the time limit for release?"

"Ummm." Michelline tried to recall the details. "One album, pop, six months."

"Okay, that's good. Not tied down." Danté thought his way through things.

"Tied down to what?" Curious, she stepped closer. "Do you think they did me a dud deal? Have I been ripped off?" Her blood started bubbling under her skin along with the alcohol.

"Not necessarily," Danté said. "But a lot of labels don't always give their new stars the best deal. They own you for the duration, and once it ends you can't go anywhere else for a year or two, and they won't let you out early if the record's a flop. We've seen it all pass through our doors with the people we've worked with."

"Worked with a lot, huh?" She sidled closer, her nerves slipping away. "All the *big* names."

"Of course." Danté watched her eyes eagerly race over him. "From my father and mother in the '80s, to myself and my brother. We've worked with many famous musicians, singers, bands. Some actors as well when writing the score for a movie." He watched her take another step and took a swig of beer.

"What's it like?" Her voice came out soft and small.

"What?"

"Being in a family like that. The wealth, the privilege, the heritage." Her voice took on a slightly snarky tone. "Must be *so* nice to not have to worry about where your next meal is coming from, or rent money, or—"

"We never had it easy," Danté's tone hardened and he stopped leaning against the railing. It was the one lie he was sick and tired of dealing with. "My grandparents were hard workers who slogged their guts out to pay their way through life. They taught my father and uncles the same rules. Work hard and you'll earn your way. They just happened to be lucky enough to receive an inheritance from Grandpa's dead relative and make something out of it. They *all* worked hard at their jobs and careers and taught us the same values."

He slammed his bottle down on the outdoor table. "That's the *one thing* above *all else* that pisses me off. That regardless of all the articles we've done over the last thirty-plus years about how hard we've worked to build our family company; someone will *always* assume we grew up with silver spoons in our mouths." He paced back and forth, his hands gesturing with his words. "We didn't. *None* of us did. *We* didn't, our *parents* didn't, our *grandparents* didn't. My mother spent four years at Juilliard after *earning* her way in, and regardless of the fact she inherited her father's estate upon his death she *never* touched it until 2007 to help fund my sister's assault centre. *That's* what the family money goes to. Doing good for the community by helping other people. *Not* ourselves."

Breathing hard, he rested his hands on the terrace railing. "We never took one cent of it for ourselves, and although our grandmother started trust funds for us all, we've all worked damn hard to make something of ourselves and rarely touched a cent of it. Most of it goes into our charities to benefit others. And I wish every-fucking-body on this planet would get that."

Silence followed, but the waves crashing on the beach broke into it.

"I'm sorry. I was just…" Michelline couldn't find the words to tell him. She was just being bitchy because he had money and didn't have to struggle, or want, for anything, and she did.

"And just because the family has money and *so-called* privilege, it doesn't stop us from dealing with everyday shit like everyone else," Danté told her, staring hard into her glossy blue eyes. "My uncle died in 1981 long before I was born, but Grandma's love and determination brought him back. *I* was nearly killed by a shark in 2007 after my sister was raped, and my cousin was assaulted and contracted HIV. In 2012 Alena nearly died in a plane crash while on tour, and Antonio and his wife were nearly killed in a car crash on their honeymoon, which I guess was prophetic as that's the way she was killed last year. My cousin Diana and her family were nearly lost in an avalanche in 2015, and I nearly lost my brother in the London bombing in 2017. I've lost my grandparents to old age, and my aunt to an illness. So, don't you *dare* fucking talk to me about privilege because of money. *We damn well fucking earned it.*"

After storming down the stairs and around the pool, he stood staring out at the ocean, listening to the waves crash in time with the pounding ache in his head. He'd loved the ocean as a kid, but the shark attack had made him hate it. Rubbing his leg, which still periodically ached, he breathed in the salty scent wafting on the breeze. After years of therapy, he'd ventured back into the water over a period of time, but still didn't go out into the bays of Mykonos, just stayed near the shore. And if they went out on the family yacht, he stayed on board and kept an eye out for sharks to protect his family which now consisted of five nieces, six nephews, and seven second cousins. The family had grown considerably.

"I'm sorry."

Turning his head towards the voice, he saw that she meant it. "I'm sorry if you had a hard life. Most people do. But while my parents had no mortgage and could buy food and pay their bills, it was because they worked damn hard for it. We *all* have. My IT business didn't happen overnight. Being a DJ and producer, or writer, didn't happen overnight. It took *years* of learning and practice and educating ourselves. Pushing ourselves to *be* better, to *learn* the next new thing that came along. We worked *damn hard* and went without."

"Without what?" Michelline asked, her blood tingling in her veins. "What did *any* of you go without while working damn hard? You had your grandparents, your parents, your siblings and cousins. A roof over your head, food on the table, a job to go into. *Your* family owns a music studio and nightclub."

"Which we built and started from the ground up," Danté snapped.

"But *you* still had it in the family to go into. That was your parents and grandparents, but all of you kids had it to walk straight into. You've never had to look for a job in your life. Never had to wonder where your next paycheque was coming from, or if all of the years you'd put into learning your craft was even going to pay off. What the hell have you gone without, you privileged brat? You've got it made and I barely managed to get myself a contract. What the hell have you had to go without in your life?" Her breath came hard and fast and she stood panting and wiping her mouth, ashamed and embarrassed that she could think those types of things, let alone say them. Especially about him.

Danté stepped over to her, took her face in his hands, and kissed her as passionately and endlessly as he'd ever kissed a woman. Fireworks blasted in his head, and when he was finished he gazed into her stunned aquamarine eyes and breathed one word.

"You."

"What," whispered out of her stunned mouth.

"I've gone without you." Danté held onto her, staring into her eyes. "All of my adult life I wondered if and when I would ever find *the one.* Like my siblings, cousins, parents, uncles and grandparents before me. When was *I* going to be lucky enough to find *my* soulmate? The one that made fireworks go off in my head. The one who I would fall in love at first sight with, the one who would make my heart thunder like a horse's hooves on dry arid soil. I've waited for all of those feelings all of my life and it took until tonight to happen." Leaning over her, her body falling into his, he breathed her in. "Have you ever fallen in love at first sight? Heard a billion fireworks go off in your head when you kissed them?"

"Yes," she whispered clutching his arms and rising on her toes. "You." Lightheaded, she was drunk on vodka, lust, and love. Yes, she'd known who he was, and yes, she'd been attracted to him. But she hadn't been expecting fireworks to explode before her eyes. No man had ever given her that reaction. Danté was the first. And something in her soul told her, the last.

Drowning in the sea of her eyes, he lowered his head and kissed her. Gently, softly, his lips played with hers until his tongue was ready to sneak out and taste the angel it had in its grasp.

Her tongue toyed with his, but unable to hold back for long, and with a desire and passion she'd never known, she clawed her way up until her arms were around his neck and his around her body.

They didn't let go. Tongues tasted, arms and legs wrapped around each other, and they fell onto a poolside lounge in heat.

Hours later, they lay listening to the ocean waves, a wayward towel draped over their lower bodies as the late-night air caressed their hot flesh.

Danté's fingers gently stroked her face as she curled into his side. "I'm sorry," he whispered, drawing in her angelic beauty.

She tilted her head to look at him. "For what?"

"Hurting you."

Puzzled, she said, "You didn't."

"My…length, can sometimes be too much for women. I thought at one point, with the noises you were making, that I'd hurt you." Hurting a woman was the last thing on his mind, and something he'd been raised to never do.

She giggled softly and snuggled into his side. "No. You didn't hurt me. Those were sex noises, you know. The grunts and groans and sighs you make when you're having an orgasm." Everything felt right in Danté's arms. The world had shifted into the right position, and all worries had slipped away. If just for a while.

"Yes…I do realise that." Danté's deep voice was soft. "I just happen to have genes that make me larger than the average man."

"You certainly do." She nestled her face into his chest, rubbing her cheek against the soft hair spread evenly across the muscular torso. "I've never had a man as big as you, but it didn't cause any issues, so don't worry. I'm fine." Kissing his chest, she slid fully onto him. "In fact, I could do that again. How 'bout you?" Gazing into his dark eyes, she brought her knees up and straddled him. Her lips toyed with his, her hands roamed and explored and he reciprocated.

Bringing his knees up, he lifted her onto his ten inches and mated with her fully. His tongue with hers. His body with hers. His soul with hers. She was the one. He knew that in every fibre of his being, so did his body, which took what it wanted from her and gave it back ten-fold.

"Ugh." Her head fell back as she came and kept coming. His penis did things to her insides no other penis had done. Her hands tangled in his hair, his mouth ravished her skin, her neck, her breasts, so full and ripe. She shuddered and collapsed into his arms.

"Oh, God," he gasped, holding her against his chest. "Oh, God, I love you. How the hell can I love someone I've only just met as much as I love you right now? How? It's just not possible. And yet it's what I've been waiting for my entire life. This. This moment, these feelings and emotions. It's all just fallen into place." His eyes took in the starlit sky. "It's all just happened in one brilliant moment."

Breathing deeply, Michelline rested against him, listening to his heart beat to its own rhythm, and realised that hers was beating in time. Two hearts beating in just one time. Relaxing her muscles, she thought about all of the men she'd dated, had relationships with, and realised that none of them had ever made her feel this way. Regardless of how much she had known about Danté Stephanopoulos before, nothing had prepared her for the emotions she was having now.

"I've never been in love like this before," Danté murmured. "It's weird."

Michelline raised her head. "What do you *mean* weird?"

He grinned softly and kissed her forehead. "It's weird how you can go through life having relationships, thinking you're in love, having feelings of love, but then boom, one day it can hit you in the face like a tonne of bricks and you can truly fall head over heels in love. Love like you've never felt before love. Love like you've never experienced before love. A once in a lifetime love that very few people get to feel or experience."

"I like the sound of that." Micheline's fingers lazily slid up and down his arm and torso. "I like the sound of it so much I think I'm actually experiencing it."

"Good. Because I can't be the only one feeling this way." Danté cupped her face and looked into her eyes. "If I'm the only one feeling this, then it's not going to happen if you're not—"

"No, I am, I am." She quickly shifted, so her face was in front of his. "I am, it's just, that it's all so new and I've never felt this way before, or so quickly…" Her voice trailed off as she tried to find the words.

"This has happened so quickly that you're lost for words and not sure what happens next," Danté said. "Because I'm not quite sure, either."

Her giggle was soft and light. "Exactly. I mean, I know *who* you are, but probably should get to know you. And you've just met me. I suppose we should actually tell each other about ourselves and get to know one another."

"Even though it's love at first sight?" he inquired. "Because I know that I'm in love with you with every fibre of my being." His gaze probed hers. "I *know* that I'm in love with you. I *know* you're the one for me. I *know* I want no one else. How many times does one get to know these things? How many people get to experience it? Very few."

"Everyone in your family," she murmured, melting into his eyes. "I've read the stories."

"Oh, I'm sure you have; so's half the planet." A grin lit up Danté's lips. "I love you. Is it okay if I say that? Because if you don't feel the same—"

"Oh, I do," she interjected and kissed him. "Oh, how I do." Pausing a moment, her smile matched his. "I just think we need to get to know each other on every other level."

"Every other level than what?" he cheekily asked.

"Every other level than sexual," she replied. "Not that I'm *not* loving *this* level. It's just—"

"Good!" Danté rolled her over so he was on top, making her squeal in glee. "Because I'm *really loving* this level."

*****

"You're what?" Nick asked the next day. "What do you *mean* you're staying here in L.A.?"

"Just that." Danté picked up half of his grilled steak sandwich. "I'm staying here another couple of weeks. Not much point me being home right now." Taking a bite, he savoured the flavours. A grilled sandwich from *Fernando's* was something he had every time he was in town. With the best meats, healthiest of ingredients, the bread as soft and light as a feather, everyone in town was after a *Fernando's* grilled sandwich.

"Is it the blonde from last night? The one you ran after. You lovesick?" Nick swigged on his beer and studied Danté's face while he ate. He knew, like the entire family did, when one of them was lovesick. And Danté had the illness.

"Yep." Danté wiped his mouth and took a long swallow of ice-cold water. "She's the one."

"One what?" Nick sat back and waited.

"*The* one," Danté replied and took another bite.

"The one, one?" Nick's brows rose. "As in, love, love? The one, one?"

Another swallow and a nod of his head. Danté replied, "Yep, *that* one."

"You're fucking kidding me!" Nick slammed his bottle onto the table and leaned forward. "*Are you* fucking kidding me? You mean you've actually met *the one*. The blonde from last night? The one that sang and you ran after?"

"That's the one." Danté finished off his water and ordered another one. "Her name is Michelline Volmeyer. She's thirty, and under contract with a label for a pop record."

"Is that all you know, or did you talk all night?"

"Oh…" Danté paused with the other half of his sandwich at his lips. "We definitely *talked* all night." With a sly grin, he bit into his food.

"Oh, you *dirty* dog." Nick shook his head and huffed. "You fucked a complete stranger all night."

"Something *you've* done yourself multiple times, so get off your high horse," Danté reminded him.

Sighing, Nick rested his chin in his hand. "Yeah, yeah. But that's *me*. I didn't expect it out of *you*. Did you actually bother to learn anything about her?"

"I know she's a pocket rocket, has porcelain skin, and a tiny butterfly tattoo."

"Where?"

"Where's none of your business." Danté's grin slid back into place. "And you'll never find out." Finishing off his food, he wiped his hands and mouth and sat back.

"You're in love, aren't you?" Nick studied him. "And I *mean really* in love. Truly, madly, deeply, impossibly in love."

"The love my grandma had with my grandpa kind of love," Danté replied. "We having dessert?" He drank a mouthful of water and looked for the waiter.

"That strong, huh?" Nick had heard the story of Spiros and Jenny countless times in his life and knew their love was legendary. All of the Stephanopoulos kids and grandkids lived on in their own version, and he hoped one day it would rub off on him.

"*That* strong." Danté sighed and sat back, his mind wandering back to last night and that morning. "We woke up in each other's arms to the sound of the waves crashing on the beach, and a new day just beginning. And I knew, just like last night, that she's the one for me. The one Grandma told me would come along when the time was right. And she did. Valentine's may have become a shitty day in my family, but for me, it's brought nothing but joy and love and happiness." Shaking his head at the devastation of the last few years, he breathed slowly to stop the flow of tears. "Let's hope we can bring back some happiness to the family. Stella's having her baby this year, and I've met the woman I want to spend the rest of my life with."

"You sound definite about that." Nick moved back as the waiter set down a plate with a huge piece of chocolate cake in front of him.

"Oh, I am." Danté eyed his own chocolate mousse cake. "As definite as I am about inhaling this cake. And you know I'm not one for desserts these days."

"Only because your grandma's not around to make them." Nick sliced off a piece of cake and ate it. "She made the best cakes and desserts."

"She did. And it still sucks that she's gone. And sucks even worse that no one can make a cake like she could." Danté grinned softly. "Not even Uncle T and Roger. They try, but just can't quite get it to taste the same."

"They're pretty damn good, though. And didn't Tomas learn from your grandma?"

"He did, and so did Roger. And they taught Tony and Cabot, and they're all good, but not as good as Grandma. It never had her special ingredient."

"Which was?"

Danté paused a moment as sadness poured through him. "Her love." Tears sprang to his eyes and he set down his fork to take a moment. "Ahh, it still hurts," he whispered and he closed his eyes for a moment.

"It would. Your grandma was everything. The glue that held the family together." Nick watched Danté while he gathered himself. "What would she think of Michelline?"

"I think she would love her. Which is why I think she sent her to me." After having a quick drink, Danté took another bite of cake.

Nick laughed. "You think your grandma did what?"

Nodding, Danté went on to tell him about the conversation he'd had with Jenny at Tomas and Roger's Armidale wedding. He'd never spoken in depth about it, just the few words mentioned at the time, so this was the first time Nick was finding out.

"Wow." Nick's brows rose. "*That's* the conversation you two had? You were backstage for ages. Even Aunt Angie started freaking out that you were gone for so long."

"Yeah, well, I was freaking out backstage after my panic attack. It just suddenly hit me that they could be gone by the time I married and had kids, and they would never get to see them. And they won't." He blinked back tears and breathed slowly. His grandmother's passing still hurt like hell four years on.

"What's the family going to think?" Nick asked softly.

"That I'm bat shit crazy." A soft smile slid across Danté's lips. "But no, they'll probably be happy for me once they see how in love I am. It's not like *their* marriages didn't happen quickly after meeting. Like Antonio's and Maria's." A subdued calm moved over them.

Nick kept his tone light. "How is he?"

"Not good." Danté took a deep breath and slowly let it out. "Which is understandable. It was a rough year on him and the girls, and then Aunt Viv died, and then Christmas and New Year's, Valentine's, and now it's March next month. Aunt Viv's birthday and the first anniversary of Maria's death, and then it would've been their twenty-first anniversary in May, along with Grandma's birthday and wedding anniversary…" He sighed. "He and Uncle Carlos are both suffering."

"I heard he'd taken to drinking," Nick said quietly.

"Yeah. But Cabot and Tony are getting in there to help. So are Diana and Papa and Uncle T. They're all trying to pull them through. We also think Izabella's doing drugs."

Nick inhaled sharply and frowned. "That's not good."

"No." Danté slid his fork into the last bite of mousse cake. "If Grandma was here she'd probably deal with it the same way she dealt with Cabot way back when. So, I guess that's what they'll do now." He raised the fork to his mouth. "Get her help." They finished up and paid the bill before walking out into the February sunshine. It may have been California, but even L.A. got a chill in the air in winter.

"Have you decided what's going to happen? Are you spending the next couple of weeks with her?" Nick asked as they climbed into their car after the attendant collected it for them. "I know we've finished our business, but we still need to work. Where to now?"

"Ah…I might pop into the studio to see Michelline. As for work, I know you'll take care of things, and we do have a manager. Take some time off for yourself. Are you seeing your sisters while you're here? Oh, that reminds me." Danté snapped his fingers. "Aleesha told me the two blondes you were making out with last night have also been hitting on your brothers-in-law. I'd watch out for them if I were you."

"My sisters, or my brothers-in-law?" Nick drove off down the street. "Where's the studio?"

"On West. *Uptown Records*," Danté replied. "And both. The girls, apparently, are getting around to all the men who can get them anywhere in life. Let your sisters know and keep an eye on Thomas and Richard. I wouldn't want them cheating on your sisters. You'd kill them."

Summer and Melody had married blockbuster action star twins To and Ro Morrow back in 2019. They had lived in L.A. down the road from the Stephanopoulos residence, side by side in matching mansions, ever since. As twins married to twins for fourteen years with three children each, their husbands still wanted to do everything together and live their lives as a mirror image. Matching wives, houses, cars, toys, you name it, they had it or did it. And thanks to Carlos making their first twenty movies before they moved onto doing everything themselves, including promoting every item they could think of as part of their branding, the boys had reached billionaire status in 2030.

"I certainly would. I'm as fiercely loyal to them as you are to yours. So, yeah, I'd kill them." Nick plugged in the GPS and slipped through traffic. "Do I get to meet the infamous Michelline, or am I just meant to drop you off and leave?"

Danté shrugged. "It's up to you. She has a car and can give me a lift home like she did this morning."

"You may as well just pack your bags and move in with her," Nick teased. "Is that an overnight bag you brought with you?"

"Yeah…" Danté trailed off as he thought about it.

"It would save you coming back and forth. We're up in the hills, and she's down the beach."

"Yeah, funny that." Danté frowned. "After Aunt Viv died, Uncle Carlos didn't want any of us staying in the house. We managed to buy the house next to it to use as our base, so they were in close proximity. And then I find out Micheline's staying next to the place Uncle Carlos used to have. Weird."

"Yep," Nick muttered. "Weird how things end up."

"Mmm…" Danté wandered off in thought until they pulled to a stop outside of *Uptown Records* and he came back to reality. "We here already?"

"We are, and I'm coming in to meet her." Nick collected his phone and wallet before getting out.

"Just don't stay long," Danté said, seeing Michelline's car. "I'll go home with her."

"*Of course* you will." Nick snickered. "Don't forget your bag."

Danté rolled his eyes and led the way into the studio where he removed his sunglasses to allow his vision to adjust.

"Ah, Danté Stephanopoulos, good to see you. What are you doing here?" Head honcho, and manager of the studio, Mike Telford, stepped forward to shake hands.

"Here to see Michelline Volmeyer." Danté extended his hand. "Good to see you, Mike. How've you been?"

"Good, good. And the family? We've all heard about your family's tragic passings."

"We're coping, thanks, Mike." Danté never said much when people offered their condolences. It wasn't his place to talk for the whole family. That was his father's and uncles' job, so he kept his replies simple. "What studio is she in?"

"Number four. Nick." Mike nodded. "Good to see you."

"Mike." Nick shook hands and followed Danté down the hall to studio four.

Danté quietly slipped into the room and stopped to listen to her sing in the booth. It was as hauntingly angelic as the night before.

"We need more sound to it. Step it up a notch," Scott Barrowman said into his mic so she could hear.

"No, you don't," Danté said. "It's perfect as is and should be kept that way." His eyes hadn't left her the whole time.

Scott spun around at the intrusion. "Danté Stephanopoulos," he muttered, and upon seeing Nick, added, "And the boy wonder. What brings you by?" He didn't need Danté in his recording studio telling him how to produce. Even though he liked the kid and his brother and parents, he just didn't like being shown up. *Or* told what to do as he'd been doing it a good thirty years of his life.

"We came to see Michelline and hear some of the album, if the tracks are down." Danté knew Scott's rep and was nonplussed. "Care to share?"

"Sure, we can play you a track or two." Scott casually sat back and saw Danté's eyes never leave Michelline. "How long have you two known each other?"

"They met last night," Nick offered when Danté didn't speak. "I haven't met her yet."

"Are we taking a break?" Michelline asked and removed her headphones before walking out of the booth. "Hey." Her eyes never left Danté.

"Hey," he replied, a small smile playing on his lips.

"Danté here wants to listen to a few tracks," Scott told her. "Care for him to listen?"

"Sure, why not. Then he can hear how they sound." She raised her brow at Danté. They'd talked a lot about her music the night before and how she wasn't happy with it.

He noticed the signal she was sending and nodded. "Yes, I'd love to hear some."

Nick rolled his eyes and stepped between them. "Hey, I'm Nick Gatos, Danté's best friend and business partner. I was at the party last night, but we didn't get to meet."

Michelline blinked at him a couple of times and smiled. "Hello. It was an interesting party, wasn't it?" Her gaze travelled around him back to Danté.

"And you clearly don't care. Okay, Scott, you were putting some songs on." Nick left the two lovebirds to it and flopped down on the couch against the back wall.

Three songs later, Danté nodded. "That's definitely your work, Scott."

"Meaning?" Scott asked. "*My* work makes money."

Danté gave a one-shouldered nonchalant shrug. "My work makes more. You're like Stock, Aitken and Waterman from the '80s. Every song sounds the same. Different title and lyrics, but they all sound the same. It's a formula, but formulas don't always need to happen. Sometimes you can make it up as you go along."

Scott bristled, but kept his temper in check. "But that doesn't always make bank."

"If that's all you're worried about," Danté replied casually, not wanting to get into a fight. "I just think, after hearing her voice, that it's not being used to its full potential."

Michelline nodded in agreement, hoping Dante's words would knock some sense into Scott.

"Potential or not, that's not what the label wants, and I'm just here to give them what they want." Ending the discussion, Scott turned his chair around to face the mixing desk, leaving his back to them. "Don't you have somewhere to be?"

Danté shook his head and indicated to Michelline to leave the studio. "Come on, Nick. I know when I'm not wanted."

"I'm just going to the ladies' since we're taking a break. I'm busting." Michelline grabbed her bag and hurried into the hallway with Danté and Nick behind her.

Walking back to the foyer, Danté said, "There's no point me sticking around, so I'm going to go as it looks like it'll be a long day. Give me your house key and I'll get Nick to drop me off."

"Sure." She hastily pulled it off her keyring. "I don't know how long I'll be, but he'll probably keep me longer now."

"Don't let him. He sits on his arse recording while you're doing all the hard work. Tell him you're leaving at ten and then make sure you do. An artist has to rest her gift." He bent down and kissed her, hearing fireworks popping in his head. "I'll see you tonight. I love you."

"Love you, too." Michelline stared dreamily at Danté.

"Love you, too," Nick mocked. "Come on, dude, time to go." He grabbed Danté by the shoulders and directed him to the front door. "Bye, Danté's future wife."

Her eyes widened in shock.

"What! Why would you say that?" Danté chastised Nick as they left and got into the car. "Why would you…? How could you…? Jesus, Nick!"

"Oh, please. Don't tell me she's *not* going to be. With the way you've gone on about her, it's a safe bet your wedding will happen by the end of the year. Now, where to?"

"Yeah, but it's not something we've discussed, yet." Danté yanked on his seatbelt.

"Why? Because you only just met her last night?" Nick retorted and pulled onto the road. "Face it. If she's the one you've been waiting for, then a wedding's going to happen. Now, *where* to?"

"Yes, but we're still getting to know each other."

"Fucking can help with that."

Danté sighed. "Nicholas, are you jealous?"

"Fuck yes!" he exclaimed. "She's fucking gorgeous, sings like an angel, nice tits and ass, and *you* fucking get her. *And* fucked her, you bastard. *Where to*?"

"You'll find yourself a woman one day. Maybe you just need to stop looking and she'll walk into your life, but for now, Michelline has walked into mine and yes, she's the one I want in my life for *the rest* of my life. And yes, we will more than likely get married—"

"It's *more* than likely," Nick cut in.

"Well, okay, yes, it will happen at some point," Danté conceded. "But *right now* we need to get the feel of each other, and find out what the other wants, and whether she wants me as her life partner as I do her."

"*Or* you just keep fucking each other's brains out until you realise you're made for each other. But seriously, when's the wedding? 'Cause you know what that means."

Resigned, Danté sighed again. "What?"

"That I beat out Dom for best man!"

*****

"Hey, I'm home." Michelline closed her front door, kicked off her shoes, dumped her bag, and walked into the kitchen to find a chilled bottle of wine and Danté cooking. "Ooh, nothing heavy. I can't eat heavy stuff this late."

"It's not heavy." Danté switched off the cooktop and removed two bowls of salad from the fridge. "I was just sautéing some bacon and pine nuts. It's just a salad and chilled wine. Unless you don't want that either."

"Oh, no, I *definitely* want that." She slid onto a bar-stool at the island bench and sighed.

"He give you a hard time after we left?" Danté popped the cork and poured two glasses. "I wondered if he might."

"Oh, *he did*." Michelline accepted her glass, knocked it back and held it out for a refill. Seeing his surprised expression as he poured, she smiled wryly. "I got the Spanish Inquisition. *When* did you meet, *where* did you meet, *how much* did you tell him, are you planning on leaving your contract for *Sync*."

"Not that any of that's *his* business." Danté sprinkled the bacon and nuts onto the salad. "Where do you want to eat?"

"Oh…" She exhaled and looked around. "On the sofa. I just want to curl up."

"Then you grab the glasses and the bottle; I'll bring the salads." He led the way over to the living area and they settled into one of the three fluffy peach couches. "Other than that, how was it?" He handed her a bowl and sat back.

"Tiring." Michelline speared the salad vegetables and shoved them into her mouth, sitting there chewing while she thought about her day. "You know," she muttered, around a mouthful. "He's a hard-ass."

"He can be," Danté agreed. "As I said last night, he's good at what he does, but that's it. Everything else is none of his business. Scott doesn't work for the label; he has no say in anything other than the production of the music." He took a sip of wine.

"Doesn't he?" She paused to look at Danté. "I thought he came *with* the label. That he worked for them and was like, some head honcho, or something."

Shaking his head, Danté swallowed before speaking. "Most producers don't. They hire themselves out to whoever wants them. That's how they make their money."

"Mmm…" Michelline ate another forkful and chewed thoughtfully. "This is nice. You can cook, too. What is it?"

"A salad," Danté said dryly before giving her a grin. "It's just a salad I threw together with bacon and nuts and some citrus dressing. One of my uncle's recipes."

"Which one?"

"Tomas. He and Roger released two cookbooks every year from

2008 to 2028, co-written by Grandma. Massive best sellers."

"Are they the ones with the gym?" Michelline asked before eating another mouthful.

"Yep. Qualified nutritionists, dieticians, and professional trainers. They know their stuff."

She nodded and tried to remember everything she'd read over the last couple of decades. "Didn't your cousin Cabot get in on it, or something?"

"He did. He and his husband Tony did workout videos with them back in 2008 to 2018 to appeal to gay men of all ages. Got their qualifications as well and are continuing it."

"And from what I've read, your family's the musical one, and Cabot's is the model movie ones. But none of them do it anymore."

"No…" Danté finished his salad and wine. "My father and mother were into music, so all four of us were, but my sister Alexis went into supporting assault and HIV victims and runs her centre. Uncle Carlos stepped back from directing and producing at *S'Reel*, his movie production company, about ten years ago, but left a manager in charge and allowed many directors and producers to work under the company banner as long as he approved of the movie and had his name on the final cut. Antonio *was* on the way to taking over, and Diana's son Adam is also into movie making and has directed many teen and young adult movies in the last decade." He paused and took a breath. "But it was never the right fit for Antonio after modelling, whereas it was for Adam. Once he hit twenty-one, he was all but running the place."

"And how old is he now?" She had been watching his face as he spoke, knowing what heartache must still be underneath.

"Ah, twenty-four, twenty-five in April. Many of us share the same month for birthdays. Dom, Alexis, Roger and Mama are also April. My father and uncles are Valentine's Day, Alena and Diana are June, Cabot and Antonio July along with Grandpa…all of the grandkids…" Frowning, he breathed slowly. "March and May won't be good months."

"Why?" She rested her hand gently on his arm.

He looked down at it, and after a moment, covered her hand in his. "March would have been Aunt Viv's birthday, and it will be the one year anniversary of Maria's death. We all know Antonio won't cope, and neither will his daughter Izabella. They're not coping now. First Maria, then Aunt Viv. Three years after Grandma, and four years after Grandpa, both in May. The day after their anniversary, two days after Grandma's birthday."

"Oh, Jesus," she murmured. "I'm so sorry."

Unable to control his tears, he felt comfortable enough to let them fall.

"Oh, Danté." Michelline placed her bowl on the coffee table and wrapped her arms around him while he sobbed, his head in the crook of her arm. "I'm so sorry. That's just so much pain to deal with. I'm so sorry, oh, my baby. I'm so sorry." Holding him until he was done, she waited for him to right himself. "You okay?"

"Not really." He wiped his face and sniffed. "I haven't cried in front of anyone since Aunt Viv's passing. It's always been in private."

"Death is hard to deal with. I've lost one set of grandparents and an aunt. It sucked every emotion out of me, but when I turned to music, it came pouring back out. I guess…" She licked her lips and tucked a strand of hair behind her ear. "I guess that's why they're so emotive. All of my emotions are in my lyrics. Like the song I sang last night. I wrote that about my grandparents."

"And it was beautiful. Like you," he said softly, gazing into her eyes. "Lyrics like that deserve beautiful music to accompany them. Have you written any?"

"Not to that one, no." A small smile touched her lips. "I don't know how to write music. I can read it, sing a melody, but being able to write notes on paper means nothing." She gave a slight shake of her head. "Funny that. I learned the notes in singing class, but never really understood how to write it. And I don't play any instruments, so can't add to it."

"I can. What if I added music to it?" Danté gazed adoringly into her eyes and saw them glisten.

"You? Really?" Shock overcame her. *"Really?"*

"Well, you *do* have a piano sitting over there doing nothing." He nodded in its direction. "How about we make beautiful music together?"

A creeping blush swept across her face and the two glasses of wine kicked in. "That sounds like quite an offer, Mr Stephanopoulos."

"I'm *offering*, Ms Volmeyer." He leaned closer and lowered his voice. "I'm offering *a lot*."

"What's a lot?" she whispered, drowning in the sea of chocolate in his eyes and hearing her heart thumping in her chest.

"The world." His voice was soft as his lips zeroed in on hers. "Let me give you the world. Let me make beautiful music with you."

Breathing heavily, she managed, "Only if we can make beautiful love first," before her eyes closed and his lips latched on.

*****

"You what!" Nick exclaimed two weeks later when he finally caught up with Danté for lunch. He'd been spending time with his sisters, nieces and nephews, partying, and fucking a hot actress he'd met. "You what!"

"I'm going to propose," Danté repeated. "I've been looking around the jewellers for the perfect ring, took a bunch of photos, and want you to help me decide."

They sat in a seaside restaurant, famous for its freshly caught ocean to plate seafood, and were enjoying the warmth of the day. "I just don't know whether to go for nothing but diamonds, or get something else like a ruby, or emerald, surrounded by diamonds."

"Why are you asking me? I've never picked out engagement rings before. Why don't you ask your family?" Nick nodded at the waiter who placed a bowl of steaming prawn pasta in front of him.

"Because it's a surprise and I don't want them knowing until I go home." Danté salivated at his seafood chowder. "I want to propose before the family find out."

"What? In case she says no." Nick smirked. "What about my sisters?"

"They'd be on the phone to Alexis first thing," Danté retorted. "They're bigger gossips than Cabot." An idea came to him. "But...*you* could ask them."

"Me?" A frown crossed Nick's forehead. "*Why me? I'm* not getting married."

"But you could say you are and need help picking out a ring. You could show them the pictures I took. I'll send them to you." He pulled his phone from his shirt pocket.

"Don't bother. They'll see through that in a red hot minute. *Me? Getting married after two weeks?*" He grinned. "They'll know it's fake and that I'm probably doing it for you. And *then* they'll tell Alexis."

Danté sighed. "I suppose you're right. Okay, here." He thrust his phone across the table. "Just tell me which one is better. Don't pick the one you *think* she'll want, pick the one that's most romantic and represents love and happiness most."

"Ugh." Nick's shoulders slumped and he took the phone. "Okay," he droned, and started flicking the pictures left. "No, no, maybe, that's nice, maybe, that's expensive, holy Jesus that's a boulder, no, no, maybe, oh…hello…" He flicked back a few as the pictures had sped past. "You want love and romance, well out of all of them nothing beats that one." Handing the phone back, he devoured a mouthful of pasta.

Danté looked at the one Nick had chosen. "Yeah, I was leaning towards that one."

"Then what the fuck did you need me for?" Nick mumbled around his food.

"Would you buy it for your girlfriend if you ever had one?" Danté put his phone away and dug his spoon into his chowder, trying to gather as much seafood onto it as he could.

"Don't know." Nick swallowed and took a swig of beer. "With the type of woman *I* date, they'll probably want that massive boulder I saw."

Danté laughed in agreement. "We *do* date different types of women."

"What are *you* talking about? *You* don't date," Nick retorted. "I don't even know the last time you *did* date."

Danté thought back. "I…" His eyes narrowed and he frowned in concentration. "Well…neither do I."

"There you go then. When are you buying the rock?"

"We can go today if you've got time."

"Can you afford it?" Nick asked and then laughed at the stupidity of the question. "Of course, you fucking can. You're mega fucking rich. Does she know that? And what are you going to do about it?"

"Yes, I guess she would have figured that out. And do what about what?"

"Prenup. You still doing it?"

"Grandma made all of the in-laws sign one, so that's what we'll do." With a shrug of his shoulder, Danté paused with his spoon in mid-air. "What if she doesn't?"

"Doesn't what?"

"Sign the prenup."

"If she loves you, she'd be nuts not to. If she loves your money more, she might refuse."

"Yeah," Danté muttered. "I guess. Hadn't thought about it before, but it's the rule Grandma set up to protect all of us and the family business."

"Look…" Nick leaned forward and lowered his voice. "Regardless of the fact that all of the in-laws get nothing upon divorce, they all still get to live well. In nice homes on Mykonos, paid for by your grandmother. They get to travel by private jet, drive nice cars, have nice things, and live *really* well. Your grandma didn't want any of you to lose what she and your dads' built. It's a family empire, and just like the others, although Marcus divorced Alexis, and Maria is gone, and well, Tony's rich in his own right, all of them signed the prenup. They know they're onto a good wicket marrying into this family. And if she loves you, she'll realise that she'll live well even if she signs it. I guess the real test will be if she signs it without reading it."

"Yeah." Danté thought about it. "I guess it would be. I've just never had to broach the subject before. I don't really know how the others did, unless Grandma did it, but she's not here, so I'll have to bring it up. Although…" He sat back and frowned. "It's a bit weird proposing to the person you love and then pulling out the paperwork and going, here babe, mind signing this first?"

"Then talk about it before you propose, so she has a fair idea of what'll happen if you *do* propose."

"What, like a conversation about prenups?" Danté's frown deepened. "I *guess* I could."

"It will help you get it across beforehand and then it'll be out of the way."

"Yeah, yeah it will." Breathing deeply because his dilemma had been solved, Danté decided to have the conversation that night. "We *have* been talking a lot about family. This will just be another part of it, I guess. In the meantime, I can't propose without a ring. So, let's finish up and get going."

Half an hour later, they were standing in the jewellery store looking at the ring.

"It *is* perfect, isn't it?" Danté marvelled at the flashes of light radiating from it. "It's perfect for the occasion, a perfect representation of our love, just…"

"Perfect," Nick replied dryly. "Does it have matching wedding bands?"

"It does." The manager pulled another tray out from under the counter. "Here we are. Matching wedding band and eternity ring for her and wedding band for him."

"What, you don't get an engagement and eternity ring for yourself?" Nick joked to Danté. "*So* not fair."

Grinning from ear to ear, Danté appraised all four rings. "I'll take them because they're perfect."

"Of *course* they are." Nick snorted. *"It's a celebration of your love."*

"Cut it out." Danté gave him a shove and went to pay.

"We taking them home? You got a safe for those?" Nick called out. "Don't want to lose them on the way home because *someone else* thinks they're *perfect.*"

"They'll be fine." Danté chuckled and accepted the nondescript bag. "Let's just get home, so you don't have to sweat it out any longer." Thanking the manager, they left, and once their car doors were shut Danté heard the lock click into place and turned to Nick. "Seriously?"

"Dude!" Nick started the engine. "You have over a million dollars' worth of rings in that bag. I am *not* taking any chances. Strap in."

Maniacal laughter burst out of Danté. "I can't believe I'm doing this."

"What? Holding over a million dollars in jewels, or about to propose?"

Danté looked at him dazedly. "Both."

*****

That night, Danté lit the house aglow with candles, fairy lights, and lanterns. Soft music floated in the air, roses littered the floor, and the aromatic scent of Tomas Stephanopoulos's world-famous *Fish à la Stefan* wafted in the air. There was a bottle of champagne chilling on the coffee table, and a bowl of chocolate-dipped strawberries in the fridge.

He glanced around the room and declared it perfect with a nod of satisfaction.

"I'm home," Michelline called from the foyer and padded barefoot into the living area. "Ooh, pretty, we having a party?" Her eyes took in every little detail and landed on Danté in the kitchen. "Smells good. Looks good. You *are* good."

A soft laugh came from him and he walked around the island bench to sweep her into his arms. His lips landed on hers and left a deep impression.

"Mmm," she sighed and wrapped her arms around his neck, melting into the kiss.

"Mmm, yourself," Danté murmured, gazing into her eyes. "I love you."

"And I love you." Her hands slid through his hair and down his neck to his chest. "If *this* is the kind of welcome home I get every time I walk in the door, then I want it *every* night." She nuzzled his chest and inhaled his strong masculine scent.

"Well…" Danté saw his opening. "Maybe we should talk about that."

"Mmm… About what?" Lifting her head, she saw the serious expression. "What?" Pulling out of his arms, she went on. "What is it? Is something wrong?"

"No, no, nothing's wrong." He smiled and took her hands, kissing them as he spoke. "It's just, I love you and you love me and maybe we should do this…*you know.*"

"Do what?" After a long day in the studio, she was not connecting the dots.

Danté's smile grew. "Be tighter. On a more permanent basis. *Live* together."

"Oh…" Her aquamarine eyes grew wide. "You mean…*permanently?*"

"Yes." He shrugged. "Let's live together. Be together, be a couple. Boyfriend and girlfriend."

"Seriously? You want to do that…with me?" Michelline couldn't believe what she was hearing after only two weeks. This incredible man wanted to be with her.

"You don't want to?" Danté saw her hesitation. "Oh…okay…well, we don't have to become that serious that quickly. It's just, I've been here for the last two weeks anyway, and I figured it would be easier to get our own place if you want to stay here in L.A., or…" He took a step back and lowered their hands. "Maybe you can come to Mykonos."

"What!" she gasped. No man had ever taken her to the Greek islands before. And here was one offering to move her there. "But…my…life…is here," she managed.

"For now." He nodded. "You *do* have a contract that you should fulfil, and need to finish off your record, but that doesn't stop us from permanently living together. We can spend our time between here and home. Although the family does get to New York and Miami a couple of times a year, and many of us fly to London, and even Australia, occasionally." He swung their hands between them in excitement. "I could give you the world, Michelline. I could give you *everything.*" He watched her reaction and saw her soften, her lips curl into a small smile, her eyes tear up. "I love you."

"I love you." Taking a deep breath, she went on. "We've only known each other two weeks, and yes, you have stayed here the whole time, but the label will kick me out when we're done and I'll be back out in the real world—"

"With me to look after you," Danté quickly cut in.

"I've had men say that to me before." She smiled wryly.

"I'm not like other men."

His tone told her he was serious and she nodded. "Oh, I know that; Danté Stephanopoulos. Your parents and grandparents raised you well, and I see you mean what you say, but…" Glancing around the room she saw the lighting, candles and roses. "I feel a bit out of my depth. I'm just a girl from mid-west USA come to L.A. for her break, and sure, I studied hard dind learnt my craft, but I've also been screwed over by men who thought they could get what they want. Not that you're like that," she quickly added when he was about to argue. "I *know* you're different, but so's your life. *You're* Danté Stephanopoulos, world-famous, mega-rich, businessman and tycoon. You're *so* far out of my league." Running her hands through her hair, she breathed deeply and walked over to the sofa, resting her hands on the back. "Is this a fairy tale?"

"No." Danté stood beside her. "It's very real and right here in front of you." He gently turned her to face him. "I love you, Michelline. I know you're the one for me and I want to make it happen. I want us to be together, live together, make beautiful music together. And I want you to want that too."

"Oh…" She melted into him. "I *do* want that too."

Just before their lips met, a ding went off.

"Ah, bugger." Danté closed his eyes. "Dinner's ready, madam." He led her over to the dining table and pulled out her chair. "Madam."

"Thank you, sir." She nodded and seated herself.

Danté quickly plated up the food and set it down on the table. "Here we go, *Fish à la Stefan*, courtesy of my Uncle Tomas and Grandma. Their recipe."

"Smells incredible." Michelline sampled some of it and savoured the taste. "Tastes incredible, too."

"It should. I made it," Danté joked and poured some wine. "I *slaved* over the oven all day."

"And dessert? Did you slave over that, too?"

"Ah…" A twinkle lit up his eyes. "You'll just have to wait and see."

"Ah…" A smile lit up her lips. "Can't wait."

They talked more about living together as dinner wore on.

"We could live on Mykonos?" she asked, catching a piece of fish with her spoon. "I know you have your studio, but I have my contract."

"True." He nodded and watched her looking into her bowl. "But it'll be done with the album, and then you'll be free to go wherever you like and sing whatever you want."

"But we'd live on Mykonos," she persisted, unable to look him in the eye. "You said we could travel."

"If a singing career is what you want to pursue, then all of your music can come out of Mykonos *and Sync*. Then tour the world when you want. That's what my sister did until she retired." He noted her hesitancy. "Do you want to be here in L.A. permanently? Is that what's worrying you?"

"Um…not really. I'm just…" Sipping some of the broth, she tried to put it into words. "If I'm to have a career here, don't I need to *be* here? I wouldn't want to wear myself out flying everywhere just for a tour or show."

"You can base your career in Mykonos, spend some time through the year here, or do it all online, these days." Danté scraped up the last of his vegetables and chewed thoughtfully. After a sip of wine to wash it down, he added, "You don't *need* to be based here. But I *am* willing to spend more time here if it's where you want to be. We do have a *Sync* studio here in L.A. I can work from here."

Surprised, Michelline paused with her glass at her lips. "You'd do that? For me?"

"Of course. I love you. We do things for the person we love." Danté's voice was soft and sweet. "My grandmother moved to Mykonos in 1967 for my grandfather. Aunt Viv moved from L.A. to New York for my Uncle Carlos, Roger moved from Miami to New York for Uncle Tomas, Papa ran away to New York with Mama, and then they all went back to Mykonos for Uncle Tomas when he was sick. It's been our home base since 1981. And even though my siblings and cousins have married, all of their partners move to Mykonos to be with them, but they do spend their time in other places. Such as Spain, London, Australia. If you want to be *here*, then I wouldn't be the first one to move for love in this family."

"You'd move here for me?" she whispered, stunned and unbelieving.

"Yes." He took her hand and gently kissed it. "I would. I'd do what my grandma did sixty-six years ago and move countries for the person I love."

A tear slid down her cheek and she inhaled a shaky breath. "No one's ever said that to me before. No one's ever been that serious."

"I'm *very* serious." Danté gently wiped her tear away with his thumb. "I've never been more serious about anything in my life. Even my family would tell you that."

"So…um…" She wiped her face and sniffled. "We could spend our time in both places?"

"We can if you want."

"I've never been to Mykonos before. I've seen it in pictures. It's beautiful." She corralled another loose tear. "I'd like to see it."

"When are you done recording?" An idea formed in Danté's mind.

"This week. And then it's mixed and produced, and a single's released, and why am I telling *you* this." She giggled softly. "You already know."

Grinning, Danté kissed her hand and collected the plates. "I do. How about dessert?"

"What is it? I have to watch my waistline." She patted her flat stomach.

"A skinny raspberry chiffon cheesecake," he replied, putting the dishes in the sink.

"Another of your uncle's recipes?" Michelline drained her glass and poured another.

"Grandma's." He pulled the cake from the fridge and looked at it. Heart-shaped, he'd covered it in raspberries, and raspberry crème filled heart-shaped chocolates surrounded it on the plate. It had a few rose petals for decoration, with a big fat engagement ring right in the middle of them.

"When would we go to Mykonos? Obviously, I'd meet your family at some point." Michelline wasn't sure if it was the wine, or apprehension making her stomach knot. "What will you call me? Will I be your girlfriend? Partner? Lover?"

Danté placed the cheesecake on the table in front of her and waited for her to notice.

"Ooh, that looks so good, but *so* fattening…" Her voice trailed off and she leaned forward for a better look, her finger gently poking the massive ruby heart ring surrounded by diamonds to see if it was real or just a decoration. Flying back in her seat as if stung by a thousand bees, and covering her mouth with both of her hands, she shakily turned to Danté who was down on bended knee.

"I hope I'll be calling you my fiancée."

*****

Danté quietly let himself through the door, paused at the sounds coming from the house, and silently closed it behind him. He saw them in the kitchen, but headed for the mantel over the fireplace first, so he could pay his respects. He did it every time he walked into that house. Murmured words of love, gave their urn a kiss, and held their photo to his heart. Just as he did now. It was hard to not shed a tear when he did this. The loss of his grandparents still bore deep scars. Far deeper than the ones on his leg.

Tomas laughed at something Pedro and Mike were doing out on the balcony and turned to Roger on his left. He saw Danté in the lounge room taking a moment and smiled softly. He did the same thing every morning when he rose. Kissed his parents' urn, said hello, and had a conversation. After having moved in over a decade ago to look after them, he and Roger stayed, as instructed by Jenny, until their own days had passed. And at night, he kissed their urn and bade them goodnight, after telling them about his day, of course. Regardless of them being gone, he still conversed with them as if they were still there.

Roger noticed Tomas gazing past him and turned to look. "He's back," he said softly, waiting for Angie to acknowledge his comment before nodding in Danté's direction.

She spun around in her seat to see Danté standing at the mantel. "Hey, sweetie. You're finally back."

Inhaling a shaky breath, Danté slowly walked over to the kitchen and stopped at the island bench with a worn out smile. "Yeah. Got back last night."

She hopped off her seat to give him a hug and he slid his arm around her and planted a kiss on the top of her head. "You're normally not gone this long. I missed you." Sensing the tension in his body, she looked up. "You okay?"

"Yeah," he murmured dejectedly and set the photo on the counter.

Angie stared at it. "Missing your grandma? So am I."

"Yeah."

Pedro and Mike came in from the balcony. "Hey, Danté when did you get back?" He shook himself off and flung an arm around his son. "Good time in L.A.?" He noticed the photo. "Missing your grandma? Yeah, so am I."

"Are any of us not?" Dan drawled. He and Derek had been permanently living in Mykonos for over a decade, had been with the family when both Spiros and Jenny had passed, and had then helped the family through Maria's and Viv's deaths.

Everyone in the kitchen looked at him and sighed.

"Guess not," Tomas replied and glanced at Danté. "What's going on? L.A. go okay?"

"Yeah, L.A. was fine, got stuff done, met people." He stared at the photo that contained the whole family. "Everyone's heard about Maria and Aunt Viv and send their condolences." He glanced at Carlos. "They send their love to you and Antonio."

Carlos sighed and threw down a peanut shell. "You thank 'em for it?"

"I did." Danté studied his uncle. He'd aged a lot in the last few years even though he was now eighty. He'd stopped dying his hair and had gone salt and pepper grey, with more of the salt than the pepper. "How are you and Antonio? I know it was Aunt Viv's birthday last week."

Sucking back a sob, Carlos held it together. "I managed."

"With help from all of us," Tomas told Danté while eyeing his brother. "We were by his side the whole day. As were Diana, Cabot and their families."

"Antonio?" Danté asked, looking from face to face.

"For a while," Pedro replied sombrely before ruffling his son's hair. "What'd you get up to in L.A.? Find any new acquisitions?"

"Maybe." Danté licked his lips and rubbed his grandmother's face in the photo. "I, uh… Nick and I went to a party at Jasmine Wetherill's house on Valentine's. She sends her condolences, and thanks Uncle Carlos for making her rich enough to own such a palatial home."

Carlos snorted. "I just directed her movies. *She* managed her money. Better than any accountant I've ever seen." He cracked a couple of peanuts in his hand and let the shells fall onto the counter, irritating Tomas who frowned and swept them into the bin.

"Yeah." Danté absentmindedly rubbed the photo.

"What happened, sweetie? Something clearly did." At seventy-four, Angie had learnt to read her children long ago, after learning from Jenny, and knew when something was going on.

"Oh…" Another sigh. "A lot happened."

"Clearly." Pedro slapped his son's back. "Spit it out."

"Remember when…" Danté took a breath and looked at his father. "In 2018 at Uncle T and Roger's actual legal wedding—"

Roger guffawed. "Are we still calling it that?"

Danté's lips lifted into a small grin. "Yeah…um, when you guys got married in Armidale and we'd walked into the reception hall and Grandma started laughing at the others because they couldn't wrangle their kids?"

"You're going back a fair way, kid. What's your point?" Carlos stopped cracking peanuts long enough to frown as he remembered back to all of the conversations about his parents dying and the reorganisation of the company that year. "What of it?"

"Well…" Danté took another breath. "I laughed and said I was glad I didn't have to deal with that, and she said I would one day, and that when I met the right person then it would be on like Donkey Kong."

Light laughter went through the kitchen.

Danté looked down at the photo, a frown crossing his brows before he continued. "And then I had my panic attack because I realised that when that happened she and Grandpa wouldn't be here, and then we talked about it backstage."

"And neither of you ever really mentioned it again." Angie had always been put off by that moment, that her son couldn't talk to her about his issues, and Jenny refused to tell her, saying it was up to Danté.

"Yeah, well…" Danté's heart beat wildly in his chest as he looked at his mother. "We just talked about life and death and love and marriage, and how it was okay if she wasn't here when I finally met someone I wanted to marry." Tears filled his eyes and rolled down his cheeks. "I didn't want her to die and she said she didn't want to either." His voice cracked under the weight of the emotions in his chest.

"Ah." Tomas wiped his tears away and turned his back for a moment.

"Neither did any of us," Carlos murmured and watched Tomas until he turned around, eyes red and watery. He'd seen how much harder Jenny's death had been on his brother, even though it hit them all hard.

"I hated the fact I hadn't married and had kids. That it didn't happen before they died. It wasn't fair for them to not see it." Danté wiped away the rivers flowing down his face. "I wish it could've happened, but Grandma told me it would happen when it was meant to whether she was here or not." Staring down at the photo he wiped away the drops that splashed on it. "But she said if she wasn't, then she would make sure the right one was sent my way, and when she came, I'd know it was because Grandma had sent her. And then it would be on like Donkey Kong," he sobbed.

"Why are you telling us this, Danté? Is it because you're turning forty this month and they won't be here? What's going on?" Pedro rubbed his son's back and squeezed his shoulder, exchanging puzzled glances with everyone else.

Danté wiped his face and looked at his father. "Besides the fact I'm nearly forty, and it won't be the same without them, or Aunt Viv, or Maria, it's because I never really believed it. Never believed it would happen. It meant nothing without Grandma here. But it *did* happen just as she said it would, and now it's on like Donkey Kong just as she said it would be." His sobs of sadness turned to sobs of masked joy as he waited for his family to understand what he was saying.

Confused, Pedro could only shake his head until a strangled sound came from his brother.

"You've found someone?" Tomas cried, covering his mouth in shock.

Danté nodded vigorously at him. "And I proposed and she said yes and we're getting married."

"What!" The startled exclamation rang out around the room.

Turning back to his parents, Danté continued. "I've met the one and I think Grandma sent her to me, and I've never felt this way about anyone before, so I know it's her and she's gorgeous and stunning, and has a perfect pitch when she sings, and oh, my God I love her so much." He finally took a breath as he was pulled into Tomas's arms for a hug.

"But when did you meet her?" Angie asked, stunned that her baby boy was engaged and it had taken until he was almost forty. And that they hadn't known until now.

"On Valentine's Day at Jasmine's…" His voice trailed off and he looked at the now sombre expressions. "Which I know sucks for you guys now."

"I turned eighty and got drunk." Carlos threw a peanut into the air and caught it in his mouth. "And my nephew got lucky. Great day for you, shit day for me. *Nothing* good ever really came out of Valentine's Day."

"Grandma would disagree," Danté said vehemently. "She had her three sons on that day, so *she'd* say that *three* good things came out of Valentine's Day, and she made damn sure to celebrate it every year that she was alive because her baby boys celebrated another year alive and on this planet. *Especially* Uncle Tomas. Look what she did for him when he was sick. She moved the *earth* for him to bring him back to the family and keep him in it."

Carlos's shoulders slumped and his eyes flitted back and forth between an ever still appreciative seventy-eight-year-old Tomas who was nodding and wiping the tears pouring from his face, and his scowling middle-aged nephew. "Mmm, I suppose."

"You suppose?" Danté said. "Grandma was always right and we always listened to her, and for the most part always did what she said. She loved her sons and loved the fact you were born on the same day two years apart. Don't *ever* forget that. She loved you three to pieces and would, *and did*, do anything and everything for you and your children."

Carlos's head nodded slightly and he finally cracked a small smile, remembering back across eighty years and the love his mother had showered upon all three of them since 1953 when he'd been born. Her love had always been pure and true. *Especially* on *their* day. A day that all three Stephanopoulos brothers shared which made them, and that day, a very sacred thing indeed. "That she did, kid. That she did."

Angie saw the tears her husband and brothers-in-law were shedding and quietly manoeuvred the conversation back to her son. "So…back to your fiancée, Danté. She *is* your fiancée, isn't she? You didn't get married already? Did we miss out on it?"

"No, Mama. She's my fiancée, but we want to get married as soon as possible." Danté took her into his arms for a hug.

"She's not pregnant, is she?" Dan asked, sipping his coffee and leaning casually against the island bench.

Danté grinned at him. "Wouldn't be the first time in this family."

Pedro's lips curled up and he slapped his son on the back. "No, it wouldn't."

"But no, she's not," Danté added. "That I know of. But I'd have no problem if she was. We want to get married soon and start a family."

"Is she willing to sign the prenup?" Carlos asked wearily.

"Already did and without reading it," Danté replied.

"That was quick." Tomas was surprised. "When are you thinking of for a date?"

"Ah…" Danté looked from face to face. "May twenty-third."

"But that's Mama's and…Papa's…" Tomas frowned. "Why?"

"To honour them," was Danté's simple reply.

"Naw!" Tomas's face crumpled and he embraced his nephew with fresh tears rolling down his cheeks. "Mama would love that."

"I hope so." Danté hugged back and looked over at all of the family photos on the wall. "I figured if she's the one who sent her into my life then we should honour her."

"And what did your fiancée think?" Angie asked. "Since it would have been *you* suggesting the date." She sat back on the stool between Carlos and Maggie, still stunned at the news.

"She thought it was sweet. She's lost one set of grandparents and an aunt, so she knows what it's like." Danté cast a glance at Carlos before continuing. "But look, she's here in Mykonos, she's finished recording her album which is why we're here now, and I thought we could have the whole family around tonight for a get together. But I wanted to introduce her to immediate family first instead of dumping all of you on her at once. And, I, ah, know everyone's in town, so maybe we could get the others over first and tell them. Then she can meet the rest of the in-laws and grandkids later."

"Uh, I'm not sure what the others are doing," Angie mumbled and pulled out her phone. "What do I tell them?"

Danté shrugged. "That it's a family emergency. Come now. Here, I'll do it." He held out his hand, and once he had the phone, quickly typed out a message to his siblings and cousins and hit send. "There, done. Now, once I tell them, I'll go and get her, so you can meet her. I've already brought her up to speed on who's who and whatnot."

Messages started dinging on Angie's phone.

Alexis - *do I have to? I'm busy at the centre*

Dom - *is it* actually *an emergency?*

Alena - *D and I are busy sticking pins in a doll. Do we need to* come?

Cabot - *be there later, why now?*

Simon - *in the middle of work, can't right now*

There was no reply from Antonio.

Danté shot out two sentences. *Your grandmother's! NOW!*

And sure enough, within ten minutes, they all piled through the door.

Dom spied Danté in the kitchen. "Hey, little D's back. When did you get here?"

"Last night." Danté saw Nick bring up the rear and close the door before finding his parents for a welcome home hug.

"Naw, here's my little brother." Alexis hugged him. "Micah's missed you. Hasn't gotten to play with Uncle Danté in ages."

"I'll see him tonight," Danté replied and hugged his way through the rest of the family.

Antonio headed for the fridge. "Got anything to drink?" He flung the doors open and stood staring into it.

"You know we rarely have alcohol in the house anymore," Tomas said quietly from behind him.

"Not even a beer," Antonio whined.

"Didn't we ban them after Cabot threw one across the kitchen in '07?" Danté snickered at his cousin.

Cabot shrugged a nonchalant shoulder. "I was a dickface then."

"Whaddya mean *then*." Antonio sneered. "So, what's this fucking emergency? Someone else die?" He slammed the fridge door and watched a laminated crayon drawing of hearts and suns surrounding a family fall from it. It was from his Izabella and Valentina to their great-grandparents and depicted all of the family members. Tears stung his eyes and he crouched down and picked it up.

Gasps went around the room and Tomas gripped him by the arms from behind. "*Don't you dare* in this house," he breathed into his stunned nephew's ear as they both looked at the drawing in Antonio's hand. "*Not* in your grandmother's house. *Do you hear me?* We know you're not dealing well with life, but that doesn't stop you from being happy for someone else. *Do you understand me?*"

Stunned that Tomas, who barely ever raised his voice, or physically accosted someone, had spoken to him and treated him that way, Antonio could only nod and release a shaky breath.

"*Not in your grandmother's house,*" Tomas warned. "Now shut up and pay attention." He spun Antonio around to face the stunned family and kept a tight grip on his nephew's arms. "Go ahead," he told Danté calmly.

"Um…" Danté could only stare at his uncle and cousin, having never seen Tomas act that way. He saw Carlos's expression and noted that it was thoughtful. *And* thankful. "Um…" He finally turned to his stunned siblings and cousins and inhaled deeply. "Ah…I thought that since it's Saturday, that we'd have a family get together tonight. You, your partners, the kids. Here. Not dinner, just drinks and nibblies. Around seven."

"Ugh, can't," Alexis complained. "I'm running the centre tonight. Can we do it to coincide with your birthday next week? Or just wait until your birthday?"

"And I'm worn out from getting the current *Haus of Stefan* collection done," Diana added. "And dealing with Mama's birthday last week." Her gaze wandered to Antonio who looked as if he were about to say something, but Tomas shut him up.

"Yeah, I'm not really up for it, little D." Cabot was watching his brother. "And Antonio's been sentenced to house arrest after that stunt he pulled."

His brother looked at him sharply and opened his mouth.

"I *meant my son*," Cabot told him and sighed tiredly. "That's the problem with having *three* Antonios in the family."

"And most of the girls are working at all of the businesses," Alena said. "I doubt we could wrangle them into the same room."

"And I've got an album to finish off by Monday. Sorry, bro." Dom shrugged. "What's the family emergency, Mama? Was this is? Hardly an emergency."

"We'll come, Danté," Simon said. "I'll let Liam, Stella and Samuel know."

"Thank you, Simon." Danté nodded. "Good to know someone in this family gives a damn about it."

Guffaws went through the room. Simon was Roger's son, but Tomas had adopted him, making him a Stephanopoulos, and he was always the one who had time for the family who'd taken him in as one of their own.

"You suck-up, Simon," Dom joked with a grin. "I gotta go. We'll catch up at some point, probably your birthday, but not tonight."

"Same here."

"Me too."

"Better go."

"So much to do."

They turned and headed for the door except for Simon and Antonio who Tomas held on to.

"Well, that's just great," Danté said loudly. "All the years you've harassed me about getting married and now that I'm engaged you walk out on me." He waited for the response.

They collided at the door as the words sank in and they turned around with their jaws wide open.

"What!" Dom took a step forward. "What!" he yelled and saw Danté grin. "You're getting married! What!" Running to his brother he wrapped his arms around his waist and picked him up. "Fucking what!"

"Danté's getting married. My little brother's getting married," Alena sang and danced around them.

"What do you mean, *your* little brother?" Alexis chastised. "*Our* little brother."

Cabot bounced on his tiptoes and lightly clapped his hands. "Danté's getting married, Danté's getting married." Even though he was fifty, old habits died hard with him.

"Ugh." Antonio slumped in his uncle's arms, sick to the stomach at the news.

"Don't you dare!" Tomas whispered. "Have the decency to be happy for your cousin. You have the ability to do that."

Heartbroken, Antonio gulped back tears and nodded. It was almost a year since his beloved Maria was killed in a car crash in Italy, four months since his mother had passed away, and now his cousin was happy and engaged. All he could do was stare down at the drawing from his daughters. "Ugh."

"Just breathe," Tomas said, his arms still around him. "Do it for your cousin. Do it for your mother who would be happy and excited at another wedding, but most of all, do it for your grandmother who would want you to be happy for him."

"Who is she, what does she do, how old is she, where did you meet her, how long have you known each other, when did you propose, when's the wedding—"

"Shut up, Alena." Alexis rolled her eyes. "Let him speak."

Laughing, Danté tried to remember the questions. "Ah, she's Michelline Volmeyer, she's a singer who's just cut her first album, she's thirty, I met her at Jasmine Wetherill's house, since Valentine's Day, I proposed on the twenty-eighth and the wedding's in May."

"Wait...you met her on Valentine's Day and proposed two weeks later?" Cabot was stunned. "Fuck, *you* work fast, too."

"Kinda like the rest of the family," Danté replied. "Except for you."

Cabot spluttered. "Yeah, well, I had a lot of growing up to do. It was the mature thing to wait."

"Ah-ha," Dom murmured, giving Cabot a sly glance. "Is *that* what it was."

"Congrats, Danté." Simon gave him a slap on the back. "When do we meet her?"

"Well, she's here, and I thought once you all got here and I told you everything, that you could meet her *now*, and everyone else can meet her later, so she's not overwhelmed by the family."

"Good idea." Cabot nodded and crossed his arms. "Go and get her."

"Okay, just..." Danté looked from sibling to cousin. "*Behave. All of you.* I know what this family's like. The in-laws know what this family's like—"

"Big." Alexis shrugged.

"Noisy," Alena added.

"Crowded," Diana offered.

"Just go and get her," Dom complained. "We don't have all damn day."

"Okay, okay." Danté headed for the door, but stopped when he opened it. "Just *be nice* and *don't* crowd her," he told them.

"Go!" Dom ordered with an outstretched arm and a point of his finger. When the door closed he spun around to question Nick. "*You* clearly know what she's like. Spill."

All eyes focussed on Nick and he blushed. "Fucking gorgeous. And sings better than some in this family."

"Hey!" Alena cried, "What's that supposed to mean?" Even though Alexis could sing, as well as some of their children, Alena was the only one who'd done it for a career so far.

"Why do you always make everything about you?" Alexis asked her.

*****

Danté ran into his house and called out to Michelline. "They're ready to meet you. We can go now."

She hurried from the bedroom where she'd changed her outfit five times trying to find the right one. Danté had bought her a whole new wardrobe and luggage set for the trip, and she'd brought everything with her, so she could set up her new home in Mykonos. "How do I look?" Twirling, she fidgeted with everything. "Is my hair okay? My outfit? My earrings, are they too big?"

"Stop fretting." Danté took her face gently in his hands and kissed her. "You're stunning, and I love you."

Michelline melted into his arms. "I love you. But I want to make a good impression."

He looked over her skinny black jeans and platform boots, soft pink shirt tied with a gold chain belt, and a matching black and pink long sleeveless cardigan vest over it. "You're stunning. And I love you. And *they'll* love you."

"Did you tell them anything?" The butterflies in her stomach were making her sick.

"The basics. So, let's go." Taking her hand, he led her outside. "They'll ask a million and one questions, want to see the ring, have probably grilled Nick about it, and will want to know every little detail." He glanced at her as she clung to his right arm looking petrified. "It will be overwhelming, but okay. They're good people. We've just been through a lot in the last year and…" He glanced at the house as they drew near. "I'll introduce you to Grandma and Grandpa. I think they'll be happy."

A soft smile lit up Michelline's face. "I hope they will be."

"Okay, we're here." He stopped at the door and looked down at her. "You ready?"

"As I'll ever be." She grimaced and gripped his arm tighter.

Grinning, he opened the door and stepped in front of her, turning to her to shield her from the family's prying eyes before she was in the house. Closing the door behind her, he flashed a comforting smile and turned around to see everyone waiting. "Ah…" He gulped and grimaced on the inside. "Everyone, this is Michelline, my fiancée."

"Hello," she murmured, her stomach somersaulting a mile a minute. She was used to being stared at, but this was unnerving. As if she were prey for a family of hungry tigers and all eyes were on her for an entrée.

Murmurs went through the family as they walked over.

"You *are* gorgeous!" Cabot exclaimed, and as always, he was the first one to step forward because he was just a plain old nosy gossip. "Hello. I'm cousin Cabot, and that drunken bum over there," he pointed to his brother who frowned in return, "is my twin brother, Antonio. Hello."

"Oh, hello." Michelline shook his hand, but wondered why he'd said such a thing, especially when the rest of the family gave him surprised looks.

"Hello, Michelline, I'm Angelina Stephanopoulos, Danté's mother." Angie came forward with open arms. "And your future mother-in-law." She was glad to see that her son's fiancée would be shorter than her without heels. "Welcome to the family." She hugged her. "You *are* gorgeous."

"Oh." Michelline blushed. "Thank you."

"Welcome to the family, Michelline. I'm Pedro, Danté's father." He shook her hand. "Looks like you've made my son very happy."

She beamed up at her fiancé who was beaming back. "And he's

made *me* very happy."

Pedro introduced her to Carlos, Tomas, Roger, Dan, Derek, Mike and Maggie who she shook hands with and made condolences to.

Dom snapped his fingers. "I know where you're from. *Ripchord Records.* Their latest find. You've been recording a new album," he said, shaking her hand.

"Oh, ah, yes." Michelline was surprised. "I didn't know anyone knew that yet."

"I recognised your name, but it wasn't until I saw you that I remembered reading an article online," Dom told her. "Perfect pitch and crystal clear. How many octaves again?"

"Six." She blushed. "I'm operatically trained."

"Impressive." Dom nodded. "Can't wait to hear you."

"Mmm," Alena quietly harrumphed, and Alexis nudged her and hid a giggle. "Care to sing for us now?" she asked before introducing herself.

"Oh, I better not." Michelline glanced at Danté. "I need to warm up first."

"Maybe later," Danté suggested. "Show everyone what you've got."

She smiled and leaned into him, sliding her hand up his arm and resting her chin on his shoulder. "Will you play?"

"God, you two are so in love it's *sickening.*" Cabot grinned and shook his head. "*Grandma* would *so* approve."

"And speaking of." Danté pulled Michelline over to the mantel. "Michelline, say hello to my grandparents, Spiros and Jenny Stephanopoulos."

And just like that, a photo fell from the wall.

"Oh, no, I hope it didn't break." Michelline gently picked it up from the mantel and looked it over. "No broken glass, hook is attached." She glanced up at the wall. "Nail's still there. It shouldn't have fallen." Replacing it carefully, she studied the photo. "Mr and Mrs Stephanopoulos, hello, how do you do. I'm Michelline Volmeyer, Danté's fiancée. But I bet you know that already." Nodding at Viv and Maria in the photo, she added, "Mrs Stephanopoulos, Mrs Stephanopoulos, nice to meet you both."

Everyone had been watching her, puzzled expressions on the kids' faces, surprise on the adults, except for Tomas. The respect she had shown his parents touched his heart and he rushed over. "Is it intact? Which one was it?"

"No glass broken," Michelline told him. "It just fell, unless your mother did it."

Tomas turned sharply to her. "Why would you say that?"

Surprised by his tone and questioning eyes, she took a step towards Danté. "My grandparents died five years ago. We think they visit when things fall off the walls, or fall over on their own. We say hello and have a chat. My aunt does it too. She'll move her favourite cat statue to show us she's around."

"Oh, you've lost loved ones, too…" He frowned slightly. "That's right, Danté mentioned it before. Well, thank you, Michelline, for showing my parents and family respect." Nodding, he glanced at Danté. "You've got a good one here, Danté. Danté?" He saw the tears rolling down his nephew's face. "Hey, what's wrong?"

Michelline slid her arms around her fiancé. "Sweetie, what's wrong? What is it?"

"That photo," he sobbed, "is from your wedding." Gasping, he leant on the mantel and grasped his grandparents' urn. "Thank you, Grandma, thank you."

Not sure of the significance, Tomas turned to the photo and wondered why it meant anything, having forgotten what Danté had mentioned earlier.

"Oh, that's when she told you she would bring the one into your life and it would be on like Donkey Kong," Michelline's voice was soft as she rubbed his back. "And here we are."

The light dawned on Tomas, and he watched Danté take Michelline into his arms and cry. And as they clung to each other, he walked back to the kitchen to give them a moment.

"What…" Carlos softly asked Tomas as the others gathered around.

Tomas shook his head and noticed that Roger had taken a hold of Antonio. "Our wedding in Aus, when he had his panic attack and he and Mama talked about meeting *the one* even if she wasn't here," he said softly.

"Ah…" went around the kitchen.

"*That's* the photo that fell off the wall, so it means something to him. They think it's a sign that Mama gave them. So do I." He nodded. "She just gave her approval."

After gathering himself, Danté and Michelline walked back over. "So, ah…drinks and nibblies at seven, here, tonight, bring everyone."

"Absolutely." Dom took his brother into his arms and held on tight. "I miss her, too."

"We all do," Alexis said from the other side. "And we'll be here as well."

"Us too." Alena sneaked in under Dom's arm.

"And, of course, we will be." Diana smiled softly.

"I'll even let Antonio out of jail for the night." Cabot gave his twin the evil eye. "*Both* of them."

"I…" barely made it out of Antonio's mouth.

"Will be here tonight even if I have to drag you up those fucking stairs myself," Tomas growled into his ear.

Antonio blinked rapidly at the change in his uncle. "Uncle T—"

"No," Tomas cut him off. "I may be seventy-eight years old, Antonio DeLuca Stephanopoulos, but I will make *damn* sure on Mama's behalf that you're here tonight to celebrate the engagement of your cousin. Do you hear me?"

Gasping back a sob, Antonio nodded and lowered his head.

Carlos nodded approvingly at his brother. "Well done, T."

"I know you don't have the energy to deal with this, so the rest of us will deal with it for you. Just like Mama would. And…" He turned back to his nephew. "Izabella and Valentina will also be here."

"I don't know where Izzy is," Antonio mumbled.

"*We* do, and we'll get her here." Tomas nodded at Pedro.

Jenny had taught them a lot over the decades, and when dealing with Cabot's attitude back in 2007, they had learned the significance of a family security team. *Especially* with everything else that happened that year, not to mention what had happened to him and his brothers in 1977. A security team was on the payroll at all times, and was one of their biggest expenses. But it was also something they would never go without. After what happened to Alexis and Cabot, every new in-law and child had a bodyguard who melted into the background and only stepped forward to act if it was necessary, no matter where they were.

"Oh, forgot to ask." Alena pulled out of the embrace. "Let's see the ring."

"Oh!" Turning as pink as her shirt, Michelline held out her hand to show off the ruby heart dazzler.

"Oh, that's gorgeous, Danté, well done." Diana admired the ring.

"Mmm, nice," Alena muttered and glanced at her own diamond ring that was relatively small compared to her future sister-in-law's.

Alexis nudged her and said, "Nice ring, bro. Cost a pretty penny?"

"Alexis!" Angie exclaimed. "We don't need to know because it's none of our business." She held Michelline's hand and moved it in the light, admiring the colours that dazzled from the ring. "It *is* beautiful, Michelline. Did you pick it out, Danté?"

A hurt expression flitted across his face. "*Of course.* I *do* know how to pick a ring out, Mama. Geez."

"Technically, *I* picked it out." Nick rolled his eyes, and when everyone turned to him, he added, "He was unsure, so showed me a bunch of photos and asked me to pick. I did. That one." He pointed to Michelline's hand.

"Yes, but I already had my eye on it—" Danté managed before being cut off.

"*Sure* you did," Nick scoffed. "*Sure* you did."

"Don't be a dickface, Nicholas," Danté said. "It's unbecoming and makes you just like Cabot." It was a name that had become a long-running joke in the family.

"Hey, don't involve me in your lovers' spat," Cabot complained and held up his hands. "Leave me out of it, coz that's all in the past for me."

"Okay, if we're back at seven then I gotta get back to the studio." Dom checked his watch. "It's twelve now, so I should be able to get a lot done." He held his hand out to shake his future sister-in-law's. "Michelline, nice to meet you. Danté," he slapped his brother on the shoulder, "congrats. See you later."

"Yes, and we'll see you later, sweetie." Diana kissed their cheeks. "Welcome to the family, Michelline."

"Thank you," Michelline murmured as Alexis and Alena followed suit.

"Don't forget to bring the kids," Danté called after them.

"We will." Cabot kissed them both and walked over to Antonio. "Say goodbye, Antonio, and I'll get you home." He helped his brother over to their cousin.

"Um…" Antonio hung his head, but managed to murmur. "Congrats, Danté. Really."

"Thank you, Antonio. I know this month is hard for you, being your mother's birthday and the anniversary of Maria's passing." Danté hugged him.

"Yeah, yeah, it is." Antonio hugged back and blinked away his tears before pulling away and looking at Michelline. "Welcome to the family. It's a bit dysfunctional right now, but, hopefully, it'll get better."

"Thank you," she murmured, tears pricking her eyes. "And I'm *so* sorry about your wife and mother. My condolences."

Unable to say anything, Antonio simply nodded and a fresh onslaught of tears pooled in his emerald eyes.

"Thank you," Cabot replied for both of them. "We'll see you tonight. Come on." He led Antonio to the door where the others had waited and they all left together.

Once the door closed Danté let out a huge sigh. "That went as well as could be expected, considering he's not coping."

"Are any of us?" Carlos asked, resting his arms on the island bench. "I'm not, he's not, Izzy's not, Valentina's not, Diana, Cabot, their kids."

Taking his fiancée into his arms, Danté held her tightly. "But hopefully, with everything we're doing, we can make it better."

*****

Just before seven that night, the family started arriving and all eyes were on Michelline.

They had told their partners and children about her and all were eager to see, not only the newcomer to the family, but the ring.

"Uncle Danté," Micah cried when he came through the door. He bolted across the room, managed to bypass his cousins and aunt who'd come in ahead of them, and launched himself into his uncle's arms.

"You're back. Did you bring me a present?" At seven, along with his cousin Rose, they were the youngest in the family and loved spending time with cousins, aunts and uncles. He also knew it meant lots of presents.

"Hey, Micah." Danté hugged him tightly. "Yes, I did, but I'll get it to you tomorrow, okay, because now, I want you to meet someone very special. This is Michelline, my fiancée. She's going to be your aunt." He slid an arm around her and introduced Alexis's children. "This is Marais, Michaela and Micah. This is Michelline."

"Hello," they chorused. "You're gorgeous."

"Oh, thank you." The blush sped over Michelline's face. "As are the three of you. You clearly take after your mother." All three children had Alexis's dark hair that set off their creamy complexions.

"Oh, thank you," Alexis murmured, and admired her future sister-in-law's outfit. "Not *Haus of Stefan*, but just as good."

"Oh, no, these aren't. But I do have a few pieces in my wardrobe." Michelline nervously smoothed the sequined tunic top over her black tights. It was belted at her waist making it look even tinier than it already was. The colours from the top sparkled off the dazzling ruby earrings that were an engagement present from Danté. Her hair was fluffed around her face like a halo, and she'd kept her make-up minimal, but she'd made sure to wear stilettoes, so she didn't feel so short.

"Well, we'll have to do something about that." Alena moved Alexis out of the way and cast a critical eye over Michelline's clothes. "We'll definitely have to dress you in *Haus of Stefan*. Especially when you're promoting your new album. When's it out?"

"I…I'm not sure," Michelline murmured, feeling very much under a microscope. She lifted a shoulder in a slight shrug. "When the label wants to put it out, I guess."

"Mmm…" Alena was still put out that she wasn't the only singer in the family, but managed to introduce her family. "These are my daughters, Ava and Harper, and my sons Hunter and Skylar." She noticed her boys staring dreamily at Michelline. "Put your tongues back in your mouths, boys. They're hanging out."

Turning bright red, Hunter elbowed Skylar and both mumbled hello before rushing off.

"Ah…teenage boys." Alena sighed and shook her head. "And this here is my—"

"Luca Saint." Luca extended his hand and kissed Michelline's when she took it.

"Oh." Stunned, Michelline pulled back and saw Alena's furious expression. "Hello."

Danté took a protective step forward. Rumours had been around for years that Luca was after younger women, but so far, there was no evidence. "Fairly obvious where the boys get it from, though."

"And what would that be?" Luca asked, never taking his eyes from Michelline.

"The perverted, tongue hanging out of your mouth, eyeballs popping out of your head, behaviour," Danté replied and smoothly stepped between his fiancée and brother-in-law. "*Definitely* you. You have my sister for a wife, Luca. No need to hit on my fiancée."

Luca's eyes narrowed and he stared defiantly at Danté. "I was doing no such thing." A cold chill ran down his spine and he shivered.

"Yeah, you were. Coz *that* was Grandma *telling* you that you were, and to back off. She's still watching you, you know." He leaned closer and lowered his voice. "She's keeping an eye on you, Luca. From the grave."

Frowning, Luca took a step back, glanced at his wife's fury-filled face and walked away. He hated being in that house because he knew full well Jenny's spirit was still there watching over the family. Too many things had happened that one couldn't explain, except to put it down to a ghost. And there were *many* in that house.

Alena smiled her thanks at Danté and lightly squeezed his arm before moving over to their parents.

Danté pulled Michelline into his arms. "You okay? Luca thinks he's still in his prime and can hit on anyone. We're all careful around him."

She let out a shaky sigh. "Not the first time a dirty old perve has hit on me. Won't be the last." Smiling, Michelline added, "Your nieces and nephews are gorgeous."

"Runs in the family." His smile matched hers and he kissed her before being tapped on the shoulder.

"Hey, can I get one of those?"

Turning his head, Danté saw Dom, Davina and their kids. "Hey, guys, say hello to Michelline. This is Davina." He gave her a peck on the cheek and pointed to his nephews and niece as he introduced them in order. "And their boys, Christopher, Weston and Xander, and their daughter Rose." He held his arms open and she rushed into them.

"Uncle Danté. You're back. Did you bring me a present?"

"Argh, Rosie, my girl. Did you miss me?" Danté lifted her up and planted a kiss on her cheek. "I missed you."

Her big blue eyes stared into his brown ones. "I missed you a lot. Where are my presents?"

Laughter bubbled out of Danté. "Micah asked the exact same thing. You'll get them tomorrow, okay."

"Okay." Rose nodded eagerly and straightened her long-sleeved red velvet dress over her cream tights when he put her down. Staring up at Michelline, she said, "Hello."

"Well, hello." Michelline managed to smile at her before Davina embraced her.

"Welcome to the family. I was the fifth person to marry a Stephanopoulos, oh, seventeen years ago now, but you're the last."

"Unless Alexis marries again." Danté looked over at his sister who was hugging their father. "First one to get divorced, too."

"Sadly, not everything lasts forever," Michelline murmured as she watched Alexis. "If only it could."

Danté slipped an arm around her and stared into her eyes. "Yeah, if only."

Simon and Deidre arrived and introduced Liam and Stella, plus Stella's husband Samuel.

Diana and Charles turned up with Adam, Jaqueline, and Carys, who started to make a beeline for Harper to continue the argument they'd had earlier that day. But Diana pulled her back and pointed to Danté and Michelline. "Introductions first." They walked over and kissed them both.

"Hello, again. This is my husband Charles, and our children Adam, Jaqueline and Carys. Everyone, this is Michelline, Danté's fiancée."

Everyone shook hands and Michelline said, "Oh, you're *all* gorgeous."

From the girls' golden hair, big blue eyes, and peaches and cream complexions, to Adam's similar masculine looks, she saw it clearly came from Diana.

Diana blushed. "Why, thank you. I seemed to have passed my good genes onto my children."

"Yes, I am sorry about your mother," Michelline told her. "Danté's showed me many photos from throughout the decades; she was stunning."

"Thank you." Diana nodded. "She was, and I will now go and say hello to my father. Excuse us." She and Charles walked over while the kids went to speak to their cousins.

The door opened and Cabot pushed Antonio through. "We're here… *all* of us," he called

Tony brought the kids up at the rear and followed Cabot over to Danté.

"Hello, again," Cabot said. He had a grip on his brother's left arm and grasped his niece's right arm when Tony deposited her next to him. They'd heard the crowd quieten down just waiting for the arguments to ensue. "You met us, Cabot and Antonio before," he nodded at his brother, "well now this is Izabella and Valentina, Antonio's daughters."

"Hello," Michelline smiled softly at the two stunningly gorgeous, but clearly depressed, teenage girls before her. "My condolences for your mother and grandmother."

Izabella scowled. "What do you care? Ow!"

Cabot's fingers had dug into her arm and he pulled her close. "Don't you *dare* be a bitch in *this* household. *Not* in *my* grandmother's house. Thank her for her condolences."

Surprised, and wincing in pain, Izabella's big green eyes darted from her angry uncle to her blasé half-drunk father. Her uncle's grip tightened. "Thank you," she muttered, glancing at her father's cousin and his future wife under hooded eyes.

"Right, now, this is my husband Tony, and *our* children Antonio and Jennifer." He nodded at them and then indicated to his brother and niece. "And I'll just deposit these two with Papa and Uncle T. Excuse us." He marched them over to the kitchen where he left Izabella with her grandfather and Antonio with Tomas.

Carlos held out his arms. "Come here, Izzy B." He took his granddaughter into his embrace and held her tightly. "Be happy for them. Your grandmother and great-grandmother would want you to be. Just as they would be over the moon at another family wedding."

"It's hard," she whispered into his shoulder. "I feel so fucking miserable. How can I be happy for anyone?"

"Because you *can* be. Don't let your pain wash away happiness you're quite entitled to feel for others. He's family. *Be* happy."

Tomas came around the island bench and took Antonio into his arms. "Thank you for coming. It means a lot, and your grandmother would have wanted you to be here."

"Didn't have much of a choice, Cabot dragged me here," Antonio mumbled.

"You have a choice, Antonio," Tomas told him. "You can *choose* to be miserable for the rest of your life, or *choose* to be happy for the people *in* your life. We've all dealt with death on a personal level. You're not the only ones. Mama would want you to be happy and *she'd* tell you so."

"I miss them so much," Antonio whispered through his sobs. "Maria, Mama, Grandma, Grandpa. It sucks."

"I know," Tomas soothed him. "We know because we're dealing with it, too. But there comes a time when you choose to start living life and doing things again. This is a chance to." He pulled back and cupped his nephew's face. "For them."

"It's one year this month. I can't, not after Mama's birthday." Tears flowed down Antonio's face.

"You *can* and you *will. For them.* Do you understand me? It's Danté's birthday next week and we'll be dragging you to that, too. Because life goes on. It doesn't stop because we lose the ones we love. We rally when we have ones we love who are still alive and in need of taking care of." Tomas wiped his nephew's face. "And it starts tonight, Antonio, at your cousin's engagement party, and continues next week at his birthday party. Got it!"

Sniffling, Antonio's waterlogged eyes gazed into his uncle's and he nodded.

"Um..." Tony murmured, gazing from his frazzled husband who was sculling back a bottle of beer, to his cousin-in-law. "Sorry 'bout that. Yes, this is Antonio DeLuca III, and Jennifer, named for her grandmother."

Michelline nodded. "That's so sweet, and so many Antonios to keep straight."

A small laugh came from Tony. "It is. But we've gotten used to it. The easiest way to remember it is that *I'm* Tony, my brother-in-law is Antonio, and my son goes by his nickname of Tonio. It was nice to meet you, Michelline. Congrats, Danté. I'm off to join my husband."

"You too." Michelline's gaze moved to the three teenagers before her and saw that the girls had definitely inherited their fathers' golden-brown good looks.

"You're gorgeous." Jennifer eagerly eyed her up and down. "You bi?"

Shocked that a teenage girl could *and* would ask an adult woman that, Michelline could only mutter, "What?"

"Jennifer." Danté frowned at his cousin's daughter. "Don't go there."

"Why not?" Jennifer shrugged. "*I* might be, and Tonio here's more than likely gay." She waved a hand at her brother who was almost the spitting image of Tony. He stood with his hands in his pockets and gave a shrug of disinterest.

"Um…well, I'm not," Michelline said. "But you're a gorgeous girl. You'll find someone one day." Her eyes moved to Valentina. "You all will."

"Mmm… Maybe?" Jennifer linked her arm through her cousin's. "Come on, V, let's go talk to Marais."

Danté watched everyone wander off and mingle until he heard a small sigh and felt his right hand being gripped. He turned his head to his fiancée and pulled her into his arms. "What's wrong? What is it?"

"I…" She glanced around to see who was listening and kept her voice to a whisper. "Everyone seems to be okay, except for those affected by your aunt's and cousin's deaths. Which I get. But…" She toyed with the buttons on his shirt.

"But?"

"But isn't it taking a long time for them to deal with this? They're so angry," she continued. "And then Cabot and your uncle being just as angry back at them. It's a little…*unnerving*."

"Yeah…" Danté sighed and rested his chin on her head. "I know. But they were dealing with Maria's death when Aunt Viv passed, so it just doubled all of the emotions everyone was already feeling. And it sucks, and I'm sorry you came into the family at this time."

She pulled her head back to look up at him. "What does *that* mean?"

"I'm *not* sorry you came into the family," Danté corrected. "I'm sorry you had to come in at *such an emotional time* that a lot of us aren't exactly dealing with properly. That's all."

"It can't be helped." Her hands slid up to his face and caressed it. "Losing loved ones is hard and it takes however long is necessary to deal with it. But we'll try and make the most of it."

"We will." Danté kissed her gently.

Summer and Melody barged into the house. "We're here, did we miss anything?"

"Hey, my girls are here," Maggie cried out and rushed over to hug her daughters. "Why have you come now? Are the kids with you?"

"No, but how could we *not* come?" Summer replied and hugged Alexis and then her father. "When Nick said everyone was headed home, we wondered who everyone was and texted him."

"And all he said was, you might want to come home," Melody added. "So, we packed a bag, got a babysitter, and jumped on the jet. And then Alexis called and told us about it en route."

"You *told* them?" Danté turned to his best friend with disappointment on his face.

"*I* didn't, but *Alexis* clearly did," Nick argued. "I just told them they may want to come home. They're part of the family, too. They may have wanted to be here for the big announcement."

"Oh, Danté, finally." Melody and her sister rushed over to meet the newest member of the family and chat for a few minutes.

Once everyone had drinks and nibblies, Danté called for attention. "Okay, everyone. I have a few announcements. I need your attention." Once he had it, he went on. "We're not sending out invitations to my side of the family because, well, you're all here. So, we'll just tell you now to lock in May the twenty-third for our wedding."

Dom frowned. "But that's Grandma and Grandpa's—"

"I know." Danté put up his hand to quieten his family. "I want to get married on that day to honour them, and all they mean to me *and us* as a family." He saw his sisters and Diana tear up. Even Cabot pouted and wiped away his tears. "I know it's quick, but it's not the first time someone in this family met at Valentine's and married soon after." He glanced at Antonio who gave a strangled cry. "Grandpa proposed to Grandma on Valentine's Day in 1952, and the only day Grandma could book the church for was May twenty-third. Two days after her birthday. Which will also be Cousin Jennifer's fifteenth birthday as she is Grandma's namesake." He watched her primp for the crowd around her. "Just like her father, look at her." Danté chuckled and saw Cabot raise a brow of distaste at his daughter and try and calm her down. "She takes after you *so* much, Cab. Anyway, I am honouring them, and all they stood for, and taught us, as the last member of the family to get married, by marrying on the same date."

Murmurs went around the room and he smiled softly. "Now, while they married in Australia, and it would be even harder to get this family over there for a wedding now, we discussed it," he glanced at Michelline and took her left hand in both of his, "that it would be just as sweet to honour them, and my parents and uncles, by marrying in the church they were married in here on Mykonos. Just like Diana, Alena and Alexis did." He saw stunned and surprised faces. "And we're having the reception at *The Windmill Hotel*, just like they did fifty-five years ago, and my siblings and Diana did."

"Oh, Danté," Angie murmured. "My baby." Wiping away her tears, she hurried over to him and slipped into his embrace.

"Mama." He hugged her fiercely, but looked at all of his family over her shoulder. "Make sure you lock in that date and we'll celebrate Grandma and Grandpa's anniversary as well as Grandma's birthday." He watched his nieces, nephews and cousins scan their devices to see if they were available, and added, "I don't care if you have something on, change it. That date will always be sacred and you know it." The younger members of the family stared at him and shrugged, as those dates just weren't as important to them as to the generations before them.

"You know *we're* always free over those three days," Tomas called from the kitchen. "Have you booked the church and hotel, yet?"

"I did. It's locked and loaded," Danté replied.

"Do you have a dress, Michelline?" Diana asked, moving over to converse. "We could make you one."

"Oh, that's so sweet of you." Michelline flashed her a smile. "But I already have one. Thank you for the thought, though."

"Clearly not interested in *Haus of Stefan* then." Alena scowled and crossed her arms.

"Alena," Danté said sharply and glared at his sister. "Can it."

Alena's blush raced across her skin. "Sorry," she mumbled. "Just being a bitch for no reason. I didn't mean it."

Bristling, Michelline replied coolly, "*Actually,* it *is* a *Haus of Stefan* from ten seasons ago. I fell in love with it when it first came out, but couldn't afford it, like *most* people on no budgets, but managed to track one down a couple of years ago. It's been in my closet ever since waiting for the day I marry." Seeing Alena's blush deepen with embarrassment, and everyone snigger at her, Michelline turned her gaze to Danté and her smile beamed around the room. "Little did I know I'd be marrying the brother and cousin of the designers."

Danté's face lit up. "Small world. I know you'll look beautiful in it." Kissing her lightly, he whispered, "Well done on putting her in her place. She *can* be a bitch, sometimes."

"So I see," Michelline whispered back before they were interrupted by bickering.

"Oh, for God's sake, Harper, you're just like your mother," Carys argued. "You want everything your own damn way and to hell with everyone else."

"And you're a fairy princess who thinks her mother's the fricken queen. Well, *she's not!*" Harper argued back. "Get off your damn high horse, so I can knock that fucking crown off."

"Oi!" Dom boomed, directing an angry frown at his niece and cousin who were not the only ones startled by the loudness of his voice as it reverberated around the house. "*There are children in the room. Enough with the language.*"

"Girls!" Angie reprimanded. "*Not* around the children."

"*What* has gotten into you two?" Diana stared at both of them. They were exact replicas of her and Alena at those ages.

"We were *not* like that," Alena complained. "And *what do you mean* she's just like me?"

"*Exactly* like you," Alexis drawled and then lowered her voice so only Alena could hear. "Bitch, bitch, bitch, bitch, bitch." Seeing her sister's scowl, she grinned. "Calm your farm, the girls have *always* been like you. Even at Uncle T and Roger's wedding they were pushing and shoving."

Laughter burst out of Diana at the memories. "They both wanted to sit in front of Grandma so badly they were shoving each other out of the way."

Everyone else that was there started laughing, bar Antonio. And before long, they regaled the girls with stories of fights throughout the last eighteen years. When the tears of laughter had been wiped away, and the argument ended, Danté sat at his grandmother's piano and ran his fingers over the keys.

Within moments, everyone was quiet, and he paused to look up at Michelline who was standing beside him and beaming back, before nodding. His fingers started playing the music he'd written to her lyrics weeks earlier, and when ready, she started singing pure and pitch-perfect. Her vocal ability stunned everyone, and the lyrics brought tears to everyone's eyes.

Even Rose wandered over and tucked her hand into Michelline's and she stood staring up at her future aunt.

Michelline gazed at her while singing, saw the big blue eyes and dark brown curls, and touched a finger to her cherubic rosy cheek.

"Oh, nice," Dom muttered as the high notes came, knowing they'd have to get her signed to *Sync* as soon as possible as she'd be one hell of an acquisition.

Alena mumbled beside him and crossed her arms, annoyed that she and Ava weren't the only ones in the family who sang for a career anymore.

"You're just jealous that she's better than you," Ava whispered in her mother's ear. "Pitch-perfect, six octaves, and gorgeous."

Alena flashed her daughter a furious frown before being elbowed by Dom, and she turned that frown to him and his grin before Danté and

Michelline finished the song.

The crowd broke into thunderous applause and watched as Danté kissed Rose before kissing his fiancée. Finally happy after all these years.

"Well, that's the entertainment factor for the night," Danté called. "Let's celebrate."

*****

On May 23, 2033, the Stephanopoulos family gathered in the Greek Orthodox Church in Mykonos along with Michelline's parents, her father's parents, aunts, uncles, and cousins, for what was the next family wedding.

In the groom's room, Nick and Dom were putting the finishing touches to Danté's suit. Tying his tie, putting on his initialled cufflinks, and giving him a brush down.

"Mama would be so proud of her last baby right now," Tomas said from the doorway. He was accompanied by Pedro and Carlos. As the three remaining eldest Stephanopoulos heirs, it was their duty to carry out whatever needed doing. And giving Danté his pep talk was one of them.

"I remember," Pedro walked over to his sons, "When your Uncle Carlos married. Tomas and I gave him his cufflinks." He held his son's right arm and studied the black onyx and white gold creations. "And then for *my* wedding, they gave me mine."

"And for *my* wedding, they gave me mine." Tomas extended his left arm, as did Carlos who put his hand over Tomas's.

Pedro laid his hand on top of theirs. "We gave Papa a pair that Christmas, and Mama gave us all initialled luggage sets."

"It seemed to be a craze we started because we gave Mama her diamond initial bracelet as well," Carlos murmured. "We've continued it ever since with you boys receiving cufflinks for your weddings, and the girls receiving bracelets for theirs." He gazed at the emerald gentleman's ring on his left pinkie finger. It had been Spiros's which the family had given him for his and Jenny's fifty-fifth wedding anniversary in 2007. Now it belonged to Carlos.

"And we hope you'll continue it with your boys." Pedro looked up from Carlos's hand. All three of them had received a couple of pieces of their father's jewellery to hand down to their sons one day.

"I've got mine." Dom finished fastening Danté's left one. "And now Danté's got his. And Roger gave Simon his set for his tenth anniversary present, and we have nine boys between us to go, until Danté and Michelline populate the country. That's gonna be a lot of cufflinks."

"And diamond initial bracelets for the girls," Tomas added. "Deidre also got hers for her tenth wedding anniversary."

"Diana's is full. She's had to get another one as there are so many initials." Carlos pushed his hands into his pockets. "You ready to go, kid?"

"When did you start calling me kid, Uncle Carlos?" Danté couldn't even remember.

"Don't know. But it's making me feel real damn old," Carlos muttered, his face wrinkled with age, time, and heartache. "If you're ready, we'll go and make sure everyone's seated."

Danté patted his pockets. "Ah…yes. I am."

"Good. Now, everyone's here, and so far so good." Tomas straightened Danté's bowtie.

"Antonio?" Dom asked, a little on edge. "If he causes problems—"

"He's sober," Tomas cut him off. "Considering Cabot and Tony dragged him and the kids off to Africa for two months right after Danté's birthday to work with the poor and needy. It seems to have done both Antonio and Izabella some good. Cabot says Antonio hasn't touched a drink since, even after getting home last week. And from what they can tell, Izzy hasn't been on drugs, either. So far, they both seem okay."

Dom huffed and crossed his arms. "Still, if either one causes problems I'll have no problem taking them out." He may have been a year younger than Cabot and Antonio at fifty, but he was still in prime shape and would teach his cousin a lesson if needed, because *no one* was going to ruin his only brother's big day.

"You have no need to beat up my son and granddaughter, *Dominic.*" Carlos scowled. "*Especially* after what we've been through."

"You can't use that as an excuse forever, Carlos," Tomas informed him. "No, there will be *no physical violence.*" He glared at Dom until he received a relenting nod. "But we won't tolerate their bad behaviour, either. Hell, Cabot was slapped by Mama, maybe one of us should have done it with Antonio."

"I never expected him to ever go off the rails," Pedro said. "After Cabot, we figured it would always be *him* because Antonio was always the strong one, the one who did as he was told, the one always in charge of Cabot."

"Now, it's the other way around," Tomas murmured. "Antonio's falling apart and Cabot's stepping up to support his brother and get him through by looking after him the way Antonio did for him."

"The way you stepped up for Mama and Papa in their old age," Carlos said.

"Yeah." Tomas nodded. "It's what Mama always said we do. Love, protect, defend."

"And drag us up from the bottom of hell," Carlos muttered. "Now Cabot's doing it for Antonio as he once did it for him."

"Which is surprising," Danté said. "With Antonio being the older and mature one, and Cabot being the stupid one, we all figured it would be him needing help the rest of his life."

"Antonio?" Tomas frowned at the comment. "No, Cabot's the oldest."

"No." Pedro shook his head. "No, it's definitely Antonio." He and Tomas looked from each other to Carlos who was between them.

Carlos sighed, resigned by life. "Don't look at me. I don't even remember."

"Wait, how do we not know this?" Pedro was perplexed. "*Surely* we know this? Who's the oldest? It's Antonio, right?" He saw Angie walk into the room. "Babe, who's the oldest out of the twins. Antonio or Cabot?"

"Ah…" Angie stopped and thought about it. "I don't *exactly* know. Isn't it Antonio? He's the mature one. Normally."

"I thought it was Cabot," Tomas said. "But you're right. How *do we* not know this? We'll have to ask them."

"*Really, Uncle T?* It's my wedding day," Danté complained.

"Don't worry, we'll go and ask when we make sure everyone's seated,"

Tomas placated him. "It'll take no time at all. You're about done anyway."

"Yeah, I am. Is Michelline done, Mama?"

"She was putting the finishing touches on when I left. Not long now." She straightened his tie. "My baby boy's getting married at forty. You about gave me a heart attack, Danté."

"What for?" He kissed the top of her head. "It just took me a little longer is all."

"I know, and I'm grateful that I'm still here to see it. And I know your grandma's watching over all of us, so *she'll* see it." Smoothing out his jacket she smiled sadly. "She's here."

"I know." Danté gave her another kiss. "Now, all of you get out so I can finish up."

Tomas and Pedro took that as their chance to leave, and walked out and into the church where they found Antonio on the aisle end of the pew with Cabot next to him.

Izabella was on Cabot's right with Valentina, Tony, Jennifer and Antonio taking up the rest of the pew. They were seated behind Diana and her family.

"Ah, boys, we need to ask you something?" Tomas stopped beside Antonio and rested a hand on his shoulder. "Which one of you is the oldest? Born first?"

"We all thought it was Antonio, but Tomas thinks it's Cabot." Pedro glanced between the twins and saw Cabot's arms linked through his brother's and Izabella's, gripping their hands and making his knuckles white.

Everyone in the pews turned to look.

"What?" Antonio's face puckered. "It's Danté's wedding day and you're worried about which one of us was born first?"

"Wait, you mean you don't know? After nearly fifty-one years?" Cabot was confused. "Doesn't *everyone* know?"

Diana had turned around in her seat to listen. "*I* don't. In all these years I've never actually known which one of you came first. I just always assumed it was Antonio because he was the mature one." Her eyes darted back and forth between her brothers and landed on Cabot. "*You* definitely weren't."

"Geez, thanks, sis. Just because it took me a lot longer than everyone else to mature, doesn't mean I'll be the same for the rest of my life," Cabot complained. "How do y'all not know after all these years? *You were there.*"

A chuckle came from his left and he looked at his twin to see him laughing. "Good to see you finally having a laugh. Even though it's at *our* expense."

Antonio couldn't stop, but looked up at his uncles and father who'd joined them. "Of all days to be thinking about it, and the irony with what's happened in the last year." He wiped his eyes and kept laughing.

"It's good to see you laughing." Tomas kissed his head. "It's good to see that you're okay."

"What's going on?" Alena and Alexis leaned back over their pews.

"Do you girls know who's oldest out of the twins?" Pedro asked.

"Antonio," they both said. "Why?"

Antonio laughed harder, getting stares from Michelline's side of the church.

"Daddy, is Antonio the oldest out of him and Cabot?" Diana asked her father as he leaned heavily on the back of the pew in front of them.

"What's going on?" Roger leaned forward. "*Why* is this conversation happening now?"

Tomas shrugged at him and turned to his brother. "You *should* know."

"Eh…" Carlos shrugged with the weight of the world on his shoulders. "Viv would know. She had them."

"*You were there, Daddy,*" Diana chastised lightly. "You *should* know."

"And in the dark recesses of my mind I'm sure I do, sweetie," Carlos told her. "But it's fifty-one years ago and I've long forgotten those things." His eighty years on the planet had aged him. Because it had been a long, incredibly eventful, eighty years.

Danté, Dom, and Nick came into the church and strode over to them.

"All right, which one is it?" Danté asked. "Antonio, right? Hurry it up, we haven't got all day, I need to get married."

Antonio laughed harder and shook his head at all of the family looking their way. "*Why* do you all think it's me?"

"Because you *were* the mature one." Dom planted his hands on his hips.

They had all seen the change in Antonio after being away for two months, but even this was a bit hard to fathom.

"Oh, for fu-ff's sake," Cabot quickly corrected himself since there were children around and they were in church. "*It's me by one bloody minute.* It's on our birth certificates. Jesus Christ. Oops!" Even though he wasn't religious, he crossed himself and murmured his apologies to the cross in the lead stained window above the altar.

"What!" the family exclaimed as a whole.

"Yes!" Tomas fist pumped. "I knew it."

"Aw, thanks, Uncle T?" Cabot primped.

"Are…"

"You…"

"What?!"

The adults all looked at each other in shock.

"Maybe it's because they were always together, so you automatically registered them as one unit and forgot that one had to be born first," Dan suggested. He was sitting in the pew behind Roger's family with Derek, Mike, Maggie and their girls.

The family, as a whole, gazed at Dan and then back to the twins to see Cabot nodding enthusiastically.

"Good point. Now, we have a wedding to watch. Get up there, Danté." Cabot nodded towards the altar and Danté, shaking his head in disbelief, walked off to get things started with Dom and Nick following.

"Well…I'll be blowed," Carlos muttered and sat heavily next to a shocked Diana. "Wasn't expecting that."

Cabot rolled his eyes while Antonio kept laughing. "*Seriously, Carlos!* You helped create us and were there when Mama brought us into the world. You and Mama not only *made* us, you *named* us." He tried to remain serious, but one glance at his brother and he burst out laughing.

Carlos turned around as everyone else took their places. "Maybe so, but considering everything you two've done, it's escaped my mind." He watched Antonio wipe his face and gasp between laughs. "Good to see you're back to normal."

"A long way from it," his son replied. "But I'll get back to some form of it."

Nodding, Carlos turned towards the front and took Diana's hand in his. "You are as beautiful as your mother."

A soft smile crossed her lips and she kissed his cheek. "Thank you, Daddy."

*****

In the bride's room, Michelline's sister and best friend were putting the final touches on. A touch of make-up, straightening the veil and train, making sure her jewellery sat just right.

Her sister, Emmaline, handed her the bouquet. "Are you ready?"

Gazing into the mirror at her reflection, Michelline noted how well the dress still fitted three years after buying it, although she had basically starved the last five years to make it in Hollywood. The off-white silk material draped elegantly from the lace on the bust, shoulders, and arms, to skim down over her tiny waist and hips and drape softly to the ground into a gorgeous train. Beads, sequins and Swarovski crystals decorated the lace into the v neckline that ended just between her breasts. Beaded tassels hung from the seam between the lace and silk creating a tiny musical effect as she moved. Breathing in deeply, she exhaled slowly. "I'm ready."

"Okay, let's go." Emmaline, and Michelline's best friend, Sophia Newstead, held her train while she walked from the room and around to the entrance hall. She saw Dom and Nick waiting and smiled nervously. "Is Danté ready?"

Dom nodded his approval. "He is." Waving to someone to start the music, he and Nick lined up and prepared to walk down with the bridesmaids.

"My darling." Brannock Volmeyer held out his arm for his daughter to take and wrapped his hand over hers. "Are you ready?"

"More than I'll ever be," she replied and nodded to her bridesmaids and groomsmen. They slowly walked ahead, and when they were at the altar, Michelline and her father proceeded down the aisle, her eyes never leaving her husband-to-be.

Danté felt the air leave him, snatched by her breathtaking beauty. And never once taking his eyes from her, he couldn't wait until she was beside him and becoming his wife.

Alena watched her walk past and mouthed to Diana *that one*, giving it a thumbs up.

Diana nodded and murmured, "Beautiful." Remembering how much work and love had gone into that dress, she was glad to see someone wearing it.

Michelline stopped beside Danté and tilted her head for her father to kiss her cheek, and then handed her bouquet to her sister. Turning to her husband-to-be, she smiled through her veil as he took her hands in his.

He smiled back. "You're beautiful," he said softly and saw her beam.

"Ladies and gentlemen, we are gathered here today for the wedding of Danté and Michelline, if anyone has any objections, please state them now or forever hold your peace."

Danté turned around and gave everyone the evil eye. "Don't you dare," he said, making everyone laugh. When no one objected, the wedding went on.

"Do you, Danté, take Michelline, to be your lawful wedded wife? To have and to hold, for richer, for poorer, in sickness and in health, till death do you part."

Antonio inhaled sharply and squeezed his eyes shut while Cabot squeezed his hand.

"I do," Danté said.

"And do you, Michelline, take Danté, to be your lawful wedded husband? To have and to hold, for richer, for poorer, in sickness and in health, till death do you part."

"I do," she breathed.

The priest went on to read from the bible passages both Danté and Michelline had chosen, including the passage from Corinthians that had been read at all of the weddings since his grandparents'. A few Greek traditions were upheld, and rings were exchanged, at which point they spoke their vows.

"Michelline, when I heard you sing, I knew you had the voice of an angel." Danté stared into her big blue eyes. "And when I saw you, I knew you *were* one. I knew my grandmother had sent you to me, and I had to grab you with both hands and run and run and never let go. *You* are the one I've waited for. You are my heart, my blood, my breath, my soul. Every fibre of my being, you are in it. My body, my love, my psyche, every emotion I experience, you are in it. You *are* it." He saw the tears roll down her angelic cheeks. "I love you. I'm *in* love with you. And you're the one I want to spend the rest of my life with. You're the one I *will* spend the rest of my life with. I love you."

"Aw, my baby," Angie gasped from the front pew and dabbed at her face.

Laughter filled the church and Danté turned around. "Hush, Mama."

Michelline inconspicuously pulled a tissue from her wrist-length lace sleeve and dabbed at her face. "That was so beautiful," she stuttered. "I don't know what to say after that."

"Whatever comes into your heart and soul," Danté murmured, rubbing her arms.

"Oh, goodness." She patted her tears and drew a shaky breath. "I love you." Staring up at him she could see all of his family watching. "I'm *in* love with you. And I've never felt this way about any man before. When you kissed me that first night, and fireworks went off in my head, I just knew that someone had sent you to me. I thought it was *my* grandma and grandpa, and you think it's *your* grandma and grandpa, well, maybe they're in cahoots somewhere and both made it happen." She scored a grin from him. "But what I know for sure is, that *you* are the one that I want. The one I want for my husband, my partner, my lover, the father of my children, my future. *You* are the one I have waited my entire life for, and who knows how many lifetimes before that. But I get to spend the rest of this one with you. Right here, right now. I love you, Danté, and I am *so* glad to be your wife."

Danté breathed in a shuddering gasp. "So am I."

With everyone in the church crying and dabbing their faces, especially Antonio, they turned back to the priest.

"By the power vested in me, I now pronounce you, husband and wife. You may kiss the bride." The priest closed the bible and waved a hand for them to kiss.

With shaky hands, Danté lifted her veil and set it back to reveal her face. "Oh," he breathed. "You're so beautiful."

With a tear-gasping smile, she reached up and laid her hands on his chest as he kissed her. Fireworks went off in her head as they did every time they kissed, and her hands slid around his neck as he slid hers around her body.

"Whoa, yeah, Danté!" Cabot yelled and stood to applaud before everyone else.

To much applause, Danté and Michelline broke apart and walked hand in hand down the aisle and out the door.

The family's chauffeured vehicle took them to *The Windmill Hotel* where they freshened up in the grand suite.

"God, I love you." Danté twirled her around until she giggled.

"I love you too, oh, stop, I'm getting dizzy."

Pulling her into his arms, he kissed her. "I love you, Michelline Stephanopoulos."

"Mmm…" She melted into him. "I love the sound of that."

A knock at the door interrupted them.

"Go away," Danté yelled.

"Danté," Dom yelled back. "Everyone's here. Time for photos."

Sighing, Danté threw his head back in defeat. "Coming." Smiling at his new bride, he said, "I love you. Have I told you that?"

Her giggles continued. "Only about a million times. Let me freshen up first." Michelline hurried into the bathroom, fixed her hair and make-up, added a touch of perfume, and then rushed out. "Come on, let's go." She led him downstairs and out into the garden where the photo shoot was taking place.

It was a beautiful spring day with not a cloud in the sky and was a balmy twenty-five degrees Celsius. But corralling all of the family to take those photos was an entirely different matter altogether. After two hours, they finally made it to the reception hall attached to the hotel.

"Oh, that was so much fun," Michelline gasped as they made their way to the head table.

"I just thank God we don't have babies in the family at the moment." Danté pulled her chair out for her and helped her settle in. "The noise would be intolerable." He stayed standing while the rest of the families were seated by the manager and staff, and the bridesmaids and groomsmen were by their sides. Once everyone had their place, and he had their attention, he started.

"Ladies and gentlemen. Stephanopoulos and Volmeyer families, friends, thank you all for being here on this incredibly meaningful day. Meaningful in more ways than one." His gaze drifted over the one hundred plus guests and came to rest on his parents and uncles. "Way back in November 1977—"

"Oh, no," Dom groaned and looked up at his brother. "*Really?* Do you *have* to?"

"Who's wedding is this? Shut up," Danté scolded and turned back to their parents to see them laughing. "Way back in November 1977, my family spent three days celebrating three weddings here in Mykonos. They married at the church Michelline and I just married in, and had their reception in this very hall. My Uncle Carlos married my Aunt Vivian, my father married my mother, and my Uncle Tomas married Roger." He watched the beaming grins spread across their lips, but only a tight smile touched Carlos's. "My grandmother, Jenny Stephanopoulos, had arranged all three weddings and receptions because her baby boys were getting married."

"Oh, God." Pedro laughed and shook his head. "Get on with it."

"And that's the reason I always wanted to marry in the same church, and have the reception in the same hall."

"Because the family owns it," Cabot called out.

Danté nodded. "Not just because the family owns it, but because it has meaning. We've celebrated every anniversary here since 1983, so it will *always* have meaning. And *this* day has *another* meaning." He scanned the crowd and caught a vague glimpse of a couple he thought he recognised at the back of the hall.

"In Australia, on Valentine's Day 1952, Spiros Stephanopoulos proposed to Jennifer Marsh after going steady for a year. They married fourteen weeks later on May twenty-third. This year, 2033, it would have been their eighty-first wedding anniversary. Grandpa would be one hundred and eight in July, and Grandma would have turned one hundred and five two days ago. When they died, the world changed. I've only been in this family for forty years, but Grandma and Grandpa had held it together and kept it going for forty-one years before me. And they, especially my grandma, held it together like the superglue she was. Through times tougher than anyone will ever know, that her sons, and then her grandchildren, put her through. She was the rock that we clung to, and was a beacon on a stormy night."

Cabot nodded and wiped away his tears. He knew exactly what Danté was talking about. 2007 had been a bitch of a year, and the worst in his life. If not for his beloved grandmother Jenny, and his twin Antonio, he'd be dead. And they all knew it.

Dom sighed and glanced up at his brother, remembering back to almost losing him to a shark. It had snapped him out of his stupidity and made him a *real* big brother. The one his grandmother had expected him to be. 2007 had been a bitch of a year, and he would never forget it was the year he almost lost his only brother.

Alexis clutched her daughters' hands as they sat either side of her. She prayed neither of them were ever assaulted and she had made them train at self-defence; something she wished she'd known when her rape occurred. And that one rock she had throughout, was her grandmother. The life raft she'd clung to to get her through the worst time, and year, of her life. 2007 was a bitch of a year, and one she would one day tell her children about.

Diana glanced at Charles and thanked God her grandmother had been able to find him when she needed him the most. When she was pregnant with his child and he had disappeared on assignment, only for her to find out he'd been kidnapped and tortured. If it wasn't for her grandmother, Charles would be dead, and she'd be without the man she loved. 2007 was a bitch of a year and one she would never forget.

"And I for one will never forget the lessons she taught us, the stories she told us, the fierceness she protected us with. And I've seen all of us hand that down to the next generation." He stared at his family and saw his siblings and cousins nodding their heads. "For those of the next generation that knew her and loved her and learnt from her, never forget it. *Or* her. Your great-grandmother was an incredible woman who would do *any*thing for her family, and so would we. Your aunts and uncles and grandparents. *We* learnt from the best, and now we will continue to teach you and *your* children, and hope you pass down the values, lessons, and respect to *your* grandchildren one day. Because if it weren't for Grandma and Grandpa, *none of us* would be here. So, raise your glasses." He lifted his and waited until everyone else did. "This may be *our* wedding day, and we'll move on to celebrating that in a moment, but for *this* moment, we're going to celebrate the two most incredible people I've ever known. My grandmother and grandfather. To Spiros and Jenny." He looked through the crowd and swore he saw his grandparents standing at the back of the hall smiling over the family.

"Spiros and Jenny."

About the Author

L.J. has been writing since 2006, when her first of many novels, ***The Road To Vegas,*** was born. In 2016 she created the ***Porn Star Brothers*** series about three sizzlingly hot Australian born Greek Island raised brothers who became the hottest porn stars in '70s America.

L.J. lives in Australia, loves '80s music, disaster movies, and collecting Jackie Collins books as Jackie is her inspiration and mentor.

L.J. Diva is the adult pen name for author Tiara King. You can find more about Tiara on her website; follow her on social media, or visit her publishing house, Royal Star Publishing.

Socials

tiaraking.com.au/ljdiva

royalstarpublishing.com.au

Sign up for *Tiara's* Newsletter…

Make sure you're always in the know and never miss free exclusives, the latest news, book updates, and so much more with newsletters from…

tiaraking.com.au

Have you read these?

The Porn Star Brothers Series

Porn Star Brothers
Forever
Love Never Dies
Stefan: The New Generation
DeLuca
Spiros & Jenny
And Always

The Illicit Things Series

Her
Him
Madam X

A Novel Investigations Series

Designs in Crime
A Killer Plot
Murder on the Set
A Novel Investigation (omnibus)

Or these?

NOVELS

Burning Desires
Anything for You
Falling for London
The Road to Vegas
Hollywood Dreams
The Billionaire's Dirty Little Secret

SHORT STORIES

The Body
The Perfect Plot
The Star of Your Own Crime Scene